With degrees in English and Hi⋯ of Regency and Victorian times committed anglophile, who, at l⋯ up teaching to devote her energ⋯ husband knew what he was doing.

Silent on the Moor is Deanna's third novel in the **Silent** series featuring the effervescent Lady Julia Grey and the enigmatic private investigator Nicholas Brisbane.

Deanna is currently hard at work on her next book from her home in Virginia.

Find out more online at www.mirabooks.co.uk/ deannaraybourn

SILENT on the MOOR

Deanna Raybourn

MIRA

MIRA is a registered trademark of Harlequin Enterprises Limited, used under licence.

Published in Great Britain 2009
MIRA Books, Eton House, 18-24 Paradise Road,
Richmond, Surrey, TW9 1SR

© Deanna Raybourn 2008

ISBN 978 0 7783 0304 6

54-0709

MIRA's policy is to use papers that are natural, renewable and recyclable products and made from wood grown in sustainable forests. The logging and manufacturing processes conform to the legal environmental regulations of the country of origin.

Printed in Great Britain
by Clays Ltd, St Ives plc

ACKNOWLEDGEMENTS

One of the loveliest aspects of being a writer is having the opportunity to acknowledge the debts I owe. Great appreciation and tremendous thanks:

To my family: my daughter who provides endless companionship, laughter and very often food, my mother who tidies everything up – including my manuscripts, and my husband who makes it all possible.

To my agent, Pam Hopkins, a woman of tenacity and good humour whose skills at hand-holding, negotiating, and talking her writers down from ledges is unsurpassed.

To my editor, the stylish and demanding Valerie Gray who never rests unless she has my best.

To my friends, particularly those who travelled great distances, hosted me, shepherded me through their cities, or made multiple trips to events, most especially Vanessa, Sherri, Kim, Stephanie, Jerusha, Suzanne, Kristin, David, Tyler, Sali and my beloved godfather, Billy.

To those who have given technical assistance and shown exceptional professional generosity: Chris Wallbruch, Dr Sandra Hammock, Shea Titlow, and Dr Gregory Davis.

To all of the unsung heroes and heroines of publishing, the many hardworking people through whose hands my books pass and are made better and who work so tirelessly to get my books into the hands of readers – editorial, marketing, sales, public relations, and production. Most particularly, I would like to thank Emily Ohanjanians and Nancy Fischer for their elegant and attentive contributions to the editing process.

To the many booksellers who have shared their enthusiasm with their customers and converted them to readers.

To the readers of blog and books who have been so generous in their praise and kind in their compliments. I have shared my stories with you, and in return you have shared your stories with me. Thank you.

This book is dedicated to
Courtenay James Jones,
a far better father than any
I could have written.

THE FIRST CHAPTER
London, 1888

For now sits expectation in the air.
—William Shakespeare
Henry V

"Julia Grey, I would rather see you hanged than watch any sister of mine go haring off after a man who will not have her," my brother Bellmont raged. "And Portia, I am thoroughly appalled that you would not only condone such behaviour, but abet it by accompanying Julia. You are her elder sister. You ought to set an example."

I sighed and stared longingly at the whisky decanter. Portia and I had known that the summons to our father's London townhouse was a thinly-veiled ambush, but I do not think either of us had expected the attack to be so quick, nor so brutal. We had scarcely taken our seats in Father's comfortable library before our eldest brother launched into a tirade against our proposed visit to Yorkshire. Father, ensconced behind his vast mahogany desk, said nothing. His expression was inscrutable behind his half-moon spectacles.

Catching my wistful glance, Portia rose and poured us both glasses of whisky. "Take this, dearest," she urged. "Bellmont is in rare form. He will surely rail at us until supper unless he has an apoplexy first," she finished cheerfully.

Bellmont's already high colour deepened alarmingly. "You may well jest about this, but it is unacceptable for Julia to accept an invitation to stay with Brisbane at his country house. He is an unmarried man, and she is a widow of thirty. Even if you are there to chaperone, Portia, you must admit, it would be a complete violation of propriety."

"Oh, Julia hasn't been invited," Portia responded helpfully. "I was. Julia rather invited herself."

Bellmont clicked his teeth together and drew in a deep breath, his nostrils going white at the edges. "If that is supposed to offer me comfort, it is a cold one, I assure you."

Portia shrugged and sipped at her whisky. Bellmont turned to me, deliberately softening his tone. At more than forty years of age and heir to our father's earldom, he had long since grown accustomed to having his own way. It was only with his eccentric family that his success was mixed. With a cunning blend of sternness, cajolery, and logic, he was sometimes able to bend us to his will, but just as often he found himself not speaking to more than one of his nine siblings. Now he attempted an appeal to my reason.

"Julia, I understand you were quite bereft when Edward died. You were very young to be a widow, and I am sympathetic to the fact that you felt compelled to search out your husband's murderer." I raised my brows. He had not been so sympathetic at the time. When I had unmasked my husband's killer in a dramatic scene during which my town-house was burned down and I nearly lost my life, Bellmont had actually stopped speaking to me for two months. Apparently, murder is a failing of the middle classes only. Aristocrats are supposed to be above such unpleasantness.

He went on. "I realise your connection with Mr. Brisbane was a necessary evil at the time. He has proved himself a thoroughly capable inquiry agent and, mercifully, a discreet one. But your association with this man cannot continue. I do not know what Father was thinking to invite him to Bellmont Abbey at Christmas, but it was badly done, and it has given you ideas."

"And God knows women mustn't have *ideas*," Portia murmured into her glass. Bellmont did not even bother to look at her. We were well-accustomed to Portia's pointed asides.

I looked helplessly at Father, who merely shrugged and poured himself a glass of whisky. If Bellmont continued on we should become a family of inebriates.

"Monty," I began, deliberately sweetening my tone, "I do appreciate your concern. But Father has already explained to you Brisbane was there to pursue an investigation. He left before the family arrived for Christmas. You did not even see him. I have never invited him to accompany me to your home, nor have I ever foisted him upon you in any social situation, although he would not be entirely out of place. His great-uncle *is* the Duke of Aberdour, you know."

Bellmont rubbed a hand over his face, smoothing the furrows that marked his handsome brow. "My dear, his antecedents are quite immaterial. He is in trade. He is a half-

Gypsy vagabond who makes his living by dealing in the sordid miseries of others. His exploits are fodder for the newspapers, and we have been dragged through those rather enough at present," he finished, shooting Father a look that was ripe with bitterness.

Father waved an indolent hand. "Do not blame me, boy. I did my best to sweep the entire matter under the carpet, as did Brisbane." That much was true. The newspapers, through Father's influence and Brisbane's connections, had taken little enough notice of the events at Bellmont Abbey, although a few rather distasteful morsels had found their way into print.

Bellmont swung round to face Father while Portia and I huddled closer to one another on the sofa and drank our whisky.

"I am not unaware of your efforts, Father. But the press have always been interested in our little peccadilloes, and you have simply not done enough to keep them at bay, particularly when you were so indiscreet as to entertain your mistress at the same Christmas party as your children and grandchildren."

"A hit, a palpable hit," Portia whispered. I stifled a giggle. Bellmont was being rather unfair to Father. He had exercised as much authority over the press in the matter as he could. Considering what had actually transpired at the Abbey, we were lucky it had not become the scandal of the century.

"Madame de Bellefleur is not my mistress," Father said, puffing his cheeks indignantly. "She is my friend, and I shall thank you to speak of her respectfully."

"It does not matter what she *is*," Bellmont pointed out

acidly. "It only matters what they *say* she is. Do you have any notion how damaging such stories could be to me, to my children? Orlando is considering a run for Parliament when he is established, and Virgilia is to be presented this season. Her chances for a good match could be completely overthrown by your conduct, and it will not improve matters for her aunts to be seen chasing off to Yorkshire to stay with a bachelor of questionable reputation."

Portia stirred. "I should think the fact that I live openly with a woman would be far more damaging to her chances for a society marriage," she remarked coolly.

Bellmont flinched. "Your relationship with Jane is something to which I have become reconciled over these past ten years. It is a credit to Jane that she lives quietly and does not care to move in society."

Portia's eyes glinted ominously, and I laid a warning hand on her wrist. "Jane is the love of my life, Bellmont, not a pet to be trained."

Father held up a hand. "Enough. I will not have you quarrelling like dogs over an old bone. I thought we buried that particular issue long ago. Bellmont, you forget yourself. I have permitted you to abuse your sisters and me quite long enough."

Bellmont opened his mouth to protest, but Father waved him off. "You have a care for your sisters' reputations, and that does you credit, but I must observe for a man so often hailed as one of the greatest brains of his generation, you are remarkably obtuse about women. You've been married going on twenty years, boy. Have you not yet learned that it is easier to pull a star down from the heavens than to bend a woman to your will? The most tractable of women will kick over the traces if you insist upon obedience and, in case it has escaped your notice, your sisters are not the most tractable of women. No, if they are intent upon going to Yorkshire, go they will."

Portia flicked a triumphant gaze at Bellmont who had gone quite pale under the angry wash of red over his fair complexion. I took another sip of my whisky and wondered not for the first time why my parents had found it necessary to have so many children.

"Father," Bellmont began, but Father rose, straightening his poppy-coloured waistcoat and raising a hand.

"I know. You are worried for your children, as you should be, and I will see that their chances are not damaged by the actions of their aunts." He paused, for dramatic effect no doubt, then pronounced in ringing tones, "Your sisters will travel under the protection of their brother, Valerius."

Portia and I gaped at him, stunned to silence. Bellmont was quicker off the mark. Mollified, he nodded at Father. "Very well. Valerius is thoroughly incapable of controlling them, but at least his presence will lend the appearance of respectability. Thank you, Father." He turned to leave, giving us a piercing look. "I suppose it would be too much to ask that you conduct yourselves like ladies, but do try," he offered as a parting shot.

Portia was still sputtering when the footman shut the door behind him. "Honestly, Father, I do not see why you didn't have him drowned as a child. You've four other sons, what's one at the bottom of the pond?"

Father shrugged. "I would have drowned him myself had I known he would turn out Tory. I know you want to remonstrate with me over the suggestion of travelling with Valerius, but I want to talk to your sister. Leave us to chat a moment, will you, my dear?" he said to Portia.

She rose gracefully and turned, pulling a face at me as she went. I tried not to fidget, but I felt suddenly shy and uncertain. I smiled up at Father winsomely and attempted to divert the conversation.

"Valerius will be simply furious with you, Father. You know he hates to leave London, and he is devoted to his work with Dr. Bent. He's just bought a new microscope."

It might have been a good diversion under other circumstances. Father could rant easily for an hour on the subject of Valerius and his unsuitable interest in medicine. But he had other game afoot.

He turned to me, folding his arms across his chest. "Do not look to distract me," he said sternly. "What the devil do you mean by hunting Brisbane like a fox? Monty is right, though I would not give him the satisfaction of saying so in front of him. It is damned unseemly and shows a distinct lack of pride. I reared you for better."

I smoothed my skirts under nervous fingers. "I am not hunting Brisbane. He asked Portia to come and help him sort out the estate. Apparently the former owner left it in a frightful state and Brisbane hasn't any lady to act as chatelaine and put things in order." I opened my eyes very wide to show I was telling the truth.

"Nicholas Brisbane is entirely capable of ordering his own bedsheets and hiring his own cook," he commented, narrowing his gaze.

"There is nothing sinister afoot," I assured him. "Brisbane

wrote in January to accept Portia's offer to help arrange his household. He told her to wait until April when the weather would be more hospitable. That is the whole of it."

"And how did you become involved?" Father demanded.

"I saw the letter and thought springtime on the moors sounded very pleasant."

Father shook his head slowly. "Not likely. You mean to settle this thing between you, whatever it is."

I twisted a bit of silken cushion fringe in my fingers and looked away. "It is complicated," I began.

"Then let us have it simply," he cut in brutally. "Has he offered you marriage?"

"No." My voice was nearly inaudible, even to my own ears.

"Has he given you a betrothal ring?"

"No."

"Has he ever spoken of marrying you?"

"No."

"Has he written to you since he left for Yorkshire?"

"No."

My replies dropped like stones, heavy with importance. He waited a long moment and the only sounds were the soft rustling of the fire on the hearth and the quiet ticking of the mantel clock.

"He has offered you nothing, made no plans for the future, has not even written. And still you mean to go to him?" His voice was soft now, free of judgment or recrimination, and yet it stung like salt on a wound.

I raised my gaze to his. "I must. I will know when I see him again. If there is nothing there, I will return to London by the first train and never speak of him again, never wonder what might have been. But if there is a chance that he feels for me—" I broke off. The rest of it need not be spoken aloud.

"And you are quite determined?"

"Quite," I said, biting off the word sharply. He said nothing for a moment, but searched my face, doubtless looking for any sign that I was less than resolute and might be persuaded to abandon my plans.

At length he sighed, then drained the last of his whisky. "Go then. Go under Valerius' protection, however feeble that may be, and find out if Brisbane loves you. But I tell you this," he said, folding me into his embrace and pressing a kiss into my hair, "I may be above seventy years of age, but I still fence every day and if the blackguard hurts you I will hunt him down and leave a stiletto in his heart."

"Thank you, Father. That is very comforting."

Dinner that evening was a peculiarly quiet affair. Portia was a charming hostess and kept an admirable table. She was renowned for the quality of her food and wines as well as the excellence of the company. She knew the most interesting people and often invited them to little suppers arranged to show them to perfection, like gems in a thoughtful setting. But that night there were only ourselves—Portia, her beloved Jane, and me. We were all of us occupied with our own thoughts and said little, our silences punctuated with phlegmy snorts from Portia's vile pet, Mr. Pugglesworth, asleep under the table.

After one particularly nasty interlude, I laid down my knife. "Portia, must you have that dog in the dining room? He is putting me quite off my food."

She waved a fork at me. "Do not be peevish just because Bellmont took you to task today."

"Puggy is rather foul," Jane put in quietly. "I will remove him to the pantry."

She rose and collected the animal, coaxing him out with a bit of stewed prune. Portia watched her, saying nothing. They were a study in contrasts, each lovely in her own way, but different as chalk and cheese. Portia had a fine-boned elegance, coupled with the classic March family colouring of dark hair faintly touched with red and wide green eyes. She dressed flamboyantly, in colours suited to the pale alabaster of her skin, always in a single hue from head to toe.

Jane, on the other hand, seemed determined to wear all the colours of the rainbow at once. She was an artist and scholar, and her face was modelled along those lines, with handsome bones that would serve her well into old age. Hers was a face of character, with a determined chin and a forthright gaze that never judged, never challenged. People frequently offered her the most extraordinary confidences on the basis of those eyes. Deep brown, touched with amber and warm with intelligence, they were her greatest beauty. Her hair, always untidy, was not. Dark red and coarse as a horse's mane, it curled wildly until she grew tired of it and thrust it into a snood. It resisted all other confinement. More than once I had seen Portia, laughing, attempting to dress it, breaking combs in its heaviness.

But she was not laughing as she watched Jane remove Puggy to the pantry. She merely took another sip of her wine and motioned for the butler to fill her glass again.

"When do you think we ought to leave—" I began.

"Tomorrow. I have already consulted the timetable. If we leave very early, we ought to make Grimsgrave by nightfall. I have sent word to Valerius to meet us at the station."

I blinked at her. "Portia, my things are not yet packed. I have made no arrangements."

She looked down at the pale slices of pork on her plate. She poked at them listlessly with her fork, then signed for the butler. He removed the plate, but she kept hold of her wine.

"There are no arrangements for you to make. I have taken care of everything. Tell Morag to pack your trunk, and be ready at dawn tomorrow. That is all that is required of you."

I signalled to the butler as well, surrendering my wine, and wishing Portia had done the same. She did not often drink to excess, and the extra glass had made her withdrawn, icy even.

"Portia, if you do not wish to go to Yorkshire, I can go alone with Valerius. I am offending propriety well enough as it is. I cannot think that travelling without you will make much of a difference."

She stared into her wineglass, turning it slowly in her palms, edging the dark, blood-red liquid closer to the crystal rim.

"No, it is better that I should go. You will need someone to look after you, and who better than your elder sister?" she asked, her tone tinged with mockery.

I stared at her. Portia and I had had our share of quarrels, but we were extremely close. She had offered me the use of her townhouse when I was in London, and my stay had been a pleasant one. Jane had welcomed me warmly, and we had passed many cosy evenings by the fireside, reading poetry or abusing our friends with gossip. But every once in a while, like a flash of lightning, brief and sharp and hot, a flicker of something dangerous had struck between us. I was not certain why or how, but a new prickliness had arisen, and more than once I had been scratched on the thorns of it. A word too sharp, a glance too cold—so subtle I had almost thought I had imagined it. But there was no imagining the atmosphere in the dining room. I glanced at the door, but Jane did not return.

"Dearest," I began patiently, "if you want to remain here with Jane, you ought to. I know Brisbane invited you, but he will understand if you decide to stay in London."

Portia circled the glass again, the wine lapping at the edge. "To what purpose?"

I shrugged. "The season will be starting soon. You might organise a ball for Virgilia. Or give a dinner for young Orlando, introduce him to some of the gentlemen of influence you have cultivated. If he means to run for a seat in Parliament, he cannot begin too soon."

Portia snorted and her hand jerked, nearly spilling the wine.

"Our niece's mother would never permit me to throw a ball for her, as you well know. And the gentlemen of influence would have little interest in meeting our nephew at the dinner table, and I have little interest in meeting our nephew. He is a dull boy with no conversation."

She was being far too hard on Orlando, but I knew that recrimination would only provoke her. "And you hope to find good conversation in Yorkshire?" I teased, hoping to jolly her out of her foul mood.

She stared into the glass, and for just a moment her expression softened, as though she were prey to some strong emotion. But she mastered it as swiftly as it had come, and her face hardened.

"Perhaps there is nothing to find," she said softly. She

tilted her hand and a single crimson drop splashed onto the tablecloth, staining the linen with the finality of blood.

"Portia, leave off. You will ruin that cloth," I scolded. The butler moved forward to scatter salt over the spill.

Portia put her glass down carefully. "I think perhaps I have had too much to drink." She rose slowly. "Julia, do enjoy dessert. I will retire now. I must supervise Minna whilst she packs. If I leave her to it, she will hurl everything into a bedsheet and knot it up and call it packed."

I bade her a quiet good-night and told the butler I wanted nothing more except a strong cup of tea. He brought it scalding and sweet, and I sipped it slowly, wondering why the trip to Yorkshire, which had filled me with elation, should now cause me such apprehension. It was not just Portia's antics that alarmed me. I knew very well that Brisbane had not invited me to Yorkshire. Moreover, I knew his uncertain temper and how scathing his anger could be. He was entirely capable of packing me onto the next train to London, my purpose unresolved. I knew also his stubbornness, his pride, his stupid, dogged persistence in blaming himself for my brush with death during our first investigation together. I had told him in the plainest terms that the idea was nonsense. If anything, Brisbane had saved my life and I had told him so.

Whether he had listened was another matter entirely. The whole of our acquaintance had been an intricate, twisting dance, two steps toward each other, three steps apart. I was tired of the uncertainty. Too many times I had abandoned myself to the exhilaration of his company, only to be thwarted by circumstance or his own stubborn pride. It seemed a very great folly to attempt to force a declaration from him, but it seemed a greater folly to let him go. If there was a single chance at happiness with him, I was determined to seize it.

But determination was not enough to silence my jangling nerves, and as I put the cup onto the saucer, I noticed my hand shook ever so slightly.

Just then, Jane returned. She resumed her place, giving me a gentle smile. "I do apologise about Puggy. He is not a very nice dinner companion. I have often told Portia so."

"Think nothing of it. With five brothers I have seen far worse at table," I jested. Her smile faded slightly and she reached for her glass as I fiddled with my teacup.

"I wish you were coming with us," I said suddenly. "Are you quite certain your sister cannot spare you?"

Jane shook her head. "I am afraid not. Anna is nervous about her confinement. She says it will give her much comfort to have me in Portsmouth when she is brought to bed, although I cannot imagine why. I have little experience with such matters."

I gave her hand a reassuring pat. "I should think having one's elder sister at such a time would always be a comfort. It is her first child, is it not?"

"It is," Jane said, her expression wistful. "She is newly married, just on a year."

Jane fell silent then, and I could have kicked myself for introducing the subject in the first place. Anna had always been a thorn-prick to Jane, ever since their father died and they had been cast upon the mercy of Portia's husband. Younger than Jane by some half-dozen years, Anna had made her disapproval of Jane's relationship with Portia quite apparent, yet she had happily reaped the benefit when Portia had insisted upon paying the school fees to have her properly educated. Portia had offered her a place in her home, an offer that was refused with the barest attempt at civility. Instead Anna had taken a post as a governess upon leaving school, and within two years she had found a husband, a naval officer whom she liked well enough to enjoy when he was at home and little enough to be glad when he was abroad. She had settled into a life of smug domesticity in Portsmouth, but I was not surprised that she had sent for Jane. Few people were as calm and self-possessed, and I hoped that this olive branch on Anna's part would herald a new chapter in their relationship.

I almost said as much to Jane, but she changed the subject before I could.

"Are you looking forward to your trip into Yorkshire?" she inquired. "I have never been there, but I am told it is very beautiful and unspoilt."

"I am not," I confessed. "I should like to see Yorkshire, but I am rather terrified to tell you the truth."

"Brisbane?"

I nodded. "I just wish I knew. It's all so maddening, the way he drops me entirely for months on end, then when we are brought together, he behaves as though I were the very air he breathes. Most infuriating."

Jane put a hand over mine. Hers was warm, the fingers calloused from the heavy tools of her art. "My dear Julia, you must follow your heart, even if you do not know where it will lead you. To do otherwise is to court misery." There was a fleeting shadow in her eyes, and I thought of how much she and Portia had risked to be together. Jane had been the poor relation of Portia's husband, Lord Bettiscombe, and society had been cruel when they had set up house together after Bettiscombe's death. They had a circle of broad-minded and cultured friends, but many people cut them directly, and Portia had been banned from the most illustrious houses in London. Theirs had been a leap of faith together, into a world that was frequently cruel. And yet they had done it together, and they had survived. They were an example to me.

I covered her hand with mine. "You are right, of course. One must be brave in love, like the troubadours of old. And one must seize happiness before it escapes entirely."

"I will wish you all good fortune," she said, lifting her glass. We toasted then, she with her wine, I with my tea, but as we sipped, we lapsed into a heavy silence. My thoughts were of Brisbane, and of the very great risk I was about to take. I did not wonder what hers were. It was only much later that I wished I had spared a care for them. How much might have been different.

THE SECOND CHAPTER

O mistress mine, where are you roaming?
—William Shakespeare
Twelfth Night

rue to Portia's intention, we left early the next morning, but we did not achieve Grimsgrave Hall by nightfall. The journey, in a word, was disastrous. Jane did not accompany us to the station, preferring instead to bid us farewell at Bettiscombe House. It was just as well, I thought. Between Portia and myself, there were two maids, three pets, and a mountain of baggage to be considered. Valerius met us on the platform, arriving just before the doors were shut and lapsing into his seat with a muttered oath and bad grace.

"Good morning, Valerius," I said pleasantly. "How nice to see you. It's been ages."

The corners of his mouth were drawn down sullenly. "It was a fortnight ago at Aunt Hermia's Haydn evening."

"Nevertheless, it is good to see you. I know you must be mightily put out with Father for asking you to come—"

He sat bolt upright, clearly enraged. "Asking me to come? He didn't ask me to come. He threatened to cut off my allowance *entirely*. No money, ever again, if I didn't hold your hand on the way to Yorkshire. And worst of all, I am not permitted to return to London until you do. I am banished," he finished bitterly.

Portia gave a snort and rummaged in her reticule for the timetable. I suppressed a sigh and gazed out the window. It was going to be a very long journey indeed if Val meant to catalogue his wrongs. The refrain was one I had heard often enough from all of Father's younger sons. Although the bulk of the March estate was kept intact for Bellmont and his heirs, Father was extremely generous with his younger children.

Unfortunately, his generosity seldom extended to letting them make their own choices. They were expected to be dilettantes, nothing less than gentlemen. They might write sonatas or publish verse or daub canvases with paints, but it was always understood that they were strictly barred from engaging in trade. Valerius had not only struggled against this cage, he had smashed the bars open. He had at one time established himself, quite illegally, as physician to an expensive brothel. His dabbling in medicine had violated every social more that Father had been brought up to respect, and Father had very nearly disowned him altogether. It was only grudgingly and after a series of violent arguments that he had consented to permit Valerius to study medicine in theory, so long as he did not actually engage in treating patients. This compromise had made Val sulky, yet unsatisfactory as his work had become, leaving it was worse.

He lapsed into a prickly silence, dozing against the window as the train picked up speed and we began our journey in earnest.

Not surprisingly, Portia and I bickered genteelly the entire morning, pausing only to nibble at the contents of the hamper Portia's cook had packed for us. But even the most delectable ham pie is no cure for peevishness, and Portia was in rare form. By the time the train halted to take on passengers at Bletchley, I had had my fill of her.

"Portia, if you are so determined not to enjoy yourself, why don't you leave now? It can easily be arranged and you can take the next train back. A few hours at most and you can be in London, smoothing over your quarrel with Jane. Perhaps you could go with her to Portsmouth."

She raised a brow at me. "I have no interest in seeing Portsmouth. Besides, what quarrel? We have not quarrelled."

Val perked up considerably at this bit of news, and Portia threw him a vicious glance. "Go back to sleep, dearest. The grown-ups are talking."

"Do not attempt to put me off," I put in hurriedly, eager to avoid another squabble between them. "I know matters have not been right between you, and I know why. She is not easy about this trip. Perhaps she will simply miss your company or perhaps she fears you will get up to some mischief while you are away, but I know she does not like it. It does her much credit that she has been so kind to me when I am the cause of it."

Portia wrapped the rest of her pie in a bit of brown paper

and replaced it in the hamper. Val retrieved it instantly and began to wolf it down. Portia ignored him. "You are not the cause, Julia. I would have gone to Brisbane in any event. I am worried for him."

My heart thudded dully in my chest. "What do you mean? Have you heard from him?"

She hesitated, then fished in her reticule. "I had this letter from him last week. I did not think to visit Grimsgrave so early. When he first invited me, I thought perhaps the middle of April, even May, might be more pleasant. But when I read that…" Her voice trailed off and I reached for the letter.

The handwriting was as familiar to me as my own, bold and black, thickly scrawled by a pen with a broad nib. The heading was Grimsgrave Hall, Yorkshire, and it was dated the previous week. I read it quickly, then again more slowly, aloud this time, as if by hearing the words aloud I could make better sense of them. One passage in particular stood out.

And so I must rescind my invitation to come to Grimsgrave. Matters have deteriorated since I last wrote to you, and I am in no humour for company, even such pleasant company as yours. You would hardly know me, I have grown so uncivilized, and I should hate to shock you.

I could well imagine the sardonic little twist of the lips as he wrote those words. I read on, each word chilling me a little more.

As for your sister, tell her nothing. She must forget me, and she will. Whatever my hopes may once have been, I realise now I was a fool or a madman, or perhaps I am grown mad now. The days are very alike here, the hours of darkness long and bleak, and I am a stranger to myself.

The letter dropped to my lap through nerveless fingers. "Portia," I murmured. "How could you have kept this from me?"

"Because I was afraid you would not go if you read it."

"Then you are a greater fool than I thought," I replied crisply. I returned the letter to its envelope and handed it back to her. "He has need of me, that much is quite clear."

"He sounds as if he wants to be left alone," Val offered, blowing crumbs onto his lap. He brushed them off, and I rounded on him.

"He needs me," I said, biting off each word sharply.

"It was one thing to arrive as my guest when I was invited," Portia reminded me. "Does it not trouble you for both of us to arrive, unannounced and unwelcome? And Valerius besides?"

"No," I said boldly. "Friends have a duty to care for one another, even when it is unwelcome. Brisbane needs me, Portia. Whether he wishes to own it or not."

Portia's gaze searched my face. At length she nodded, giving me a little smile. "I hope you are correct. And I hope he agrees. You realise he may well shut the door upon us. What will you tell him if he bids us go to the devil?"

I smoothed my hair, neatly pinned under a rather fetching hat I had just purchased the week before. It was violet velvet, with cunning little clusters of silk violets sewn to the crown and spilling over one side of the brim to frame my face.

"I shall tell him to lead the way."

Portia laughed then, and we finished our picnic lunch more amiably than we had begun it. It was the last truly enjoyable moment of the entire journey. Delays, bad weather, an aimless cow wandering onto the railway tracks—all conspired against us and we were forced to spend an uncomfortable night in a hotel of questionable quality in Birmingham, having secured three rooms by a detestable combination of bribery and high-handed arrogance. Portia and I shared, as did the maids, and as penance for securing the only room to himself, Valerius was forced to spend the night with the pets.

After an unspeakable breakfast the next morning, we resumed our journey with its endless changing of trains to smaller and smaller lines in bleaker and bleaker towns until at last we stumbled off of a train hardly bigger than a child's toy.

"Where are we?" I demanded. Portia drew a map from her reticule and unfolded it as I peered over her shoulder. Behind us, Morag and Minna were counting bags and preparing to take the dogs for a short walk to attend to nature.

Portia pointed on the map to an infinitesimally small dot. "Howlett Magna. We must find transport to the village of Lesser Howlett and from thence to Grimsgrave."

Val and I looked about the tiny clutch of grey stone buildings. "There is something smaller than *this*?" he asked, incredulous.

"There is," Portia said crisply, "and that is where we are bound."

Portia was in a brisk, managing mood, and the arrangements for transportation were swiftly made. Valerius and

I stood on the kerb surveying the village while Portia settled matters.

"It looks like something out of a guidebook of prospective spots to catch cholera," Val said, curling his lip.

"Don't pull that face, dearest," I told him. "You look like a donkey."

"Look at the gutters," he hissed. "There is sewage running openly in the streets."

I felt my stomach give a little lurch. "Val, I beg you—" I broke off, diverted.

"What is it?" Val demanded. "Someone bringing out their plague dead?"

I shook my head slowly. "No, there was a man walking this way, but he saw us and ducked rather quickly into the linen draper's. I have never seen such a set of whiskers. He looks like Uncle Balthazar's sheepdog. They are certainly shy of strangers, these Northerners." I nodded to the doorway of the shop opposite. The fellow had been nondescript and rather elderly, wearing rusty black with a slight limp and a tendency to *embonpoint*. A set of luxuriant whiskers hid most of his face from view.

"Probably frightened away by how clean we are," Val put in acidly.

I turned to him, lifting my brows in remonstrance. "You have become a thorough snob, do you know that? If you are so appalled by conditions here, perhaps you ought to do something to make them better."

"I might at that," he said. "God knows I shall have little enough to do in any case."

There was an edge of real bitterness to his voice, and I suppressed a sigh. Val could be difficult enough when he was in a good mood. A peevish Val was altogether insufferable.

Portia signed to us then, her expression triumphant. The blacksmith at Howlett Magna had business where we were bound and agreed, for a sum that seemed usurious, to carry us, with maids, pets, and baggage, to the village of Lesser Howlett. From there we must make other arrangements, he warned, but Portia cheerfully accepted. She called it a very good sign that we had engaged transport so quickly, but I could not help thinking otherwise when I laid eyes upon the blacksmith's wagon. It was an enormous, rocking thing, although surprisingly comfortable and cleaner than I had expected. In a very short time, we were settled, maids and bags and pets in tow, and I began to feel marginally better about the journey.

The countryside soon put an end to that. Each mile that wound out behind us along the road to Lesser Howlett took us further up into the great wide moors. The wind rose here, as plangent as a human voice crying out. Portia seemed undisturbed by it, but I noticed the stillness of Valerius' expression, as though he were listening intently to a voice just out of range. The blacksmith himself was a taciturn sort and said little, keeping his attention fixed upon the pair of great draught horses that were harnessed to the wagon. They were just as stolid, never lifting their heads from side to side, but keeping a steady pace, toiling upward all the while until at last we came to Lesser Howlett.

The village itself looked grim and unhygienic, with a cluster of bleak houses propped against each other and a narrow cobbled road between them. A grey mist hung over the edge of the village, obscuring the view and making it look as though the world simply stopped at the end of the village road. We alighted slowly, as if reluctant to break the heavy silence of the village.

"Good God, what is this place?" breathed Valerius at last.

"The far edge of nowhere, I'd say," came a sour voice from behind us. Morag. She was laden with her own enormous carpetbag as well as a basket for my dog, Florence, and the cage containing my pet raven, Grim. Her hat was squashed down over one eye, but the other managed a malevolent glare.

In contrast, Portia's young maid, Minna, was fairly bouncing with excitement. "Have we arrived then? What a quaint little place this is. Will we be met? The journey was ever so long. I'm quite hungry. Aren't you hungry, Morag?"

Portia, deep in conversation with the blacksmith, called for Minna just then and the girl bounded off, ribbons trailing gaily from her bonnet.

Morag fixed me with an evil look. "All the way, I've listened to that one, chattering like a monkey. I'll tell you something for free, I shall not share a room with her at Grimsgrave, I won't. I shall sooner lie down on this street and wait for death to take me."

"Do not let me stop you," I said graciously. I pinched her arm. "Be nice to the child. She has seen nothing of the world, and she is young enough to be your granddaughter. It will not hurt you to show a little kindness."

Minna was a new addition to Portia's staff. Her mother, Mrs. Birch, was a woman of very reduced circumstances, endeavouring to rear a large family on the tiny income she cobbled together from various sources, including washing the dead of our parish in London and laying them out for

burial. Minna had always shown a keenness, a bright inquis-
itiveness that I believe would stand her in good stead as she
made her way in the world. It had taken little persuasion to
convince Portia to take her on to train as a lady's maid. Our
maids, Morag included, were usually taken from the reformatory our aunt Hermia had established for penitent prostitutes. It seemed a luxury akin to sinfulness to have a maid
who was not old, foul-mouthed, or riddled with disease. I
envied her bitterly, although I had grown rather fond of
Morag in spite of her rough edges.

Portia at last concluded her business with the blacksmith
and returned, smiling in satisfaction.

"The inn, just there," she said, nodding across the street
toward the largest building in the vicinity. "The innkeeper
has a wagon. The blacksmith has gone to bid him to attend
us to Grimsgrave."

I turned to look at the inn and gave a little shudder. The
windows were clean, but the harsh grey stone gave the place
a sinister air, and the weathered signpost bore a painting of
a twisted thorn and the ominous legend "The Hanging Tree."
I fancied I saw a curtain twitch, and just behind it, a narrow,
white face with suspicious eyes.

Behind me, Valerius muttered an oath, but Portia was
already striding purposefully across the street. We hurried
to catch her up, Morag hard upon my heels, and arrived just
as she was being greeted by the innkeeper himself, a dark
young man with the somewhat wiry good looks one occasionally finds in the Gaels.

He nodded solemnly. "Halloo, leddies, sir. Welcome to tha
village. Is i' transport thee needs?"

Portia quickly extracted a book from her reticule and buried her nose in it, rifling quickly through the pages. I poked her sharply.

"Portia, the innkeeper has asked us a question. What on earth are you doing?"

She held up the book so I could read the title. It was an English phrasebook for foreigners. "I am trying to decipher what he just said."

The innkeeper was staring at us with a patient air. There was something decidedly otherworldly about him. I noticed then the tips of his ears where his dark curls parted. They were ever so slightly pointed, giving him an elfin look. I smiled at him and poked my sister again.

"Portia, put that away. He is speaking English."

She shoved the book into her reticule, muttering under her breath, "It is no English I have ever heard."

"Good afternoon," I said. "We do need transportation. We have been told you have a wagon—perhaps you have a carriage as well, that would be far more comfortable, I think. There are five in our party, with baggage and a few pets. We are guests of Mr. Brisbane."

"Not precisely guests," Portia said, sotto voce.

But her voce was not sotto enough. The innkeeper's eyes brightened as he sniffed a bit of scandal brewing. "Brisbane? Does thou mean tha new gennelman up Grimsgrave way? No, no carriage will coom, and no carriage will go. Tha way is too rough. It must be a farm cart."

Portia blanched and Morag gave a great guffaw. I ignored them both.

"Then a farm cart it will be," I said firmly. "And do you

think you could arrange such a conveyance for us? We are very tired and should like to get to Grimsgrave as quickly as possible."

"Aye. 'Twill take a moment. If tha'll step this way to a private room. Deborah will bring thee some tea, and thee can rest awhile."

Valerius excused himself to take a turn about the village and stretch his legs, but I thanked the innkeeper and led my dispirited little band after him upstairs to private accommodation. The inn itself was like something out of a children's picture book. Nothing inside the little building seemed to have changed from the days when highwaymen stalked the great coaching byways, claiming gold and virtue as their right. Still, for all its old-fashioned furnishings, the inn was comfortable enough, furnished with heavy oak pieces and thick velvet draperies to shut out the mists.

The innkeeper introduced himself as Amos and presented a plump young woman with blond hair, Deborah, who bobbed a swift curtsey and bustled off to bring the tea things. We did not speak until she returned, laden with a tray of sandwiches and cake and bread and butter. A maid followed behind her with another tray for Minna and Morag, who perked up considerably at the sight of food. They were given a little table in the corner some distance from the fire, but Portia and I were settled next to it, our outer garments whisked away to have the dirt of travel brushed from them.

When the tea things had been handed round, Deborah seemed loath to go, and at a meaningful glance from Portia, I encouraged her to linger. We had not spoken of it, but it occurred to me—and doubtless to her as well—that it might be a good idea to glean what information we could from the locals about the state of affairs at Grimsgrave Hall.

For her part, Deborah appeared gratified at the invitation to stay. Her blue eyes were round in her pale face, and she refused Portia's suggestion that she send for another cup and share our tea.

"I could not do tha," she murmured, but she patted her little mob cap, and a small smile of satisfaction played about her mouth.

"But you must sit a moment," I persuaded. "You must be quite run off your feet." That was a bit of a reach. The inn was clearly empty, and although it was kept clean enough and the food was fresh and ample and well-prepared, there was an air of desolation about the place, like a spinster who was once the belle of the ball but has long since put away her dancing slippers and resigned herself to the dignity of a quiet old age.

Deborah took a small, straight-backed chair and smoothed her apron over her knees. She stared from me to Portia and back again.

"You seem terribly young to run such an establishment," Portia commented. "Have you been married long?"

Deborah giggled. "I am not married, my lady. Amos is my brother. Will thou have another sandwich? I cut them myself."

Portia took one and Deborah's face suffused with pleasure. "I help him run the inn when we've guests." She looked at us wistfully. "But thee'll not stay here. Amos will take thee to Grimsgrave Hall."

"Is the Hall a very old place?" I asked, pointedly helping

myself to another slice of cake. The girl did have a very light touch. I had seldom had one so airy.

"Oh, yes, m'lady. 'Twas built in the time of the Stuarts, but there was a manor at Grimsgrave since before the Conqueror came."

"Really? How interesting," Portia remarked. "And did it often change hands?"

"Oh, no, m'lady. The Allenby family did own that land in Saxon times. They kept it until last year, when Sir Redwall died and it were discovered there were no money. 'Twas sold, to a newcomer, Mr. Brisbane. He is a friend to thee?"

"He is," I put in smoothly. "We thought to surprise him by paying a visit. Spring on the Yorkshire moors is reckoned to be a very lovely thing."

"Aye, it is," she agreed. "The daffodils are out, and all across the moors you can hear the sounds of the little lambs bleating out their first cries." She hesitated, and I flicked a glance at Portia. This was the time to press the girl.

"Is the Hall a very large establishment? Are there many places in the household for villagers?"

Deborah drew back. "No, m'lady. They've a half-wit girl to do the rough, and a few lads from the farms will help Mr. Godwin with the lambing and shearing when he has need of them. And, of course, Mrs. Butters is cook-housekeeper, but there be no household there like the old days."

"Mr. Godwin?" Portia asked, pouring herself another cup of tea.

Deborah dropped her eyes to the work-roughened fingers in her lap. "Mr. Godwin was a sort of cousin to the late Sir Redwall. His part of the family was never so exalted. They were honest farmers, managers and stewards to the Allenby gentlemen. Mr. Godwin is the last of the Allenby men left. He still has a care for the sheep."

I darted a glance at Portia. This was a curious development. Perhaps this last scion of the Allenbys was the source of Brisbane's difficulties in his new home.

As if intuiting my thoughts, Portia asked, "What sort of man is Mr. Godwin?"

To my surprise, Deborah blushed deeply, not a pretty rose colour, but a harsh mottled red. "He is a fine man, m'lady. He is tall and accounted handsome by the village lasses."

I hid a smile behind my teacup. There was no mystery about Mr. Godwin. He was simply the village Lothario. I wondered if he had ever misbehaved with Deborah, or if she had merely wanted him to. Making a mental note to observe him carefully when we arrived at Grimsgrave, I turned the conversation again.

"And is Mr. Brisbane often seen in the village?"

Deborah shook her head. "Never, m'lady. He keeps up the Hall, and if he has need of something, Mr. Godwin comes. We have not seen him since January past."

This I did not like. Brisbane was an energetic, dynamic man. If he had holed up at Grimsgrave like an animal in its den, it meant he was either brooding or had fallen prey to the vicious migraine headaches he had battled most of his life. I was not certain which was the greater evil.

"Well, we will soon change that," Portia said with forced jollity. "It is such a charming village. We must make certain he enjoys all its natural beauties." I stared at her. What little we had seen of the village had been depressing in the extreme. Dark stone houses clinging together against moor mists and the bleak winds that howled down from the barren heights above, pale folk with pinched faces and suspicious eyes peering out from peeling door-ways. True, Amos and Deborah had been courteous enough, but how much of that had been genuine, and how much had been in anticipation of the coin they might earn?

But Portia's remark had the desired effect. Deborah smiled deeply, revealing a few dimples in her plump cheeks, and she hurried out to see how her brother was coming along with his preparations with the farm cart.

Portia and I each poured another cup and regarded one other. "I do not like this, Julia. Did you see the curtains twitch in the windows as we made our way to the inn?"

"Perhaps they get so few visitors," I began, but gave up when I looked at Portia's cynical face. "No, you are right. I do not like this either. It does not even feel like England anymore, does it? We are strangers in a strange land here."

"If you think this is strange, you havena been to Scot-land," Morag snorted.

We drank our tea and said nothing more.

Some little while later, Amos collected us while Deborah fussed over our things and helped us into our freshly-brushed garments. We thanked her for the tea and paid her handsomely, and as we ventured out into the dying sunlight, I wished we might linger just a bit longer by the friendly little fire in her sitting room. Now that I had nearly reached Grimsgrave Hall—and Brisbane—my courage ebbed a bit, and I wondered what I had been thinking to come so far on a fool's errand.

Portia, sensing my mood, pushed me along, manoeuvring me into the cart and sitting heavily on the edge of my skirts, pinning me in place. "No running back to London, pet," she murmured. "Time to pay the piper now."

If she had shown me any sympathy, I might well have run. But her cool common sense was just the prop for my failing nerve. Valerius joined us then, settling himself before the maids were handed in, the pets coming last in their assorted baskets and cages. I turned my face toward the windy moors and bade Amos drive on.

The drive itself was interminable, and with every turn of the wheels, my stomach gave a little lurch of protest. Amos said little, but did manage to point out the lay of the land. He explained that the village lay at the edge of Grimsgrave Moor and that the Hall itself was on the other side. The road skirted the moor, but he nodded toward a footpath that led over the moor from the churchyard in Lesser Howlett.

"Tha's the quickest way to the Hall. By foot it's more'n an hour. The road goes the long way round, and horses can never make more than a slow walk on account of the steepness and the stones. Two hour, maybe a bit more, and we'll be there."

I shook my head, astonished. I had never imagined that anywhere within our tiny, crowded island, such isolation could still exist. The nearest railway was half a day's journey, and even that was the smallest possible branch line. I had been reared in the South, where all roads led inexorably, and quickly, to London.

I marvelled in silence at the landscape, in contrast to Minna, who chattered about anything and everything. Mercifully, the wind drowned her out, and though I could see her lips moving, I heard very little of what she said. Morag shot her a few filthy looks and attempted to sleep. The bench was unpadded wood and there was little support, but she managed, doubtless a skill she had learned in her days as a Whitechapel prostitute, paying a fraction of a penny to sleep upright lashed to a bench in a doss house.

The dying daylight softened to thick grey shadows over the landscape. Val looked straight ahead, his face set to the wind, while Portia and I gazed out over the moors, watching the grasses move and shift over them like restless waves on a vast inland sea. A lopsided waning moon rose to shed a pale, unreal light over the scene as we continued on, winding our way ever higher, leaving the village far behind.

At length we saw a tiny, ghostly light flicker in the distance. Amos pulled the reins and we stopped a minute. He raised his whip and pointed to the little light.

"Tha's Grimsgrave Hall." The words sent a little chill into my heart. It crouched at the end of a long drive, straight over the moors, unmarked by tree or bush, save a few small, twisted thorns. We passed through a gate, and I could just make out the contours of the house itself, looming low and dark, like some beast crouching in the shadows. Just in front lay a flat, glassy spot—a reed-fringed pond—its black waters barely ruffled by the moor winds. Behind the pond, a wall of black stone rose against the night sky, three pointed arches fitted with windows. As I stared, I saw the moon rise through these windows, as if the moon itself dwelt in the house. And then I realised the wall stood alone, remnant of a ruined wing.

"My God," I murmured. There was no time to point out

my discovery to Portia. Amos had drawn the cart to a stop at the front door of the house and had alighted to hammer upon the great oaken door. I alighted as well, grateful to be out of the cart, but the twist in my stomach did not leave me. All of the nerves I had suppressed in the bustle of the journey rose up with a vengeance, and I found it difficult to swallow, my mouth suddenly dry as tinder.

Chiding myself for a coward, I brushed the dust from my skirts and went to stand behind Amos, feigning a courage I did not feel. I glanced about Brisbane's new home as we waited, wondering why it was impossible to reconcile the urbane gentleman with this dark and forbidding place. The tiny, welcoming light seemed too small, too feeble now. It glowed from a single window leaving the rest of the house shrouded in darkness. Behind me I could hear Minna's little voice reciting the Lord's Prayer, and I very nearly bade her say one on my behalf as well.

After an eternity, the door swung back on its hinges, and the tiniest woman I have ever seen, withered as a winter apple, stood in the doorway.

"Aye, Amos?"

"Ladies and a gennelman to stay wit' Mr. Brisbane," he called over his shoulder as he stalked to the cart and began flinging out baggage. There were a few protesting barks from the dogs and Grim, the raven, made an ominous noise in the back of his throat, but the pets were the least of my worries. I moved forward, inclining my head.

"Good evening. I am terribly sorry to descend upon you without warning. I am Lady Julia Grey. This is my sister, Lady Bettiscombe. Our brother, Mr. Valerius March." Val and

Portia both nodded to the little winter apple who instantly stepped back into the hall.

"Oh, ye must come in out of the wind," she said, her expression one of profound bemusement. "Visitors indeed! We've not had so much excitement since the day the new schoolmaster came to Howlett Magna. Of course we must offer you shelter. Ye might be angels unaware, as the Bible does tell us! Come in, come in!"

We did, and I noticed she wore a mob cap on her fluffy little white curls and a wide pinafore over her striped gown. The entrance hall itself was as old-fashioned as its inhabitant—all heavy oak panelling and great paving stones. A dark carved staircase stood at the back of the hall, its shadows pierced by a single candle on the landing.

"I am Mrs. Butters, the cook-housekeeper," she began, but before she could finish her introduction, I was aware of a presence on the staircase. Mrs. Butters must have seen my glance over her shoulder, for she paused and turned as the vision descended the stairs.

And a vision she was. In spite of the severity of her hairstyle and the plainness of her clothes, she was the most beautiful woman I had ever seen. She was graceful, with a light, dignified step as she descended the staircase slowly. She moved into the light of the hall and I realised she was both older and poorer than I had first thought. She was well over thirty, with a gown that was twenty years out of fashion, its full skirts sweeping the stones of the hall as she walked. Even in the fitful light I could see the faint lines at the corners of her eyes, and at the seams of her dress where it had been turned more than once. But her gaze was calm and level and she looked at us as equals do, her chin high and her expression one of gentle reproof, perhaps at the lateness of the hour.

Mrs. Butters drew back another step. "Guests at Grimsgrave, Miss Ailith. Lady Julia Grey and Lady Bettiscombe and Mr. Valerius March. They are friends of the master's."

The cool, appraising look rested briefly on me, then my sister, lastly Valerius. She stared a long moment, as inscrutable as the Mona Lisa and just as arresting. Her features were beautifully sculpted; no Renaissance master could have fashioned her better. The skin was luminous as alabaster; the eyes wide and impossibly blue. Her brow was high and unmarked, and her corn-gold hair was parted severely in the centre, plaited, and wound round her head like a coronet. Upon a lesser woman, it might have seemed fussy, silly even. On her, it was a Madonna crown, light enough for that lily-neck to bear. Only her hands were unpleasant, red and rough as any laundress', the nails bitten to the quick.

"Welcome to Grimsgrave Hall," she said at last. Her voice was beautifully modulated, with none of the Yorkshire brogue that marked the local folk. "I am sorry we have not prepared a proper welcome for you. We did not expect you," she commented.

"I am certain accommodation can be arranged quickly enough," I returned with a smile. "If you would be so good to tell Mr. Brisbane we've come. And you are?"

Her expression remained sweetly serene as she dipped a suggestion of a curtsey. "I am Ailith Allenby, my lady. Welcome to my home."

I stared at her in confusion. The innkeeper's daughter had told us that Mr. Godwin was the last of the Allenbys, had she not? Then I recalled her words, *the last of the Allenby men,* she had said. No mention of a daughter of the house, I thought with a touch of exasperation.

Portia moved forward, extending her hand as coolly as a duchess. "Miss Allenby," she said, extending a hand. Miss Allenby shook hers gravely, and mine as well. She nodded demurely to Valerius, then motioned for us to follow her. "Amos, leave the baggage in the hall and mind your way back to the village."

Before I could think better of it, I spoke. "It is so late, and it is so far across the moor to the village. Surely a bed could be found for Amos here." I finished with a winsome smile, but I knew at once I had overstepped myself. There was a sudden stillness in the room, and I heard the sharp intake of breath from Mrs. Butters.

Miss Allenby regarded me steadily for a moment, as if she had not quite understood my words, and I half wondered if I ought to offer her Portia's phrasebook.

"There be no proper barn here," Amos put in quietly. "And 'twould not be fit for me to sleep in the house." His tone was edged with harshness, but as he turned away, he gave me a quick nod and I knew he would not forget.

For her part, Miss Allenby seemed determined to pretend I had not spoken. She turned to the rest of us. "If you would care to step into the kitchen, there is a fire kindled. Mrs. Butters, something warming for our guests. Then we must see to their rooms."

Amos took his leave and shut the door behind him as Portia raised a brow at me. We had seldom been entertained in kitchens. But before we could move, the door opened again, flung hard on its hinges. The moor wind gusted inside, flaring the candles as a man strode over the threshold.

"Brisbane," I said, my voice catching. He saw me then, and I think his expression could not have been more surprised if he had seen a ghost. In fact, he stopped a moment and put out his hand, as if to prove to himself I was no wraith.

"You cannot be here," he said finally. His hair was the longest I had ever seen it, witch-black and tumbled to his shoulders. His eyes, black as his hair, were fixed on mine, and he had gone pale under the olive of his skin. His black greatcoat hung carelessly from his shoulders, and as we stood, staring at one another, it slid unheeded to the floor. He wore neither neckcloth nor waistcoat. His white shirt was open at the neck and tucked loosely into his trousers, but it was not the unseemliness of his attire that made me gasp. His shirt and his bare forearms were streaked with blood.

"Brisbane!" I darted forward. "You are hurt."

He shied, stepping aside sharply. I did not touch him. "It is not mine." His voice was hoarse and strange, and for the space of a heartbeat he seemed utterly unknown to me, a stranger in a familiar person. We were inches apart, yet we did not touch, did not speak for a long moment. He was struggling to say something, or perhaps not to say it. His lips parted, but he held his silence. He snapped his mouth closed again, grinding his teeth hard against each other. Unlike the Brisbane of old, whose emotions had been so carefully in check, this man's face wore a thousand of them, warring with each other until I could not tell if he wished to kiss me or throttle me.

"Will you not bid me welcome?" I asked quietly, lightly, forcing a smile. I put out my hand.

He looked down at it, then at my face, and I saw that the mask had settled into place again. The emotions I had seen, or thought I had seen, were mastered once more.

"Welcome," he said coolly, shaking my hand as a stranger might, barely touching my fingertips. "I hope you enjoy your stay at Grimsgrave."

He nodded formally at Portia and Valerius, but said nothing. He brushed past me, stalking toward the staircase. He did not ascend. There was a door underneath it I had not seen in the dim light. He slammed it behind him as he left me standing in the hall, unwanted as a discarded toy.

I smoothed my skirts and turned to follow Portia, averting my eyes from Valerius'. They had heard, of course, as had Miss Allenby. Our hostess did not look at me as we moved into the kitchen, but I knew from the pained expression of her lovely features she pitied me, and in spite of her elegant manner and her beauty, I decided then, quite deliberately, to dislike her.

THE THIRD CHAPTER

Two women placed together makes cold weather.
—William Shakespeare
Henry VIII

To her credit, Miss Allenby said nothing and schooled her expression to serenity by the time we were seated round the fire. She helped Mrs. Butters in cutting and buttering bread and pouring tea, never hurrying, never moving with anything less than perfect composure. It was oddly soothing to watch her, every gesture carefully chosen. I could not imagine her untidy or rushed. And thinking of Miss Allenby prevented me from thinking of Brisbane. My thoughts were so disordered I could not even manage polite conversation. I signed to Portia behind Miss Allenby's back, and nibbled at my lip.

"You must forgive my confusion, Miss Allenby," Portia said with forced politeness. "I thought there were no more Allenbys at Grimsgrave."

Miss Allenby smiled serenely. "The Allenbys built Grimsgrave. We have lived on this land since the days of the Saxon kings. Now, only my mother and sister and I are left. And Cousin Godwin, although he is not of the family proper."

A thousand questions tumbled in my mind, and doubtless Portia's as well, but she kept her queries courteous.

"Ah, a mother, too?" Portia remarked. "And a sister? When will we have the pleasure of making their acquaintance?"

Miss Allenby laid the slices of bread and butter onto a thick brown plate and placed it on the table. There was no cloth, only smooth, scrubbed wood. "My sister, Hilda, is not yet returned from a walk on the moor."

Portia blinked at her. "She must be a very singular sort of person to walk the moors at night."

Miss Allenby's smile deepened. "We were reared on Grimsgrave Moor. It holds few terrors for us, even in darkness. She is often wakeful, my sister. Walking helps to order her thoughts."

A slight shadow passed over the lovely features, and she hurried to leave off the subject of her sister. "My mother is upstairs, abed with a rheumatism. She will be sorry to have missed your arrival, but we did not expect guests. I am afraid Mr. Brisbane did not mention you." She smiled to take the sting out of her words. It worked—almost. "I am quite certain my mother will be better tomorrow. Perhaps you will meet her then." I heard the hesitation in her voice, and I knew precisely what it meant. She had her doubts whether Portia and I would even last the night under a roof where we were so clearly unwelcome. This last thorn-prick was too much.

I rose and yanked at the strings of my cloak, jerked off my hat and tossed them both at Morag. "See to these."

"But your tea, Lady Julia," Miss Allenby began.

"Tea would be very nice, Miss Allenby, but I have a bit of unfinished business to which I must attend first. Do excuse me."

Valerius rose as if to remonstrate with me, but I gave him a silencing look. He lapsed back into his chair and shrugged. His role had been to offer his sisters protection during the journey. What we did once we arrived in Yorkshire was our affair, and he knew he was powerless to interfere.

I made my way to the door Brisbane had used and knocked soundly, not even pausing to gather my courage. There was no reply, and after a moment, I tried the knob, rather surprised to find that it turned easily in my hand. I had half-expected a barricade.

I pushed through and found myself in a large chamber, crowded with indistinct shapes. The light was poor, and it took a moment for me to realise everything in the room was covered in dustsheets. Packed nearly to the ceiling, the shapes left only a narrow path leading to a door in the wall opposite. This door was slightly ajar, flickering light spilling over the threshold. I threaded my way through the dust-sheets, careful to disturb nothing. I hesitated at the door, then pushed it open. I had not troubled to disguise my foot-steps; he would have known I was coming.

The door gave onto a smaller room furnished simply with a bed, a small writing table, and a single chair. A second table, tucked into a corner, had been carefully draped with a piece of linen to cover something, but I did not stop then to wonder what. A little fire burned in the hearth, scarcely large enough to drive the chill from the room.

Brisbane was busy at a basin set upon the deep window-sill. He had stripped off his blood-streaked shirt and was naked to the waist, scrubbing at his hands and forearms until the water went quite red. I had first seen him partially undraped in a boxing match on Hampstead Heath. The effect was still rather striking, and I cleared my throat.

"I am glad you are not hurt," I said, motioning to the impressive breadth of his chest. He was muscular as any statue I had seen in my travels in Italy, and yet there was a sleekness to his flesh that no cold marble could hope to match. Black hair spread from his collarbones to his hips, and I put my hands behind my back lest I be tempted to touch it. High on one shoulder there was a round scar, still fresh, from a bullet he had taken quite deliberately to save another. A different man might have worn the scar as a badge of honour. To Brisbane it was simply a mark of his travels, a souvenir of his buccaneer ways.

He reached for a thin linen towel and wiped at his face. "I might have known it would take more than a closed door to keep you out."

"Yes, you might have." I closed the door behind me and moved to the chair. I did not sit, but the back of it was sturdy and gave me something solid to hold.

I waved at him. "Do carry on. Nothing I have not seen before," I said brightly.

"Do not remind me," he returned with a touch of asperity. "My conduct toward you has been ungentlemanly in every possible respect," he added, turning away.

I blinked rapidly. "Surely you do not reproach yourself? Brisbane, whatever has happened between us has been as much my doing as yours."

"Has it?" he asked, curling his thin upper lip. He moved to the travelling trunk that sat at the foot of his narrow bed. He threw back the lid and reached for a clean shirt. It was a mark of his fastidious ways that he knew precisely where to find one.

I tipped my head to one side and began to enumerate on my fingers. "You did partially disrobe me to question me about the circumstances at Grey House, although I should add that you asked permission first. You kissed me on Hampstead Heath, but as I kissed you back, you can hardly count that amongst your crimes. You gave me a piece of jewellery, highly inappropriate, but I kept it, which is equally inappropriate. We have been together unchaperoned, both at your lodgings and mine, upon numerous occasions. I have seen you in a state of *dishabille* more than once, but on none of those occasions was I specifically invited to view your nakedness. If anything, my misbehaviours quite outnumber yours. I would say we have compromised each other thoroughly. Steady, Brisbane," I finished. "You are about to tear that shirt."

He muttered under his breath as he pulled on his shirt, and I looked away to afford him a chance to settle his temper. When I looked back, he was as tidily dressed as any valet could have managed, his cuffs and collar perfectly smooth, a black silk neckcloth tied neatly at his throat.

"You astonish me, Brisbane. I should not have thought you bothered by the conventions of gentlemanly behaviour."

He turned to face me, his expression betraying nothing

but deep fatigue. "Every man should have something impossible to which he aspires."

"You look tired, Brisbane. What takes you abroad on windy nights and leaves you covered in blood that is not your own?"

He canted his head, his eyes searching my face.

"Sheep. I was assisting a ewe at a difficult lambing. Quite a comedown, isn't it? I am a sheep farmer now."

He crossed his arms over his chest, immobile as any sculpture of antiquity.

I shrugged. "Any man of property who owns livestock could say the same. It is a very great change from your investigations in London, but I do not see why you think it objectionable."

He gave a short, mirthless laugh, sharp and unpleasant. "You do not see. No, you do not. You will see a great deal more when the sun comes up. Folk in the village say this place is accursed, and I am beginning to wonder if they are right."

"Nonsense," I said briskly. "Of course, it is a little remote—"

He laughed again. "Remote? Julia, I do not want you here, and I cannot even compel you to leave because I have no means of sending you back to the village. No carriage can manage these heights, and there isn't even a farm cart left here. The entire property is in shambles. Only the façade of the east wing remains; the rest of it has crumbled to dust. The gardens are overgrown to wildness. Everything of value has been stripped from the house and sold. There is nothing left here except ruin."

"And you," I said, emboldened by his excuses. Brisbane was more determined and more capable than any man I had ever known. Had he really wanted me to leave, he would have carried me to Lesser Howlett on his back and put me on the first train back to London. His pretexts told me everything I ought to know: Brisbane needed me.

His expression was bitter. "I? I am the most ruined thing of all." He turned to face the fire, and for a long moment I watched the play of light over the sharp planes of his face. There was something new in his expression, something careworn and bedevilled that I did not like.

"How did you come to be here?" I asked at length. "I thought you were to receive the viscountcy of Wargrave from the Prime Minister."

I trembled to hear the answer. I had interfered with Brisbane's investigation at Bellmont—interfered so badly it had taken tremendous work on his part to salvage the situation. He had been engaged in business for the government, and the title had been offered as incentive for his involvement. When the promised viscountcy had not materialised, I had blamed myself.

He rubbed at the dark shadow at his jaw. From the look of it, he had not shaved in some days. "Prime Minister was perfectly willing to give me the viscountcy. Then I discovered this property was available. When the previous owner, Sir Redwall Allenby, died, his mother and sisters were forced to sell. Lord Salisbury pointed out that the income from this estate was not sufficient to support the style of a viscount, but when I offered to take the estate in lieu of the viscountcy, he made the arrangements to purchase the property on my behalf."

"But why would you want this place at the expense of the Wargrave title?"

He gave me a long, level stare. "Because it suited me."

That he was concealing something, I had no doubt. But Brisbane could be solitary as an oyster when it pleased him.

"And the Allenby ladies? I presume you have extended your hospitality to them because they have nowhere else to go?"

"Something like that," he said, his eyes flickering away from mine.

Silence stretched between us and I glanced around, noticing for the first time the delicate frieze painted upon the walls. Stylised palms and lilies reached toward the ceiling, and here and there a bird took flight, its wings gilded with a touch of gold paint.

"It is an interesting room," I offered. "The decoration is most unusual."

"Sir Redwall was an Egyptological scholar. His rooms were decorated to suit his tastes."

"Very pretty," I remarked. I drew in a deep breath and moved closer to him. The firelight flickered over his face, casting shadows and lifting them again, making his expression impossible to read. I could see the lines etched at the corners of his mouth, lines I knew too well. I put out a fingertip to trace one.

"You have been in pain. The migraines?" He did not brush my finger away. He closed his eyes a moment, then shook his head.

"I have kept them at bay, but not for much longer I think. I can feel one circling on wings. There is a blackness at the edge of my vision."

"All the time?"

"Most." This time he did brush my finger away, but gently.

"What do you take? Do you still smoke the hashish?"

He shook his head. "Too much trouble to procure it here. Nothing but a glass of whisky before bed."

I clucked at him. "That will never serve. You require something far stronger than that."

"Don't fuss, Julia," he said, but his tone was soft.

I put out my hand again, cupping his cheek. He exhaled sharply, but did not move.

"Brisbane," I murmured. "If you really want me to leave you, tell me now and I will go and you will never see me again. Just one word, that's all, and I will remove myself. Forever."

I stepped closer still. He closed his eyes again and covered my hand with his own. "You smell of violets. You always smell of violets," he said. "You've no idea how many times I have walked these moors and smelled them and thought you were near. On and on I walked, following the scent of you, and you were never there. When I saw you in the hall tonight, I thought I had finally gone mad."

He opened his eyes, and I saw a world of heartbreak there I had never expected. My own eyes filled with tears, and his image shimmered before me.

"You should leave," he said finally, his voice thick. "It would be so much the better for you if you did." His hand tightened over mine.

"But do you want me to go? Will you send me away?"

"No."

I sagged against him in relief, and his arm came around to catch me close to him. I could feel the beat of his heart under my ear and it was the pulse of all the world to me.

Suddenly, he drew back and slid a finger under the chain

at my neck. He tugged gently, and a pendant slid out from under my gown, a coin struck with the head of Medusa and incised with a code Brisbane had chosen at the end of our first investigation. Those few strokes of the engraver's steel told me everything about Brisbane's regard for me that the man himself could not. He turned the pendant over in his hand, then slid it back under the neckline of my gown, his finger warm against my flesh.

"You will regret it," he said finally. "You will be sorry you stayed, and you will come to blame me."

I stepped back and shook my head. "You said the last time we met I was more your equal than any woman you had ever known. Whatever is amiss here, I am equal to it as well. Good night, Brisbane."

He did not bid me good-night, but as he turned to the fire, I heard him murmur, "Forgive me."

And I wondered to which of us he was speaking.

THE FOURTH CHAPTER

She speaks, yet she says nothing.
—William Shakespeare
Romeo and Juliet

"I am afraid there is no other suitable chamber," Miss Allenby apologised when she showed us up. "I have given you my sister Hilda's room. She can share with me, and there is a little closet where Mr. Valerius can be accommodated."

She meant closet in the medieval sense of the word, a small, panelled room with a narrow bed fitted into the wall and a tiny tiled stove for warmth. Valerius gave me an evil look and slammed the door behind him. He had already shown little grace in carrying up the bags, and I decided to leave him be. Perhaps a good night's sleep would smooth his ruffled temper.

Portia and I demurred politely at Miss Allenby giving up her sister's room to us, but she shook her head. "Oh, but you must have Hilda's room. It has a pretty view over the moor, and the bed is bigger than mine. We have so little, but we must make you as comfortable as possible." There was a gentle dignity about her, even as she admitted that the family had fallen on hard times. She showed us to the room, and I was relieved to see it was passable—more heavy, dark oak panelling with furniture to match, what little of it there was. The room appeared to have been stripped of its furnishings save the bed, an enormous monstrosity far too large to fit through either the door or casement. Some long-ago estate carpenter had doubtless assembled it *in situ*, never dreaming anyone would wish to remove it. There was a small chest beneath the window, and a handful of books stood propped upon the sill, leaning haphazardly against one another. I brushed a fingertip over the first, a heavy volume of green kid.

It was a compendium of Egyptian hieroglyphics, and rather an advanced one from the look of it. Miss Allenby smiled. "My sister is a devotee of Egyptian history," she explained. "It is not a very ladylike pastime, but so long as she does not read her books in front of Mama, no one troubles her."

"Indeed," Portia remarked kindly, "Julia's literary tastes are far more shocking, I assure you."

I pulled a face at her, but Miss Allenby said nothing. She was already moving to the fireplace where a fire had been laid in the cold hearth. A warming pan was procured, and Morag heaped it with coals from the kitchen fire and thrust it between the sheets. Within minutes clouds of steam were billowing from the bed, and Miss Allenby had the grace to look abashed.

"It is difficult to air things properly. It can be rather damp on the moor," she murmured. She left us then, and it was just as well. I would have hated a stranger to hear the imprecations uttered by Morag when she inspected the tiny adjoining room and realised she would have to share with Minna.

"Do be quiet, Morag," I instructed. "I am far too tired to listen to you tonight. Finish the unpacking and I promise you may abuse me as long as you like in the morning."

She yanked a gown from my trunk and spun slowly on her heel, surveying the near-empty room. "And where do you suggest I unpack *to*, my lady?"

I sighed. "Very well, I take your point. Not so much as a peg to hang a hat upon. Just fling me my nightdress and go to bed. We will sort it out in the morning."

She snorted and did as she was bid, banging the connecting door to register her displeasure. Minna had already retired, having done twice the work in half the time, and Portia and I were left alone. We made our preparations hastily and scrambled into bed.

"It reminds me of the Great Bed of Ware," Portia observed in ominous tones.

"Not quite so large, but certainly as forbidding," I agreed. "At least the bed curtains are still in evidence. We should freeze otherwise."

She looked around the room, shaking her head slowly. "Steaming beds, no paraffin lamps, and I do not like to look under the bed to make certain, but I *believe* that is a chamber pot."

"Do not speak of it, I beg you," I said faintly.

We stared at each other a long moment. "It is like something out of the Middle Ages. I had no idea people actually lived like this anymore."

"Hush," I warned. "I should not like Miss Allenby to hear you. She has been most hospitable. Clearly, their means are reduced. I am certain it is not their fault."

She pressed her lips together. "Just because they are in *res angusta* doesn't mean the rest of us have to endure it."

There was no possible reply to that, so I did not attempt one. Portia blew out the candle and I drew the bed curtains, shutting out the pale, tattered remnants of moonlight. We huddled together for warmth, careful to keep our toes well clear of the steaming bed warmer.

"Are you going to tell me what he said?" my sister whispered into the darkness.

"No. But we are staying."

"For how long?"

"I cannot say. As long as he needs me, I suppose. Or until I grow tired of bashing my head against the wall."

She reached out and took my hand, saying nothing. We had not slept in the same bed since we were children, and I had forgot what a comfort it could be to have a hand to hold in the dark. Just as I was dropping off to sleep I heard a door close nearby, and female voices—one raised in impatience, the other low and soothing. Ailith was telling her sister of the new arrivals, I surmised. At length they quieted, and I heard nothing more.

The next morning I rose early, feeling better than I had since I had left London. True, Brisbane was bedevilled, and the accommodations were far from comfortable, but the sun was shining, Brisbane had not sent me away, and I had slept surprisingly well. I woke feeling rested and a little stiff from the chill of the room. Portia slept on and I slipped through the curtains, careful not to rouse her. The fire had died, but sunlight was streaming through the window. I pushed it open, breathing in great gusts of fresh moorland air. The moor stretched as far as the eye could see, green and brown, and purpled with heather in a few brave patches. There were dark shadows where the bogs lurked, but the moor had lost the sinister feeling of the previous night. Tufts of grasses spotted with tiny flowers rippled like waves, beckoning me out of doors, and I longed to explore. But first there was breakfast, and I was happily anticipating a hearty meal—my first proper sustenance since we had left London.

The hygienic arrangements were primitive at best. I daubed a bit of cold water about my person and dressed in a warm costume of soft tweeds edged in crimson braid. The skirt was full enough to make walking easy, and there was a divine little pair of low-heeled kid boots—just the thing for scrambling over the moor, I thought. I felt very smart as I descended to breakfast, following the delectable smells to the kitchen. Mrs. Butters was bustling from stove to table, bearing bowls of porridge and hot stewed fruits, racks of toast, and plates of hot, crispy sausages. Behind her scuttled a fey little creature, barely as tall as Mrs. Butters, with an untidy nest of black hair and wide, childlike black eyes. She took one look at me and scurried to the corner where she sat on a tiny stool, peeping over the corner of her apron.

Mrs. Butters leaned close, pitching her voice low. "Pay her no mind, my lady. Tha's Jetty, tha is. She's a halfwit, but a harder worker or a quicker hand you'll never find. Her father is a farmer over Lesser Howlett way. She comes to do the rough. She'll not speak to you, not at first. I pray you'll not take offence, for she means none. She's tha afraid of strangers, she is. But she is blessed in her own way, for the Lord does tell us that the meek shall inherit the earth," she finished firmly.

"Certainly, Mrs. Butters." I glanced at the quivering girl, still staring over the edge of her apron. I gave her a small smile, but she merely threw the apron over her head entirely. I surrendered my efforts to encourage Jetty and turned my attention to breakfast.

"How delicious it all smells, Mrs. Butters," I offered.

She smiled at me, wiping her hands on her apron. Dressed in a striped skirt and an old-fashioned cap, she looked like something out of a picture book. Her cheeks were flushed pink with the heat of the stove, and her little curls were tight from the steam.

"I would offer thee coffee or tea, but we've only tea, so tha must do."

"Tea is perfect, Mrs. Butters. Thank you."

She motioned me to take a chair and I obeyed, charmed by the contrast between this humble kitchen breakfast and the elaborate morning meals I customarily took in London. The kitchen itself was tidy and well-organised, with a neat larder tucked to the side. Through the open door I could see row upon row of bottles, jewel-bright with fruits and vegetables put away against the winter. Although it was nearly spring, there was still a good supply of the previous year's harvest which spoke of good housewifery, in spite of the condition of the rest of the estate. It was a place to be proud of, and I wondered idly what the pantry in my London house had looked like before the place was burned down. It had never occurred to me to inspect it, and I made a mental note to be more diligent with my next home.

Mrs. Butters brought a tray with pots of jam and little plates of butter, and a few other delights. "Thee'll be thinking this is very different from London."

I reached for a piece of toast. "I begin to think you must have a touch of the witch about you, Mrs. Butters. I was indeed pondering that very thing."

She gave a little start. "Say no such thing, my lady! Witches indeed, such a thing is not to be borne. Has tha not read the Bible?"

I hastened to make amends. "It was simply a jest, Mrs. Butters," I soothed. "This jam is quite delicious. Did you make it yourself?"

Her ruffled feathers settled themselves quickly. "No, bless you. Her ladyship always saw to her own stillroom. Comfits and preserves, a great one she was for those. Bottling fruits and mushrooms and brewing wines. Miss Ailith helps her with it, now she has grown frail. Ah, here is my lady."

She nodded toward the door where Ailith Allenby was following an elderly lady into the room. But Lady Allenby was unlike any elderly lady I had seen before. She was every inch as tall as her daughter, and even in old age her face bore traces of great beauty. She carried herself with the bearing of a queen, and I rose to my feet to greet her.

"Lady Allenby, I am Lady Julia Grey."

She smiled gravely as she approached the table. A single glance at her hands revealed why she had not offered one in greeting. They were gnarled like old vines with odd lumps and swellings, the marks of lingering rheumatism. There were lines etched by pain at her eyes, but those eyes were warm with welcome. "My dear, I am so pleased to make your acquaintance. Please sit. Do not allow your breakfast to get cold."

Miss Allenby and I exchanged nods and innocuous remarks about the weather. She looked a little embarrassed as she accounted for her sister's absence.

"Hilda is tending the chickens, and Godwin is out near Thorn Crag this morning. One of the rams has gone missing," she told me. She did not speak of Brisbane and I did not ask. I should see him soon enough, and I was buoyed by the thought that now I had ensconced myself at Grimsgrave Hall, I should have all the time in the world to settle matters between us. As far as Hilda was concerned, a girl who was more interested in her chickens than in visitors from London was not likely to offer much in the way of conversation, I mused. There would be plenty of opportunities yet to make her acquaintance.

Lady Allenby settled herself into a chair as Ailith plumped a cushion behind her. "You must forgive us for clinging to the old customs here, my lady. We are not so fashionable as you southerners. Here we eat in the kitchen, and do our needlework and reading by the fire. We must have our economies," she added with a solemn sort of dignity. A lesser woman would have apologised for her poverty, but not Lady Allenby.

I hastened to reassure her. "I am not fashionable in the least, I promise you, Lady Allenby. I do not dine with the Marlborough House set, and it is years since I went to Court."

She shook her head at the mention of the Prince of Wales'

companions. "Disgraceful. A pack of German upstart prince-lings. They are not of the old blood. Not like your family," she said approvingly. "I had a peek in Debrett's before you awoke. A fine old English family, yours is."

I tried not to think of all the French and Irish scapegraces who had married into the Marches. "Yes, well, I suppose we have been here rather longer than some folk."

Lady Allenby smiled benevolently. "And not as long as others. There have been Allenbys here since the time of Edward the Confessor."

"Indeed? I shall be very interested to hear the history of this place."

She gave me a gracious nod. "Whatever you should like to know, you have only to ask. Of course, it is not my place to show you the house. You are Mr. Brisbane's guest, and the honour will fall to him."

It seemed an awkward patch in the conversation, and I hastened to smooth it over. "I am certain Mr. Brisbane cannot possibly do justice to its history compared to yourself, Lady Allenby."

She inclined her head again, putting me greatly in mind of a queen granting a boon to a serf.

"It is very nice for Mr. Brisbane to have visitors. One worries about the bachelors of the species, they are too often solitary creatures," Lady Allenby said with an effort at delicacy, I thought. Clearly she wondered about our presence, and I felt compelled to at least try to be forthright with her.

"I am afraid the situation is not quite as we thought," I began cautiously. I was not entirely certain how much to reveal. I was deeply conscious of Ailith Allenby hovering nearby as she prepared her mother's plate. I had no desire to make my private affairs fodder for Allenby family gossip, but we were living cheek-by-jowl with them as it were, and it seemed silly to ignore the situation altogether.

"My sister and I were rather precipitous. We thought that, as a bachelor, Brisbane was in need of some feminine assistance in ordering his household. We did not realise you and the Misses Allenby were in residence."

Lady Allenby spread her hands. The joints were thick and swollen, but still elegant, and on her left hand she wore a thick band of gold, braided with baroque pearls and old-fashioned, lumpy rubies.

"My dear lady, you must not think Ailith and I will be in your way, and Hilda is positively useless at domestic matters. We are simply guests of Mr. Brisbane's while he kindly oversees the refurbishment of one of the outbuildings for our use. He has been exceedingly generous to us. There was no provision under the terms of the sale of Grimsgrave Hall for my daughters or myself. What he does for us is solely out of his own sense of charity."

As there seemed no possible response to this, I did not attempt one.

While I finished my toast, I darted glances at Ailith, attempting to make out her character. I realised that in spite of her remarkable beauty, Ailith Allenby's life had likely not been an easy one. I felt ashamed of my first impulse to dislike her, and determined to make an effort to befriend her.

I smiled at her briefly, then turned to her mother. "I do hope you are quite recovered, Lady Allenby. Miss Allenby told us last night you were suffering from a rheumatism."

"The last year has been a trial," she said softly. "My rheu-matism is grown much worse now. My hands, my hips. Some days I can scarcely rise from my bed. Still," she said forcefully, "we are given no trials over which we cannot triumph with the aid of the Divine." She touched the chain at her belt, and I realised it was a rosary. I suppressed a sigh. Between Lady Allenby's devoutness and Mrs. Butters' fondness for Holy Scripture, I feared I would find their company a trifle tedious. My father had once famously stated in Parliament that religion was as intimate as lovemaking and ought to be as private. The thought was not original to him, but it reflected his views quite accurately. While we had attended church, it was seldom with any true regularity, and God was seldom discussed in our family except in a very distant sort of way, rather like our cousins in Canada.

Lady Allenby lifted a crooked hand to her daughter. "Ailith, dearest, I find I am in need of St. Hildegarde's ointment." Lady Allenby turned to me. "We are fortunate at Grimsgrave to have a Gypsy woman who lives in a cottage out on the moor. She is a skilful healer and a most interesting woman. Perhaps you would care to make her acquaintance?"

"I will go this morning and fetch more ointment," Ailith said. "If Lady Julia would care to accompany me, she would be most welcome." She darted a quick, birdlike glance at me from under her dark gold lashes. She spooned out some fruit for her mother and broke a piece of toast into manageable bits. "You must keep up your strength, Mama," she murmured.

Lady Allenby gave her daughter a fond look. "Thank you, child. Yes, I will eat it all, I promise."

They made a game of it, with Ailith filling her plate slowly with tempting morsels, and Lady Allenby finishing it a bit at a time until she had at last eaten a full breakfast. She managed quite well so long as she used both hands to steady her utensils. Ailith herself had merely nibbled a piece of dry toast, and I wondered if she cared for her mother at the expense of herself.

After I finished the last of the rather excellent fruit compote, we excused ourselves, and I went to look in on Portia. She was still slumbering peacefully, one arm thrown over her face as she slept. I did not bother to pause at Val's door; I could hear the snores reverberating through it well enough. The maids were making their way down to breakfast, Morag muttering all the while about the laxness of some establishments that did not even provide morning tea. I might have pointed out the laxness of maids who did not rise in time to attend their mistresses, but it was far simpler to ignore her and gather my things to meet Ailith in the hall as we had arranged.

Just as I reached the bottom of the stairs, Brisbane emerged from his rooms, impeccably dressed and carrying a small portmanteau, his greatcoat draped over his arm. He caught sight of me just as he pulled the door closed.

"Good morning," he said smoothly. He nodded toward the shawl in my hand. "You will want something warmer than that if you mean to venture out on the moor. The sun is out, but it is deceptively chilly."

I swallowed hard, my fine breakfast suddenly sitting like a stone in my stomach. "Don't let's talk about the weather when you are clearly leaving. Did you even mean to say goodbye?"

He shrugged. "I am bound for Scotland for a few days upon business."

"Business! I thought you had given up your inquiries."

"Never. I have merely closed my rooms in Half Moon Street for the present. I am conducting my investigations from Grimsgrave unless circumstances demand my presence. Such is the case I have undertaken in Edinburgh."

"Why cannot Monk look to this investigation?" Monk was the most capable of his associates, acting as confidant, valet, and majordomo for Brisbane as circumstances demanded. He was also a skilled investigator in his own right, and I had wondered at his absence from Grimsgrave. As a former military man, he ought to have had the place wholly organised and functioning smoothly in a fortnight.

"Monk is already engaged upon a case, and I cannot spare him," he replied, tidying his already immaculate cuffs. "I must see to this myself."

"And you thought to creep away whilst I was upstairs," I observed coolly.

His nostrils flared slightly with impatience. "I thought it would be rather easier if I left without a formal leave-taking."

"Easier upon whom?" I asked, wincing at the touch of acid in my voice.

Brisbane noted it as well. "You're playing it quite wrong," he advised. "You ought to be disdainful and remote and tell me that you plan to go back to London and if I wish to see you, I will have to follow you there."

"I never manage to keep to a proper script," I admitted. "I've too little pride in this instance. Oh, you are a devil, Brisbane. You knew last night you were leaving, didn't you? That is why you did not pack me back to London by the first train. You thought you would slip out this morning and I would be so outraged at your behaviour I would leave of my own accord."

"Well, it was worth the attempt," he conceded. "You do have a rather spectacular temper when you are roused."

"I do not," I countered hotly. "I am the calmest, most collected—" I noted the gleam in his eye then and gave him a shove. He caught my hand and pressed it against his shirt-front. The linen was soft under my fingers, and just beneath it I could feel the slow, steady beating of his heart. I felt the heat rising in my face and pulled my hand away.

"Do not think to distract me. You have business here as well, Brisbane. There are things that must be settled between us," I said, sounding much more decisive than I felt.

He opened his mouth to respond, but suddenly, his gaze shifted to a point just over my head and he dropped my hand. "Ailith is coming," he murmured.

I turned to greet her. She had donned a warm cloak of fine blue wool and draped a shawl of the same over her head. She looked like a Madonna fit to grace any master's canvas.

"You are dressed better than I for the moor wind, I think," I told her. "Brisbane was just saying—" I turned, but the hall was empty, the door swinging wide upon its hinges. "Where the devil did he go?" I demanded.

Ailith dropped her eyes at my language, and I made a mental note to exercise a bit more decorum.

"I saw no one," she said. I did not doubt it. Brisbane had certainly heard her step upon the stair and seen the distinctive blue hem of her gown. All it had taken was a moment's misdirection on his part, skilful as any conjurer, and my attention was diverted long enough for him to make his escape.

"Blast him," I muttered. But I had no intention of discussing the matter with Ailith Allenby, and it occurred to me that Brisbane's absence might be a perfect opportunity for me to take the lay of the land. Brisbane had been terribly mysterious about his doings at Grimsgrave, and I was very keen to know the full extent of his troubles.

I looked at Ailith and realised I was still grumbling to myself, for she was looking at me with the gentle, quizzical glance that nurses reserve for mentally defective patients.

"Never mind," I said, forcing my voice to cheerfulness. "I believe I am poorly dressed for an excursion on the moor."

She looked at the tiny feathered hat perched atop my head and frowned. "I am afraid that will never do, my lady. The moor wind will whip it away, and your ears would be quite chilled. And that thin shawl will not keep out a bit of the wind. Let me find you a proper shawl."

She hastened off, returning a moment later with another heavy length of blue wool and a pair of alarmingly ugly rubber boots. I stood very still as she wrapped my head with the scarf, trying not to think about how trying blue was against my complexion and trying not to breathe too deeply. The shawl still smelled of the sheep it had been shorn from. She wrapped it tightly, unlike her own elegant drape, and tucked the ends firmly into my skirt, plumping my waist unbecomingly.

She clucked over my boots, insisting I remove them on the grounds they would be instantly ruined in the mud. Flat boots or pattens, she advised me, although rubber boots were by far the best. She fitted me with a pair that pinched a little—in spite of her height, Miss Allenby had tiny feet—and declared us ready. She looped a basket over her arm and we left the house by the kitchen door, and as we walked it suddenly occurred to me to wonder why Brisbane had referred to Ailith Allenby by her Christian name.

THE FIFTH CHAPTER

My flocks feed not, my ewes breed not,
My rams speed not, all is amiss.
—William Shakespeare
"The Passionate Pilgrim XVII"

We passed into a garden, or rather, what had once been a garden. Sheltered by high stone walls, it was a peaceful place that had clearly once been a productive one as well. Gnarled old fruit trees sprawled against the walls, but it was easy to see the bones of where they had once been espaliered. Beds, edged in crumbling brick, were thick with weeds and overgrown bushes, and just at the edge, sheltered in the recess of a wall, a set of beehives stood quiet and empty. A small plot was still in cultivation, but it had been planted with an eye to industry rather than beauty. It bore none of the traces of elegance that lingered yet in the rest of the garden.

Miss Allenby saw my interest and the faintest of blushes

tinged her cheeks. "The gardens of Grimsgrave were once renowned for their beauty. Even the kitchen garden was lovely. It has been many years since we have had gardeners to tend them. Godwin does what little he can with this plot, and Mama still has a tiny garden for her flowers." She gestured toward a sunny spot where a listless bunch of daffodils struggled limply out of the dark, peaty soil. "Most of our vegetables are delivered by folk who used to be our tenant farmers," she added, her tone edged with emotion—nostalgia perhaps?

She motioned toward the far end of the garden where a rotting wooden door sagged in the stone wall. I turned back, eager to see Grimsgrave Hall in the clear light of day. It was almost as forbidding as it had been by moonlight. The native gritstone, once handsome no doubt, had weathered to blackness, giving the entire façade a gloomy cast. The ruined wing put me in mind of a skeleton, its flesh rotted away from the bones. But the structure itself, Jacobean in design, was elegant if old-fashioned. Properly rebuilt and with thoughtful landscaping, it might still be redeemed.

"It would take a miracle from God and more money than I will ever see in my lifetime to rebuild it," Miss Allenby commented, intuiting my thoughts.

"It is a handsome place," I offered, following slowly as she led the way to the wooden door.

"Handsome, but rotten through and through. I have a model of the house, as it used to be. It is a doll's house really, but it was built by an architect who came to make a study of the house. He presented it to my grandmama when she was still in the nursery, and eventually it was given to me to play with. It is a lovely thing, but it makes me quite sad sometimes to see how it used to be. Mind your step here, my lady. A bit of stone has come loose," she warned.

I followed her into a pleasure garden, this one derelict as well. It had been well-planned and probably well-executed, but little that was recognisable remained. Woody old vines choked a statue of an ancient king, and here and there a few scattered bits of stone spoke of ornaments long since destroyed.

"That is King Alfred," Miss Allenby informed me, gesturing toward the decrepit old king. "He is an ancestor of the Allenbys. We are of ancient Anglo-Saxon stock," she said proudly. Her chin was tipped high, and I could well see the resemblance to old royalty in her profile. I had read long before that the athelings, the children of Saxon royalty, had been reckoned by the conquering Normans to be the handsomest people they had ever seen. It was not so difficult to believe Miss Allenby was of this tribe. I said as much to her and she laughed, clearly pleased.

"There is an old tale that Pope Gregory once saw a group of Angle children for sale in the Roman slave market at Deira. He was so struck with their beauty, he asked who they were. He was told they were Angles, and he replied, 'Non Angli, sed angeli.'"

"'Not Angles, but angels,'" I translated.

"Precisely."

We passed through the pleasure garden and beyond another crumbling door. As soon as we crossed the threshold, I gasped, for stretching before me was the moor, vast and rolling, empty and endless as the sea. It was beautiful, and yet inhospitable as well.

Miss Allenby stood next to me. "When I was a little girl, I was frightened of the moor. The way the wind always rises, keening like a human voice. The local folk call it a speaking wind. One is never entirely alone on the moor. That wind always blows, and that voice is always there."

"I can well imagine it," I murmured.

"But it can be a great comfort as well," she said, turning aside. Her expression had not changed, but I noted the black of her gown and remembered the brother whose death had necessitated the loss of her home. Did she mourn him still?

A narrow path wound its way through the moor grasses, here quite straight, there bending a little to skirt a bit of rock or a boggy patch. There was just enough room to walk abreast and we did so. I had thought the moor empty, but as we moved farther from the Hall, I noticed the occasional bird, beating its wings to rise above the grasses, or heard the bleating of sheep carried on the wind.

She pointed out the dark, peaty waters that swirled and sucked in boggy places, ready to close over the unsuspecting. She warned me sternly against straying from the path, and lifted her arm to point out a shimmering expanse of black water in the distance.

"Grimswater. It is an ancient place, that lake—full of magic. They say the god who lives there gave this moor its name."

"Really? I should have thought the name Grimsgrave quite appropriate in any event."

Miss Allenby gave a quick, light laugh. "The moor is not so sinister as that. Grim was a Saxon god, and *grave* merely means pit or shaft. This moor was mined in ancient times, even through the Roman occupation. Silver and lead run deep under these lands."

She nodded toward the surging waters of Grimswater. "They say there was once a town there, where the waters now stand. It was a rich place, with fine houses and proud people. One day a poor man searched the town for shelter and food, but none would offer him succour. Only the poorest farmer would give him a crust and a bed. When he had taken the farmer's hospitality, the poor man, who was a god in disguise, raised his hand and cursed the town."

Miss Allenby paused a moment, her eyes closed. Then she opened them, spread her arms and intoned,

> *"Grimswater rise, Grimswater sink,*
> *And swallow all the town save this little house*
> *Where they gave me food and drink."*

Her voice was commanding as a priestess' and I shuddered a little. It was too easy to imagine her, clad in the robes of a pagan witch, conjuring spirits to do her bidding.

She smiled then, and the effect was lost. "It is atmospheric, isn't it? They say the waters rose at once and covered the town, drowning everyone. The Saxons used to throw sacrifices into the lake to keep the gods happy. Even now, when the wind is coming off the waters, you can hear a bell tolling under the lake. It is said to presage a death in my family," she finished softly.

"The moor is full of old legends, isn't it?" I asked faintly. There was something quite otherworldly and a little unsettling about Ailith Allenby. Talking to her was rather like conversing with a faery or a unicorn.

"Oh, yes. There are soft places where the souls of those who have been sucked into the bogs cry for help."

"Is that all?" I demanded. "They don't drag folk down into the bog with them or carry off one's children?"

"No," she said, her tone edged with peevishness. "I think you are making sport."

"Not a bit," I told her truthfully. "We have the most useless ghosts at my father's house. I always think if one is going to be haunted, it's rather nicer to be haunted by something *useful*, don't you think? Your tolling bell, for example. Quite helpful indeed. An Allenby would hear that and know he ought to change his ways or at the very least make a proper confession if he is to die soon."

She turned wordlessly and led the way across the moor. I realised my tongue had run away with me and thought to make amends, but the wind rose and rendered conversation impossible. We trudged along, here and there helping each other over the muddiest bits, until we reached a crossroads in the path. A direction board pointed out the proper way to the village, but Miss Allenby struck out toward the left, taking a smaller path that wound higher up on the moor. I followed now, struggling to catch my breath as Miss Allenby led the way, unruffled as ever. If my flippancy had offended her, she had decided to overlook it, and I relaxed a bit, enjoying the glorious fresh air and the spectacular views.

After a few minutes, we came over a rise and I saw, sheltered just below us, a cottage sitting beside another crossroads. It was a tumbledown little place of faery-tale proportions, with a high-peaked roof that sagged in the middle and a profusion of roses twining about the doorway, although the flowers themselves would not bloom for another two months. The cottage was set apart from the path by a low stone wall, and within its shelter lay the most enchanting garden I had ever seen.

In spite of the cold and the mud there was a profusion of green, a whole world yearning toward the sunlight and spring. Set into the stone wall was a little wicket gate, and Miss Allenby pushed through, scattering a few fat, speckled chickens as she walked. They clucked at her but continued to scratch at the ground contentedly. A fragrant plume of smoke issued·from the chimney, and welcoming lights glowed at the leaded windows.

Before Miss Allenby even raised her hand to knock, the door was thrown back.

"Miss Ailith!" cried the woman on the threshold in welcome. "You have brought me a visitor," she said, stepping forward and taking my hand in her own. She was an extraordinary creature. Her colouring, like most Gypsies of my acquaintance, was dark, all olive skin and striking black eyes. Her black hair was loose, curling to her waist and threaded thickly with silver. Gold coins hung at her wrists and ears, and long chains of them were wrapped around her neck. A single thin band of gold circled her marriage finger. She wore several skirts, each more colourful than the last, and a becoming blouse with a deep ruffle at the elbow. Her hand was warm over mine, and her smile was genuine.

"You are Lady Julia," she pronounced in tones of great import.

I gave her a cool, deliberate smile. "It is no great feat of clair-voyance to listen to neighbourhood gossip," I said blandly.

She laughed at this, displaying beautiful white teeth. "Come in, lady. I am Rosalie Smith. Come along, Miss Ailith."

She ushered us into the cottage. It was as charming within as without. A single room, it was comfortably fur-nished for any possible use. A cheerful fire burned on a wide brick hearth, an assortment of pots and pans ranged around it on iron hooks. Bundles of herbs and flowers hung from the rafters well away from the fire, their fragrances mingling to something spicy and delicious in the warm room. There was a scrubbed table, large enough to seat four, and com-fortable chairs with freshly-woven rush seats and gaily pat-terned cushions. A snug bed had been pushed under the window and tucked neatly with a spread of patchworked cottons and velvets edged in bright taffeta. A black cupboard, beautifully painted with pastoral scenes, stood in the corner, and next to it stood a small table with a violin and a sheaf of music.

The Gypsy woman held out her hands for my wraps. "Come and warm yourself by the fire. I will make a tisane for you. Something to warm the blood."

I struggled out of the blue shawl and various other bits and pieces and took a chair, grateful to be out of the wind. Miss Allenby rested her basket on the stone-flagged floor at her feet while our hostess busied herself with cups and saucers and little pots.

At length she joined us at the table. "Miss Ailith, black tea with a bit of raspberry leaf," she said, passing her a tiny teapot. "Lady Julia, a tisane of borage." I peeked into the pot and was enchanted to find a pale green decoction, spotted with just a few tiny, starry blue flowers.

"How lovely," I said. Rosalie Smith gave me an enigmatic smile.

"All herbs have their purpose, lady. They can heal or kill, but one must know their secrets."

The conversation seemed mildly sinister to me, and I glanced sharply at my harmless-looking tisane before changing the subject.

"I confess, Mrs. Smith, I am surprised to find a Romany living so settled a life. You are far removed from the road up here, are you not?"

Another might have taken offence at the question, but not Mrs. Smith. She merely gave me one of her inscrutable smiles and poured out her own cup of tea. Very strong and black, she took it with no sugar, straining the leaves through her teeth as I had so often seen the women of her people do.

"I am here because it suits me, lady," she said, her tone friendly. "I have a purpose here. When it is served, I will rejoin my own folk."

"A purpose?" I sipped at the borage tisane. It was delicious. The flavour was light and reminded me of tea, but greener somehow, with a thread of something I could not quite place.

"Cucumber?" Mrs. Smith hazarded, watching me.

"Yes! It is quite refreshing," I told her. She smiled again, clearly gratified.

"I make many tisanes, for many ailments. The villagers and farmers have learned to come to me for their troubles."

"Are there no doctors? Not even in the village?"

Mrs. Smith shrugged, and Miss Allenby put down her cup. "There is one, but he is quite elderly. His hands tremble, and he is very often the worse for drink."

"Besides," put in Mrs. Smith, "the old ways are often the best, do you not agree, Lady Julia?"

I shrugged, thinking of Val's enthusiasm for the latest advances. "They can be. I think there is much to be said for modern medicine as well."

Mrs. Smith laughed. "You are a complicated woman, I think. You look with one eye to the past and another to a future you cannot yet see."

"Doesn't everyone?" I asked coolly. I was well-accustomed to the Gypsy tendency to make mystical pronouncements.

Mrs. Smith turned to Ailith Allenby. "How does your lady mother?"

"Better, thank you. She asked me to fetch more of the ointment for her joints and more of the meadowsweet and liquorice tea. Her hands have been troubling her of late."

Mrs. Smith nodded. "I will send along some quince jelly as well. Tell her to take a spoonful every day. And you will take her some fresh peppermint from the garden. Steep a handful in hot water and tell her to sip it slowly. It will stimulate the appetite." She cast an eye over Ailith's slender figure. "Drink a cup yourself. You will not last out another winter if you do not put meat upon those bones."

To my surprise, Miss Allenby did not seem to resent the observation. She merely smiled and sipped at her tea. Just then there was a scratching at the door and a low, pitiful moan. I started, but Mrs. Smith waved me to my chair with a laugh.

"'Tis only Rook," she said, opening the door to admit a

white lurcher. He was thin, with sorrowful eyes and a clutch of long, pretty feathers in his mouth.

"What have you brought me, little one? A fat pheasant for the pot?"

He dropped it and gave her a worshipful stare. She patted him and waved him toward the fire. He stretched out before the hearth, giving a contented sigh as he settled onto the warm stones.

Mrs. Smith put her prise into a basin and laid it aside.

"I will clean it later. Perhaps your ladyship would like the feathers for a hat?" she added hopefully.

They were lovely feathers, and I knew she would haggle tirelessly over the price.

"That's quite illegal, you know," Miss Allenby commented, nodding toward the basin. "That dog is a poacher."

Mrs. Smith roared with laughter, holding a hand to her side. "Bless you, lady, of course he is! All Gypsy dogs know the value of a fat bird. He was of no use to my husband because he is white, but he suits me well enough."

I had heard before that the Roma never kept white dogs as they were too easily detected when they were thieving, but I was more interested in the other little titbit Mrs. Smith had revealed.

"Your husband? Does he travel then?"

"Aye, lady. He travels with our family, but I keep a place for him here when the caravans come this way. That is his violin," she said, nodding toward the instrument on the little table. "And the bed is wide enough for two."

She roared with laughter again while Miss Allenby and I looked politely away. Had it not been for Miss Allenby's company, I might have joined in her laughter. I had always had an affinity for such women—comfortable and at ease in their own skin—and I had known a few of them. My father's particular friend, Madame de Bellefleur, and Minna's own mother, Mrs. Birch, came to mind. But Miss Allenby was cool to the point of primness and I did not like to shock her.

She reached for her basket then and presented it to Mrs. Smith. "Godwin slaughtered a lamb, and Mama has sent along a small joint. I hope that will be sufficient?" It was a question, but only just. It was apparent from her tone that she considered the haunch a fair trade for the medicinals she had come to fetch.

Mrs. Smith peered into the basket, inspecting the lamb carefully. She put it aside and handed the basket back to Miss Allenby. "It will do," she said at length. "The dew will be dry now. Go and cut an armful of mint. I will fetch the ointment of St. Hildegarde and the quince jelly."

Miss Allenby rose and took up her wraps and basket. Rook the lurcher raised his head lazily when she opened the door, then laid it back down.

"He is a lazy one," Mrs. Smith commented with a fond look at the dog. "But his company suits me."

"It must get lonely for you," I ventured, "alone up here, with only the odd villager for company."

Mrs. Smith shrugged. "I told you, lady, I have a purpose. If one has a purpose, life is bearable enough, do you not think so?"

I did think so, in fact. I had spent the better part of my widowhood searching for one.

"But I think you will be lonely here," she said suddenly,

leaning toward me and pitching her voice low. "And when you are, you must come to Rosalie. You will have no greater friend on the moor. Do you understand?"

I did not, but I smiled at her, wondering if she had perhaps become a bit unhinged living in such isolation.

"How very kind of you," I began, but she waved me off.

"I am not kind," she said firmly. "My family is known for its gifts, but I do not have the sight. I do not see the future, although I do feel when danger is about. I feel it now, and it hovers over you, like a creature with great black wings."

I stopped myself from rolling my eyes in annoyance. I had heard such things before, always from a Gypsy fortune-teller who wanted her palm crossed with silver.

"I do not wish to have my fortune told, Mrs. Smith, and I am afraid I have no coin on me at present."

To my astonishment, she grabbed my hand and held it firmly in both of hers. Her hands were warm and smooth and I could catch the scent of herbs on her skin. "Lady, I do not want your money. I speak honestly of friendship. You must call me Rosalie, and you must come to me whenever you have need of me. Promise me this."

I promised, albeit reluctantly. She rose then and rummaged in the black-painted cupboard. She returned with a tiny pouch of brightly-patterned red cotton. She pressed it upon me.

"Carry this with you always. It is a charm of protection."

I must have looked startled, for she smiled then, a beautiful, beneficent smile. "I am a *shuvani*, lady. A witch of my people. And I want you to know I will do everything I can to protect you."

I took the little pouch. It had been knotted tightly with

a silken thread and it held several small items, nothing I could recognise from the shape. "I do not know what to say, Mrs. Smith—"

"Rosalie," she corrected. "Now keep that with you and show it to no one."

Obediently, I slipped it into my pocket, and only then did she resume her lazy, good-natured smile.

"I think Miss Ailith is ready to leave," she commented, nodding toward the window. "Have you finished your tisane?"

"Yes, thank you." I collected my wraps and bent to pet the lurcher. He gave a little growl of contentment and thumped his tail happily on the floor.

"Tell me, Rosalie," I said, twisting the unbecoming shawl over my hair, "if all herbs have a purpose, what was the point of giving me borage?"

Rosalie smiled her mysterious smile. "Have you never heard the old saying, lady? Borage for courage."

I collected Miss Allenby from the front garden and we bade Rosalie farewell. She pressed the jar of quince jelly and a tin of ointment upon Miss Allenby who thanked her graciously. As we passed through the wicket gate, I fell deeply into thought, pondering what Rosalie had told me. Perhaps she belonged to a more subtle variety of Gypsy than those I had yet encountered. Perhaps, rather than overt offers to tell fortunes or lift curses, Rosalie's methods were more insidious. I had not paid her for the little charm, but who was to say that on my next visit she might not insist the danger was growing nearer and that only a costly amulet might hold it at bay? It was a cynical thought, but one that bore consideration, I decided as I tripped over a stone.

Miss Allenby put out a hand to steady me, aghast. "My apologies, Lady Julia. I would have warned you about that stone, but I did not imagine you could have missed it."

She was right about that. It was nearly a yard across, a marker of sorts at the little crossroads in front of the cottage, and though it stood only a few inches proud of the earth, it was enough to catch an unwary foot.

"I was woolgathering," I said apologetically.

She nodded. "I can well understand, although I have never found the moor a good place to think—the wind seems to drown out my very thoughts. But my brother used to walk the moor quite often when he was puzzling out a problem, and my sister still does. Perhaps you will find it a restful place as well, should you stay for some time."

As a conversational gambit, it was blunt and inelegant. I rose to it anyway and replied with perfect truth. "I do not know how long I shall be at Grimsgrave. Some weeks at least, I should expect." Heaven only knew precisely when Brisbane would return, and it could take some time after that to settle matters between us.

She nodded, as if I had confirmed some private conviction of hers. "It is a great distance to travel for a shorter visit," she observed.

"That it is," I agreed.

We moved down the path toward the turning for Grimsgrave Hall. The wind had died a little, and I seized the opportunity to take a better measure of Miss Allenby's situation.

"Your brother was Sir Redwall Allenby?"

She nodded, her face averted.

"I understand he was an Egyptologist, a scholar," I ventured.

She paused, but still did not turn to me. "He was. He made quite a name for himself in certain circles."

The lovely mouth was thin now, the lips pressed together as though to hold back some strong emotion. Impulsively, I put out a hand.

"I believe his death was fairly recent, and I can see that it grieves you still. Please accept my condolences on your loss."

She opened her mouth to speak, then shut it, sudden tears shimmering in her eyes. After a moment she composed herself and turned to me.

"You are very kind, Lady Julia. It was sudden and you are quite correct. It does grieve me still."

She started slowly down the path and I hurried to keep up with her longer stride. "Everything changed when Redwall died. I had no idea the house had been mortgaged. His death left us paupers, Lady Julia, beggars in our own home. My mother and sister and I are dependent upon Mr. Brisbane for every crust of bread." She stopped to take a breath, her hands fisted at her sides. "We are to remain at Grimsgrave until a home can be fitted out for us."

I felt a rush of pity for her then. I could only imagine how difficult the past months had been for her. To lose a beloved sibling, a home, and a fortune was too much to be borne. I could only hope Brisbane was not making the situation more difficult in his present bad humour.

"I do hope Mr. Brisbane is proving a hospitable land-lord," I offered.

She shot me a questioning look over her shoulder, and I

quickened my pace. "I simply mean that he can be terribly short-tempered. But his bark is much worse than his bite. If there is anything you need, you have only to ask him. He really is quite generous. To a fault at times."

She turned abruptly, fixing me with an appraising look. "How well do you know Nicholas Brisbane?" she asked without preamble. I nearly stumbled again, this time into a rabbit hole.

"As well as anyone could," I told her. "He is a singular sort of person. I would imagine it would take a lifetime to know him completely."

She paused again, raising delicate gold eyebrows. "Really? I have not found him much changed."

I stared at her, and for some unaccountable reason, I felt the chill of the moor wind as I had not felt it before. "You knew him? Before he came to Grimsgrave?"

Miss Allenby nodded slowly. "We were children together. Didn't he tell you? He was a boy in this place."

She turned and led the way back to Grimsgrave Hall. The wind had risen again, and conversation was impossible. It was just as well. Ailith Allenby had given me much to think about.

THE SIXTH CHAPTER

Crabbèd age and youth cannot live together.
—William Shakespeare
"The Passionate Pilgrim XII"

hen we reached Grimsgrave, Miss Allenby and I went our separate ways. She left her basket in the hall, inclining her head graciously toward Valerius who passed her upon the stairs.

"Are you just now rising?" I asked him. He yawned broadly.

"I am. I have not slept so well in years. Something about the air up here, I think," he commented, smiling.

"I am suspicious of you, Valerius. You look entirely too cheerful for a person whose presence here has been secured by means of extortion."

He shrugged. "I am of a gentle and pleasant disposition," he said mildly.

I opened my mouth to argue, but he held up a hand. "I am in no mood to quarrel, Julia. I have a mind to walk out over the moor, perhaps to the village. I am rather curious about how they manage for a doctor in Lesser Howlett."

"Not very well," I told him. I quickly related what Rosalie had revealed about the village doctor.

He rolled his eyes. "I am not surprised. Any medical professional with the slightest bit of acumen would have had something done about the drains in Howlett Magna. I mean to see if they fare any better in Lesser Howlett. Good drains are fundamental for public health," he added. I hastened to divert him before he warmed to his theme and we spent the better part of the morning discussing public hygiene.

"And you might like to stop for a chat with Rosalie Smith whilst you're out," I advised. "She seems quite knowledgeable about folk remedies." We parted then, Val full of schemes for his entertainment, and I felt a little deflated. With Brisbane gone there was nothing pressing, and I looked about the hall for something to do. Ailith had taken herself upstairs. Portia and Lady Allenby and the mysterious Hilda were nowhere to be seen, and I was seized with a sudden, childlike urge to explore Grimsgrave on my own.

I crept to the nearest set of doors, enormous, panelled things, and pushed one open, holding my breath as it creaked in protest upon its hinges. I moved into a handsome hall of excellent proportions, the walls panelled, the plaster ceiling worked in a repeating pattern of lozenges and crowns. The room was impressive, not the least because it was entirely empty. Not a stick of furniture nor vase nor picture warmed the room. It was a cold, austere place, and I shivered in spite of myself.

I turned to leave, surprised to see that I had been quite

wrong in thinking the room was bereft of decoration. Hung just next to the great double doors was a length of tapestry, bordered in flame stitch, and fashioned as a sort of genea-logical chart. The names and dates had been worked in thick scarlet wools, and far back, just near the top of the tapestry, several of the names were surmounted by crowns heavily stitched in tarnished gold thread.

I moved closer to read the names. Those at the top were Saxon royalty, the kings of England before the Conqueror came from across the sea. From them descended an un-broken line, all the way down to Lady Allenby herself, married to Sir Alfred Allenby, I noticed. Peering intently, I could just make out that they had been first cousins, and that Lady Allenby had been orphaned quite young.

"I wonder if that was arranged," I murmured. It seemed too neat otherwise, the orphaned heiress of the old blood royal married off to the sole heir. Rather like royal mar-riages of old, I thought irreverently, keeping the bloodlines and the family fortunes secure. Still, the notion of an arranged marriage left me cold, and I hoped it had been one of affection instead.

I traced the line between them, and down to where Sir Redwall's name had been stitched, the year of his death still bright and untarnished. Some distance apart was Ailith, and between them a place where another name had been re-corded but had clearly been unpicked by a careful needle. After Ailith was Hilda, the letters quite narrow and cramped, looking rather like an afterthought. My eyes returned to the empty spot between Redwall and Ailith.

I passed then to a smaller room, the dining room I suspected, a similar chamber with panelling and plaster ceiling, its furniture also missing. In these panels I noticed the crowned initial *A* carved over and over again, endless reminders of the once-royal blood that still flowed in the Allenby veins.

I clucked my tongue at the carvings. There were royals within my own family, but most of them were not the sort worth remembering, I reflected wryly. For all our exalted history, the Marches were very much country gentry, deeply connected to the land and its people. We had a gallery of painted ancestors, but as their exploits were always of the wildly eccentric and deeply embarrassing sort, I had learned to ignore them. I was much more attached to the modern, American idea of finding merit in one's efforts rather than one's birth. But I had little doubt the Allenbys would find such a notion heresy.

I crossed the hall again, feeling very intrepid indeed as I made my way into the dust-sheeted room next to Brisbane's bedchamber. I crept through, scarcely heeding the ominous, ghostly shapes in the half-light. I was bound for Brisbane's inner sanctum, for reasons that did me no credit.

"Curiosity is a dangerous pastime," I reminded myself as I edged into his room. But then so is love. I sat on the edge of his bed for a long moment, breathing in the scent of him. It was an easy thing to imagine him there, lying with his black hair tumbled across the soft white linen of the pillow. I put out a hand to touch it, then drew it back in haste.

He had made his bed, skilfully as any housemaid would have done, and I was suddenly glad of it. I had been seized with such a tremendous sense of longing I might well have lain down.

I surged up from the bed, realising I had strayed into

rather dangerous territory. I had not come to build castles in Spain, I told myself firmly. I had come to find some clue as to Brisbane's state of mind as master of Grimsgrave.

His trunk yielded nothing unexpected, save a copy of Socrates in Greek, the endpapers heavily marked in Brisbane's distinctive hand. I had known he had a facility for languages, but I had not realised Greek was among them.

I tucked it neatly back into his travelling trunk, along with a small leather purse full of what seemed to be Chinese coins, and a set of false white whiskers so realistic I started back in fright at the sight of them. I had seen Brisbane in them once before and had not known him, I reflected with a smile. We had come quite far since then, and yet not far at all.

I rose and moved to the covered table in the corner, lifting the linen cloth carefully. A set of scientific instruments reposed there, some chemists' glass, a scale, and most impressively of all, a microscope even finer than Valerius'. "No wonder Brisbane keeps that under cover," I mused. "He would never know a moment's peace if Valerius suspected this was here."

"Talking to oneself is the first sign of a disordered mind." I whirled to find Lady Allenby standing in the doorway, leaning upon her rosewood walking stick, her expression gently reproving.

I dropped the cloth and straightened. "I was just—"

Her expression softened and she held up a hand. "There is no need to explain, my dear. I was once your age. And I was in love."

I took a deep breath. "Is it so obvious?"

"Only to someone who has also suffered."

I dropped my head. "It isn't always dreadful, you know. In fact, it is rather wonderful most of the time."

She gave me a moment to compose myself. I took a deep breath and forced a smile.

"I was looking over the other rooms as well. The dining room and the great hall. They must have been magnificent."

"There were Jacobean suites of furniture in each of them, the finest English oak, carved by a master's hands. They were sold along the way, with the Flemish tapestries and the French porcelains," she added with a sigh. "So much of this place lost. It will be a mercy, I think, to leave it behind."

I marvelled at her courage, twisted and wracked with pain, forced to leave the only home she had ever known.

"I hope you will be happy in your new home," I said impulsively. It seemed a stupid sentiment. Who could be happy in such circumstances, torn up by the very roots?

"God will provide. As will Mr. Brisbane. He might have turned us out into the streets to starve, you know. We must be grateful that he is a generous man."

"Or perhaps he feels kindly toward old friends," I ventured, watching her closely. She blinked a little, but her expression of gentle kindliness did not falter.

"Ah, I suppose Ailith has told you they knew each other as children? Well, do not be misled by that. Their acquaintance was of short duration. Mr. Brisbane was, er, travelling, with his mother's family at the time," she said, neatly glossing over the fact that the gentleman who now owned her house had once been a wild half-Gypsy boy. She went on smoothly. "They passed through, every spring. And you know what children are, always swearing eternal friendship, then quite forgetting one another when the season has passed. Ailith did not even know him when he first arrived here in January, he is so changed."

I remained silent, wondering whether Ailith's attachment to Brisbane had been deeper than her mother knew.

Lady Allenby looked around her for the first time, taking in the small room and its tidy complement of furnishings. "This was my son's room," she said suddenly.

She turned away then, and I knew she was thinking of the son she had lost so precipitously. "I wonder if you would like to see Redwall's things," she said, almost hopefully.

Nothing could have appealed to me less than sorting through the possessions of a dead man, but Lady Allenby had been very gracious, and I did not like to offend her.

"Of course."

We entered the long room I had passed through the previous night. She busied herself lighting a few lamps to throw off the chill and the shadows. Without the gloom, the room seemed more inviting, the shrouds less sinister. The tops of the walls were decorated with the same frieze as the small bedchamber—a riverbank, edged with marsh grasses and flights of birds taking wing. Here and there a lily bloomed, pale and fragile against the delicate green grasses, and near the corner a graceful gazelle stopped to drink from the river. It was beautifully done, and I remarked upon it to Lady Allenby.

"Oh, yes. Ailith painted that. She's rather clever at such things, and it was a present for Redwall after he returned from his travels in Egypt. He was quite taken with the decorations of the tombs, and brought back many drawings, and even a few plates taken by the expedition's photographer."

"Egypt—how exciting! I should love to travel. I have only been to the Continent, but Africa seems another world entirely."

She smiled, her expression nostalgic. "It was to Redwall. He was never happier than when he was reading his books about the pharaohs or working on his models of the tombs and temples. I am afraid it was rather difficult for him to leave Egypt behind. I believe Ailith thought he would pine less if he had something of the place here in his private rooms. Let me show you something."

She moved toward the nearest dustsheet and tossed it aside with a theatrical flair. I swallowed a gasp. There was a long, low couch, fashioned of thin strips of woven leather and held aloft by a pair of golden leopards.

"Astonishing," I breathed, moving closer. I dared not touch it. The gilt of the cats' spots was alternated with blue enamel, the eyes set with great pieces of amber that glowed in the lamplight.

"It is a fake, of course," she told me, regretfully, I fancied. "Redwall purchased many treasures in Egypt. He wanted to furnish all of Grimsgrave in the Egyptian style. Much of what he purchased is of no value—modern reproductions of the furniture of the pharaoh's tombs, although I believe some of the smaller pieces and the papyri may be worth something. And there is some jewellery as well. I seem to recall a few pretty things amongst these bits." She gestured toward the other shrouds in the room, and I turned slowly on my heel, thinking rapidly.

"All of these dustsheets are covering his antiquities?" I asked her.

"Most of them. The others are covering boxes of smaller statues and amulets, boxes of jewellery, his collection of scholarly works and publications. My son travelled for many years, you understand. He often sent things back and we stored them as best we could. This was his workroom, then beyond, in the room Mr. Brisbane uses as a bedchamber, was Redwall's private study. When Mr. Brisbane came, Redwall's things were moved into this room to give him a bedchamber on the ground floor. One must observe the proprieties, even here," she finished with a wan smile.

I took a deep breath and plunged into what I was afraid might be a colossal piece of impudence.

"Lady Allenby, I do hope you will forgive me for speaking so frankly. You have given me to understand that your son's death has left you and your daughters in rather straitened circumstances."

She opened her mouth to speak, but I hurried on, afraid both that she would accept my proposal and that she would reject it. I had suddenly seen how the Allenbys might be made solvent again, and I was certain that in some fashion I was conspiring against some larger scheme of Brisbane's. I had no notion *how*, precisely, only that I was very sure he would not have cause to thank me for what I was about to do.

"It is entirely possible that within this room may lay your salvation. Have you a catalogue of what pieces Sir Redwall brought from Egypt?"

She shook her head. "No. I have his letters, and in those he talks about a few of the larger items, but if he kept an inventory, I do not know of it."

"Then one must be made," I said boldly. "You told me that

Mr. Brisbane was preparing a home for you. Surely you will have no room for this collection there."

"No, of course not," she said slowly. "I confess I hoped not to. The Egyptian things have never been to my taste. I find them rather gruesome. It was something of a relief to be able to put them all in here and close the door."

I felt a glimmer of hope. If she had been relieved not to see the things, she might well have no objections to my plan.

"This room will have to be cleared for Mr. Brisbane's use eventually, and you will not be able to keep the things. Why not let me prepare a catalogue and make some inquiries for you? My brother, Lord Bellmont, is rather good friends with the director of the British Museum. Perhaps he can arrange for the museum to purchase some of the items. Or, failing that, we could no doubt interest one of the antiquities dealers in London in mounting an exhibition with an eye to selling the entire collection. Scholars will certainly be interested in his papers and books and the papyri, and collectors will be terribly keen for the rest of it. Even society ladies will go mad for the reproductions. Egyptian décor is rather in vogue just now, you know."

I paused, and for a long, terrible moment Lady Allenby said nothing. Then she swallowed hard and looked down at the dustsheet still clutched in her knobby fingers.

"You are very practical, my dear. And as I suspected, very clever. It might well be an end to all of our money troubles. But I do not think—"

She broke off and pressed the back of her hand to her mouth, stifling a sob. Just as quickly as she had broken down, she composed herself, her posture once more erect, her eyes dry.

"I do not think I could bear to touch his things, nor could

Ailith. Hilda might, if you could ever run her to ground, but I fear we would be of little help to you."

I felt a surge of relief. "I do not care about that, I assure you. If I have need of assistance, I am quite certain I can persuade my brother, Valerius, to lend a hand. I would be happy to take this on, and if you will permit me, I will write to Bellmont tonight to set things in motion."

Lady Allenby paused another long moment, then nodded. "In that case, I accept your generous offer with one caveat. Do you think it would be possible to arrange the sale without bringing the Allenby name into it?"

I started to protest, but she held up a hand. "I realise the interest would be much greater if Redwall's name was attached, but it has been so difficult already, with the sale of the house, and being dependent upon Mr. Brisbane's good graces. The sale of our furnishings has been discreet. We have so few visitors. Very few know how dire our situation has become. I should not like it to be known that we were forced to sell Redwall's things."

I laid a hand on her arm. "Of course. I shall make certain the entire affair is handled with discretion."

She smiled then, and for an instant I saw the staggering beauty she must once have been.

"Thank you, my dear." She glanced about the room, her expression unfathomable. "I only hope you do not come to regret your generous offer."

I laughed at the time, but much later I realised that had I never offered to arrange for the sale of Redwall Allenby's possessions, nothing that followed would have happened, and one of the few inhabitants of Grimsgrave Hall would still be alive.

THE SEVENTH CHAPTER

Youth is hot and bold; age is weak and cold.
—William Shakespeare
"The Passionate Pilgrim XII"

I passed the rest of the morning attending to the various grievances and demands of the maids and the pets. Morag complained bitterly about sharing her room with Minna, and the dogs, my own Florence and Portia's Puggy, demanded to be walked. Minna cheerfully offered to attend to the animals, even to the extent of feeding my raven, Grim, when she was finished with the dogs.

"Thank you, Minna," I told her. "Mind you wrap up well when you take them out, and keep to the moor path. They needn't go far, and Florence will want her little coat."

She bobbed a curtsey. "And what about Puggy, my lady?"

"God himself could not kill that dog. I doubt a little cold air will do him any harm. Take a shawl for yourself as well, my dear. We don't want you taking a chill."

Minna smiled her dimpled little smile and hurried off to her charges. I turned to Morag who was busy plumping the bedpillows.

"You might take a leaf out of her book," I advised her. "Minna is always ready to lend a hand, no matter if it is her job or not."

Morag gave a deep sniff. "I am making the bed, am I not? Not that I've a choice." Her voice dropped to a mutter. "No chambermaids. What sort of household is this, I ask you?"

"A poor one," I told her severely. "Now mind your tongue. The Allenbys cannot help their reduced circumstances."

Morag tipped her head, a sudden malicious light in her eyes. "But the Allenbys dinna actually own Grimsgrave, now do they? It's Mr. Brisbane who ought to be hiring the maids, isn't it?"

I flicked a glance at the bed. "You've made a mess of those sheets. The bed will have to be completely made over."

She was still complaining under her breath when I left her, but as that was Morag's customary state, I paid her scant attention.

I found Portia at length on the staircase. She had paused on the landing and was sitting in the panelled window embrasure, looking out over the vast stretch of moorland.

"Brisbane has gone," I said, settling in next to her.

She blinked at me. "You must be jesting—no, it cannot possibly be a jest. It isn't funny in the least."

"He has gone to Edinburgh on business, and said he will return in a few days, which may well be a fortnight or longer for all I know."

"Oh, isn't that just like a man to ruin a thrilling romantic gesture by leaving as soon as you've come rushing up here to sweep him into your arms and declare your love for him?"

"What a revolting image. You must stop reading novels, Portia. They are ruining you."

Portia snorted. "Do not ask me to believe you weren't thinking precisely the same thing. You expected him to take one look at you and fall to one knee and propose instantly."

I smoothed my skirts primly. "Yes, well. Brisbane has never done what was expected of him. I did, however, make it quite clear to him before he left that I intended we should settle the question of our connection once and for all upon his return."

"And you think he will hurry back for that, do you?"

"Sometimes I wonder why I bother to confide in you," I told her irritably.

I fell to nibbling my lip in silence, and Portia stared out at the ceaseless, restless moor.

"This is the most desolate place I have ever seen," she said tonelessly.

"Oh, it isn't as bad as all that," I replied. "Miss Allenby took me for a walk this morning, and I thought the moor quite pretty. Desperately cold, of course, but pretty. You ought to come out with me after luncheon."

Portia rolled her eyes. "There is no luncheon. It is called dinner here, or hadn't you heard? And they sit in the kitchen, *and* they take every meal there, like savages."

I pinched her arm. "Hush. The Allenbys keep country ways. They cannot afford to heat the dining room."

"Ah, but *Brisbane* is now responsible for the cost of heating this place," she corrected, echoing Morag's sentiments.

"It makes no difference," I told her repressively. "They sold the furniture. There is nothing to sit upon and no table to set, so it is the kitchen for you, my girl. Pretend you are at Wuthering Heights. Everyone there ate in the kitchen."

Portia affected a faraway look and shivered, calling in a high voice, "Heathcliff, where are you? I'm so coooooooold."

I shoved her. "Don't be such an ass."

She rose with a sigh. "I fear lunch, er, *dinner* will be something quite provincial. Game pie and boiled cabbage, unless I am very much mistaken."

I linked my arm through hers and drew her down the stairs. "You are a terrible snob, Portia. Have I ever told you that?"

"Frequently."

The rest of the household had already assembled in the kitchen by the time we arrived. Mrs. Butters was scurrying between oven and table, and although Portia raised her eyes significantly at the sight of the game pie and the bowls of boiled cabbage, I thought the table looked extremely inviting. A clean cloth had been laid, and although it had been mended, it was done with great skill and care, the stitches tiny and precise. A cheap glass vase had been filled with an armful of nodding daffodils, lending an air of gaiety to the room. The serving dishes were pewter rather than silver, but the mellow glow served the room, I decided, and the food itself smelled wonderfully appetising.

Besides the pie and the cabbage, there were dishes of pickles and a large fresh cheese, a great cottage loaf of new bread, and a clutch of boiled eggs. There was even a bowl of newly-picked salad greens, lightly dressed, and a tiny dish of mushrooms fried to crispness.

Lady Allenby was already seated, her walking stick braced against her chair. She motioned to me and I took the chair next to her, while Portia seated herself opposite. Ailith Allenby was helping Mrs. Butters, moving smoothly to carry the last few dishes and to pour a pitcher of beer for the table. In the corner, Jetty was scraping scraps into a basket by the sink, her mouth slack as she looked Portia over carefully from head to foot. I could not blame her. Portia was dressed in a particularly luscious shade of cherry that became her exceedingly well. I had no doubt Jetty had ever seen such a garment in this grey and gloomy corner of England.

Just then the kitchen door opened and a tall man entered, shrugging off a worn tweed coat and doffing his flat cap. He paused a moment to hang his things on a peg by the door, and I took the opportunity to study the newcomer. He was Brisbane's opposite in almost every way. Though they were both tall men and muscular, this man was blond, with startling blue eyes and lines on his face that marked where he smiled, deeply and often. They were of an age, but it was clear to see from their faces that they had lived very different lives. This was an outdoorsman, a simple man, with simple tastes, I decided; one who would be happy with merely a roof over his head and a fire in his hearth.

He glanced up then, and caught my eye, smiling. I looked away, but he strode to the table, offering his hand.

"You must be one of the ladies from London. Lady Julia or Lady Bettiscombe?"

Before I could reply, Lady Allenby thrust his hand away from mine. "Godwin, manners! You must wait to be presented to a lady, and you have not yet washed."

His smile did not falter. He withdrew his hand and contented himself with a wink. "I will go and make myself presentable then," he said, casting his glance wider to include my sister. Portia raised her brows at him as he moved to the sink, dropping a kiss upon Mrs. Butters' cap as he reached for the cake of soap. "Hello, Jetty, my love," he said to the bashful hired girl. "Have you had a pleasant morning?" To my astonishment, the mockery had dropped from his tone, and there was only gentle affection.

The little maid flushed with pleasure and smiled, a great wide smile that showed a mouthful of crooked teeth as she giggled.

Mrs. Butters laughed and scolded him for being in the way, but Lady Allenby was not so forgiving.

"I do hope you will excuse him, Lady Julia," she murmured. "We have despaired of teaching him how to conduct himself. I am afraid we are so isolated here, it is difficult to maintain the proper distance. And he is family, I suppose," she trailed off, and I thought about the tapestry in the great hall. I had not seen his name stitched there, but then I had not looked for it. I made a mental note to investigate after the meal and hurried to reassure Lady Allenby.

"Think nothing of it, Lady Allenby. I completely understand."

Godwin finished washing himself and hurried to take a seat at the table. He had his pick of either the chair by Portia or the one next to me, but he chose to partner Portia, offering her his handshake, which she accepted with lazy grace. He complimented her costume and was just moving on to how well it suited her complexion when Ailith sat between her mother and Portia, leaving two empty chairs for Valerius and the mysterious Hilda.

As if thinking had conjured him, Valerius entered then, nodding graciously toward Lady Allenby, and casting a hasty glance over the rest of the table.

"My apologies. Miss Hilda was showing me her chickens," he explained hastily.

I stared at him in astonishment. I had not even seen her, but Valerius had already befriended the mysterious Hilda in the poultry yard. I ought not to have been surprised. Val, like all the March men, was singularly personable, with both charm and good looks to recommend him. I longed to ask him how he had met her, but before I had a chance to speak, a young woman hurried in, throwing herself down breathlessly in the remaining empty chair.

"Sorry, Mama," she said shortly. The woman, who I took to be Miss Hilda, filled her plate and began to eat with as much vigour as a farmhand.

"Hilda," her mother said sharply. "You have not made the acquaintance of Mr. Brisbane's guests. You will kindly greet Lady Bettiscombe and Lady Julia Grey, and pray they will forgive your churlishness."

Hilda laid down her fork and gave two short nods, one in my direction, one in Portia's, and shot a quick smile at Val, then took up her fork and began to eat again with astonishing rapidity.

"Lady Bettiscombe, Lady Julia, I hope you will overlook my daughter's poor manners. I assure you she is more gently bred than she has given you cause to believe."

If Hilda was annoyed at her mother's criticism, she gave

no sign of it. She merely continued to eat, working her way rapidly through a second piece of pie before the rest of us had finished the first. She did not look up from her plate, but there was an awareness, an energy that fairly vibrated from her that made me wonder if she were not as curious about us as we were about her.

I scrutinised her closely as she ate, observing that she was nothing so pretty as her sister. Where in Ailith long limbs and a slender neck had given an appearance of elegance and delicacy, in Hilda they were coltish and awkward. Her elbows flapped as she ate, giving her the demeanour of a restless grasshopper. Her eyes were fixed upon her food, but I had seen a glimpse of their muddy grey hue when she had glanced in my direction, and I did not think I was mistaken in believing I had detected a keen intelligence there. Her clothes were appalling. One might expect that of an impoverished woman, but hers were particularly nasty, of masculine cut and carrying with them the distinct odour of the poultry yard. I thought I saw Val's nostrils twitch ever so slightly, but he was too well-bred to offer less than perfect courtesy to a lady. He made some low remark to her and she replied with a grunt and a shrug of her shoulders while her mother and sister attempted to make polite conversation.

Lady Allenby nodded toward the enormous pie. "Have you enough there, Mr. Valerius? There is plenty, and you have only to let Ailith know if you would like something more. I am afraid we must serve ourselves," she finished. As we had settled into our meal, Mrs. Butters had filled plates for herself and the maids, then retired to her room to entertain them.

I remarked upon it, and Lady Allenby smiled apologetically. "An unconventional arrangement, but it was the most suitable we could devise under the circumstances. When we dine alone, we do not trouble if Mrs. Butters joins us at table, but of course it would not do to have the maids. One doesn't like to dine with staff," she finished on a deliberately cheerful note.

"No, one doesn't," Hilda echoed, throwing a meaningful look at Godwin.

He put his head back and roared with laughter. "Shall I take my plate and eat in the sheepfold then?"

Lady Allenby's face had gone quite white and pinched. "Hilda! Godwin! That is enough. What will our guests think of you—" She broke off then, doubtless remembering that she was no longer mistress of Grimsgrave. I felt a surge of pity for her. The pattern of her life would have been settled and predictable before her family's fortunes had fallen so dramatically. The question of where to put the servants for meals would never have arisen during the simpler times of her youth.

I turned to Ailith. "Tell me, Miss Allenby, what do you do for amusement?"

She patted her lips with a napkin and replied, but I was not listening. For some unaccountable reason I felt a desperate urge to keep the conversation civil, and I asked dozens of questions, most of Ailith and Godwin, determined to keep attention away from the prickly Hilda.

Ailith Allenby, I noticed, ate little, and what she did eat was consumed in tiny, delicate bites, and chewed very slowly. In contrast, Godwin filled his plate three times, eating heartily and laughing loudly. He was no gentleman, but he was merry and friendly, and if he was overly-familiar, it was an easy fault to forgive. The pale atheling looks that were so striking in the elder Allenby ladies had darkened to a gilded sort of masculinity in him. His hands, broad and thickly callused, were surprisingly graceful, and his features, although not as finely-limned as Ailith's, were every bit as arresting.

More than once I found my eyes drifting to his over the meal, and more than once he shot me a mischievous wink when he thought no one else was paying attention. He put me a little in mind of Lucian Snow, the curate at the parish church at my father's country estate at Bellmont Abbey in Blessingstoke. I could only hope Godwin Allenby made a better end than Mr. Snow, I thought with a shudder.

After the midday meal, the gentlemen left again—Godwin to attend to his sheep while Valerius struck out to explore the moor. Hilda scurried away as soon as the last spoonful of pudding had been swallowed, and the other Allenby ladies retired to their rooms. "A little repose just after dinner is the best thing for digestion," Lady Allenby said, although I suspected she needed the rest more for her twisted joints than as an aid to digestion. She had eaten almost as much as Godwin, and I marvelled at her still-slender figure. Perhaps Rosalie's mint tonic had been just the thing to spur her appetite.

Mrs. Butters bustled in to clear the dinner things, and Portia and I left to take a turn in the garden. I warned her to bundle up, but the sun had come out, and the afternoon was warmer, if not exactly pleasant. We strolled aimlessly, exploring the various gardens, arguing mildly over what each of the ruins had been. We finally settled on a water garden to the east of the house, fed by the reedy pond that lay just in front of the main façade, and an orchard farther on, the trees now badly overgrown and desperately in need of attention.

Portia brushed a litter of dead leaves from a crumbling stone bench and sat heavily. "The entire place is a wreck. I wonder that Brisbane even took it on. He could not have known what he was letting himself in for. It will take a fortune to make it right again, and the passion of someone who wants to reclaim it."

"Oh, I don't know," I said thoughtfully, turning slowly on my heel to survey the entire orchard. "Really, it wants a lot of pruning and perhaps some repairs to the walls. The paths need to be marked out freshly, of course, and it could do with a new ornament or two. That cupid is quite nasty," I finished, nodding toward a derelict statue that looked more like a small devil than the embodiment of Love.

Portia sighed. "I meant the estate, dearest, not the orchard. There is hardly a room fit to live in, and the entire east wing has fallen into disuse. Lady Allenby gave me a tour of the place whilst you were about with Ailith."

"I poked about the public rooms earlier," I confessed, coming to sit beside her. "Did you see the tapestry? All those little stitched crowns?"

Portia nodded, her expression faraway. "They are a bit ancestor-mad, I think."

"But why? I mean, we've kings and queens perched in the family tree, and we do not go about putting it on the walls for everyone to see."

"Because we have never lost it," Portia pointed out patiently. "The Allenbys haven't been royal since the time of Canute. Do I mean Canute? Was he Saxon?"

"Danish, I think." It was difficult to remember. We had had several governesses, none with a very firm grasp of history.

Portia shook her head. "In any event, the Allenbys probably lost everything except their royal blood when the Normans came in and upset the apple cart. They've no grand titles. They are marooned out here like Robinson Crusoe and Friday, with no proper company and a house that is threatening to fall down over their heads at any moment. Is it any wonder they cling to what little prestige they once had? If nothing else it gives them something to lord over the neighbours."

"Speaking of neighbours…" I began. I told Portia about Rosalie Smith, describing her little cottage in great detail, and finishing with our mysterious conversation.

When I had done, I pulled the little charm from my pocket and dropped it into Portia's palm. "What do you think she meant? What protection should I require? And why should she be a friend to me?"

Portia pressed it back into my hand. "Julia, you have seen enough Gypsies to know their tricks. She means to frighten you. I'd wager a fiver the next time you go, she will speak of death stalking your shadow and promise to banish him for a pound, and ensure your good health if you buy a candle for another shilling."

I replaced the charm carefully in my pocket. "You've grown cynical in your old age."

"And you are still foolish in yours," she returned, though not as harshly as she might have. "That Hilda is rather beastly, don't you think? She smells of the poultry yard. Dreadful clothes."

"I suspect they are suitable for her purposes," I said slowly. "But she seems highly put out that we have come. I wonder if we are somehow upsetting her apple cart?"

Portia shrugged. "I cannot imagine how. Lady Allenby told me all she does is keep chickens and walk on the moor. God knows I shan't interfere with either of those occupations. Perhaps she's just peevish. Like Nerissa."

The mention of our crabby elder sister set both our mouths twitching.

"What do you think of Godwin?" Portia asked.

I tipped my head, thinking of his handsome face and warm smile. "A rogue, but not a serious one. He seems a merry sort, doubtless wanting for company here," I said, casting a look about the deserted ruin of the orchard.

"But Deborah, the innkeeper's sister, said he was popular with women. He must go into the village. I wonder," she trailed off.

"Yes?" I prodded her.

She shook her head, casting off her reverie. "I wonder if he is entirely trustworthy about women. I am worried for Minna."

I laughed aloud. "Minna? Our little Cockney cabbage? Why on earth should you worry for her?"

"Because she has never been out of London. Because all the men she knows are pale and thin and weedy. Because Godwin Allenby is a big strapping man who radiates health and animal good looks and would be very attractive to a girl of Minna's class."

I considered. "I suppose you are right. I hadn't thought

of it, but he is very different from the London lads. The accent alone would make him seem exotic to her."

Portia snorted. "I can scarcely make out one word in three. What the devil was he talking about at luncheon?"

"Dinner," I corrected. "He was talking about the view from Thorn Crag, and telling us we ought to make our way up there on a fine day. He claims we could see all the way to Scotland, which I highly doubt, but it is enticing."

Portia goggled at me. "You learned all of that from the gibberish he was talking? How on earth did you make him out?"

I shrugged. "After Morag, I imagine I could understand anyone. In any event, you needn't worry about Minna. I shall tell Morag to keep an eye open, and we will all have a care for her. I am very fond of Minna, as I know you are. Besides," I finished with a shiver, "I should hate to be the one to explain to Mrs. Birch how we let her eldest daughter stray from the path of virtue. I am rather frightened of Mrs. Birch."

Portia nodded solemnly. "As are we all." She was silent a long moment, then she seemed to gather herself and rose from the bench. "I suppose we had better make some plans to put the house in order," she said. "We must tread carefully. I know Brisbane owns the house, but I cannot help but feel the Allenbys are still very much mistresses here."

I thought of Ailith and her corn-gold hair and wide blue eyes, her exquisite grace and her easy self-assurance. And I thought of Brisbane, immured here for the long cold months of winter with nothing to do but sit opposite that beautiful face and marvel at its perfection.

And I felt a surge of determination.

I rose and shook out my skirts, brushing the odd leaf from their folds. "Do not worry, Portia. They may have held sway here in the past, but this is a new day."

THE EIGHTH CHAPTER

He that dies pays all debts.
—William Shakespeare
The Tempest

After our conversation in the orchard, Portia retired
to rest whilst I made excuses to remain downstairs. She shrugged and went on her way, and I
scurried to make certain no one was lingering in the hall as I
slipped into Sir Redwall's study. I had little doubt Brisbane
would not appreciate my efforts to help the Allenbys, and until
I knew why, I had no intention of letting him discover it.

I could hear Mrs. Butters humming a hymn tunelessly to
herself and the occasional giggle from Jetty as they scrubbed
the kitchen, but once I closed the door behind me there was
only the cool silence of the deserted room.

Deserted, and yet populated with treasures I could only
imagine. I scarcely breathed as I moved between the dust-
sheeted heaps, wondering which held riches from a pharaoh's

tomb, and which the crude trinkets fashioned for picking a tourist's pocket. And I wondered if I should be able to tell the difference. I had no experience with Egyptology beyond attending a few lectures in London and the unrolling of a mummy that a certain duchess had arranged as an entertainment. It had been a gruesome evening, but thrilling nonetheless, and as I picked my way through Sir Redwall's possessions, I wondered what I would do if a mummy lay amongst them.

I twitched aside a dozen dustsheets, tantalised by the glimpses of polished stone and gilded wood, the flashes of gold—or perhaps something baser. I itched to fling them all aside, but I knew there was no method to that, and if I was not a properly-trained Egyptologist, at least I knew enough to have a care with the items. Since I did not know which was truly valuable and which was worthless rubbish, I decided to handle them all as though they were priceless, a sensible precaution under the circumstances, I thought. And I would catalogue the items as I found them. I would have preferred to group them like with like, but the conditions of the room made that impossible. There simply was not sufficient space to alter the current arrangements, and as it was, moving the furniture and statuary would require a great deal of muscle—muscle I had no inclination to find at present. In spite of my assurances to Lady Allenby, I did not wish to involve Valerius before it was absolutely necessary. I had little doubt Godwin would be happy to help, but it seemed prudent to keep a bit of distance until I knew him better, and as for Brisbane, the less he knew of my plans for the present, the happier I would be, I was convinced.

After a lengthy search I found the desk, an enormous thing

with dozens of drawers and a handsome bit of carved detail. There was nothing of Egypt about this piece. It was of good English oak and more than a hundred years old, judging by the patina. I ran a hand over its surface, smooth as satin from years of careful polishing. The pigeonholes still held paper, and I found a few sheets of foolscap to begin my notes.

As I opened the drawers, searching for a pen or bit of pencil, I realised the desk had not been cleared out after Sir Redwall's death. His diary lay open to a date from the previous summer, the page annotated in a spidery masculine scrawl. It took a bit to decipher it, but it was a note to himself: *Unwell today. Dosed twice with q.* I flipped to the previous page and there was the note: *Felt poorly. Single dose.* I continued to flip back and each page had a note about his health and sometimes estate business, each item marked with a little tick, presumably after he had concluded the matter. *Speak to Godwin about gardener's cottage. Arrange sale of little pasture. Letter from SB.* Some of the days were noted with tiny drawings, hieroglyphs from the look of them. His handwriting had grown progressively more feeble over the weeks before his death, a sign of his deteriorating health, no doubt. But had he realised he was dying? He had, by his own hand, arranged for the sale of one of his pastures. Surely he had known the failing state of his fortunes. Had he planned some retrenchment before his death and been unable to carry it out?

I closed the diary and moved on through the pigeonholes and little drawers, finding nothing of value but everything of interest. There were no letters from SB, nothing to indicate if this had been an *inamorata* or a business associate or even another scholar of Egyptology. I would have expected letters from creditors, but there were none. I found a tiny scarab, its enamel long since lost, and a small ball of bits of twine, carefully saved and wrapped neatly. There was a penknife, a handsome thing marked with the initials *AA*. I took it to be his father's, Sir Alfred's, saved for sentimental reasons, or perhaps simply because it was an item of good quality. The dockets for correspondence were neatly labelled, *To be answered, To be read, To be filed,* but empty save for a few mouldering issues of periodicals pertaining to Egyptology. I scanned them for articles penned by Sir Redwall, but found none. This was not entirely unexpected. Many gentlemen preferred to use a *nom de plume* when writing professionally. I laughed at the obviously false soubriquet St. John Malachy-LaPlante, and those I laid aside. It was not entirely impossible that Sir Redwall had written them himself.

The rest of the desk revealed nothing of note. If Sir Redwall had left debts, someone had removed the bills, perhaps with an eye to satisfying the creditors. I assembled a few items I should need—paper, ink, pen, blotting paper, gluepot, even a clever little notebook that had never been used—and tidied the rest away, thinking to put them in the largest bottom drawer. I opened it, and realised I had missed something. There was an album of sorts wedged into the bottom, and I prised it loose with the aid of the paperknife. It was an old-fashioned leather album covered in black kidskin. I opened it and read the inscription: *The property of Redwall Allenby 1858*. I did the subtraction quickly. The album was a child's then, begun when he was still a schoolboy.

I glanced through the first few pages, past the reports of

his tutors, pasted carefully in with little notes from his father and clippings from newspapers. They were yellowed and crumbling and I smiled at the thought of the boy carefully cutting the columns and pasting them into his album. Most were pieces about Sir Alfred, lauding his career and praising the Allenby family. Clearly the boy had shared his mother's pride in their name and accomplishments.

And then, sadly, a death notice, heavily bordered in black, mourning the passing of Sir Alfred. I worked the dates again and realised Redwall would not have been more than twelve, so young to have lost his father. I knew what it meant to lose a parent in childhood, but as I had been only six when my mother passed, I felt Redwall's loss must have been keener. I hardly remembered my mother—only a rustle of taffeta, the scent of her perfume. At least Redwall had had his album to comfort him.

I turned faster now, skimming quickly. There were letters from Lady Allenby, addressed to Redwall at university, then in care of *postes restantes* abroad, as well as various hotels. Then came notices in the newspapers announcing his appointment to the Egyptological expedition mounted by Lord Evandale and seconded by St. John Malachy-LaPlante, the Comte de Roselende. So the silly name was authentic after all, I mused, and not a pseudonym of Redwall's. I wondered how Redwall had felt at being selected for the excavation party. Had he been thrilled to finally see the ruins he had studied for so long? Or had he been apprehensive, a stranger in a strange land, uncertain of himself so far away from his native heath? Perhaps his years of travel had inured him to the exoticism of Egypt. The differences between the windy

Yorkshire moors and the burning desert sands of Egypt did not bear thinking about.

The rest of the book was blank. If Redwall had kept a journal of his adventures in Egypt, it was elsewhere, and I hoped I would discover something of the sort as I cleared out his things. He was an interesting character, I decided, and I would like to know more about him.

There was another volume, this one slender and bound in scarlet kid, a collection of love poems of the Egyptians in translation. The paper was thin and soft, perhaps with much handling, for the cover was worn so badly that the gilt of the title was almost completely obscured. I thumbed a few of the pages, struck by the passionate language.

"This will be further reading," I murmured, and tucked the volume into my pocket.

Suddenly mindful of the time, I tidied away a stray curl and bundled my supplies into the drawer, stuffing the scrapbook into its place on the bottom. It would make excellent reading for some rainy day, I had no doubt, but the room had suddenly grown much darker and I realised how long I had been about my task.

After supper that night, the household sat by the kitchen fireside. Godwin was apparently not expected to tarry with the family, for he left directly supper was finished and did not return. Ailith Allenby said little, her golden head bent over her needlework. Portia had taken a book of poetry from her pocket, but it sat on her lap, unread, the pages unturned. Valerius chatted to Hilda about his discoveries regarding the drains in Lesser Howlett, and she listened with little grace, nodding once or twice and deigning to speak a syllable or two when she thought no one else was listening. It was left to Lady Allenby and me to carry the conversation, and we did so by discussing the garden. She described it as it had been in her youth, lush and bountiful, providing more than enough food for the family and the staff.

"Of course, we had more than just Mrs. Butters then," she said with a little laugh, "although she was with us. That was long before she married Butters. She was just little Martha the kitchenmaid then, with hair in two great plaits down to her waist and clumsy hands. Cook used to curse her for breaking plates, if I remember. But she grew quite skilled in time, and eventually she married Mr. Butters, a tradesman in the village. I always thought it a great pity they had no children. She would have been a wonderful mother. But they were not blessed, and then Mr. Butters took ill and died. So much has changed since then." She broke off, her eyes misty with reminiscence.

"Little of it for the better," Hilda put in suddenly. She ignored the reproving glance of her mother.

"How long has Mrs. Butters been a widow?" I queried.

"Oh, it must be thirty years past. She and Mr. Butters had the cottage on the moor as their own. They kept it so nicely. Butters dearly loved to putter in the garden when he was not wanted in his shop. But when he died, it seemed better for Mrs. Butters to stay here in the main house rather than out on the moor by herself."

"The cottage on the moor? Do you mean the one where Rosalie Smith lives?"

Lady Allenby nodded. "Yes. She has been there a very long time," she added dismissively.

A long time indeed, I thought rapidly. If Rosalie had

moved in directly Mrs. Butters had left, she had lived in the little cottage for thirty years, and yet she looked scarcely more than forty.

"Gypsies age better than we," Hilda put in, correctly interpreting my thoughts. "Perhaps they have some pact with the devil."

"Hilda!" her mother said sharply. She crossed herself and kissed the rosary at her belt. Hilda looked down at her work-roughened hands, but I saw that a tiny smile played over her lips. Portia and Ailith had heard the remark and let their own conversation lapse. Lady Allenby looked from Portia to me.

"Sometimes my daughter confuses pertness with wit," Lady Allenby observed coldly.

If Hilda was disturbed by her mother's cutting remark, she masked it well. She merely turned to stare into the fire, her conversation with Valerius clearly at an end. My brother busied himself with a newspaper a fortnight out of date, but I fancied he heard everything.

"Think nothing of it." Portia waved a lazy hand. "We are an irreligious family."

Lady Allenby's expression stiffened. "I am sorry to hear it. I think there can be no true satisfaction in a life that is not virtuous."

Portia flashed her a winsome smile. "Oh, I manage. If you will excuse me," she said, rising, "I am feeling a trifle unwell. I think I would like to retire early this evening."

It was the grossest discourtesy to excuse herself early, but Lady Allenby's disapproval melted instantly, and she was solicitous, determined to send for Minna to tend to Portia.

"Not necessary, I assure you. It is only a headache. A good

night's sleep will put me to rights, and I am certain the moorland air is cure enough."

Lady Allenby smiled warmly at this observation, and I marvelled at Portia's ability to offend on one hand and ingratiate on the other.

Ever attentive, Ailith rose and lit a candle for Portia, leading her into the darkened hall and bidding her good-night.

Lady Allenby leaned near to me whilst she was away. "I do hope you and Ailith will become friends. I know it is presumptuous of me to say it, but she has so little opportunity for good company here. She suffers so from loneliness."

If I was taken aback by the words, the sincere warmth beneath them won my sympathy. I glanced to where Ailith's natural companion, her own sister, sat sullenly staring into the fire. "I would like that, too, Lady Allenby."

She smiled and I introduced the topic of chickens then, and when Ailith returned we were peaceably debating the merits of brown eggs versus white. Almost against her will, Hilda was drawn into the conversation, chickens being her one passion. She warmed a little, but she was nothing as hospitable as her sister, and when she had had enough of the talk, she merely rose and left without preamble or farewell, even to Valerius.

Lady Allenby shook her head. "I do not know what will become of that child."

"She is no child," Ailith put in sharply. "She is thirty years old, and can mind her tongue well enough if she chooses. She simply has no sense of duty."

Lady Allenby made a fretful noise. "I blame myself. She was a babe when Sir Alfred died, and I was left to raise my

poor fatherless children alone. I was too soft with her. I
ought to have remembered the Scriptures. I ought not to
have spared the rod."

I shuddered at the thought. Father had had the raising of
ten children without benefit of a wife, and yet never once
had he raised a hand to any of us in anger.

"Perhaps not, Lady Allenby," Val ventured quietly. "They
say the most spirited horses are the most easily broken in
temperament. You would not like to have your daughter's
spirit broken, I am sure."

Lady Allenby's eyes were stern as they fixed on my brother.
"It is a mother's duty to perfect her children," she said coldly.
"And I have failed all of mine."

Her eyes went to Ailith, who paled visibly. But nothing
else in her demeanour changed and when she put out her
hand, it was perfectly steady.

"Come, Lady Julia. I will light you to bed."

THE NINTH CHAPTER

I'll to thy closet and go read with thee
Sad stories chanced in the times of old.
—William Shakespeare
Titus Andronicus

The next few days were passably diverting, although there was little enough in the way of either company or amusement to hold my interest at Grimsgrave in Brisbane's absence. I thought of him often, and when no one was about, I sometimes crept to his deserted room simply to be near his things, as if proximity to his possessions meant some sort of connection to the man himself. I longed for and dreaded his return. As difficult as uncertainty was to bear, at least it offered the consolation of hope. So long as Brisbane stayed away, there was a chance of happiness. Once he returned, matters would be decided once and for all.

My mood was not a sociable one, but I did my duty by the household. Supper was taken early each evening, and we sat by the kitchen fire for an hour only before we were lighted up to bed. Ailith and Portia and I sometimes attempted three-handed whist, although Lady Allenby never played. I wondered if it was because of her swollen hands or if she simply disapproved of cards on principle. I had noticed a few more signs of piety about her, and she was punctual with her prayers, pausing several times each day at times that corresponded to the old hours marked by the religious houses.

Valerius had fallen into the habit of reading of an evening, as had Hilda. They sometimes talked a little, perhaps of drains or chickens, I thought nastily. But they spoke only in low tones I could not overhear, and once or twice I saw her unbend so far as to smile at him, as if their conversation had strayed to warmer matters. If her glance happened to catch mine, she instantly dropped her eyes and flushed in irritation. Clearly, she had decided not to befriend me.

Ailith was a little more companionable. She was never demonstrative, but we had taken to walking together over the moors each morning, and it was a pleasant diversion. The more time I passed in her company, the better I liked her in spite of her reserve. I spent a great deal of time with her as Portia had become increasingly preoccupied and snappish. She had formed the habit of striking out on her own across the moors, usually taking a protesting, wheezing Puggy with her as an excuse for walking, and ignoring her plans to refurbish the house entirely.

Valerius busied himself each day in the village, sitting in the public room of The Hanged Man and attempting to win the villagers' confidence. When I asked him why, he would only say, "I have thoughts I wish to share with them regarding public hygiene." I could not bring myself to pry further, and left him to his own devices, although I could not fail to notice he spent much of his time sketching what appeared to be a very elaborate poultry house.

As for the maids, Minna—sadly neglected by her mistress—was left to her own devices much of the time, and I set her to helping Mrs. Butters. I reasoned if she were properly trained she might aspire to the post of housekeeper herself in time. It would lend her less glamour than a lady's maid but more authority, and as I explained to her, a skill once learned is never wasted. She agreed with alacrity and spent most of her mornings in the kitchen, learning how to roll pastry and prepare simple sauces and roasted meats under Mrs. Butters' tuition. She even persuaded Jetty, by sheer dint of her own good humour, to clean her fingernails and put on a clean apron after she had done the rough.

The most pleasant aspect of this arrangement was that it stopped Morag from continually complaining about Minna. Mrs. Butters did not seem to mind the girl's chatter, and Morag was free to get about her business without distraction, although there was precious little for her to do. My hems were invariably crusted with peat mud, but I seldom changed, and often wore the same costume from morning to night, quite a difference from London where I might wear six ensembles in a single day. After Morag had tightened every button in my wardrobe and polished my boots over and again until she seemed in danger of wearing through the leather, I gave her leave to read the books I had brought with me. She was not a proficient reader, having come late to her letters, but she was an enthusiastic one, and had a taste for low romances. I had tucked a few into my trunk for just this sort of occurrence, and it was not uncommon to find her holed up in her tiny room, feet stretched to the fire, happily tossing titbits to Florence as she devoured the further adventures of Miss Melanie Lovelady and her lover, the Count of Rompollion.

My afternoons were spent in Sir Redwall's study, with Grim the raven for company, carefully compiling the detailed catalogue of his collection. I had written to my brother Bellmont straightaway, encouraging him to use his influence with the museum to explore the possibility of purchasing the items Sir Redwall had brought home from Egypt. Even to my untrained eye there were a number of quite fine pieces, and I managed to tidy things enough to begin setting these aside. The obvious tourist tat went into another pile, and I was very pleased to find an excellent assortment of books, some scholarly, some written for the more casual traveller, but all in better shape than I might have expected given the haphazard method used to store them. A few mice nibbles here and there, a bit of wear on the covers, but all in all a very comprehensive collection. There was even a first edition of the *Description de l'Égypte,* commissioned by Napoléon after his conquest of Egypt and running to several volumes—twenty-three to be precise. It had been a massive undertaking, written by more than one hundred and sixty scholars, all presenting the most comprehensive knowledge of Egypt at the time of the Napoleonic conquest. Father had the second edition in his library at Bellmont Abbey, and it had been one of my favourite pastimes as a child to while away long afternoons tucked in the window embrasures, studying the plates of illustrations.

This edition was, if possible, even more exquisite, and I toyed with the idea of making Lady Allenby an offer for the set myself before I decided such a gesture might be too fraught. One would not wish to insult Lady Allenby by offering too little, but neither would one wish to spend too much above the value. Better to let them go, I decided. I put them carefully aside and moved on to the lesser volumes, including one or two extremely distasteful tomes on mummification with very nasty illustrations. They were disgusting enough to fetch a very high price, I had little doubt.

In all, the work was very interesting, but it could only divert me so long from the question of Brisbane. More than one moonlit night had found me perched in my window embrasure, reading breathless verses of quite stimulating Egyptian love poetry from the little red volume. And several times I collected myself, pen poised halfway through a word, staring out of the window and across the moor as if I expected him to come striding toward me through the heather.

Finally, one afternoon when I had stared at a collection of *shawabtis* so long their features had blurred, I threw down my pen and fled the house on my own. I had learned to dress for the moor. My fetching hat with the violets had been torn to pieces by the wind, and I knew better now than to leave the house without a thick shawl. I borrowed one of Morag's, a warm black affair knitted of the best wool, and wrapped it over my head, tucking the ends carefully into the waist of my skirt. On an impulse I asked Minna for one of the little cakes she had baked that morning and she presented it to me proudly, wrapped in brown paper and tied with a pretty ribbon. I tucked it into a basket and set off on the moorland path from the kitchen garden, raising my face to the sun.

"Thee'll get wrinkles on tha' pretty face," came a good-humoured voice from behind me. I whirled to see Godwin emerging from the kitchen garden. He was smiling at me and carrying a canvas sack. I waited for him.

"Hello, Mr. Allenby. Running off to join the circus?" I asked, nodding toward the sack.

He laughed, his face crinkling into a mass of weathered lines. His eyes were lit with amusement, and I fancied for just a moment if he were properly dressed and groomed, he would give any of the finest gentlemen in society a fair bit of competition. But even as he was, grimy and unkempt and shaggy as a moorland pony, he was arrestingly attractive. He raised the sack.

"Tha's a bit of dinner for myself. Minna is a fair hand with the cakes now," he told me. We walked together slowly, and when we came to a boggy bit, he took my elbow, letting his hand linger perhaps a moment too long on my arm.

"Thank you, Mr. Allenby."

"Thee must not be so formal. I am Godwin. 'Mr. Allenby' is too grand for the likes of me."

"Very well, Godwin. Where will you be taking your dinner?"

He paused and stepped behind me, raising his arm just over my shoulder to point out a steep rocky outcropping rising high over the moor. "The heights up there on yon crag. Thorn Crag, it's called. 'Tis a good enough place to survey the whole of the moor. I must collect the sheep. 'Tis nearly time to dip."

I was acutely aware of his arm still stretched out beside me, his rough sleeve brushing my cheek. I stepped neatly aside.

"Surely you alone cannot dip the entire flock."

He smiled at me again, holding no grudge though I had evaded him.

"I'll have a few of the boys from the next farm over to help. But mind you stay away. A nasty business tha' is, the dipping of sheep."

Of that I was only too aware. When I was twelve, I had pestered my brother Benedick to let me help him dip Father's flocks at the Home Farm. Finally he agreed, without bothering to tell me the dip was mixed up of a few extremely nasty things, including arsenic. It took me the better part of a month to wash the smell away.

"And where are you off to, my lady?" Godwin asked, raising his brows at the cake in my basket.

"I thought I would pay a call upon Mrs. Smith," I told him, slanting a quick glance to gauge his response.

"She'll not tell a fortune, but she has a potion for anything that ails you," he advised me. We did not speak for several minutes as we climbed higher on the moor. Godwin was a comfortable sort of person, surprisingly respectful given the impropriety of our situation. When we had nearly reached the crossroads of the moor paths, he turned to me.

"Lady Allenby says tha' you are clearing out Redwall's things," he said. I noted the lack of Sir Redwall's honorific, and the omission intrigued me. I remembered then the note in Sir Redwall's diary about his plan to speak to Godwin regarding the gardener's cottage, and I wondered if the interview had ever taken place.

"Yes, I think he had some rather fine pieces, and Lady Allenby gave me to understand the funds from their sale would not be unwelcome."

Godwin nodded. "Tha's true enough. They've not two pennies to rub together, save a few sticks of furniture and that old rag in the hall."

"Oh, you mean the tapestry. I did not notice, is your name stitched there?"

He threw back his tawny head, his laughter ringing out. "Bless you, no. They've no use for the lesser mortals in the family. I am but a younger son of a younger son of a younger son. We've been farm managers for the Allenbys for two centuries, and every last one of them has hated tha' we bear the same name as they. Sir Alfred even offered my old da' a thousand pounds to change it."

I nearly stumbled over a tussock. He put out a strong hand to steady me. "Careful there, lady."

"Sir Alfred? You mean Sir Redwall's father? He actually offered your father money to change his name?"

"Aye. But he would have none of it. Sir Alfred had an apoplexy and died soon after, and all the better for us. He would have chucked out the lot of us, tha's for certain, and left us to starve. If the Allenbys have any gift, 'tis for dying when you want them to."

I opened my mouth to question him further, but we had reached the crossroads by then and he raised his hand to point up the path. "Tha's the way to Rosalie's. You mind you know it well enough? And back again? I can come and collect you if you don't. 'Twould not serve you to get lost on the moor."

"No, thank you, Godwin. I know my way."

"Then I'll be off. Good day to thee, my lady."

He sketched a little parody of a courtier's bow and left me, whistling a merry tune. I walked slowly, turning over what he had said in my mind. So many interesting little titbits, and so many questions unanswered. I was so preoccupied that I tripped over the rock just in front of Rosalie Smith's cottage for the second time, cursing roundly as I did so. There was a laugh from just over the stone wall of the garden.

"Lady in looks, but not in speech," Rosalie said, smiling as she opened the gate.

I waved a hand at the stone. "You might have that thing removed. That is the second time I have tripped over that stone. It could be dangerous in the dark."

She shrugged. "Everyone knows it is there. And if you ever come to me at night, I will know it is you by the swearing."

I proffered the cake and she took it with thanks.

"Come in and we will slice it for tea."

I accepted, and in a very short time we were settled at her comfortable hearthside, sipping our tea and nibbling at heavy slices of fruitcake. It was moist and rich and thick with fruit that Mrs. Butters had set to steep in tea and whisky many weeks before. She had guided Minna through the mixing of the batter and the girl had outdone herself.

Rosalie and I talked for a few minutes about nothing in particular, then fell silent. As with Godwin, it was a comfortable silence, and I realised, not for the first time, that my most companionable moments were often found in the company of those whom society would have me shun. Other ladies of my station would simply never have considered walking with the farm manager or taking tea with a Gypsy witch. Nor would they have considered any possibility of a romantic entanglement with a man of questionable parentage who made a living in trade, I reflected ruefully.

"Penny for your thoughts," Rosalie murmured.

"If you were gifted with the sight, you would already know them," I teased her.

She shook her head, her expression darkening. "I have seen those with the sight, lady. It is a cruel gift, one that takes as much as it bestows."

I thought of Brisbane with a shiver. He resisted his flashes of insight, his inexplicable ability to see things he should not, and to know things he could not. This refusal to accept himself for what he was sat at the root of his migraines, vicious and torturous. He held them at bay with all manner of evil things, and I suspected his current regimen of a whisky at bedtime would not serve him for long. It had occurred to me that his music was some solace, but I knew that it would never be able to stem the tide of pain forever. Sooner or later, the pain or his visions would win out, if only they did not destroy him in the meantime. Shortly after our last investigation at my father's home in Sussex, I had visited a Gypsy woman of my acquaintance, Magda, who had known Brisbane's family, and his ill-fated mother, Mariah Young.

The one man Mariah Young loved was not a Romany. He was a rogue, come from an old and proud Scottish family, and his people hated Mariah. But he must have loved her in spite of his wicked ways, for they married and after seven full moons had passed, she gave birth to a child, a boy with his mother's witchcraft and his father's wildness. But blood will out, and the noble

*rogue left his wife and son. Mariah did not grieve for him. His
love of drink and other women had killed her love, and when
she saw she was rid of him she danced as she had not danced
since she was wed. She took her boy to her people, tried to teach
him the ways of the travellers.*

*But the child was a halfling, born between two worlds, be-
longing to neither. When he was but ten years old he ran away,
leaving his mother behind and, for the first time in her life,
Mariah Young knew what it was to have a broken heart. She
cursed her own son. She gave him the legacy of her sight,
knowing he would fight against it, knowing it would destroy
him slowly from within.*

It was a horrible tale, tragic and violent, and it had gone
down as legend amongst their people. I wondered if Rosalie
had heard of her as well, if perhaps she knew Brisbane for
what he was. I very nearly asked her, but she offered me
another slice of cake then and the moment passed.

The lurcher, Rook, came and sat with his head on my knee
as we talked, and I petted him absently.

"He does not like many folk, and none who are not Romany,"
Rosalie told me. "You must have some Gypsy blood, lady."

I smiled and gave the dog a good scratching behind the
ears. "I think dogs know those who like them. He is a
handsome fellow. Why do you call him after a black bird,
though? His coat is white as new snow."

"'Rook' means tree in our language. Rook was cast off by
his mother and my husband, John-the-Baptist, found him
curled up under the roots of an oak tree, shivering with cold.
He put him into his waistcoat and kept him there, although
we do not keep white dogs."

Poaching, of course. That was the primary function of Gypsy dogs, and as she had indicated before, a white animal would be of no use in the dark.

"John-the-Baptist thought I would like some company here when he is away. So he kept him alive by giving him to suckle at a goat. And when the pup was strong enough, he came here to live. He is a good watchdog, although little enough stirs on the moors."

"Except perhaps ghosts," I joked, thinking of the bleak grimness of the place when the sky was iron grey and the clouds seemed to lower just overhead.

"Oh, yes. The ghosts," she said soberly. "But the dead do not always lie quietly, do they, lady?"

I thought of the people I had known who had died. I had never seen a ghost, but I had known the unquiet dead.

"No, they do not," I agreed. I hurried to change the subject. "John-the-Baptist is an unusual name."

"He is an unusual man. Perhaps you will meet him. He will come this way again soon. Always in the springtime," she said, and for an instant I fancied I caught a note of wistfulness in her tone. I could not imagine her living so long removed from her people, seeing her husband for a few weeks of each year.

I thought again of Magda. She had been banished from her Gypsy family and had spent some time as my laundress in London before rejoining her people. It was not impossible that Rosalie had been banished as well. I knew the Gypsies had many taboos for which the punishment was always banishment.

"You said you are a—what was the word?" I asked her.

"*Shuvari*. The English call me a witch, but among my own kind I am a healer."

"And the villagers here, the English, they do not bother you? I would have thought them inclined to be superstitious about such things."

She shrugged. "They remember the old ways here, when there was always a village wise woman to help babies into the world, and ease the passing of the dead. They trust me because I soften their sorrows and because I have the gift of potions. There is not a condition I cannot remedy, if a person wants my help."

"A gift indeed," I observed. "You are lucky, Rosalie. Not many people have the good fortune of knowing their purpose so clearly."

She tipped her head to one side, as I had often seen my raven, Grim, do. Her eyes were dark and bright with interest. "You speak as though you wander, lady. But you should not. Your path is one you put your feet on some time ago. And even though you cannot see the way for the shadows, you must know these shadows will not always cloud your vision."

I toyed with the Medusa pendant at my throat, turning the coin over in my fingers. Rosalie looked at it curiously, but said nothing. I tucked it away lest she ask about it. My relationship with Brisbane was complicated enough without trying to explain it to a virtual stranger. "You speak like a fortune-teller now. I thought you did not have the sight."

"I may not read tea leaves or palms, my lady, but it is easy enough to read faces. Yours is a questioning face, always looking for answers, always seeking the truth, for yourself and for others."

I smiled at her. "I think that is a very polite way of saying I am curious as a cat. And we all know what happened to the cat—curiosity killed her."

Rosalie took the last slice of cake onto her plate. "Yes, but you forget the most important thing about the little cat," she said, giving me a wise nod. "She had eight lives left to live."

I hurried my steps as I returned to Grimsgrave Hall. Dark clouds had gathered, and though it had not begun to rain, the wind was freshening, whipping my skirts and shawl about me and dragging my hair free from its pins. I cursed it as I struggled down the moor path, so intent upon my unruly hair that I did not see Brisbane approaching until he was nearly upon me.

"You've come back," I said stupidly, so stunned was I to see him there, conjured like something out of a dream. He was dressed for travelling, his suit perfectly neat, his cuffs crisp and white. How he managed to keep himself so fastidious was one of the mysteries I had yet to solve.

He fixed me with a humourless look. "You ought to be inside," he scolded. "There is a storm coming." He was scant feet away, but I could scarcely hear him for the wind.

"I know," I told him, exasperated. "Where do you think I am going?"

He took my arm just above the elbow, his fingers warm even through the wool of my clothes. He nudged me along the path, guiding me toward the house.

"Well, considering you are the most contrary woman of my acquaintance, you might just as well have been headed for the crag."

I pulled a face, but when I opened my mouth to remonstrate with him, I thought better of it. There were lines of fatigue at his eyes and mouth, and for this brief moment, it was enough simply to be near him.

After a moment, he turned sharply to me. "Are you quite all right?"

"Yes, perfectly. Why do you ask?"

"Because I have just called you contrary and you did not bother to contradict me. I thought you might be ill."

He was watching me intently, and in that moment, every feeling I had ever nurtured for him rose up within me.

"Do shut up, Brisbane," I told him. I raised myself on tiptoe and pressed a kiss to his cheek. I meant it to be a trifle, a little thing to tease him with. I ought to have known better. One cannot taunt a lion and walk away unscathed.

In the space of a pulsebeat his arms were around me and we forgot the wind, the coming storm, the sad ruin of a house before us. We forgot everything except this electric thing that bound us, sparking a reaction whenever our flesh touched. He smelled of leather and wool and tasted of apples and I could have died in that moment and counted myself happy. He groaned my name when I put my lips to his neck, and then he kissed me again, wrenching the shawl from my head completely to bury his hands in my hair, scattering pins to the ground.

It might have been only a minute, it might have been a hundred years we stood there. It was not until the thunder rumbled directly overhead that we broke apart. Brisbane was breathing heavily, his broad chest rising and falling like a man who has just run a great distance. He stepped back sharply, then gathered up my shawl, fairly flinging it at me.

"For God's sake, Julia. You were a fool to come and a greater fool to stay," he shouted over the wind. "Why do you not go back to London?"

As calmly as I could manage with shaking fingers, I laid the shawl over my head and tied it securely. "Because you need me. You said so yourself."

He thrust his hands into his hair, tearing at it. "I was wrong. I did not mean it. I do not need you. Do you hear me? *I do not need you.* Go away, Julia. Go back to London and take your silly romance with you. I want none of it."

He turned then and left me standing in the middle of the moor, the vast empty moor that tore his words to pieces on the wind. It was a long time before I followed him, but when I did, I saw Hilda's pale, watchful face peering from the window on the stairs.

THE TENTH CHAPTER

The smallest worm will turn, being trodden on.
—William Shakespeare
Henry VI, Part 3

I slept poorly that night, my dreams full of misty moors and storms breaking over Thorn Crag. I wandered, lost and sodden, crying out to Brisbane. He stood at the top of Thorn Crag, laughing, his black greatcoat tossing on the wind as he circled an arm about Ailith Allenby. I woke and buried my head under the pillow in disgust. I could not imagine a more pathetic scene. It was something straight out of melodrama, and it occurred to me that the setting of Grimsgrave Hall was bringing out all of my worst tendencies to sentimentality.

"I loathe myself," I muttered.

"Do not talk to yourself, Julia. It makes me fear for your sanity," Portia said dryly.

I peeked out from under the pillow, surprised to find her sitting on the edge of the bed, fully dressed in head-to-toe velvet the colour of pale seawater, and holding a packet of envelopes.

"The post!" I cried. We had had no correspondence since we arrived at Grimsgrave. There was no delivery arrangement for the Hall, and Godwin's trips into the village to collect from the postmistress were few and far between. Valerius had offered to fetch it himself, but the postmistress had declined to give it to him as he was a stranger. He had sulked the better part of a day over the insult, but I had little doubt it would be forgot once he had had the pleasure of his letters.

Portia handed me mine and I thumbed through them eagerly, delighted to see that Father had written, as well as a number of my siblings and my dear friend, Hortense de Belle-fleur. There was also a letter from Bellmont, and I put it carefully aside to read later. I could not stand to open it yet lest he disappoint me by not agreeing to help the Allenby ladies.

Portia had opened her first letter and was staring at it, her complexion quite pale.

"Dearest? Is something wrong?"

She shook her head and pocketed the envelope. "No, just those damned Riche brothers. I told them I needed a proper riding costume before I left London and they've sent me nothing but apologies. Difficulties with the woolen mill in Scotland, or some such nonsense."

She fell to reading her letters again, and I sank into reverie. Memories of the crushing scene between Brisbane and me on the moor rolled over me and I thrust them back. This was not the time to let a trifling setback discourage me. He had told me the first night that he needed me, and after seeing how shattered he was by one kiss, I believed his actions rather than his words. He had not appeared for supper the previous night, nor to sit with the rest of the household. He had kept to his room instead, carefully locking the door behind him as he went. I would have been affronted at this precaution had I not realised that he knew me very well indeed.

Resolutely, I rose and began my toilette. I chattered to Portia about my plans for the day, scarcely noting her quiet answers.

"I only hope Bellmont won't be completely horrid about helping the Allenby ladies," I went on, dithering between my violet tweed ensemble and a smart black velvet suit more appropriate for town. "You know how stubborn he can be. I must say, I did not expect to like Ailith. One cannot like a woman so perfect, even if her clothes look like something out of a primer on modesty, but she has proved to be quite amiable, although that Hilda is quite foul. But I do quite like Lady Allenby and I mean to do all that I can for them. How is the organising going, by the way? They do not seem to mind you taking a hand in things, and you really ought to get on, you know."

Portia shook herself, as though she had been a thousand miles away. "Oh, they are cordial enough. As yet I have only made lists. Linen to be bought, furniture, plate. The builders will have to be brought in to see about the collapsed wing. It may not be feasible to repair it. Brisbane will have to decide."

I caught sight of her then in the looking-glass. She had taken the letter from her pocket again, and she looked as I had never seen her look before. She was pale to the lips and her expression was one of utter loss. I turned and went to her, laying a hand on her shoulder.

"Portia."

Her brave façade crumbled then. She turned her face up to me, tears sparkling on her lashes. Even in grief she was beautiful. "She's left me, Julia. Jane has left me."

"Of course she hasn't left you. She has gone to Portsmouth for her sister's confinement. She will return when Anna is recovered from the birth."

"No, Julia," she corrected fiercely. "She will not return to London. She is gone."

I collapsed onto the bed next to her, unbelieving. "Jane? She cannot have left you. She loves you."

"She did once. Perhaps she still does. I like to think so. But she is gone," she repeated.

Portia's fingers were knotted over the letter, creasing it. "When?"

"I knew she had been troubled by Anna's condition. Jane wanted children so desperately, you see. She was so deeply envious of Anna's happiness. She had begun to wonder if she had done right in living with me. I told her she ought not to go to Portsmouth, but she said she must, it was her duty to help her sister. I offered to come with her, but she refused. She made me come—wanted time to think, she said. We quarrelled that last morning."

I remembered the sharp silences, the tense, wordless moments that had flashed between them, and I realised how utterly stupid I had been. "I thought she was upset at you leaving her," I ventured.

Portia's lovely mouth twisted bitterly. "No. She was upset because *she* was leaving *me*. She did not want to, you know. Not really. But she is tired of it all. She is tired of being sneered at by polite society. She is tired of being a laughing-stock. She thinks we are a joke, Julia. And she wants babies of her own."

"Where has she gone?"

Portia gave a little laugh that ended on a sob. "She is going to India as soon as it can be arranged."

"India? Good God, why? She has no money. What possible reason can she have for wanting to go there?"

She swallowed hard, then forced the words out through stiff lips. "She is to be married. That is the real reason she's left me, you know. She met him in Portsmouth, some connection of Anna's husband. He is going to India to make his fortune, and she will go with him. She wants children, you see. And she will not have them with me."

I put my arm around her, gathering her close. "Oh, my dearest. I am so sorry."

"We had prospects, I told her. I even offered her Valerius for a stud if she really wanted a child. It did not seem such a terrible notion. He is handsome enough, and we would have been raising my own niece or nephew. She told me not to be vulgar," Portia said. There was no emotion to her words now, just a flat recitation, as though she wanted to get all of the horror of it out and away. "We quarrelled over that. We quarrelled over taking a child from an orphanage or workhouse. I thought it was a noble idea. She told me it was no substitute for having a child of her own. I accused her of being selfish, reminded her that we had enough money to take a hundred orphans to raise if we liked. I think I may have made reference to Oliver Twist."

"Oh, Portia, you didn't."

"Of course I did. I was angry and sarcastic and stupid. I said things she will never forgive, and even if she could, I cannot take away the fact that although I love her more than my own life, I cannot give her the one thing she wants most of all."

I held her as she cried, aching for her as her shoulders shook with violent sobs. She wept noiselessly, stifling her sorrow against the neck of my nightdress. I rocked her as if she were a child, and when she was spent, I dried her tears with my own handkerchief and told her to blow her nose and attend to her face.

"Tell me, how much do you love her?" I asked when she had repaired the worst of the damage with a damp sponge and a powderpuff.

"Enough to follow her to the ends of the earth in a white petticoat," Portia said sadly.

"Careful, dearest. That's what Mary, Queen of Scots, said about Lord Bothwell and look what a nasty end she made."

There was not a flicker of a smile on my sister's face.

"What do you mean to do?" I asked.

She took a deep breath, exhaling slowly. She seemed calmer now, resolute. "I must go to Portsmouth. Immediately. Today in fact."

She rose and began to gather her possessions. I stared after her, mouth agape. "Portia, you cannot be serious. You cannot leave, not now."

She collected her books from the little writing desk, tossing them into an untidy heap next to me. "Sort those, will you? I shall want the Scott for the train ride. No Brontë. I've had quite enough of moors to last me a lifetime."

I shoved the books aside and rose. "Portia, listen to me. You cannot just rush to Portsmouth this instant. You don't even know when the train is leaving."

She shrugged and tossed a pair of stockings at me. "Bundle those. It doesn't matter when the train is leaving. There is bound to be one today sometime. Wherever it goes, I will go. Any station is bigger than the one in Lesser Howlett. There will be connections elsewhere. I do not care where I am bound, so long as I am *moving*. I will take Valerius with me. I will send him back directly I've arrived, I promise."

I knotted the stockings together and dropped them onto her books. "Portia, you promised Brisbane you would organise his household. You've hardly begun."

She flapped a hand at me. "That was just a stratagem to bring the two of you together. Now you're here, the rest is up to you."

"Stratagem? You never intended to put the house to rights?"

"God, no. I loathe doing that sort of thing."

"But—but you are brilliant at it!"

She shrugged and yanked two shawls from the bedpost where she had flung them earlier. "I am rather good at speaking German. That does not mean I enjoy it. I offered because I knew you would never be able to resist the chance to play the coquette and thrust yourself at Brisbane."

I folded my arms over my chest. "That is quite possibly the most hurtful thing you have ever said to me. I am not *thrusting* myself at Brisbane."

She tucked the shawls under her chin and began to fold them haphazardly. "Yes, you are, and you would be no sister of mine if you didn't."

She took my hands in hers and I could not tell whose were the colder.

"Julia, you do not need me. You have come here because you know in your heart he loves you. This is your chance to have what you always wanted. Seize it, and do not let him go. He is confused and wounded and I think he has more secrets than the Sphinx itself, but he is a good man. And I believe he loves you in ways you cannot possibly fathom. Stay, and make him see you. I cannot give up Jane without a fight, and you must not give up Brisbane." She lifted her chin. "We are Marches, and our motto is *Audeo. I dare.* Dare to take the life you want in your own two hands and do not let it go, do you hear me?"

She was weeping now, and my own eyes filled as she clasped me to her. "Go," I told her, drying my eyes on her sleeve. "Go and give Jane my love. Oh," I said, suddenly thinking of Portia's little maid. "You must tell Minna. She'll not be packed."

Portia shook her head. "She is quite happy here, and I've no time to wait. I mean to fill a portmanteau, and she can send my trunk along when she has had time to pack it. You can bring Minna with you when you return to London. I will take Morag instead."

I agreed and we hastily packed Portia's things, enlisting Minna to bring a few odds and ends while Morag complained bitterly about the high-handedness of some people, ordering her back to town just when she was happily settled in the country.

"Do shut up," I hissed at her. "You do not fool me. I see that gleam in your eye. You would rather cut off your left arm than stay here another minute. Mind you take better care of Lady Bettiscombe than you do me," I finished, thrusting Portia's muddied boots at her. "Scrape these down and wrap them in brown paper." She stalked off to do as she was bid while Minna scurried about, trembling but excited at the news she was to stay behind.

There was a spirited discussion over the custody of Mr. Pugglesworth, but as I refused to keep the revolting animal, Portia had no choice but to tuck him under her arm as she left. She had sent Minna to ask Godwin to arrange for transportation, and by the time she and Morag and Valerius were ready to leave, packed and swathed in a travelling veil, a farm cart borrowed from a neighbour was standing at the end of the drive. Valerius appeared, pale and unshaven, yawning broadly as he collected Portia's portmanteau along with his own. He raised a hand to me in farewell, and I blew him a kiss. His expression was sober, and I knew he would feel as wretched as I. Jane had been a sort of sister to him as well. Portia did not turn, but I leaned from the casement and watched until she was out of sight.

She had left it to me to make her excuses to the rest of the household, and I did not relish the task. I met with Brisbane first. He had just emerged from his room when I descended.

"Portia is gone," I told him without preamble.

"Without sorting my linen cupboard?" he asked with a touch of asperity.

"Don't, I beg you. I am quite miserable enough."

Instantly, he moved to me, his hand heavy on my shoulder. "What is the trouble?"

"Jane has left her. She means to marry and go out to India."

Brisbane said nothing, then gave a low sigh, his hand tightening upon my shoulder. "Odd, really. I would have counted them the happiest couple of my acquaintance."

I gave a little sound, half sob and half laugh. I covered his hand with my own. "That is the difficulty. They were happy. They are so well-suited to one another, and yet Jane wanted something more. She has left Portia in order to have a family."

His gaze was hard upon mine. "Can you blame her?"

"What do you mean?"

"Only that Jane has never known a proper family of her own."

"She has known Portia!" I countered hotly. "Portia has been everything to her, has given her all that she has to give."

"And perhaps it was not enough," he said quietly. His expression was so grave, I felt my heart thump painfully in my chest.

"I wonder, Brisbane, are you talking about Jane and Portia, or do you speak of something else entirely?"

The little muscle in his jaw that twitched whenever he was impatient jumped. "I am simply endeavouring to point out that no matter how much one wishes for something, no matter how desperately one might love someone, there are no guarantees."

I stared at him, taking in the coiled tension of his stand, the shadows under his eyes. "What happened in Edinburgh?"

He dropped his hand from my shoulder. "Julia, this is not the time—"

"I think it is. You were reconciled to my presence here before you left. I think you were even happy to see me, in spite of the circumstances. But you came back changed and I would know why. What happened in Edinburgh?"

"I was shot at," he told me flatly. "A ring of counterfeiters, passing false notes on the Bank of Scotland. Their leader was a son of a bosom friend of the Prince of Wales. I was asked to retrieve him and return him to his family so they can deal with him privately. He did not come quietly."

I felt cold, from my head to my feet, a sweeping cold that almost stilled my breath. "You are unharmed?" I could scarcely force the words through stiffened lips.

"I am. The bullet grazed my coat," he said, pointing to a tidy little scar at the collar that had been neatly mended. My eyes filled with hot tears.

"If that bullet had been a hairsbreadth to the left," I said, unable to finish the thought. The bullet had passed within a shadow of his throat.

"I know," he told me. "Believe me, when the tailor was stitching my coat, all I could think of was how lucky I had been. How many times I have been lucky," he said, his voice trailing off.

I thought of the bullet that had torn through his shoulder when he had saved the life of one dear to me in Trafalgar Square, and I shuddered.

He reached for my hands and held them fast in his own. "Julia, I have spent the better part of my life seeking adventure and having very little care if I woke the next day or not. I have lived freely and with no one to whom I must be beholden or accountable, no one to consider if I died." I thought of his devoted manservant Monk, and knew that Brisbane was wrong. Monk loved him like a son, and had anything befallen Brisbane, Monk would have mourned him like a lost child.

Brisbane continued. "I have led a selfish life, and I have enjoyed it. I cannot imagine a life without my work, and I cannot imagine a life without you, and yet I cannot reconcile the two." My heart, which had given a joyous leap in the middle of his speech, faltered now as I realised what he was trying to say.

"I never thought to ask you to give up your work," I began.

"But how can I ask you to sit idly by and wait for me to return when every time I kiss you goodbye might be the last?"

"Oh, don't!" I told him, fully enraged. "How dare you blame your cowardice upon me?"

His lips went white, as did the tiny crescent moon scar high upon his cheekbone. "I beg your pardon?"

"Cowardice," I said distinctly. "You hide behind this pretence of fine feeling because you will not declare yourself directly and this gives you a perfect excuse, does it not? Spare poor Julia the horror of being widowed a second time. Put her up on the shelf and keep her out of harm's way whilst you amuse yourself with your dashing adventures."

He opened his mouth to speak, but I stepped forward, tipping my head up to rail at him. "I am quite disappointed that you have revealed yourself to be so thoroughly conventional in your philosophy. Have I not proven myself a capable partner?" I demanded. "Have I not stood, side by side, with you, facing peril with equal courage? If you thought for a moment that I would be the meek, quiet, obedient sort of woman who would sit quietly at home mending your socks while you get to venture out into the world on your daring escapades, you have sorely mistaken me."

I turned on my heel and left him then, gaping after me like a landed carp. It was a very small consolation.

I made an effort to settle my temper and made my way to the kitchen. Lady Allenby was still at table, finishing the remains of her breakfast, when I appeared. To my surprise, Hilda was with her, absently cutting a piece of ham for her mother.

"My hands are rather worse today," Lady Allenby said by way of explanation.

I expressed my sympathy and gave her the broadest sketch of why Portia had fled without so much as a farewell, telling her only that there was a family difficulty and she was wanted and that Valerius would return after he accompanied her safely to Portsmouth.

"But if the difficulty is a family one, should you not be there as well?" Hilda asked, her tone cool. She thickly buttered a piece of toast, oblivious to her mother's reproving frown.

"Not at all," I said smoothly. "The business concerns a cousin of her late husband, Lord Bettiscombe." That much was true at least.

Lady Allenby redirected the conversation quickly. "How lovely that you were able to stay behind. The moorland is quite beautiful in spring, you know. It is a shame to miss a single day of it."

"I have heard, and I am happy to be staying as well," I replied. Mrs. Butters laid a plate before me, steaming eggs and sausages and a clever little savoury pudding full of cheese and herbs. I lifted my fork just as Hilda shot me a smiling look. Doubtless she was remembering the scene she had overlooked the previous afternoon, Brisbane embracing me, then shouting at me to go home. She would not have heard his words, but how many of his gestures would she have interpreted correctly? I returned the smile and stabbed viciously at the pudding.

The rest of breakfast was consumed in silence, the only sound the click of cutlery on the plain china plates and the gentle hiss of the pan simmering on the hob.

I rose when Lady Allenby did and left by the kitchen door, intending to take a walk on the moor. Just as I reached the gate, I heard Hilda's voice behind me.

"Is it not enough that you have designs on Brisbane? Must you drive Mr. Valerius away as well?" she demanded.

I turned on my heel to find her staring at me, her hands balled into fists at her sides, her pale complexion splotched unbecomingly with red.

"I do beg your pardon?" I said with icy calm.

She moved nearer, but I stood my ground. "You should have gone with them. No one wants you here. You should have gone with your sister and left Mr. Valerius. He is the only one of you worth speaking to."

"I assure you, Miss Hilda, the arrangements were not of my making. I am terribly sorry you have been inconvenienced."

The tips of her nostrils had gone white with anger. "Do not patronise me. I will not be talked down to, as though I were an imbecile like Jetty. My blood is quite as good as yours, my lady," she said, larding the last word with sarcasm. "My ancestors were kings in this land when yours were still wiping the boots of a bastard in Normandy."

I sighed and folded my arms over my chest. "Hilda, this

is tiresome. You are far too old for childish insults, insults I don't even think you believe. And you are far too sensible to put any credence in that Saxon royalty nonsense."

She gaped at me, clearly torn. In the end, her sound common sense won out. "Oh, very well, it *is* ludicrous. I would burn that stupid tapestry if I could. No one cares about such things anymore. I've tried to tell Mama that. She won't listen, and neither will Ailith. But I had to say something," she added, giving me a defiant glare. "I've nothing else to fight you with."

"Good heavens, why should you want to fight me at all? I should think you would far rather prefer a little civil conversation."

"With you?" She made no attempt to disguise the scorn in her voice. "I can assure you we have no point of commonality."

"Nonsense. We are both ladies, gently born. We are both in this remote place. We might talk of anything, the people here, the landscape, or the books," I said, feeling a sudden surge of inspiration.

She eyed me warily, as a whipped dog will do to a hand raised to it, even in friendship. "What books?"

"The ones you had in your room. The Egyptology books. You would be quite mad for the ones in your brother's study, I'm sure. Did you know he has the entire set of the *Description de l'Égypte*? It is in remarkably good condition."

If I had thought her angry before, it was nothing compared to her rage now. She could scarcely speak, and when she did, her voice was rough.

"You have been in Redwall's room? Going through his things?"

"Yes, I had your mother's permission, of course. If you would like to see them, I would be happy—"

"You would be happy?" She stepped forward, and for one terrible moment, I truly believed she would strike me. I balled my fist behind my skirts and set my shoulders. If she did strike me, I would not be unprepared. "You would give me permission to look at what by rights *belongs to me?*"

Relieved, I put out a hand to placate her. "Miss Hilda, really, there is no need—"

"There is every need," she said, biting off each word sharply. "You are a meddlesome bitch, and the sooner you go back to London, the better."

She turned on her heel then and left me standing in the mud.

THE ELEVENTH CHAPTER

A great reckoning in a little room.
—William Shakespeare
As You Like It

After the high drama of my encounters with both Brisbane and Hilda, I lost my enthusiasm for a walk on the moor. I returned to Sir Redwall's study, determined to make some headway. I had forgot Bellmont's letter in the confusion of Portia's departure, but I retrieved it, wishing fervently that he had pledged his help. The news was not encouraging. I skimmed hastily through his lectures on my wilfulness, my stubbornness, my lack of femininity, until my eyes glazed and the words ran together on the page. It was not until the third page that he came to the point.

As to countenancing any sort of exhibition regarding Sir Redwall Allenby, I can only think that you are attempting to make a poor jest. His name is anathema in Egyptological circles, for reasons that do no credit to any scholar or gentleman. Of course, in the interests of scholarship and patrimony, the collection should be turned over at once to the British Museum, although this could well ignite a heated and insoluble round of debate regarding the provenance and current rights of ownership. The absolutely wrong thing to do would be to remove the collection in its entirety to London for appraisal and private sale before anyone can get wind of what you are about. I, naturally, would counsel against such action, particularly as any more scandal would not reflect well upon our family at this time. My eldest, Orlando, is proposing marriage to the daughter of the Duke of Driffield, and anything that could puncture his happiness is of course of the greatest concern to me.

I tossed the letter aside, vastly irritated. Bellmont had always been a pompous prig, but he usually managed to be helpful in the end. If he was busy helping Orlando court the Duke of Driffield's daughter, however, there would be no help from that quarter whatsoever. The Driffield title was an insignificant but old one, and Monty would be positively swooning at the idea of marrying his heir to Driffield's daughter. Any escapades on the part of any of the Marches at this point would be severely frowned upon. There were political hopes as well for Orlando, and I had no doubt Bellmont was keeping an eagle eye on all his wayward siblings at present.

There was nothing for it then, I decided. I would have to arrange the evaluation and sale myself, although I was vastly

pleased Bellmont had dropped that little nugget of information about Redwall Allenby's disgrace in the Egyptological
community. I would have to tread carefully to dispose of his
collection without alerting the circles in which he had once
travelled. As to what Redwall had done that was so ungentlemanly and unscholarly, I would simply have to add
that question to the others tumbling in my mind.

I had just turned my hand to noting the condition of a
pretty little chest painted with ibises when the door opened.
I started, nearly dropping the chest. I knew Brisbane would
find out soon enough what I was about, but I had been reluctant to tell him of my scheme to help the Allenby ladies.
I needn't have feared. It was not Brisbane approaching softly
through the gloom. It was Ailith, her slippered feet silent on
the stone floor. Her expression was serene, her hands clasped
loosely in front of her.

"Lady Julia. My mother told me I might find you here."

I cleared my throat and set down the little chest with
infinite care. "Yes. I am cataloguing Sir Redwall's collection.
Your mother is interested in placing it for sale." It seemed
the most tactful way to phrase the matter.

She said nothing for a long moment, but looked around,
taking in the dusty shrouds of furniture, the painted
ceiling, the little notebook on my lap. She smiled then, a
sad, vacant thing.

"You have one of Redwall's notebooks. He was never without
one, always jotting notes, drawing little sketches in them." I
said nothing and she hurried on, almost as though the words
were being forced from her. "I have the others, you know."

"The others?"

"The notebooks. The ones he kept in Egypt. They might prove useful to you when you are cataloguing. He wrote about his acquisitions sometimes. Where he found them, the name of the dealer, that sort of thing."

"That would be a tremendous help. There is no provenance for many of these articles. If he kept a diary of sorts, it would at least give me a place to start."

"Come with me then, to my room. I will give them to you."

I laid aside my pencil and notebook and followed her upstairs. I had not yet seen her room, but as soon as I crossed the threshold, I realised I would have known it for hers out of any bedchamber in the house. The walls were painted a soft greyed blue, and the colour was repeated throughout the room. She had a four-poster bed hung with the same striking shade, the silk brittle and shredding. The walls were peeling in spots where the damp had seeped in, and the furniture, save a few small painted wooden pieces, was missing. It was a room that, like the lady herself, had once been extremely elegant and feminine. But time had taken its toll. I saw the fatigue here of watching the family fortunes dwindle, of isolation and loneliness. Only one object livened the room—a doll's house, large and imposing, and I realised it was the one she had told me about. Her description had been thoroughly accurate. It was a perfectly rendered replica of Grimsgrave itself.

"How lovely," I breathed, bending to see into the little rooms. It was beautifully furnished, down to the last detail, and I saw for the first time how stately the public rooms had once been with their oaken panelling and heavy carved furniture. There was even a tiny replica of the tapestry from the hall, and I squinted to make out the stitches.

"There are only flowers on the branches of the tree," Ailith explained. "The names would not fit." I noticed, though, that a crown of gold thread had been stitched at the top. Even in miniature, the royal lineage must not be forgot. I traced the branch where Ailith and her sibling had been commemorated. Three blossoms hung there and I thought at once of the unpicked place in the tapestry downstairs.

"You are clever, Lady Julia," Ailith told me. "That was my sister, Wilfreda. We do not speak of her, and I beg you not to ask Mama about her."

I stepped back, embarrassed to have caused her distress. "I am sorry. I did not mean to pry."

Ailith smiled her serene smile. "All families have skeletons in the cupboard. Some of them are bound to come tumbling out. I do not mind talking about her. The doll's house was hers, a gift from our father. When she left, I begged Mama for it. It is the only thing of hers that was not destroyed."

She paused and went to the writing table, opening the drawer. She extracted a few notebooks, identical to the one I had found in Redwall's study. "Here. I should like them back when you have done with them."

"Of course. I shall take excellent care of them, I promise."

She smiled again, this time indulgently, as an adult will to a precocious child. "I know you will. There is something else I should like you to see."

She reached into the drawer again and withdrew a photograph in a small leather frame, the sort of thing a traveller might carry. She put it into my hands and I stared at the photograph. It was of a man, dressed in travelling clothes, an exotic background behind him. It was Cairo, the minarets just visible through the latticed window. There were a few potted palms at his elbow, and a great stuffed crocodile at his feet. But it was not the props that had captured my attention. He was the most beautiful man I had ever seen. There was an elegance, a perfection to his features that was unrivalled. The lips, beautifully moulded, were slightly curved into a smile of invitation to the viewer. The bones, carved with a master's hand, spoke of centuries of good breeding. His was the sort of face that would have been beautiful even in extreme old age. Even in death.

I turned to Ailith and she was not looking at the photograph. She was studying my reaction to it.

"A very handsome man. Your brother, I presume?" The question was unnecessary. The resemblance was profound. They might have been twins, the similarity was so great.

"That was taken in Egypt," she told me. "He had been gone from home almost thirteen years by then. He wanted us to see how he had changed. He ought to have cut his hair." I turned back to the photograph. True, his hair was overlong, curling at his collar and temples, but I understood why he had not cut it. It would have been heresy to spoil those silky locks.

"Was his colouring the same as yours?" I ventured.

"Oh, yes. The same gold hair and blue eyes. All Allenbys are the same, save for Hilda. Her colouring is so dull. You might have seen Redwall's portrait, had Mama not burned it. An excellent likeness, although I think this one is better."

I blinked at her. "Lady Allenby burned his portrait?"

Ailith retreated a little, stepping back and smoothing her

cuffs. "It was an unhappy reminder to her. The artist who painted it is the man who ran away with my sister."

She had resumed her cool façade, and I knew the time for confidences was at an end. I rose and gathered up the notebooks.

To my surprise, she handed me the photograph. "You might like to keep this while you work on his things. Perhaps it will help you to remember that although he was not always a gentleman, he was always a great man."

If I was startled, I tried not to show it. The mysteries around Redwall Allenby continued to deepen, I thought as I slipped the photograph into my pocket. I moved to leave the room, then paused, my hand on the knob.

"I am truly sorry for your loss, Miss Allenby. I know what it is to love a brother, and I can only imagine how difficult this has been for you." As much thought as I had given to drowning my brothers when we were children, I would have been bereft at the loss of any of them. Even Bellmont.

She inclined her head, and did not reply.

Perhaps it was all the talk of loss and regret, but I felt the atmosphere of the house was thick with ghosts that afternoon, and I hurried from Grimsgrave and across the moor to the one place I knew could soothe my restlessness.

Rosalie opened the door as I smoothed my windblown skirts. She had tied a bright patchwork apron about her waist and was holding a spoon.

"I hope I have not disturbed you," I began.

She waved me inside. "I was working in my stillroom. Come, lady."

She beckoned me to follow her through a tiny door into a room no bigger than a pocket handkerchief. It was lined with shelves, each neatly stacked with dark glass bottles, closely stoppered and labelled with names like Syrup of Poppy and Remedy for a Toothache. There were jars of unpleasant-looking, desiccated things and bunches of herbs and grasses hanging in plaits from the beams, so low they brushed our shoulders as we moved.

There were cans of oils for making her embrocations, tins of powders, and a very fine set of scales. Bowls for mixing, various wooden implements, and a wickedly sharp knife marked with the initials *RY* were tidily arranged to be close at hand. The knife was a pretty thing, but no lady's trinket. I touched a finger to the carved initials and wondered what exotic second name her parents had given her. Yolanda? Yasmine? I moved on to peruse the rest of the shelves as Rosalie took down a bottle and a sturdy stoneware bowl. She retrieved a tin of goose fat, an assortment of bones and motioned for me to hand her a small, pointed silver spoon and the knife marked with her initials. She drew it from its sheath, exposing a long, sawlike blade. I pulled a face as I looked at the macabre collection.

"Today I am to mix St. Hildegard's ointment," she told me.

I leaned over her shoulder to watch her work.

"St. Hildegard's," she said, drawing me around to stand next to her. "This is an ointment for swollen joints. It soothes rheumatisms. The receipt is a very old one. It is from Germany, and it is very specific."

Through the course of the next half hour, she never referred to a book or scribbled bit of paper. The receipt had been committed to memory, and I watched carefully as she assembled the mixture. She measured by the palmful, four parts gin to two parts goose fat to two parts deer marrow. Extracting the marrow was the most tedious part, requiring patience and no small skill in order to keep the mixture free of bone slivers. It was messy work and the smell was appalling, but she seemed pleased with the salve she produced.

"Now, for this to work, it must be rubbed firmly into the swollen joints. The rheumatic must sit in front of an elmwood fire. Raw quince is the best food for drawing out the pain of rheumatism, but if that is not to taste, then a pudding or pie of quince or even quince wine will work as well."

She spooned the salve into a fresh jar and sealed it. Together we tidied up the stillroom and as we worked, I ventured a question.

"Rosalie, Miss Ailith has told me of the customs of the moor. Have you ever heard the bell that tolls under Grimswater?"

To my surprise, she smiled. "I would have thought you immune to village superstitions, Lady Julia."

I shrugged. "This superstition is not confined to the village. The folk at Grimsgrave claim to have heard it."

"What makes you think the Allenbys are any more sensible than the villagers? They have been here for too long. It is not good for the blood of a family to be unmixed. They have dwelt here on this moor, marrying their cousins and producing beautiful children for a thousand years. They ought to have travelled, married fresh blood and learned a little of the world."

"Sir Redwall travelled," I pointed out. "He went to Egypt."

She tipped her head, her bright gaze searching my face.

Then she smiled. "No, lady. I do not mean only the travelling that takes a man into a new country. I mean the travelling that takes a man into a new place here." She touched her heart lightly. "Too many Englishmen go to a new country and bring with them the same clothes, the same tea, the same food, the same books. They try to bring England itself with them, and then they are dissatisfied when they are foreigners in a foreign land."

"True enough," I admitted, "but Gypsies marry their own and keep their own ways, in spite of their travels."

"When have your kind ever wanted to share our ways?" she asked without rancour.

"I suppose you are correct. I should be quite hopeless at that sort of thing. What I know of Sir Redwall suggests a man who would like his comforts. But I wonder what caused him to leave Grimsgrave and venture abroad when no one else in his family had ever done so. Was it purely the love of Egyptology?"

"Who can say? It was a difficult time in the village, and the Allenbys were not very popular just then."

"The village?" I prompted.

"Those who do not farm here used to work the mines. Lead mostly, a little silver. The last mine on Allenby land played out shortly before Sir Redwall left. Folk did not take it well when he closed the mine and refused to survey for another vein. He ought to have paid for someone to look properly, but he would not. He claimed he had no money, then left for Egypt, sending back a stream of expensive artefacts. He was not received warmly when he returned."

"What happened?"

"He were pelted with rotten eggs when he came, and folk chased him from the village clear out onto the moor, throwing stones and threatening him."

I stared at her, aghast. "Their own benefactor?" I could scarcely fathom it. The relationship between the largest house in the area and the country folk was a throwback to the feudal age, with protection in difficult times and opportunities for work provided by the big house, and strong backs and willing workers provided by the villagers. It was astonishing to me that the relationship could have broken down so completely at Grimsgrave, but then northerners had a reputation for the sort of independence southerners would never countenance.

She shrugged again. "He denied them work, took food from their children's mouths. He was no benefactor to them. When he closed the mine and refused to survey for another, it caused a great deal of suffering. The estate began to fail, and he sold off some of the farms. He turned out the farmhands, sending them back to their homes, and sent the maids home as well. Many of those young people had depended upon their wages at Grimsgrave Hall to sustain entire families with their fathers out of work and younger brothers and sisters to feed. But the Allenby fortunes were in decline. Sir Redwall had spent himself into oblivion, and when he realised what he had done, he turned his face to the wall and died."

I thought of the handsome, charismatic face in the photograph and shook my head. "It seems impossible," I murmured.

"Do not think a handsome face may not hide a weak will," Rosalie advised me. I thought of my late husband and was forced to agree.

"What of his sister?" I asked suddenly. "The one who eloped with the portrait painter? Miss Ailith told me of her this afternoon. She made her escape from here."

"Did she? No one knows what became of her. She simply disappeared one night. Yes, the painter left as well, but was he forced to leave? Did he abduct the girl? Or did either of them ever leave that house alive?"

I stared at her, not quite comprehending. "Are you suggesting there has been murder done at Grimsgrave Hall?"

She smiled her enigmatic smile. "I suggest nothing. But Grimsgrave Hall is a house of secrets, and there will be no peace there until every one of them is brought into the light of day."

It was late when I left her, the shadows lengthening on the moor, the sun sinking below the horizon in a blaze of red and gold. I watched the sunset for just a moment, tearing myself away from the magnificent display when I remembered how long a walk still lay before me across the chilly moor. I set off toward Grimsgrave Hall, but I had not gone more than a dozen steps before I turned back. I stood very still, uncertain of what I had heard. And then, as the brisk moor wind rose, I heard the unmistakable sound of a bell, tolling low and mournful beneath the black waves of Grimswater.

THE TWELFTH CHAPTER

Ay, but to die, and go we know not where,
To lie in cold obstruction and to rot.
—William Shakespeare
Measure for Measure

I was not surprised Brisbane made no appearance at supper, and I was just as glad he did not. I was still smarting over his silly attempt to push me further away, and deeply frustrated that I could not discuss the matter with Portia. I went to bed early with a headache, and woke feeling only marginally better.

The next morning I closeted myself in Redwall's study directly breakfast was over. I took Grim in his cage to keep me company as usual, leaving Florence curled up in Minna's apron. It was warm there, and Minna used her for a place to rest her mending, so they were both satisfied with the arrangement. I placed the cage in its accustomed spot on the desk, but this time I opened the door to give him the run of the place. Grim bobbed his head excitedly.

"Mind you don't upset anything. Some of these artefacts are terribly valuable," I told him. He hopped out of the cage and began strutting round the room, pausing now and again to peer at something shiny. I slipped Redwall's photograph from my pocket and propped it on the desk. I told myself it was for a bit of inspiration, for the work could be tedious and grimy, but the truth was there was something arresting about that face, and wherever I turned, his level gaze seemed to follow, the mouth turned up in amusement at something I had done. I put his Egypt notebooks into a drawer to peruse later, and set to work. I had finished the books and was thrilled to be cataloguing the last of a set of delicately-wrought *shawabtis*. They were tiny statues of servants, waiting to do their master's bidding in the after-life. It amused me to see them ranged there, each with slightly different features or a different drape to his linen kilt. The artist had been so skilled, I could almost sense the watchfulness of each, the willingness to anticipate the needs of the master and respond. They were remarkable, and oddly charming.

I had just finished describing the last when Grim put his glossy black head around the edge of the desk and quorked at me.

"Are you hungry?" I rummaged in my pocket for a tin of sweetmeats, tossing him a sugared plum. He tore into it greedily and I threw him another.

"Oooh, that's for me," he said in his odd little croaking

voice. The first time Grim had spoken to me it had been a revelation, but I was accustomed to him now, and more than once his little sayings had been frighteningly *apropos*.

"Yes, that's for you, dearest." I rose and tidied up the box of *shawabtis*, then cast around for the next item to be catalogued. There was a couch I had been longing to put my hands on, but the *shawabtis* had been stacked atop it. Now, if I just shifted a set of ebony chairs, I could reach it properly. It was not an easy proposition. The chairs were precariously balanced and surprisingly heavy, their legs resting on the edge of the couch and braced by the brickwork of the fireplace. The fireplace backed the one in Brisbane's bedchamber, the two flues sharing a single chimney. I put my back to the brickwork and pushed against the first chair to edge it up in order to get a proper grip on it.

Just then Grim quorked loudly, startling me. I dropped the chair and stepped back heavily, catching my elbow on the side of the brickwork of the chimney breast.

"Damnation," I muttered, rubbing at my elbow and praying I had not damaged the chair.

Grim tilted his head up at me. "Damnation."

"Do not repeat that," I told him severely. "Or if you must, tell people Valerius taught it to you."

I examined the chair and breathed a sigh of relief. Even after a few millennia in a desert tomb, my clumsiness had not harmed it. The chimney breast was not so lucky. My elbow had dislodged a bit of it, and I bent to retrieve the piece of brick, surprised to find it was a neat slice rather than a crumbled lump. I moved to fit it back into place, and as I did so, I saw a tiny ring-shaped handle sitting slightly proud of the mortar beyond, just large enough to admit an index finger. I slid my finger inside and twisted.

To my astonishment, the mechanism worked perfectly. The side of the chimney breast swung open noiselessly, and I saw that the brick here was not solid at all. The entire panel was covered in thin slices of brick, a perfect *trompe-l'oeil* to trick the eye into believing it was as solid as the rest of the construction. It was beautifully done, each part of the mechanism fitting to within a hairsbreadth. A master had been at work here, I mused, but to what purpose?

"Of course," I murmured to Grim. "The Allenbys are Catholics. It's a priest's hole!"

He ignored me and toddled off, quorking quietly to himself, but I was intrigued. I had read of them, these odd little spaces fitted perfectly into Roman households for the purpose of hiding recusant priests. They had been hunted after the Reformation, and for a few centuries after, I recalled. But Catholics had had a stronghold in the north, and many of the manor houses had sheltered the priests who clung to the old ways and refused to recognise the Anglican church.

The spaces were invariably tiny, so as not to attract the attention of the men who searched for the priests. Some barely accommodated a fully-grown man, and there was no question of comfort. Priest's holes were for survival, and this one was no bigger than one might expect. Fitted directly against the fireplace, it must have been uncomfortably hot, stifling even, although a tiny speck of daylight high in the back wall showed where a supply of clean air might be had. There was even a silver tube still hanging next to the hole, a clever device to enable the priest to draw in the fresh air deeply.

But it was not the accommodations of the priest's hole that had captured my attention. Wedged tightly into the hole was an anthropomorphic box, the wood gilded and painted, as bright and beautiful as the day an Egyptian artist had last put his brush to them.

I leaned closer in the dim light to look at it, and felt a rush of excitement. This was what I had been searching for, a treasure from a pharaoh's tomb, the coffin of a king.

Or a queen, I decided, looking more closely at the painted face. The features were delicate and feminine. I touched a fingertip to the gilding, scarcely daring to breathe. It seemed impossible that Redwall Allenby could have spirited home the mortal remains of a pharaoh's wife, but the more I thought on it, the less outlandish it became. He was a passionate student of Egyptology, and what part of that discipline commanded more devotion than the study of its mummies? I had already learned enough of his character to know he could be impulsive and opportunistic. If he had been forced from Egypt in disgrace, might he not have taken the chance to purloin a magnificent trophy as a reminder of his travels to a beloved land?

I put out a hand and tested the weight of the coffin. It was futile to think I could move it myself, but I realised that the lid rocked a little against my palm. Without pausing to consider the consequences, I went to the desk and retrieved the knife. The blade slid easily between the lid and the coffin, and I silently blessed the work of good Yorkshire craftsmen. A lesser blade would have snapped as I rocked the lid free, but this held true, and I stepped back sharply as the lid dropped free of the sarcophagus. I peered behind it, prepared to look upon the linen-wrapped features of a long-dead queen.

Instead, there were two tiny bundles, each less than two feet long, positioned snugly in the sarcophagus, one where the lady's torso ought to have been, one in place of her legs. For one gruesome moment, I thought the lady had been dismembered, her body laid to rest in separate wrappings, but as I looked more carefully, I realised the bundles were two separate persons. I could make out the contours of heads and shoulders and legs, and each had been wrapped with all the care one would expect in an ancient burial, presided over by embalmer-priests. And to my horror, I knew precisely what they were.

I stepped out of the priest's hole and took several deep breaths, peeking once or twice to make certain the coffin was still there. Grim had found the tin of plums and pried it open, greedily helping himself to the contents. I no longer cared. My hands were still shaking as I closed the panel, careful to mark where the mechanism was as I slotted the brick into place. I was calmer by the time I put Grim back into his cage. He clucked irritably at me as I fastened the clasp.

"Damnation," he said, fixing me with a beady eye.

"Oh, do shut up, Grim," I returned.

I hurried to the hall and snatched up the first garment I found, a cloak of Hilda's, rusty black and so heavy I could barely stagger with it on. I was halfway across the moor path before I finally managed to tie its strings, picking my way toward Thorn Crag. I did not know where Brisbane was to be found, but it made sense to try the highest point in hopes I would be able to spy him from there.

As I drew closer, I fancied I heard his voice, and just as I rounded the top he came rushing from the other direction, nearly knocking me flat.

"Julia, what the devil are you doing up here? These rocks are dangerous," he scolded, putting a firm hand under my elbow and guiding me to firmer footing.

"Is there someone here? You were talking to someone," I prodded.

"Myself," he said, setting me onto my feet. "Why have you come?"

I pulled my elbow away and rubbed at it. It was the one that had collided with the brickwork, and it was still tender.

"You have mummy babies," I blurted without preamble.

He stared down at me, his dark brows furrowed. "I have what?"

"Mummy babies. In the house, in Redwall's study. He kept them jammed into a priest's hole behind the fireplace. I found it, entirely by accident," I said quickly. "I was cataloguing the contents of his collection for Lady Allenby, and—" I broke off, realising with a rush of annoyance that I had just told Brisbane something I had not meant to reveal. I hurried on in the hopes he would not notice. "I found them, hidden away in a wooden sarcophagus. They are horrid."

He continued to stare at me, his bright black gaze as inscrutable as Grim's. "Coffin," Brisbane corrected finally.

"I beg your pardon?"

"Coffin. You said it was wood. Sarcophagi are made of stone. They hold coffins, which are made of wood and gilded and painted."

"Brisbane, this is no time to be pedantic. Come and

look at them." I tugged at his sleeve, our earlier quarrel quite forgotten.

To my surprise, he did not demur. He simply glanced around casually, then gestured for me to descend the crag behind him. I scrambled over the rocks with a great deal less grace than I had ascended, but at length I reached the bottom, Hilda's cloak only slightly the worse for wear. Brisbane touched it lightly.

"Taken to wearing Hilda's things, have you?"

I pulled a face. "It is vile. I only wore it because it was the nearest thing at hand."

"It does not suit you. You are too short by half to wear it," he observed.

I snatched the trailing hem out of the mud and shot him an evil look as I stalked away. "Thank you for that. Hurry up, will you?"

He came along mildly, as unconcerned as if we were on a picnic. I think he may have even whistled a tune at one point. I ignored him until we reached the Hall, pausing only to slip Hilda's cloak back onto the peg. I made a note to have Minna brush it for her, then hurried on to the study, Brisbane following.

I noticed he closed the door behind us.

"Hullo, Grim," he said, catching sight of my pet.

"Good morning," Grim returned cordially.

"Brisbane," I said, tapping my foot. He joined me, watching as I slipped the slice of brick from its careful slot, then twisted the small iron ring and opened the panel.

"Very clever," he murmured, studying the mechanism.

"Brisbane, you can admire the craftsmanship later. The mummies," I pleaded.

He heaved a sigh, then stepped around me to study the coffin. After several minutes, he stripped off his coat and tossed it to me. In spite of a day spent upon the muddy moor, his waistcoat was smooth, his sleeves perfectly clean. He unpinned his cuffs and folded them back, baring strong brown forearms. He fitted the lid back into place, then tested it to make certain it would hold long enough to withstand a move. He positioned himself then and after a few aborted attempts managed to get a proper grip upon the coffin, removing it carefully to the storeroom floor.

"It is marvellous," I breathed, watching the lamplight play over the gilded wood.

"Quite," he murmured. He ran his hands over the coffin as carefully as a lover, testing the surfaces, for what I could not imagine. Only after he had gone over every inch of it did he straighten. He slid a hand into his boot and retrieved a knife. I blinked in surprise, but he carried on, sliding the sharp blade between the lid and the body of the coffin. As it had done against my blade, the lid eased open and Brisbane slid his fingers underneath. A few moments' careful manoeuvring and it was open. We both peered into the shadows of the coffin.

"Mummy babies indeed," he murmured, studying the little forms intently.

I shuddered. "But why babies? It's so horrid."

"Some collectors prefer to purchase the remains of children. They are usually less expensive, and the decorations on the coffins can be quite beautiful, although in this case, that was clearly not the motivation. The coffin was designed for a grown woman," he said reasonably.

I pulled back and gave him a reproving look. "Are you not outraged? Those are someone's children! And he *bought them,* like they were trinkets in a bazaar!"

Brisbane shrugged. "Most likely they were. That is where most tourists in Egypt purchase their souvenirs, Julia. He was probably walking through the *souk* one day and thought they would be an interesting memento of his travels."

"I do not care," I said fiercely. "Dead people ought not to be souvenirs."

"No, they would not be my first choice of keepsake," he agreed mildly, "but I only know of one person who has returned from Egypt without some bit of mummy. Everyone wants a mummy, even if it's only a cat."

I thought of an unrolling of a mummy I had attended, given by a duchess to amuse her friends. It had seemed a diversion, an entertainment then. I had had no sense of the person beneath the wrappings. Just a bundle of withered skin and bones, a few bits of dark red hair still plaited into a tidy arrangement.

But this… I leaned over again to peer once more into the coffin. The bundle was neatly wrapped, the linen strips woven into a perfectly-executed pattern of lozenges. It was so beautifully done; I could imagine the painstaking care to make certain each fold was just so. And it was heartbreakingly small. The child could not have been more than a few days old at most. The other was almost precisely the same size, and I wondered if perhaps they were siblings or if

Redwall had merely begun his macabre collection out of whichever stray mummy babies he could find.

"It is horrible," I said finally. "One oughtn't collect people as though they were curiosities."

"I happen to agree with you—" He paused, dropping his arm. He had stepped closer to the desk, but not to look at the mummy. His gaze was fixed on the photograph of Redwall Allenby. He arched a black brow at me in inquiry. There seemed no possible explanation without revealing to him my purpose in being in Sir Redwall's rooms.

Instead, silence stretched between us, taut as a bowstring, until Brisbane bent to retrieve the lid of the coffin. He replaced it, shutting the tiny remains from sight. He returned the coffin to the priest's hole and slid the panel neatly back into place.

"Brisbane, you cannot leave them there!" I made to move toward the priest's hole, but he turned and placed himself squarely between me and the resting place of those sad little bundles.

"I can, and I shall. There is no reason to disturb them at present. Carry on with your cataloguing," he said, his tone oddly cold.

I gave a little sigh of resignation. "I knew you would not like me poking about in here, but the Allenby ladies have so little, and they cannot have these things with them in the cottage. I suggested to Lady Allenby—"

"You suggested? I might have known. And here I thought you were meddling in here at her request," he observed, his tone acid.

I blinked at him. "You knew?"

"Of course I knew. You were careful to replace the dust-sheets, but there were signs things in here had been disturbed. And you will forgive the observation, I am sure, but it did occur to me if there were someone snooping about, the likeliest culprit was by far yourself."

He folded his arms over the breadth of his chest and I thought of the implacable expression of a particularly imperious pharaoh I had just catalogued. In his current mood, Brisbane might as well have been fashioned out of the cool black basalt himself.

I took a step toward him, deliberately gentling my tone. "There is no need to be cross. The Allenby ladies must have some means of keeping themselves. The sale of this legacy might well be the making of them."

"Oh, that it might," he said agreeably, "save that it is not their legacy to sell."

I blinked at him. "I beg your pardon?"

He leaned close so there would be no mistaking his words, each syllable clipped and impersonal. "This house and everything in it with the exception of the personal effects of Lady Allenby and her daughters is mine."

"I do not understand."

"Then let me be quite clear—this house and all of its remaining contents were sold. Lord Salisbury, acting as an agent of Her Majesty, purchased the estate and deeded it to me. I own every stick of furniture, every pillow, every spoon. I even own that revolting tapestry mouldering on the wall in the great hall. *It is mine.*"

I shook my head. "Brisbane, that is not possible. Lady Allenby—"

"Lady Allenby does not know. She never troubled to read the terms of the sale, and her solicitor, a drunk old devil from Leeds, never bothered to tell her. He couldn't even be bothered to travel out here to see her. He conducted the entire matter by correspondence, taking a fat fee for himself. She has nothing except the clothes upon her back."

I stared at him for a long moment, scarcely able to comprehend what he had told me. "That poor woman," I murmured finally. "To lose her home must be a complete devastation, but this as well. She has nothing, and neither have her daughters. How could you not tell them?"

He shrugged one muscular shoulder, his expression indifferent. "They will discover it soon enough. When the cottage I am preparing is ready, they may take a few furnishings to suit and their own effects. Under the law, I will have been far more generous with them than I am required."

"And what of your conscience?" I demanded. "Is there no moral law greater than those passed by Parliament? Brisbane, you cannot let them go on thinking they have been fairly treated. And you cannot let them believe this collection will be sold to their benefit. I must stop cataloguing," I finished, more to myself.

"Oh, no. Do go on. I won't want these things around, so you might as well catalogue them for me. I daresay the proceeds will more than recompense me for the repairs I have put into the cottage."

I took a step still closer, searching his face, but to no purpose. I did not know him. "You are a stranger to me," I said softly. "I never imagined you could treat a defenceless lady with such callousness. This is not you."

"Perhaps you do not know me," he returned.

"Oh, it would please you to think so. You do enjoy the masquerade, don't you? The mysterious, the enigmatic Nicholas Brisbane, living in shadows and secrecy. But I do know you. I know you as well as I know my own name. You are not a man who would torment any woman, no matter her offence. You are not cruel or malicious or vengeful, and yet you pretend to these things because you have some secret purpose you do not care to share with me."

Brisbane curled a lip at me, his smile scornful. He jerked his head at the photograph on the desk. "Blame him. He is the one who left them with nothing. The sale was arranged before his death."

I shook my head, trying to make sense of a senseless situation. "No, the sale was concluded after his death, when the ladies had no choice, when they had sold all of the important furnishings."

"The sale was arranged before Redwall's death," Brisbane repeated. "He did not have time to complete it, but the papers were presented for Lady Allenby's signature, and she did not trouble to read them properly. He was the one who put them into this situation. And anything I do for them, *anything*," he said, his voice low and brutal, "is more than he would have."

He straightened and cast another glance at the photograph. "Not such a handsome face now, is it?"

He brushed past me, collecting his coat as he went. I sank down onto the chair, desperately trying to understand. I had never known Brisbane to be so cold, so distant, but neither could I comprehend a man who would leave his closest relations penniless. I picked up the photograph and searched the face, looking for something, anything that would offer some insight. There was nothing. Just the same beautiful features, the same winsome smile, the same exotic background. I did not replace it on the desk. Instead I tucked it carefully into one of the drawers. If nothing else, I did not want Brisbane to dispose of it in a fit of pique. For a stranger, there seemed to be an inordinate amount of antipathy on Brisbane's part to the previous owner of his house.

And then, I realised what I ought to have known since the first conversation I had had with Ailith Allenby. Redwall was no stranger to Brisbane. They had been children together on this very moor, and whatever had passed between them, it angered Brisbane still.

THE THIRTEENTH CHAPTER

How many fond fools serve mad jealousy!
—William Shakespeare
The Comedy of Errors

After a quiet luncheon taken by myself in the kitchen—Lady Allenby felt unwell, Hilda had disappeared onto the moor, and Ailith had sent word to Mrs. Butters not to expect her—I wanted nothing more than to get right out of the house. I buttoned myself into a snug coat of heathered green tweed and tucked a scarf of soft bottle-green wool into my collar. The day was not quite so cold and the wind had died to a dull murmur, like gossiping voices whispering over the moor. I left by the front door this time, skirting the reed-fringed pond. The front wall sheltered the pond from the wind, its green surface barely rippling. I heard a frog croak and then a little splash as I walked past. The reeds shivered where something had disturbed them, and I hastened my steps a little, making my way around the ruined wing and onto a narrow path that led to a little copse of ash trees.

Just as I reached the edge of the copse, a shadow fell across the path and I started, my hand at my throat.

"'Tis only me, my lady. Thou art skittish as a new colt," Godwin said, smiling as he came near, an axe swinging from his hand.

"Oh, no. You just startled me. I did not realise anyone was about. I have never taken this path before."

"You'll not get lost," he promised. He pointed over his shoulder. "Tha' way lies the gardener's cottage where I sleep. Just beyond is the graveyard and the chapel ruins, and from there the path to the Bear's Hut, but mind you don't go tha' far. Mr. Brisbane's given orders it's not to be disturbed while the repairs are being done."

"The Bear's Hut? Were there really bears kept there?"

"Aye, though tha's quite before my time. 'Tis a cottage now, and has been for many a year. The roof is rotten through, and 'tis a dangerous place. When it is fitted up good and tight against the weather, 'twill be a fine home for the Allenby ladies. 'Tis quiet there and far from the bleating of the sheep."

"Rather inconvenient lodgings for you at the gardener's cottage," I remarked, keeping my tone deliberately light. "So far from the moor and the flock."

"Tha' it is, particularly when the ewes are throwing lambs and the weather is grim, and it's twice as broken-down as the Bear's Hut. The wind fair roars through some nights, and I can hear my own name in it." He paused a long moment, then hefted the axe in his hand. "I must be getting on," he said, edging around me on the narrow path. "If there is aught you need, make use of the cottage. Whatever I have is yours," he added with a gallant little bow. There was a twinkle in his eye, and I waved in response, turning my back and setting off down the path without looking back. His manner was one that puzzled me exceedingly. He was friendly to the point of flirtation, but for what reason I could not fathom.

I was still turning over the question of Godwin's familiarity when I rounded a bend in the copse and came upon the gardener's cottage. The little stone house, which must once have been quite snug and handsome, was in a state of pitiful decay. Half of it had come down, although the other half, considerably newer by the look of it, seemed sturdy enough. Judging from its size, it would just admit a single room, enough for a bachelor's needs, but whatever would they do if Godwin decided to marry?

But that was Brisbane's problem, I realised with a little stab of annoyance. However high-handed he was about the Allenby ladies, Godwin was his responsibility as well, and I wondered if he meant to make any better accommodation for his farm manager. I moved on, thoroughly irritated now and beginning to get a little chilled. I had been optimistic in thinking it was growing warmer, or perhaps it was the trees that made a difference. The ashes had given way to larger trees, oaks and elders and a few conifers, planted thickly and blocking out much of the sunlight. It was much darker now, and I had the sensation of venturing into a faery-tale forest, one out of myth and perhaps populated with dangerous creatures. It seemed difficult to breathe in that little wood, as if the trees themselves had robbed the place of air.

"Rubbish," I said stoutly, tugging my coat more tightly about me and straightening my shoulders. "They are just *trees*." I walked on for some distance, the path winding ahead of me, always turning one direction and then back on itself so I could never see far ahead. Suddenly, the path opened abruptly and I was in a large clearing on the edge of a hill, the ground sloping down and away toward a river. I took a deep breath and the feeling of constriction in my chest eased. It was peaceful, partially because of the gentle rushing of the river, for once drowning out the constant murmur of the moor wind, but also because of the little graveyard nestled against the stone wall of a chapel. The building itself was in ruins, only the barest structure remained, and a bit of tracery in a window where stained glass must once have been fitted. It was perfectly situated to capture the dying light of an afternoon, and I wondered what story had been memorialised there.

"It was King Alfred burning the cakes," came a low voice from behind a gravestone. I turned to see Ailith rising, holding her cloak tightly about her. She nodded toward the broken stone frame in the chapel wall. "Not appropriate for a chapel, really, but the Allenbys never wanted anyone to forget whence we came," she remarked, picking her way over the stones to where I stood.

"A lovely spot," I remarked, nodding toward the sloping hill and the pretty sweep of the river as it tumbled over the rocks.

"One of the prettiest in Yorkshire," she agreed. "It is no surprise our family chose to bury its dead here rather than build a house for the living." The words were laced with wistfulness and I wondered if she knew precisely how much the Allenbys had lost.

She stepped forward, lifting a graceful hand to gesture toward the ruined chapel. "There was an arched roof there, and even a few tiny flying buttresses to support it. It was meant to be a cathedral in miniature. It was quite a work of art in its day. I am told architects used to come from all over Europe to study it."

We began to walk, choosing our steps carefully amidst the broken stones. "What happened to it?"

She led me around to where the interior of the chapel must once have stood, and I gasped. The stones here were scorched deeply.

Ailith shook her head sadly. "That is what your neighbours will do when a family insists upon sheltering priests."

I put out a tentative hand to touch the blackened stones. "The villagers did this?"

"In the time of Elizabeth. Our family had known some prominence during the reign of the first Mary, but with her death, our hopes for a Catholic restoration were dashed." She nodded toward the chapel stones. "The queen sent agents north, ferreting out all of the recusants they could find. They tore houses apart looking for them. Sometimes local people helped in order to curry favour. Here, the villagers decided to take matters into their own hands. After they found the priest's hole in the house and dragged our poor priest screaming from its sanctuary, they turned him over to the queen's men. He was burned alive."

I started at her mention of the priest's hole, but she went

on, her face expressionless as her voice. She was reciting a story she had been told, but its horrors did not touch her.

"After they had burned the priest and all the Roman articles of worship, they burned the chapel. They dared not lay hands on the family, but they destroyed everything we held most dear. The statues of saints, the Alfred chapel, the tapestries depicting the life of the Virgin Mother. All were destroyed."

"That is dreadful," I told her, trying and failing to imagine the peaceful people of Blessingstoke ever turning upon Father or laying a hand against his estate at Bellmont Abbey. But then, Father had always looked to their benefit, and I wondered not for the first time at the antipathy that seemed to exist between the Allenbys and the villagers who ought to have owed them a livelihood.

Ailith turned then and left the shelter of the ruined chapel. "Come, Lady Julia. I should like to show you something," she called over her shoulder. I obeyed, coming to stand beside her where she had paused in front of a gravestone. Unlike the other Allenby monuments, some grand, all beautiful, with weeping angels or statues of saints, this was a plain slab, the chiselled words sharp and black against the dark grey stone.

Sir Redwall Allenby 1848-1887
Let not be shut in my soul
Let not be fettered my shadow
Let be opened the way for my soul and for my shadow
May it see the great god.

A gay little bundle of daffodils rested on the stone, and I knew Ailith had laid them there. She nodded toward the inscription. "It is an Egyptian funerary text. Redwall used to read me poetry sometimes, and funny little fables. But once he read to me a darker book, one that spoke of death and the passage of the afterlife. I remembered it, and told them to carve it into his gravestone. He was ill when he came home from Egypt, you know. I think his travels destroyed him. I think he knew he would not leave this place."

Her cool composure had not deserted her—her voice did not tremble, nor did her calm gaze waver—but I saw her hands tighten until the knuckles went quite white. I had never pitied her more. She had lost her beloved brother, and as nearly as I could surmise, had no idea that he had arranged to leave her penniless. It seemed likely she had never seen the macabre little relics hidden in the priest's hole either. They had been close then, as I was to my own brothers, but he had only permitted her to know that much of his business as it suited him to reveal. I longed to ask her about the financial arrangements at Grimsgrave, or about the gruesome little mummies, but when I turned to her, I saw the beginnings of a tear shimmer on her lashes. I could not do it.

I pressed her arm instead and offered her a kindly smile. "It is a lovely quote, and a fitting one for a gentleman who was so devoted to his studies."

Ailith nodded and blinked furiously. Ever mindful of her dignity, she would not weep, not in front of me, and I tactfully bent over and pretended to fuss with my bootlace to give her time to compose herself.

I wandered to the next stones, a series of small markers, identical down to the tiny cherub carved in each.

"Those were Mama's," Ailith said, coming up behind me.

"She calls them her 'disappointments.' Most of them were born after Redwall and I, one came after Hilda."

"How tragic," I breathed. "There must be five, no, six of them."

Ailith nodded. "Yes, all of them dead at birth. Mama said they were taken justly, as a punishment for her sins, hers and Father's."

There seemed no possible response to that. I knew the notion was a popular one, but I had little use for any divinity that would punish innocents for the crimes of their parents. I bent and put a fingertip to the last in the row, the smallest cherub in the graveyard, barely larger than my palm. It was beautifully carved, and I wondered if it had given any comfort to Lady Allenby, or if she denied herself the solace of visiting her children's graves.

After a moment I straightened and we left the little grave-yard together. The wood seemed friendlier now that I had a companion, and as we walked, Ailith pointed out the things I had missed—a clump of violets blossoming in a bit of moss, a pretty bird with red wings I had never seen before. I did not take note of its name, but she seemed very knowl-edgeable about the creatures of the small wood, and I com-plimented her on her understanding of the wild things.

"It is my kingdom," she said, her voice lightly mocking. "The wood, the graveyard, the moor. There is not an inch of it I do not know, not a foot of it I do not command."

We had passed Godwin's cottage and were just emerging from the wood onto the moor path back to the Hall.

"Do you not wish to travel? Have you never been to London?"

"What could I possibly desire there?" she demanded. "A dirty city full of strangers?" She drew a great deep breath of moorland air. "Everything I require is here."

I thought of her sister, running away from Grimsgrave with the travelling artist, her brother venturing to faraway lands, even Hilda, retreating into her books, and it seemed sad to me that Ailith had been nowhere, had seen nothing.

But just then the path turned and I could see Grimsgrave, and for an instant I saw it, not as it was—an age-blackened house falling to ruin—but as it had been, a gracious and elegant manor house, lording its austere beauty over an even more austere and beautiful moor. And I thought of the unbroken line of the Allenby family, stretching back in time, tethered by the blood of kings, and I marvelled that they had held their little domain for so long. Viewed in that light, it seemed tragic that it had slipped from their grasp.

I paused on the path and Ailith turned, her expression quizzical. "It is a fine view," I told her, nodding toward the house.

"Very little to admire now," she commented without rancour. She might have been a property agent assessing an investment. "But it was once magnificent. There was a painting over the fireplace in the dining room, commissioned just after the east wing was added, and it was a very good likeness, my grandmother used to say. She knew the house before the wing crumbled. Hers was the last generation to know the house whole."

Ailith began to describe it for me as her grandmother must have done for her: ladies trailing silken hems over the wide lawns, swans gliding gracefully over the glassy pond, gentlemen in velvet breeches waving plumed hats as they spurred blooded horses home from the moor.

"They did not mix with the neighbours, you understand," Ailith told me carefully, "but they hosted parties for their cousins and more distant relations. That is how the masters of Grimsgrave chose their brides and kept the bloodline of Allenby unblemished. Not a single bride was ever taken who did not bear some strain of Allenby blood."

I raised a brow, but did not comment. Father had often said that the wild eccentricity of the Marches was due to too many generations of close breeding. He had insisted upon tracing my mother's ancestry for twenty generations to prove they shared no kin. "Fresh blood," he always said, "is the key to good breeding, in horses or in children. Someone ought to tell the queen that," he would invariably add. He did not approve of the heavy concentration of German blood in the royal family, and I doubted he would approve the Allenbys either.

"So many weddings celebrated here," Ailith went on. "So many births, burials. So many centuries, and still it stands."

"It is a noble tribute to the Allenby family," I told her.

"Noble once, and it will be again," she said, darting a meaningful glance at me.

I chose my words carefully. "I believe Mr. Brisbane can make a very worthy contribution to its heritage. He would never destroy the integrity of such a place. He would only restore it to its former grandeur."

Brisbane had not said precisely that, but I refused to believe he would do something as ludicrous as pull the entire house down and put up a modern monstrosity of red brick with crenulated towers. It might be the fashion, but Brisbane only chose those fashions which suited his aesthetic, and I could not believe modern architecture was one of them.

"Of course he would put it to rights," Ailith said, tipping her head winsomely. "Hilda shall never permit him to do less."

I struggled to understand her meaning, but she did not wait for a response. "She will take over all of the restorations herself when the time is ripe. He will want her to, and it would be her duty as the mistress of Grimsgrave."

I did not speak. There were no possible words. She started up the path and I walked next to her, meek as any lamb to the slaughter.

"Of course, he has not asked her, but that is merely a formality these days. A woman knows when a man has intentions, don't you think?"

The beautiful cornflower-blue eyes that looked into mine were entirely guileless. She was merely repeating what her sister had told her, and I realised, as I ought to have realised before, the true cause of Hilda's antipathy. She might prefer my brother's company, but she was determined to save her home for her family. The little snippet had set her cap at Brisbane and meant to drive me away.

"And has Brisbane given any indication of his intentions?" I asked, certain of the reply.

"Oh, no, but then he would do the thing properly, would he not? He would wait until he has secured Mama's blessing, and I think she would demand rather a lot. Of course, he ought to ask me as the eldest, but I should never accept him."

I resisted the urge to smile. "Would you not?"

Ailith laughed and linked an arm through mine in a rare

gesture of friendship. "Of course not. That was finished many years past." She paused, then laughed again at my obvious bemusement. "Has he not told you? We were not just playmates together. I was the first girl he ever loved."

THE FOURTEENTH CHAPTER

With a green and yellow melancholy
She sat like patience on a monument
Smiling at grief.
—William Shakespeare
Twelfth Night

The next day I carried the midday meal up to Lady Allenby. She was abed with another attack of her rheumatism, and as Mrs. Butters and Minna were busily occupied extinguishing the pudding Minna had managed to set alight, I offered to take the tray myself. Neither Ailith nor her sister were to be found, and I was glad of it. After Ailith's pronouncement of the day before, I was not certain I could manage civility. Ailith had not struck me as an unkind woman, but I could not make her out, and the more I thought about our conversation, the more confused I became. Surely she knew of my attachment to Brisbane. My very presence in the house was of such monstrous impropriety it must have shouted news of my affections from the rooftops. Ailith could not have repeated her sister's intentions innocently.

But perhaps it had been meant kindly. We had become friends after a fashion, and it was entirely possible that Ailith knew something I did not about her sister's scheme. Hilda had shown herself to be impetuous and coarse. What treachery was within her sights? If Ailith suspected some mischief, she might well warn me simply out of her own natural kindness, and perhaps out of some lingering affection for Brisbane, her childhood playmate. Of their youthful dalliance, I could not even begin to think. My mind positively reeled at the thought, and I decided to turn my efforts to the situation at hand.

It had occurred to me that with a little deft questioning, I might learn something from Lady Allenby, and a nice little chat over her marrowbones might be just the thing.

Mrs. Butters thanked me profusely as I took up the heavy tray. "Oh, that is a kindness, my lady! It saves my hips, it does. Stairs are unkind to an old woman. I think you must be a Sumerian!"

I thought for a moment before I realised she had meant Samaritan. I smiled at her and sniffed appreciatively at the tray. There was a plate of marrowbones, a sauce boat full of thick gravy, and a rack of toast, along with a few other little dishes of tempting morsels—pickles and radishes and some of her favourite bottled mushrooms. Lady Allenby exclaimed with delight when I appeared in her room, pushing herself up onto her pillows.

"My dear, how kind of you," she began. I hastened to put

the tray down and slid a careful arm behind her to help her settle more comfortably. She was dressed in a worn velvet bedcoat, its silken ribbons shredded a bit, but still a beautiful blue that flattered her eyes. Her hair had not been dressed, but she had donned a simple lace cap, the old-fashioned lappets framing her face. Altogether she looked like a queen of old, receiving statesmen in her bed of state as courtiers looked on.

I settled the tray and poured out the tiny glass of quince wine that Rosalie had recommended. Lady Allenby looked a little scandalised, but pleased. "A bit is just the thing for rheumatism," she agreed. She nodded toward the window. "Would you draw back the curtains, my dear? I see a bit of sunlight peeking round the edges."

I obeyed, careful not to tear the fragile draperies from their rings. Sunlight spilled over the windowsill and into the room, motes dancing in the warm, buttery light. I glanced down and realised her bedchamber overlooked the kitchen garden. I could see the few little beds still struggling to produce, and the ruins of the beehives tucked into the crumbling stone wall. I commented upon them to Lady Allenby.

"They must have been charming in the day," I finished. "I have never seen any quite like that, with such detail."

She smiled wanly. "And the bees appreciated it, I am certain they did. They gave tremendous amounts of the sweetest honey. I tended the hives myself until last year." Her smile faded and her expression took on a faraway look. "They were quite my little companions, so brave. They gave their lives to assuage my pain," she said, rubbing at her swollen joints.

"I beg your pardon?" Surely I had not heard her correctly.

"The sting of a bee is a sure remedy for rheumatism. When my hands were at their worst, I used to thrust them into the hives. The bees stung me and after the first shock of the pain, there was relief, blessed relief. But I never forgot it cost them their lives to do it. I always felt so terribly guilty afterward. And then last summer after Redwall died, it seemed the proper time to let them go. One windy day, I opened the hives and destroyed the queen's chamber. The hive fled, and my bees have never come back. That is why the garden failed, you know. No bees to work it, and they will never return here."

The sunlight had fallen on her face, cruelly, for it revealed the furrows and wrinkles of her ruined beauty. I wondered if Ailith ever looked at her and mourned what she would become. Or if Redwall had ever looked upon a mummy queen and thought of his mother, I thought with a shiver.

"You ought to eat before the toast goes quite cold," I told her.

She did not hear me, or at least she gave no sign of it. "I did the right thing by sending them away. My hands are quite ruined, but pain purifies, that is what God teaches us," she said with a nod behind me. I turned to see a *prie-dieu,* ebony with a cushion of the finest needlework I had ever seen. A prayer book lay open upon it, and overseeing all was a representation of Christ upon the cross, dripping with the gore of Crucifixion.

I said nothing, and Lady Allenby nodded. "You are not of the Roman faith, my dear. You would not understand. To suffer is to understand Him, and His suffering for our sins and the sins of the world."

I felt faintly embarrassed, as I always do when earnest people discuss religion. My brothers and sisters and I had been raised Anglican, of course, and all of the momentous events of our lives had been celebrated within the ceremonies of the Church. But we seldom attended of a Sunday, and discussions of spirituality were few and far between. We were far likelier to argue over the whereabouts of Shakespeare's lost play or the plight of prostitutes in Whitechapel, both pet subjects of Father's and Aunt Hermia's. God was rather far down on the list of our personal interests.

"You are young yet," Lady Allenby assured me. "Many do not turn to God until life has revealed all of its bitterness and the promise of the hereafter is the only solace left. There is a natural order, you know. Ordained by God. It ought not to be disturbed by man."

I thought of her children, the runaway eldest daughter, the opportunistic dead son, the peculiar daughters left to her, and I agreed that she knew far better than I of the suffering of the world.

She struggled a bit with her utensils, and I offered to spread the marrow onto her toast. Lady Allenby assented graciously, with a regal nod of the head as though she were granting a royal favour. I handed her each slice as it was spread, pausing a little so the toast should not become sodden if I prepared it too soon.

"Quite delicious, will you not join me?" she offered. I declined. "The very thing for joints." She sampled the other dishes as well, exclaiming over the crispness of the radishes and the excellence of the mushrooms. "So few pleasures left at my age," she said at last, patting her lips with a napkin. "It seems almost sinful to enjoy one's food so completely."

"I think a greater sin would be to fail to enjoy it if you are privileged enough to have it," I said, wondering if I had overstepped myself.

To my astonishment, she laughed, a rusty, wheezing sound, as if she had not laughed properly in a long time. It ended badly, with a little fit of choking, and it was several minutes before she was settled again on her pillows.

"I am sorry. I ought not to have said it." I busied myself with tidying the tray to hide my embarrassment.

"Dear Lady Julia, you are such a charming girl. Little wonder Mr. Brisbane is so taken with you," she said, fixing me with those knowing blue eyes.

I folded the napkin carefully. "Do you think so? Ailith seems to be under a different impression."

Lady Allenby sighed. "Did she tell you Hilda means to marry him?"

"Words to that effect," I admitted.

Lady Allenby motioned for me to sit on the edge of the bed. I did so, gingerly, so as not to disturb her. She twisted the edge of the coverlet in her gnarled hands.

"You must not mind my daughters, Lady Julia. It has been difficult for them, living here, so far removed from appropriate society."

I tipped my head. "Ailith at least seems to relish it. I believe she even referred to herself as queen of this domain," I said lightly.

The strong silvery-white brows knitted together. "Oh, my poor girl. You see, she was devoted to her elder sister and her brother. The loss of both was difficult, *is* difficult, to bear." She hesitated, then went on, each word clearly painful for her. "My older children were born very close together. Only two years separated my eldest and my youngest. Redwall and Ailith were even born the same calendar year, one in January, the other in December. They always said it made a bond between them, like twins. Their sister, Wilfreda, was a little apart. She was bookish and solemn, a contemplative, competent child, rather like Hilda, but with a ready laugh. Redwall and Ailith were wild as moor wind. I never knew where they were or what they were about. Wilfreda was always at the graveyard or up on Thorn Crag, book in hand, preferring her own company save for the times she bullied Godwin into taking her riding. Wilfreda always knew her own mind, and once she had determined to do something, it was as good as done. I did not realise until it was far too late that she had decided to leave us."

Lady Allenby talked on, spinning out her tale.

"When the children were nearly grown, Wilfreda was eighteen, Redwall seventeen and Ailith very nearly, I engaged an artist to paint them. Not Hilda of course. She was but a child. It was tradition for the Allenbys to be painted upon maturity. There used to be an entire gallery of excellent paintings in the east wing," she said ruefully. "Until necessity compelled us to sell them, and the wing itself fell into decay. But the children, I wanted them painted, and the artist I engaged was one of fine reputation. He began with Ailith and Redwall, they insisted upon being painted together. The artist objected, but Redwall had his way. He told me he did not trust the artist, he thought the man a blackguard and felt he was not to be left alone with young ladies. He was quite right to be concerned. Ailith was painted with Redwall, but Wilfreda would have none of it. She and Redwall quarrelled terribly over it, but she had her way in the end. And she left this house with him, one moonbright night. I have not seen her since," she finished, her voice faltering just a little.

I put a gentle hand to hers. "I am so very sorry."

Her smile was mournful. "I was so angry when she left, I burned the painting of Redwall and Ailith. I ought not to have done it. It was an excellent likeness of them both. There was nothing of Wilfreda's painting to burn. Only a blank canvas he had never touched with paint. He must have talked to her during her sittings, plotting with her to carry her off. I made inquiries of course, but there was nothing to be done. The trail had gone quite cold, and I did not like to make a scandal. Perhaps it would have been different if my husband had still been alive. It was so difficult after his death, everything. The house, the children. So much to look after, and I had never been taught to."

She trailed off then, and I saw her eyelids, heavy now as she wandered in the past. I slipped off the bed and drew the curtains over the window, dimming the room. She gave a little sigh and settled deeper into her pillows. I took up the tray and tiptoed to the door, glancing behind me to see the mournful eyes of Jesus looking down at me from the bloodied cross. It was a gruesome thing, and I did not know how she could bear to sleep with it in her room.

Once I left Lady Allenby, I returned her dinner things to the kitchen feeling quite irritable, nervy and cross, and I was not fit company for anyone. Ironically, it was company I longed for. I had begun to miss Portia terribly, and Brisbane's insistent avoidance of me was verging on insult. He could not have been more pointed in his evasion if I had had boils and a leper's bell.

And to complicate matters even further, I was not at all inclined to carry on with the work in the study until I had spoken to Brisbane. I could not entirely believe his assertion that he meant to keep the proceeds of the sale of Sir Redwall's collection, but experience had taught me Brisbane was nothing if not unpredictable.

A dozen other questions circled in my brain, about Hilda's intentions toward Brisbane, the mysterious disappearance of Wilfreda, until my head ached and I could not stand to be inside a moment longer. The sky had been lowering all day, but I resolved to take my chances. I was in the hall buttoning my coat when Minna ran me to ground, smelling of smoke and burnt currants, a plump Florence resting languidly in her arms.

"There you are, my lady," Minna said, thrusting the little dog at me. "I do wish you would have a look at Florence."

I stopped buttoning and peered at my little pet. I stroked her head and she gave a soft moan. "She's got terribly fat, Minna. What have you been feeding her? I imagine it's just a bit of indigestion."

She shook her head, her eyes wide with alarm. "I do not think so, my lady. I think she is—" She dropped her eyes modestly. "I think she is in pup."

I looked closely at Florence, and I fancied her large, woeful eyes were slightly embarrassed. "But by whom? She does not go out, she does not mix with neighbourhood dogs."

Minna primmed her lips. "That rascal, Mr. Pugglesworth."

"You cannot be serious. Puggy is half-decayed. I do not see how he could manage it."

"Manage it he did, my lady! Morag said she caught them at it two months back."

"Did she? And she did not see fit to warn me at least?"

"She had to swat him with a slipper to get him off of poor Florence. She thought she had parted them in time, but I think she did not," Minna added.

I considered Florence with her fine-boned, shivery elegance and Puggy in all his decrepitude. "How perfectly revolting. It seems rather incestuous, although I don't suppose such things matter to dogs." I cupped my hand under Florence's chin. "My poor darling. What frightfully ugly pups you're going to have."

She licked at my hand and I scratched behind her ears. "Feed her up, then. She must keep up her strength if she's going to whelp. Prepare a quiet place, warm and safe, perhaps the bottom of a cupboard if you can find one suitable," I told Minna. "And line it with some towelling or an old blanket."

She bobbed a tidy curtsey and left me, cuddling Florence and crooning a little lullaby. I made a mental note to write the happy news to Portia. She would be greatly diverted to know of Mr. Pugglesworth's prowess.

As soon as I left the house, my feet turned toward the poultry yard, almost before I realised I intended to go there. Hilda was there, wrapped in a shawl and tossing kitchen scraps from a pail as she clucked her tongue at a plump chicken, muttering under her breath.

"Leave off, you great fat brute. You've not even given a single egg in a fortnight. I ought to put you in the cookpot."

"You have the countrywoman's gift for poultry, Miss Hilda," I called. "I do not think I have ever seen such plump birds."

She looked up, scowling, and threw the rest of the scraps out in a single motion. She stood for a moment, uncertainty rising in her face, then she made a sound of resignation and crossed to where I stood.

"I suppose you want an apology for what I said." Her eyes were wary, and I made no move toward her.

"Not unless you mean it. I've always hated telling someone I was sorry because I ought to."

She said nothing for a long moment, her eyes fixed over my shoulder as she turned the matter over in her mind. I nodded toward her little flock.

"I meant what I said. They are very fine birds. You ought to be proud of them."

I turned to leave her, but she snorted, a derisive sound, but not one that was intentionally insulting, I fancied.

"Any fool can raise a chicken," she retorted.

"I assure you that is not so. My brother Benedick once attempted to keep a flock to raise egg money. He managed to forget to shut the henhouse the same day Father acquired a new mastiff. Poor chickens."

Her lips twitched, but she did not smile. "You have brothers then? Besides Valerius?"

"I am the youngest daughter of ten children. I've five brothers altogether. Believe me when I say you have met the best of them."

She fell silent again and it occurred to me that she was

simply unused to conversation. Lady Allenby had mentioned that Hilda was seldom to be found and rarely engaged with the rest of the household. It was entirely possible she had never had a proper friend.

"Valerius is by far the most easygoing of my brothers," I continued. "I wonder, is he anything like your brother, Redwall, was?"

She shook her head slowly. "You must have heard tales of Redwall by now. You must know what he did to the villagers. He was thoroughly spoilt and undeserving." Her complexion was mottled again, a sure sign she was becoming distressed.

I cast about for a safe subject, then decided recklessness might serve as well. "I understand from Ailith that you mean to marry Mr. Brisbane."

Her mouth gaped, then she closed it with an audible snap. "I suppose you think I am a fool. You've come to taunt me."

"I assure you, Miss Hilda, I am in no position to taunt anyone. But Brisbane hardly seems like a good match for a young lady of solitary temperament. I merely wondered if you had thought the matter through."

She jerked her head angrily. "Of course I have. I don't really *want* to marry him. You must know that."

"Naturally. You do not even look at him, so you cannot wish to marry for love of the man."

In spite of herself, she laughed, a wheezing, unfamiliar sound. "No, I most assuredly do not love him. But I want my home. And I am so deadly tired of not having money."

She kicked at her pail, rather like a tired child, and I realised that was precisely what she was.

I seated myself quietly on the step, and after a moment

she began to speak, not to me, but in a low, faraway voice, as if she had forgot I was there.

"Poverty is so wearing. I remember what it was like to have nice things. When I was a child I had the prettiest dresses. And picture books. And a pony of my own."

"There is always a pony," I murmured, but she did not seem to hear.

"But then Papa died, and Mama was never good at figures. Nothing seemed to pay as it ought to. And Redwall left, just when he ought to have been making it better. He left and travelled the world, letting the capital run through his fingers like water and here we sat, watching it all fall apart, sinking a little further each year. We turned our clothes and when that would no longer serve, we went to the attics and wore things that were half a century out of date. Who was to care? No one ever comes here. No one visits, no one even knows we exist. And then Redwall came back and for one brief, dizzying moment, I thought it would be better. I thought he would put everything to rights."

She fell silent again, lost in her memories. I ventured to ask, "And he did not?"

Her mouth twisted in bitterness. "No. He was sick, you could see it in his eyes when he arrived home. Malaria. And the treatment for it only made him worse. He lasted less than two years. He had every chance in the world, every advantage, and he squandered them all."

I thought about the entries in his notebooks, the mentions of doses of something that began with a *q*. Quinine, no doubt, to ease the symptoms of his malaria.

Hilda's gaze sharpened suddenly. "I know about the collection," she said, her voice flat. "I know it was lost with the house. Mama and Ailith think that Redwall kept it back to save us, but I know the truth."

"I am sorry for that." I paused, wishing I could give her some reassurances that Brisbane would take care of her little family, but I had none to give. Though I believed Brisbane was a man of honour, I could not speak for him. "How did you discover the truth?"

"I went through Brisbane's papers," she told me roundly.

I stared at her. "Miss Hilda, I am appalled."

"You may not judge me," she returned, her face white to the lips. "You have not lived as I have."

"You misunderstand me. I am appalled I did not think of it myself," I told her truthfully. I had spent a fair bit of time alone in his rooms, and I had not troubled to read his papers. "Although Brisbane always seems to know when I am up to mischief. I daresay he would have known what I was about."

Her colour returned, and she seemed mollified at my approval. "It is so unfair," she said fiercely, "that we should be ruled by men. They control our very happiness, and yet they do not see fit to tell us anything. We have no more consequence than these chickens," she finished, nodding toward her little flock, contentedly scratching the ground in front of their tumbledown little henhouse.

We were silent a moment, and it was the pleasantest moment we had yet passed. There was a sympathy between us, and I ventured an expression of sentiment.

"I am sorry for your loss, Miss Hilda. It is difficult when those we love disappoint us so acutely."

She gave a short laugh. "Love? I hated Redwall. He had

the life I ought to have had, the life I *would* have had if I had been a son."

"And you think you can still have that life, that independence, if you marry Brisbane?" I asked her gently. "It will never work, you know. He will not marry for money and he cannot marry for love because he loves me."

Her eyes narrowed and I shook my head, intuiting her thoughts. "I know what you are thinking and believe me, it will not work. He cannot be tricked into marriage by compromising his honour."

"Why?" she demanded. "Hasn't he any?"

"Oh, yes, and he guards it rather ferociously, but his notions of honour are quite different from ours. If you were to climb into his bed and arrange for, say, Godwin or Mrs. Butters, to find you, he would simply shove you onto the floor and go back to sleep. He has very little tolerance for deceit."

Her hands tightened, creasing the unbecoming tweed of her skirts. "If I do not marry him, I will have no life at all."

I rose, brushing the dust from my skirts. "I am sorry you believe that, Miss Hilda. I can think of no worse reason to marry than that, and I speak from experience."

Uncertainty clouded her eyes once more. "But you want to marry him. You must—why else would you have come?"

"Oh, yes. I mean to marry him. But not because I want him to give me a life. I want to marry him to share the life I already have. The difference, I think you will find, is a significant one."

THE FIFTEENTH CHAPTER

A devil, a born devil, on whose nature
Nurture can never stick.
—William Shakespeare
The Tempest

I set off for Rosalie's cottage then, my ears constantly
straining for any sound from the Grimswater bell. I
ought not to have bothered. I might well have
imagined that I had heard anything at all. But I was aware now
of a sort of watchfulness, a stretched-on-tiptoe feeling of the
moor itself, as though it waited for something or someone.

I told myself it was just a fancy and hurried on, reaching
the cottage in good time. I had just set my hand to the latch
of the front gate when the door of the cottage opened, and
I heard Brisbane's voice.

I cannot answer for what I did next. Brisbane must have
known I had made Rosalie's acquaintance; I had every right
to call upon her. But instead of declaring myself, I ducked

behind the little stone wall and crept along until I rounded the corner, keeping myself tucked out of sight below the line of the shrubbery. I was careful to keep opposite the direction Brisbane would have to turn to set off for Grimsgrave, and I could only pray he would turn his steps in that direction. I did not think he would much care to find me playing the spy, nor would I care for the consequences. So I crouched in the shrubbery, concealed by the stone wall, and watched.

Brisbane emerged, his hair tumbled as usual, his black greatcoat flung over his shoulders. Rosalie stepped out with him and stretched out her hand.

"Do not forget what you came for, *chavvo*," she said, proffering a bottle. It was filled with a thick red syrup and tightly-stoppered by the look of it, doubtless one of her remedies, but I was more intrigued by their conversation. Try as I might, I could not remember what the word *chavvo* meant. Magda, my Gypsy laundress, had been rigid upon the point of never teaching me a word of her language. I would have given my right arm to know it now, I thought bitterly.

Brisbane turned back to take the bottle from her, slipping it into his pocket. At that moment, Rook bounded from the cottage, thrusting his great head under Brisbane's hand. Brisbane smiled and rubbed the dog's ears, murmuring something I could not hear. He straightened after a moment, then turned to Rosalie.

"*Parika tut,*" he told her. She nodded, and he paused, turning to look over the moor toward the crossroads and the path back to Grimsgrave. "You ought not to live here alone. Are you not frightened of the *mullo*?"

She gave him a little shove and laughed. "*Kakka, chavvo.* I have no reason to fear the *mullo,* do I?"

"I suppose you don't at that," he replied. He turned on his heel and left her then. Rook followed him as far as the gate, whining a little when he was left behind. Rosalie stood watching Brisbane until he had taken the turning at the crossroads and began to descend down the moor, his black coat billowing in the wind.

"Aren't you cold out there, *chavvi?*" she asked, turning to the shrubbery where I was hiding.

"Not a bit," I told her, rising and brushing the leaves from my hair. "I dropped my ring. I was looking for it."

She laughed, clicking her fingers for the dog to go inside. "You are a bad liar, my lady. Come inside and I will make tea to warm you."

I gave up the pretence then and followed her inside, stamping my feet to restore the circulation.

The fire was blazing merrily as usual, and the air smelled of spices and something sweet as well. I sank into a chair by the fire and something tightly coiled within me seemed to relax.

"Roses," she told me, putting her hands under my nose. I breathed deeply, feeling a rush of summer as I inhaled.

"But roses will not be in bloom for more than a month," I protested. "The scent is too pure to be dried rose petals."

"Not dried," she corrected. "The oil from the rose. Very difficult to extract, and very costly. I made my perfume today, always in spring, just before John-the-Baptist returns."

"Oh, do you expect him soon?"

She shrugged, shifting the long, dark ringlets over her shoulder. They looked darker now, perhaps a bit less silver than had been there before. I wondered if she used more than just perfume to enhance her attractions.

"A few days, a few weeks. It does not matter. He will come. Always with the spring."

Rook padded over and laid his head on my knee, gazing up at me with adoring eyes. I laid a hand on his rough head, and to my astonishment, felt a hard lump rise in my throat.

Rosalie came then and put her own hand on my shoulder.

"You are lonely today," she said softly. "Rook has a gift for sensing it. Let him comfort you."

She moved away then, discreetly, to gather the tea things, and I laid my face against the lurcher, wetting his fur with my tears. I *was* lonely and feeling appallingly sorry for myself. It was not a state to which I was accustomed. I had been lonely for the better part of my marriage, but I had never acknowledged it. I lived then wrapped in cotton wool, seeing the world through misty glass, a pretty specimen pinned to a collector's card.

But Edward's murder had stripped the scales from my eyes, and I saw things clearly now. I was no longer sleepwalking through my life, and I wondered sometimes if it was worth it, to feel so sharply the bad as well as the good. I was capable of happiness now, real happiness, and passion as well, I thought with a rueful memory of Brisbane's strong arms. But I was capable of despair as well. I missed my sister; Brisbane was being thorny. The moor was a lonely, isolated place, and there was little warmth and comfort for me there.

"This cottage sits at a crossroads," Rosalie said, bringing the tea things to the table. I lifted my head, drying my eyes quickly. "It sits at a crossroads for you as well," she added.

"How so?" I peered at the plate of oatcakes she had brought to the table. Plain and good as earth; with butter and honey they were delicious.

"Because you must decide. You have been drifting, one foot in the past, one in the present. But you must step forward into the future, or you will linger in limbo forever."

She handed me a cup of steaming tea and I gave her a repressive look. "I thought limbo was a Catholic notion," I told her.

"I do not speak of your soul, lady. I speak of your heart, of yourself. You do not wish to be as you were, but you are not entirely who you will become. It is difficult to be a stranger to yourself, is it not?"

I put the cup down, untasted. "Are you quite certain you do not practice the fortune-teller's arts, Rosalie? You have assessed me quite accurately."

She shook her head, smiling, her coins jangling at her ears. "It does not take a crystal ball to know you. I see people, lady. That is my gift. So many come to me because they are troubled. Would they come to me if they were perfectly happy? No, they come because they know Rosalie can see them for what they are, and can help them see which paths lay before them."

I sipped slowly at the tea, feeling it warm me through to my bones. "You do not give them a little nudge down the right path?"

"Who is to say what is the right path? If a girl comes to me because she carries a child but has no husband, I will offer her pennyroyal to shed the child from her womb, or raspberry leaf to strengthen the womb to carry it. The choice is entirely hers."

I toyed with an oatcake, turning over her words in my head. "I wonder. I have been stubborn, bullheaded even, and I wonder if I ought to have gone back to London with my sister."

"You doubt yourself. That is the surest way to misery," Rosalie advised. "Do not waste, lady. Eat the oatcake or give it to the dog. Do not crumble it to bits."

I began to nibble it, licking the honey from my fingers. My manners when with Rosalie were appalling, but perhaps that was part of the pleasure I took in her company.

"How am I to know, then, if I am on the right path? I have made myself miserable, and perhaps another as well." I thought of Brisbane with a guilty pang.

Rosalie was thoughtful for a long moment, sipping at her tea whilst I made a mess of the oatcake. "If I would know someone, lady, I do not listen to what they say. I watch what they do. Tongues lie, bodies do not."

I laughed aloud. "That seems a very simple formula. Too simple. It cannot possibly be correct."

She shrugged again, her expression pitying. "Why must you *gorgios* always make things more complicated than they are? Be simple, lady. Nature is simple. And we are not so far removed from the savages we once were."

I shook my head, scarcely believing that an uneducated Gypsy woman was lecturing me on what, with a little judicious handling, might well be a corollary to Darwinian theory.

"Perhaps you are right," I said at length.

She smiled, baring those beautiful white teeth.

"Perhaps. Remember, lady. If you would know a person, stop your ears to their words, but mark their actions. Think on what I have said, and you will know what to do."

I looked up at her, startled, but she rose then and went to freshen the pot of tea. I looked into the fire, considering carefully what she had said and stroking Rook's ears. He gave a little sigh of contentment.

"Would that everyone were as easy to please as you," I murmured into his fur. He did not reply.

The afternoon was drawing to a close as I left Rosalie, and the long purple shadows of Thorn Crag were lengthening across the moor. Just as I reached for the latch of the garden door, Godwin pushed it open from the other side.

"Lady Julia!" he cried. The wind must have risen a little, for the bushes behind him fluttered. I rubbed my hands over my arms, raising the blood. "May I have a word?"

I longed for the fireside after my chilly walk, but Godwin's habitual good-natured expression was serious.

"Of course."

"I have just learned that you have been working in Redwall's study."

"Yes, I have. I was hoping to write a catalogue of his Egyptian collection. It will help to sell the things when the time comes."

He shook his head, his dark gold curls waving about his ears. "You ought not to be there alone. I carried them in when they arrived, and I know how heavy they are." He brought his head closer to mine, lowering his voice. "Thee must not hurt thyself. Thou'rt too delicate for such things."

I stared at him, taking far too long to realise this was north country wooing at its finest. He reached for my hand, and I pulled it back, giving him my cheeriest smile.

"You are very good to be concerned, Godwin, but I am quite careful, I promise. I will call if I have need of you," I told him, making a note never to rely upon him if I could help it. His demeanour had always been friendly, but this impertinence was something new.

He was not abashed. If anything, my cool amiability seemed to amuse him. He smiled, and dropped his eyes to my lips, then lazily moved his gaze back to my eyes. "You do tha'," he said, then stepped back to let me pass. I did so, keeping to the edge of the path so I would not brush against him.

He sloped off the opposite direction then, whistling a little tune. Just then Brisbane stepped onto the path, arms folded over his chest, his expression inscrutable.

"If you want to rendezvous with the hired help, Julia, you ought to make quite sure you are alone," he suggested.

"Do not be foul," I said irritably. "I have no greater interest in Godwin than you have in Hilda Allenby."

His brows rose and he blinked at me. "Hilda?"

"Yes," I said, matching the coolness of his tone. "I am reliably informed that she means to marry you. So once more, I find myself offering you my heartiest felicitations on your upcoming marriage," I added, alluding slyly to the entanglement he had suffered during our last investigation.

"I would sooner cut off my own head than marry Hilda Allenby," he said flatly.

"Oh, I know that, but the lady in question seems most insistent. I suggest you look carefully under your coverlet before you get into bed. She has rather medieval ideas about compromised honour." I bit back a smile. In spite of our recent difficulties, teasing him was a delicious pastime.

But Brisbane was not laughing. He reached out and gripped my arms, his face a breath from mine. "Why do you not leave?" I noticed his pupils then, and I reached a hand to brush a fingertip over his brow, ignoring the question. We knew well enough the answer, the both of us.

"You have been dosing yourself with an opiate," I said softly. "The migraines are returning."

"More vicious than ever," he said, grinding the words between tensed jaws. "I cannot sleep now but I have dreams—" He broke off and passed a hand over his brow, catching my hand in his, crushing it.

"What sort of dreams?" I dreaded the reply. I knew only too well what grim horrors stalked his dreams, and I knew it was his desperate attempts to push these visions away that brought about his virulent headaches.

"Death," he said finally, his eyes never wavering from mine. "Every time. I see it coming, and there is nothing I can do to stop it." He closed his eyes and gave a little groan, pulling me to him. His heartbeat was slow and steady, dulled by the opiate he had consumed. "You must go, Julia. I know I cannot command it. I have known since the first moment I met you, you cannot be ordered to obey. But I can ask you, beg you, on bended knee if I must. Leave this place," he said harshly, his fingers biting into my arms.

I thought of Rosalie's words then, and I realised that all the while Brisbane had been telling me to go, he had been pulling me closer to him.

"You impossibly stupid man," I told him. I put my arms about his waist, and we stood thus, clinging together for a long time, the air turning purple around us as dusk gathered in the ruined garden.

At length he pulled away and rubbed his thumbs over my cheeks, catching my tears. "That's the second time today," I said, feigning cheerfulness. "I am becoming a regular blubberpot."

"You will not leave me, will you?" he asked at length, his tone resigned. I studied him in the fading violet light. The strong, almost arrogant planes of his cheekbones, the aggressive nose, the seductive underlip, its fullness offset by the purposeful, even cruel upper lip. There was just enough light left to see the tiny scar on his cheek, white and curved as a crescent moon.

"I cannot envisage any circumstances under which I would," I told him.

And I could not have imagined then that I would be packing my trunk the very next evening, determined never to see him again.

I catalogued for the better part of the next day, doggedly recording various items of what I assumed was funerary equipment. I found an embalmer's kit, a set of canopic jars, and a great bag of something that resembled salt. There were a few nasty bits of mummies, but nothing so horrific as the babies in the priest's hole. There was a cat, stuffed into a peculiarly long, thin coffin, and a baboon with a menacing mask complete with elongated, sharp teeth. I marked them down and put them aside as quickly as possible. Now that Brisbane knew what I was about there was no need to conceal my work. I was able to move more rapidly through the collection, taking notes and writing out descriptions. The papyri were too fragile to handle, at least for my clumsy and uneducated hands, so I left them and moved on, endeavouring to do as little damage as possible.

After several hours, I was dusty and filthy, but surprisingly absorbed in the work. Not for the first time I reflected that one of the primary components of happiness was a worthwhile occupation, a thought that would likely horrify my brother Bellmont.

But Brisbane would understand. He had established himself in trade out of necessity—his noble Scottish relations not being inclined to support him—but I had seen him often enough on the trail of an investigation to know that work was not only an obligation for him, it was a pleasure of the most satisfying variety. And I took great satisfaction myself in the thought that my little scribblings might well be the foundation of restoring the Allenbys to solvency. There was still the matter of Brisbane to get round, but I would deal with him when the time came.

In the afternoon, I took my tea in the workroom, feeding bits of crisp shortbread to Grim and sipping at my tea as I wondered about the infants' coffin. It had occurred to me that Sir Redwall must have had a reason for secreting the babies in the priest's hole.

Why, I wondered, would Sir Redwall go to the trouble to hide the coffin? He had displayed the others, the mummies of baboons and cats and whatever else lurked beneath the dustsheets. Why secrete this coffin, then? And if Redwall had purchased it, why was there no bill of sale amongst his papers? Was that the reason for hiding it? Had he obtained it illegally? Or were the babies themselves contraband? There were no laws that I knew of preventing him from taking them out of Egypt so long as they had been purchased, but what if they had been stolen instead? I made a note to search his papers thoroughly for a bill of sale for the little mummies, and his diaries for a clue to where he had obtained them. In the meantime, a closer look at the coffin itself would not go amiss, I decided.

I rose and went to the panel, working the mechanism and steeling myself for the task ahead. I scrutinised it carefully, looking it over without expectation of what I might find. I knew too little about Egyptology to draw any proper conclusions, but it seemed to be precisely what it appeared: an authentic coffin, earlier than the Greco-Roman period judging from the lack of portrait mask, and in very good shape aside from a piece of crushed wood at the top. It had been propped just below the hole provided for ventilating the priest's hole, and it looked as though moisture had dripped down, corrupting the wooden case. On the front, a cartouche was engraved with a series of hieroglyphs, a funerary inscription, no doubt, perhaps a sort of incantation for the afterlife.

I fetched the knife again from the desk and applied myself to the lid. It took several minutes and a great deal of effort to pry it open, but at last it came free, and I wrestled the lid aside. I peered more closely at the mummies. They seemed in exquisitely good condition.

Swallowing down my squeamishness, I peered more closely at the tiny, linen-wrapped forms. Someone had taken exquisite pains to make certain these children were suitably prepared to enter the afterlife, I reflected. I realised then more than just the coffin was damaged. From the little neck down, the upper mummy was undamaged, beautifully wrapped and perfectly dry. The head was a different matter. The bandages had rotted away where the coffin was pulpy, and I felt my stomach churn as I put out a hand to touch the shredded linen. I meant to tuck one of the bandages in more securely, but it was rotten and fell away in my hand. I saw the top of the child's head, and jerked backward, dropping the linen scrap.

Instantly, I replaced the lid, working feverishly until the babies were tucked safely behind the panel, hidden from sight, but not from memory. I knew I would never forget what I had seen, so long as I lived. I had endured a post-mortem with Brisbane, examining the body of a man who had had his head crushed by a candelabrum, but nothing could have prepared me for the shock of what I had seen in that small coffin. The skin had dried and darkened, pulling taut across the baby's brow in a grotesque imitation of life.

But it was not this that had shocked me. Just above the brow I had seen the child's hair, beautiful hair, perhaps an inch long. It had been loosely curled from the damp, and was gold—the bright, pure gold of a blond child.

THE SIXTEENTH CHAPTER

Unnatural deeds do breed unnatural troubles.
—William Shakespeare
Macbeth

My first thought upon finding the blond child was to go to Brisbane, but even as I replaced the lid upon the coffin I remembered that Mrs. Butters had told me he was busy in the sheep pens with Godwin. Dipping was a vile and messy job. He would not be finished for hours, and in the meanwhile, there were things I could do.

My hands were shaking, and I paused to take several deep breaths and think. What did I know? Nothing, for certain. I knew the child with the damaged wrappings was blond, but nothing more. It was tempting to speculate that the baby was English, but I had no proof, I told myself severely. I had myself seen a red-haired mummy at an unrolling. True, the majority of Egyptians bore the traditionally dark, Mediterranean colouring, but the Macedonians had introduced some fairer strains into their society. This child might have been of Roman or Greek colonial parentage, in spite of the coffin's distinctly Old Kingdom appearance. And there was no way of determining the origins of the child without a proper examination of both the baby and its coffin, as well as the other child. The person best qualified to do so was Brisbane, and I would simply have to curb my curiosity until he was present.

I wiped my hands on my skirts and collected a few items to take to my room. I had a mind to peruse a volume or two on Egyptian funerary customs to see if I could add to my store of knowledge before I spoke with Brisbane. I took Redwall's diaries, the ones Ailith had given me, and a book on hieroglyphs. The latter was almost an afterthought, but it had occurred to me that I might be able to read the inscriptions on the coffin's cartouche if I knew the symbols. I took the notebook and recorded the cartouche swiftly.

I worked the rest of the afternoon in my room, not even noticing the deepening gloom of the oncoming evening until Minna came to fetch me for supper.

"I am sorry to disturb you, my lady," she said, dropping a quick curtsey. "Mrs. Butters wondered if you would prefer a tray."

I must have mumbled a reply, for a little while later Minna appeared again with a tray of soup and bread. She laid it carefully onto the writing table and took a moment to light the rest of the candles in the room. I was deep within the book on hieroglyphs, just beginning to crack the first of them.

Nothing in Redwall's diaries had mentioned the coffin or the mummies, either their purchase or their shipment home.

And then with a moment of breathtaking clarity, I realised there was one person in the house who *must* have known about them.

"Minna, is Godwin taking supper downstairs?" I asked suddenly. Too suddenly, for the girl jumped and put her finger into the flame. She sucked it, nodding.

"Yes, Lady Julia. He is alone. Mr. Brisbane is supping in his room as well. He did not wish to be disturbed."

I waved aside the mention of Brisbane. I would deal with him later. "Tell Godwin I would like to speak with him before he leaves. He can send you up to tell me when he is finished with his supper."

She curtseyed again and fled, leaving me to my excellent soup, or what would have been excellent soup had I remembered to eat it. I had two or three spoonfuls before I pushed it aside, too enthralled with my reading to finish. The hieroglyphs were not tremendously difficult, particularly as I found the very inscriptions on the coffin's cartouche *in* the book.

"Most unusual," I murmured. How was it possible that ancient inscriptions on a lady's coffin had come to be replicated in a modern text on hieroglyphs? Either the inscription was a standard one, or the person who had inscribed the coffin *had read the book*.

I slammed it closed, very nearly certain of what had happened. I rose and hurried downstairs. Godwin was in the hall, standing close to Minna.

"My lady, I was just about to send Minna to you," he said, straightening and giving me his most winsome smile.

Minna flicked me a quick, sideways glance, then scurried back to the kitchen. I motioned for Godwin to join me in the old great hall. He took up a candlestick and followed. The candle threw up odd shadows, touching the mouldering tapestry of Allenby names with a spark here and there where the thread shone gold. Other shadows, thick and black, danced over the ceiling, and over Godwin's face. The light played peculiar tricks with his bone structure, making him look angelic one moment, devilish the next.

"What is it, Lady Julia? Is there aught I can do for you?" he asked, his gaze moving meaningfully over my face.

"Yes, you can answer a question," I told him repressively. "You said you unpacked all of the crates Sir Redwall sent from Egypt. Did you ever handle a lady's coffin? Or mummies? Tiny ones?"

He shook his head slowly. "No, not from Egypt."

I sagged a little. I had been so certain.

"But there was a lady's coffin here before he left," Godwin added.

"Before? How did he acquire it?" My eagerness was back.

Godwin shrugged. "'Twere his grandfather's, old Sir Alfred's father. He had a mummy, a lady. That were what started Sir Redwall on his foreign studies. That coffin were his most prized possession."

"You're quite certain?"

"Oh, aye. He had a great unrolling of her, when he came into his inheritance. His grandfather, he would never unwrap that mummy. Said it was sacrilege or blas-blas—"

"Blasphemous?" I offered.

"Aye, tha' were the word. When Sir Redwall finally became

master, he unrolled it in front of the whole household. I remember it because tha' were just when old Samson, the master's old saddle horse, had bitten my hand clear to the bone." He raised his hand to show me the curved scar, pale against the weathered skin of his hand. "I would have lost a finger without Rosalie Young's care. And tha' were the year the mine closed. I remember it well because I rode Samson to the village and fairly had my head bashed in when they realised I were on the old master's horse, and them with hardly any food to feed their children."

I brushed aside his village gossip and posed my next question.

"Godwin, what happened to the mummy? The lady?"

"She were rotten, through and through. Sir Redwall said she'd not been prepared proper, but he were tha' furious. He had her thrown into Grimswater up tha' moor. Folk said Grim himself did not like it, and tha's why the Allenbys have done so poorly since. Lady Allenby told him not to bring any others home. She were quite firm, told Sir Redwall it were unChristian to keep folks from a proper burial. She told him to buy all the animals he wanted, but he were never to bring home a person."

"One more thing, Godwin, and please think very hard. Do you remember if the lady's coffin lid bore an inscription?"

He rubbed a hand over the rough stubble at his jaw. "Not tha' I recall, but I am not a great man of letters. I can read well enough—"

"No, not English," I said patiently. "Egyptian writing. It would have been a series of pictures in an oval on the front."

"Ah, no. Tha' were empty. I remember it because I asked

Sir Redwall about the coffin and he explained the markings and such. He said it were quite unusual as the name had been rubbed off and the wood was smooth. Said it was a shame someone had bothered to chisel off the old inscriptions, but as they had, it made it less expensive and his grandfather could afford it, so he was not tha' put out."

"I see," I said faintly. "Thank you, Godwin. I will not keep you."

"Won't you?" he asked, his voice soft, and his lips curved into an inviting smile.

"No, I will not." I nodded toward the open door. I had left it open for propriety's sake, and now I was glad I had. "Good evening, Godwin."

He thrust the candle at me and strode off, touching his forelock as he left, a bit impudently. I ignored him, my mind racing with the implications of what he had told me. Redwall Allenby had inherited a lady's coffin and an Egyptian mummy, which he had later destroyed. At some point, he had acquired a pair of mummified babies, *blond* mummified babies, I reminded myself, which he had secreted in a coffin whose cartouche he had altered. There was nothing else to be done then, except the thing I dreaded most: it was time to tell Brisbane what I had learned.

I hurried to Brisbane's bedchamber, shuddering a little as I made my way through the study. I had closed the door softly behind me so we would not be disturbed. The door to his bedchamber was ajar, the soft gold light spilling into the study over the threshold. It was not enough light to prevent me from tripping over a chair, and I cursed as I rubbed at my ankle.

A shadow fell across the threshold, and I could make out Brisbane's silhouette.

"It is I," I told him.

"I told Minna I did not wish to be disturbed," he said. He went back into the bedchamber and I followed, my ankle still smarting.

"I know, but I had to see you. It's about the mummies, the babies," I clarified.

He puffed out an impatient sigh. "There is no hope that you will leave me in peace, is there?"

"There is not."

He waved toward the bed. "Then you might as well make yourself comfortable. I've a letter to finish. Can it wait five minutes?"

I nodded and perched on the edge of his bed, trying very hard not to think about the intimacy of sitting where Brisbane slept, scant inches from his pillow, while the gentleman himself was seated at his writing table, near enough to touch. Instead I glanced idly about the room, taking in the growing untidiness of his possessions since he had returned from Edinburgh. I had had occasion before to notice that Brisbane did not so much stay in a room as *inhabit* it. He had fashioned a little table next to the bed of books, unwieldy volumes on the care and feeding of sheep, Roman history, garden design, and even an atlas, an enormous thing bound in green calf. Nearby, the little chemist's glasses were smouldering over a tiny flame, sending off little puffs of smoke and the occasional spark, although Brisbane ignored this entirely.

I turned my gaze to the hearth and smiled to see that Minna had forgot his supper tray. It rested on the hearth, the bowl of soup scraped clean and just a few stray mushrooms left congealing on the plate. I noticed he had had a decanter of wine and felt a little put out. Mrs. Butters only ever sent me tea. She must have subscribed to the theory that ladies should not drink spirits, I thought darkly.

I continued my inventory of the room, marking the addition of a little row of pots on the windowsill resting under bell jars. As yet there were no sprouts to be seen, but Brisbane had always had an interest in botany. Perhaps he had a mind to start some experiments to be carried out in the derelict gardens. As fastidious as he was, it must have pained him to walk through that sort of decay on his way out to the moor each day.

Next to the washstand, his best boots were freshly polished and placed at a careful distance from the fire. There was a clean towel hung there, and I was glad to see Mrs. Butters had at least attended to that. His razor was dry, and I noted the fresh growth of beard at his chin. His whiskers were coal black, and I wondered how he would look with a beard. I loathed them, but it occurred to me that Brisbane might look rather piratical with one. I was just about to suggest it when I noticed the bottle on his washstand. Clear glass and full of dark ruby-red syrup—no, not full. At least an inch had been emptied from it, and I saw the spoon resting next to it.

I glanced back at Brisbane. He sat at the writing table, his profile sharp against the wall behind him. He did not look up as he wrote, his pen dashing quickly over the page in the bold hand I had come to know so well. Occasionally he paused to think, passing a hand over his brow or his jaw, and once he heaved a sigh, exhaling heavily as he scrawled his signature. He darted a glance at me, then folded the letter quickly, thrusting it into an envelope. He sealed it with a thick, old-fashioned wafer of wax and put it aside. There was no direction on the envelope, and I wondered to whom he had been writing so secretly. His colour was pale under the dark olive of his complexion, and there were dark shadows beneath his eyes, signs I had seen before when the headaches were upon him. He turned to me, his pupils quite small in the wide black iris.

"Well?" His tone was not encouraging. Doubtless he thought I meant to needle him about returning the collection to the Allenbys, and it was a mark of how well he knew me that he should think so.

"I do intend to persuade you to give the collection, or at least its proceeds to the Allenbys," I told him, "but we can quarrel about that later." I told him what I had found when I inspected the coffin, and what I had learned from my inquiry of Godwin.

Brisbane said nothing for a moment, pursing his lips. His booted legs were stretched out before him, one arm thrown over the back of the chair. "So Redwall kept the coffin, then found mummies to fill it, against Mama's wishes," he mused.

"Precisely," I said. "But there is something else, something rather more disturbing." I explained quickly about the inscription. "The cartouche was blank when Godwin last saw the coffin. At some point, Redwall Allenby chiselled an inscription, taking the text from a book on hieroglyphs, a chapter dealing with funerary customs, to be precise. He carved into the coffin a prayer for the dead."

"You found the text?" he asked, his expression one of acute astonishment.

"I did. It was rather obvious when I knew what to look for. I was prepared to translate, one character at a time, which I know is a preposterously difficult matter for someone not trained in Egyptology, but I was determined. Imagine my surprise when I found the entire text printed in the book." I preened a little at this point. I was immensely proud of my investigative accomplishments, but Brisbane wasted no time in praise.

"Show me," he ordered. We moved into the study and he quickly extracted the coffin lid, placing it carefully onto the floor. I held a candle aloft and he ran his fingers over the cartouche, tracing the characters.

"I ought to have noticed this before," he murmured. Then, to my astonishment, he began to chant in a language I had never heard, and after a moment I realised why: it was a language that had not been spoken in thousands of years.

"Brisbane! You speak Egyptian," I said, feeling quite breathless.

He flicked me a glance. "As well as anyone could be expected to. It is a dead language, after all."

I shook my head. "How do you know what that cartouche says?" I demanded, my astonishment rapidly giving way to anger.

"I conducted an investigation in Egypt," he said blandly. "I had to pass for an Egyptological scholar. My speciality was language, hieroglyphs and hieratic. I still remember bits of it, but you know what they say about losing languages you do not practise."

My hands were fisted at my sides. I forced my fingers to unclench, although I longed to throttle him with them.

"All this time, you have been letting me slave away in here in the dust and the grime, and you knew precisely what everything was. I never even needed to catalogue a single artefact, did I?"

He shook his sleek, dark head. "No," he said, his tone remarkably cheerful.

"You have been through this room already," I hypothesised. "You already knew every piece in this collection, didn't you?"

"Not the coffin, nor the mummies," he pointed out. "Those were hidden. And they weren't in the catalogue."

"The—the catalogue?" I was stammering in my rage. "There is a catalogue already?"

He had the grace, or perhaps the sense of self-preservation, not to laugh. "In my bedchamber. I slid it under the bed."

I was beyond angry. I felt the blood beating in my ears, and if he had smiled at me, I would have flown at him, regardless of his advantage in size and strength. "And you thought it would be amusing to let me toil away, doing my pathetic best to catalogue a collection I could not begin to understand, while you slept a foot away from a *proper* catalogue the whole time." It was not a question, and he did not bother to reply.

"How could you?" I asked him finally. "I thought I was helping those poor women, and instead I was being made a fool of."

He shrugged. "It was not meant to make a fool of you. It was meant to keep you busy and out of trouble."

I stared at him, my mouth agape. It was several seconds

before I could speak coherently. "Of all the arrogant, high-handed things you have done, this is by far the worst. I came here because I thought you needed me. We have faced down death and tracked murderers together, and I thought we were partners after a fashion."

I paused, feeling flat and empty, as though the breath had been knocked quite solidly out of my lungs. "How stupid I was. Of course you would have made yourself acquainted with the collection. You had months, didn't you? Long, cold winter months with nothing to do. You would have searched the books and found the catalogue easily. I daresay it was even in his desk, waiting for you. And then I came, blundering in as usual and you could not resist having fun at my expense, could you? Stupid Julia, let her play at being useful. How you must have laughed, knowing what I was doing each day, and what pains I took to make certain you did not find out."

"If you did not want me to find out, you ought not to have worn your perfume. I did remind you the first night that you smelled of violets. Next time, leave it off," he pointed out. That he chose to comment on that one matter, and said nothing of the rest, spoke volumes to me. I smoothed my skirts, and composed my expression.

"There will be no next time," I told him, my voice calm and even. "I have had my fill of your mysteries and your secrets and your tricks. I will return to London tomorrow, and I will only say that I am sorry I have troubled you. I hope the amusement I provided has more than made up for the inconvenience."

His expression did not change, except for the faintest flicker—of what?—behind his eyes. He merely inclined his head and folded his arms over the breadth of his chest, his knuckles white. I turned and took my leave of him, and it is to my credit that I did not shed a single tear, nor did I hasten my steps from the room. I walked slowly and with dignity, each footfall a death knell as I left him.

THE SEVENTEENTH CHAPTER

Death, a necessary end,
Will come when it will come.
—William Shakespeare
Julius Caesar

I went directly to the maids' room, opening the door without knocking. Minna was alone, knitting and talking to Grim and Florence. She looked up in alarm.

"Is there something amiss, my lady?" she asked, clearly alarmed.

"We are leaving. Pack your things and the animals and be prepared to leave first thing in the morning."

Unlike Morag, who would have peppered me with questions, Minna merely laid aside her knitting and rose.

"Yes, my lady. I will begin at once." She had gone quite pale, and I felt a surge of pity for her. It could not be an easy thing to live one's life always at the mercy of another's whims.

"I will pack for myself, Minna. See to yourself and the animals."

She dipped a quick curtsey and said nothing.

I left her then and went to my chilly room, pausing to poke at the fire. I shoved viciously, sending a shower of sparks up the chimney until it was blazing. I opened my trunk and began to pitch things in, not troubling to fold anything. I was too angry to do the job properly. I knew that once I gave myself time to think about what had happened, I would be shattered, and it needed all my energy to get myself, a maid, an expectant dog, and a raven back to London.

I had just hurled a pair of boots into the trunk with a satisfying clatter when my door was thrown back on its hinges. Minna stood there, panting as if she had just taken the stairs two at a time. Her round little face was dead white, and she was wearing her cloak.

"Minna, whatever is the trouble?"

She put a hand to her side, pressing a stitch, I guessed. "My lady, oh, you must come! I think he's dying!"

I blinked at her. "Who is dying? What on earth are you talking about?"

She tugged at my arm, dragging me toward the door. "I went downstairs to—oh, never mind! I heard him, at least, I heard a noise, as if something heavy had fallen. I went to his room to see if I could help, and I found him there. Please, my lady, you must come. He will die else!"

I realised then that she was talking about Brisbane. I jerked my arm out of her grasp and flew down the stairs, Minna hard on my heels. I found him in his bedchamber, collapsed on the floor between his bed and the hearth. He must have reached for something as he had fallen, for a stack of books was scattered over the floor, and the little bottle of red syrup was shattered over the hearthstones. He was lying on his side and he had been sick, comprehensively so. He was unaware of Minna, or of me, bending over him, calling his name. I pushed back his eyelids, but his eyes had rolled white, and as I watched, his muscles began to seize.

And as I looked down at him, suffering and broken, I knew that for the second time in my life, I was watching the death throes of a man who had been poisoned.

"My lady," Minna sobbed, "what shall I do?"

The world stopped then, for I knew whatever choice I made would determine whether Brisbane lived or died. He had been poisoned—deliberately, I was certain. But by whom? He needed help, and if I applied to the wrong quarter, he would certainly die. I had to *know* whom to trust with a life more precious to me than my own.

A thousand questions spun through my mind in the space of half a minute, a thousand pieces I had to fit together instantly. I thought of the bottled mushrooms, lovingly prepared by Lady Allenby. I saw the beautiful red syrup distilled by Rosalie in her little stillroom in the moor cottage. And I thought of Godwin, with his tins of arsenic for dipping sheep. Any one of them might have poisoned him, and any one of them might be waiting to make certain they finished the job. There was no hope, I thought desperately. Brisbane was going to die because I did not know whom to trust. The only possible action at that point was prayer, I decided hopelessly.

But before I could beg the Almighty's intercession, I knew. I rose and took Minna hard by the arms. "I dare not leave him, but you must go for help. Do you know the cottage at the crossroads on the moor? The one where the Gypsy lady lives?"

Minna nodded, her mouth trembling. She was trying desperately not to look at the ruined man on the floor. "I do."

"Go and fetch her. Tell her that Brisbane had been poisoned, and to bring whatever remedies she has. Tell her it was either mushrooms or arsenic, I don't know which—"

I broke off, thinking rapidly. I *did* know which. In our first investigation, Brisbane's friend, Dr. Bent, had explained to me that a victim of arsenical poisoning would expel fluids that smelled heavily of garlic. No such smell hung in the air of Brisbane's room.

"It was mushrooms, tell her it was toadstools and tell her if she wants to see him alive again, she must hurry. And if you make it there and back with her in quarter of an hour, I will give you a hundred pounds. *Go!*" I gave Minna a shove and she ran as if all the hounds of hell were at her heels.

She did not return in a quarter of an hour. It was nearer a half, and those thirty minutes were the darkest of my life. I held his head over the washbasin, but there was nothing to be done for him, nothing except hold his still hand in mine and watch him slip away. I did not speak. He would not have known me in any event. I simply sat, feeling his hand grow cold and then hot in mine, the fingers limp one moment, then so tightly grasped I thought he would break my bones. I welcomed the pain. It was the only thing tethering me to that moment. Were it not for the grinding of those little bones together, I think I might have gone quite mad, waiting for Minna to return with Rosalie, listening to the terrible sounds of the poison ravaging Brisbane's body.

At last Rosalie appeared, swirling skirts and long plaits swinging as she slipped off a man's greatcoat and pushed up her sleeves. She said nothing to me, merely bent over him and assessed him, as carefully and critically as any Harley Street physician.

"Mushrooms, eh?" she said at last. I nodded. "A nasty business. I will do all I can, and still he may not live. Will you help me, lady?"

I turned on her, angry as a cat. "Of course I will help you. Do you think I mean to sit idly by while he dies?"

She made no reply, merely turned to Minna and delivered a litany of orders. The fire must be stoked up, kettles of hot water must be brought, sheets and towels, and various other implements of nursing. Minna bobbed a curtsey and fled, grateful, I think, to have something useful to do.

Together Rosalie and I manoeuvred him onto the bed, stripping his soiled shirt off of him and saying nothing.

When Minna returned, she folded back her cuffs and poked up the fire, heaping fuel upon it until the flames blazed up the chimney. She went to fetch the first of the hot water kettles and Rosalie turned to me. "You trust me, lady?"

Her eyes were on mine, black and fathomless, and I felt a little faint at the power in them. I nodded. "Yes."

She gave one short, sharp nod. "As I said, I will do what I can to save him, but I make you no promises. We may fight like tigresses and still lose him, do you understand?"

"You will not lose him," I told her fiercely. "*I* will not lose him."

Rosalie gave another nod, then gestured for her basket. "If it was mushrooms, he must be made to vomit, as much as possible for a short period of time. It will not help the poison that has already settled in his system, and it will make him very weak, but it will prevent the rest from harming him."

She took a packet of ground herbs from her basket, a little paper twist that smelled like something rotten and decayed. She mixed it with water and told me to hold his head. "This will not be easy," she warned me. She was entirely correct.

The next hours I cannot clearly remember. There are sounds and impressions, and fleeting, sharp memories. Brisbane was sick, over and again, because we made him so, and I found myself murmuring apologies under my breath as he heaved and groaned. In between, we rubbed his chest and arms with towels soaked in vinegar. Minna worked the fire until sweat ran freely from her brow. All of that terrible night she tended the fire, saying almost nothing, but every time I looked at her, her lips were moving in inaudible prayer. She left only to brew pots of strong tea. Mine grew stone cold, as did Rosalie's. I could think of nothing but Brisbane, and even now, when I think of that terrible night, I remember Rosalie's eyes, black and determined as she laboured to save his life.

When he had been fully purged, she administered a solution of milk thistle and watched him carefully. At last, he settled into an uneasy unconsciousness, and Rosalie turned to me.

"That is all I can do for him. Milk thistle now, and weak tea later if he will take it, and as much as he will take."

Minna stretched, pushing her fists into her back and then went to the window, rattling back the draperies.

"Oh, look!" she cried. I turned to see the moor, purple-black and stretching to the ends of the earth, and just beyond, the first tinge of pink as the sun began to edge into the grey sky.

"It is morning," I said, sagging in relief. "He has survived the night. Surely he will live." I looked to Rosalie in appeal, but she shook her head. Her face was deeply lined and her eyes darkly shadowed, betraying all of her years. I knew I must look as worn. We had all of us lived a lifetime in that night. I opened my mouth to argue with Rosalie, but she held up a hand.

"This is the time of danger, lady, not the first hours. The poison may have settled too deeply, and we will not know until two, three days have passed. He is unconscious now, and he will either recover, or he will die. There is no way of knowing which, and there is nothing more to be done except to answer his thirst. We have done all that we could. It is in God's hands now."

I wanted to scream or rage or put my fist into her complacent face. But she was entirely correct. We had purged and dosed him, and there was nothing more to be done but wait.

I was surprised the rest of the household had not been raised during the night, but they had apparently slept on, peacefully unaware of our ordeal. At least, all but one of them had. Somewhere, a villainess must have lain awake, counting herself clever. I barred the door and gave Minna strict instructions that none of the household, particularly Lady Allenby, was to be admitted. Minna took it upon herself to prepare food for Rosalie and myself, although none of us ate much. That day stretched into another torturous night, and into the second day, the hours dragging past one and the same. I sat next to the bed, holding his hand, willing him to feel me there, to come back to me.

And as horrible as the entire ordeal had been, nothing was as black as the second night, when the witching hour came and went and I felt his skin growing cooler under my touch. Minna had dragged a thin mattress downstairs and was sleeping by the fire, curled like a child. Rosalie, exhausted by her efforts, was slumped in the chair, her head on the writing desk, pillowed in her arms.

Sometime in the smallest hours of the morning, I looked at Brisbane, and I saw something had changed. His features seemed different somehow, the features I had memorised, etched in my mind forever. I realised it would be easiest then to kiss him once and let him go. He was slipping away, it seemed, even as I watched. Or perhaps it was a fancy of mine, brought on by worry or exhaustion. I cannot say, even now. All I know is that I leaned close to him, whispering into his ear the things I ought to have said to him when he could hear me. I talked until my voice was hoarse, and even then I could not stop. I told him I could not imagine a world where he did not exist, and I told him how thoroughly I loved him, and even as I said the words, I realised it could be the only chance I would ever have to tell him so. The only chance, and it might well have come too late. I touched the lines of his face, his hands, every scar, every place where the world had been unkind to him and promised never to leave him if only he would come back to me.

I talked until I could talk no more. My head dropped against his shoulder and I slept, falling at last into an exhausted, fitful slumber, my head next to his, my hand tucked between his arm and his bare chest. I do not know how long I drowsed, only that it was dawn when Minna's shriek woke me. I started, blinking and rubbing at my eyes. She was pointing to Brisbane, incapable of speech.

I lifted my head and looked at him. His eyes were open and clear and he was staring at me.

I opened my mouth to speak, but the words did not come. Instead I crumpled slowly onto the spinning bed and slid gratefully into blackness as I fell to the floor.

THE EIGHTEENTH CHAPTER

Blood will have blood.
—William Shakespeare
Macbeth

T woke much later in my own bed, blinking against the flicker of the candle at the bedside. From his cage in the corner, Grim quorked worriedly, flapping a dark wing in my direction. I stirred, feeling a warm hand over mine, a hand I knew as well as my own.

"Portia?" My voice was a mere croak, but it was enough to rouse her. She lay next to me, fully dressed and on top of the coverlet, ready to rise at a moment's notice. She smiled sleepily, but the smile did not erase the new marks of fatigue upon her lovely features.

"It is quite time you woke, slugabed," she chided. She put a hand to my brow, her expression anxious. After a moment she relaxed. "No fever then. You gave us a bit of a scare, you know." Her tone was light, but there was a thread of unmistakable emotion. She had been afraid, afraid enough to return from London.

I moved to rise, but she pushed me firmly back against the pillow. "He is resting now. You have not lost him," she told me, her voice thick with emotion.

I felt something tight and painful in my chest ease. "What of Jane?" I asked.

A shadow passed over her face, and she said shortly, "She is gone. I do not wish to speak of it."

I nodded, my head feeling thick and woolly. "How long have I been asleep?"

"Two days, more or less," she told me.

"Two days!" I made to rise again, but Portia's arm and a wave of giddiness thwarted me.

"You fainted when Brisbane came around, and Rosalie thought it best to force you to rest. She dosed you with one of her potions and Brisbane sent Godwin into Howlett Magna to telegraph me. Valerius and I came at once, Morag as well, of course."

I sank back against the pillows. I felt boneless, weightless, and I wondered if my head would ever be entirely clear again.

"Brisbane?" I murmured.

"Mending quite nicely, according to Rosalie. Valerius has taken over the care of him, and said Rosalie could not have done better were she a proper doctor. She and Morag have been veritable dragons at keeping away visitors until he is fully recovered, and this morning he threw his soup plate at the wall."

"A very promising sign," I commented sleepily.

"It is indeed. Rosalie is plying him with all manner of tonics, and he is eating, although he says he is heartily sick

of soups and blancmanges. Apparently that is what precipi-
tated his temper this morning."

I struggled against the weight of sleep, forcing my eyes
open. "Food. Who is preparing his food?" I clutched at
Portia's arm, but she soothed me.

"Minna is preparing it herself, and Morag is tasting everything before she will permit Brisbane to so much as lift his
spoon. Valerius thought it a sensible precaution under the
circumstances."

I would have laughed at the notion of Morag serving as
taster to Brisbane were the situation not so horrifying.

Grim quorked again and I waved a hand at him. "Good
morning, Grim."

"Good morning," he returned politely. "Sweetie."

I motioned to the box beneath his cage. "Toss a few of
those violet creams in the cage for him, will you, dearest?"

Portia obeyed, but with an expression of distaste. Grim's
manners were impeccable, save when it came to enjoying his
food. He tore at the little sweetmeats savagely, and Portia
pulled a face.

"I always think he'd prefer a nice, juicy mouse," she commented.

"By all means, go catch him one. What of Lady Allenby?"
I asked finally.

"Withdrawn to her room. She confessed the deed at once,
and took to her chamber. She will see no one, and when
Brisbane is recovered, he will take the matter in hand. Hilda
is hiding out with her chickens and will not speak to any of
us, she is so horrified. Ailith has apologised perhaps a
hundred times, and Godwin says he can manage the estate

perfectly until Brisbane is fully himself again. They have all been quite human about the whole thing, really. I do rather feel sorry for Hilda. She is quite changed. All her old arrogance is gone. Even Valerius cannot make her talk. He plans to build her a nice new henhouse to make her feel better when Brisbane is recovered."

Portia continued to talk, but her words flowed together, soothing and soft, and after a few minutes, I heard nothing more.

I woke the next morning, feeling as if I had slept a hundred years. I longed for a bath and I was ravenously hungry. Morag carried up an enormous plate of eggs and bacon and devilled kidneys with toast and a steaming pot of tea. There were no mushrooms, I noted with a grateful shudder. I doubted I would ever be able to eat them again. I applied myself with vigour to my breakfast, and by the time I had wiped the last crumb from my plate, I was feeling entirely myself again.

I washed and dressed and emerged. Lady Allenby's door was closed, and I wondered if she were still immured in her room. I found Portia with Brisbane. He was propped up in bed, neatly dressed in a clean nightshirt, arms tightly locked about his chest as Portia endeavoured to cut his hair and Valerius attempted to take his pulse.

"Brisbane, honestly. You look quite a pirate. Now, if you will just let me trim a lock here and there, I can make you thoroughly respectable," she argued. She advanced toward him with scissors, and he held up a hand.

"I may not yet have regained my full strength, but if you

so much as lay a single blade on my head I will have Puggy stuffed and mounted to hang over my fireplace," he told her, his eyes glinting coldly. I blinked back sudden tears. I had not imagined it would be so moving to see him alive and in a foul mood, but I had come to accept that I would rather have Brisbane in a savage temper than any other gentleman with perfect manners.

"Portia, do you mind?" Valerius asked sharply. "I am trying to assess his condition, and you are agitating him."

"I would not agitate him if he would give in," Portia pointed out reasonably.

"Now, children," I said briskly. "No need to fuss. Brisbane, if you wish to go about looking like Heathcliff that is your affair. Leave him be, Portia." She subsided, and Val shot me a grateful look as he applied himself to Brisbane's pulse.

I glanced at the hearth where Mr. Pugglesworth was resting on his favourite cushion and emitting foul smells. "Ah, Puggy. I thought I smelled something decaying. Well, I am glad you've brought him, Portia. He will be on hand when Florence is delivered of his offspring."

I had not had the chance to write the news to her, and Portia blinked at me in surprise. "Mr. Pugglesworth is going to be a father? Are you quite sure?"

"As sure as ever I would want to be," Morag told her sourly from the doorway. She entered bearing a tray with a pretty little dish of custard and a soup plate of beef tea. Brisbane looked pointedly at the dark smear on the wall, the souvenir of his earlier displeasure.

"Morag, unless there is something on that tray I can chew, do not bother to come any farther." Morag sniffed and put the food on the hearth. Puggy hefted himself off of his cushion and sniffed at the custard before putting his front paws into the dish and lapping it up.

Val sat back with a decided air of satisfaction. "Strong and steady. Mrs. Smith, I have the utmost respect for your methods."

Rosalie was sitting in the little chair by the fireplace, knitting a sock of purple and scarlet wool, Rook curled quietly at her feet, occasionally looking with interest at Puggy's plate of custard.

"A bit of beef, well cooked and the broth thickened with blood, that is what you need now," she told Brisbane. "Do you not agree?" she asked Val.

He preened a little at her tact. "I will tell Minna," he said, rising and taking his leave.

Rosalie stood as well, tucking her knitting into her pocket. "I will tell Minna to bring an egg also, soft-boiled, and a glass of good wine to build your blood."

She turned to me as she passed and put a hand to my cheek. "You are well now."

"Yes. Thank you, Rosalie," I told her. I dropped my voice to a whisper. "For everything."

"We will talk later, *chavvi*," she said. She left us then, and Rook moved to sit at Brisbane's side, his shaggy head tucked under Brisbane's hand. Portia settled into Rosalie's abandoned chair, rubbing at Puggy's back with her slippered foot. Bits of hair and dandruff littered the cushion and I looked away, feeling rather queasy. Brisbane was watching me closely as he stroked Rook's ears, and I felt suddenly shy of him. I thought of all I had said to him, baring my soul and telling him things I could not imagine ever saying again in the clear light of day. My cheeks burned and I looked away.

"It is there, the book with the green kid cover," he said suddenly, his voice cool. He nodded toward the stack of books that had been tidied into a teetering pile next to the bed.

I blinked at him. "What is?"

"The catalogue," he said with the merest sigh of impatience.

I retrieved it, willing him not to remember what I had whispered to him in his unconsciousness. I opened it to find a catalogue, perfectly organised and exact in its details.

"Ah," I said. "A fair sight better than what I was about, I can promise you. If I may borrow this, I can at least compare the current collection with this and see if anything is missing."

He nodded, and as I made to rise, he put out his hand, clamping it tightly about my wrist. "I ought to thank you," he said softly. "If you had not acted so quickly and so decisively, I would be dead."

I opened my mouth, then closed it and shrugged. "It was Minna who found you. And Rosalie who knew what to do. They deserve your thanks, not me."

I left him then, clutching the book to my chest like a shield. He had not remembered then, and I was unutterably relieved. And dismayed. I had found the courage to tell him precisely what I felt for once. I did not think I could do so again.

Portia followed me from Brisbane's room, cuddling Puggy under her chin. I left the catalogue on Redwall's desk in the study, and without discussion, Portia and I took up wraps and made our way into the fresh air and sunshine of the garden. It was the warmest day yet during our time in Yorkshire, and I closed my eyes and turned my face to the sun when we stopped to a little bench in the orchard.

"It was a very near thing for him," Portia commented.

I opened my eyes and nodded. "Closer than you know. I thought—"

"I know," she said, covering my hand with her own briefly. She stroked Puggy's ears, cooing to him over his wheezing. "But why? Why should Lady Allenby want to poison Brisbane?"

I shook my head. "I am not certain, but I think it has to do with this house and with Redwall Allenby. Brisbane knew him when they were boys, and they did not get on. When Brisbane talked of him, there was a venom there, a hatred I have never seen in him." I quickly explained to her the terms of the sale of Grimsgrave and the precariousness of the Allenby fortunes.

"But killing Brisbane would not solve her difficulties," Portia pointed out. "Presumably his estate would pass to his heirs, whoever they may be. Perhaps Monk," she suggested, referring to Brisbane's trusted man of affairs and sometime valet. "Good God, where is Monk? Brisbane hasn't mentioned him, and I didn't think to ask. He ought to have been here, having a care for Brisbane."

"He is engaged upon a case. I do not know where, but I do not think he has been here since Brisbane took up residence at Grimsgrave, although he ought to be," I finished waspishly.

Portia shook her head. "Be fair, Julia. Brisbane had no notion he was in danger here, and if he did not suspect, how could Monk have known? Now, who besides Monk might benefit should Brisbane die?"

I shrugged. "Hortense de Bellefleur. He has paid her an allowance for twenty years. It would be like him to want to take care of her even after his death." It remained an interesting development that my father's dearest companion should have been Brisbane's first mistress. Though Brisbane and Hortense had concluded their liaison before Brisbane had even turned twenty, he still counted her a dear friend, as did I.

Portia pursed her lips. "I suppose. Or he could leave everything to you."

I gaped at her. "To what purpose? I have more money than Croesus. Brisbane knows that. He would not be so senseless. He would leave his assets to those who could best profit from them."

Portia and I fell silent, pondering the implications of the attack on Brisbane.

"Of course," I said slowly, "there are the Allenby daughters. Ailith claimed she was Brisbane's first love, and Hilda was quite forthright about her intentions to marry him to regain her home." Quickly I related the details of these new revelations to Portia.

She was thoughtful, stroking Puggy's swayed back. "I wonder. What if Lady Allenby knew of Hilda's scheme?"

"I know she did. I told her myself."

"Aha!" Portia jumped, unsettling Puggy. He puffed out an annoyed sigh and she settled him down again. "You told Lady Allenby that Hilda meant to marry Brisbane. What if she opposed the match?"

"But she told me she did not believe anything would come of it," I argued.

"*So she told you,*" Portia echoed meaningfully. "Just because she said it, does not mean she believed it. What if she knew of Hilda's intentions, and feared that Brisbane *would* marry her? The Allenbys do not marry outside their own semi-royal blood, do they? Lady Allenby might have viewed such an arrangement as the grossest *lèse-majesté*. Who is to say what steps she might take to prevent it?"

"Preposterous," I said roundly. "She had only to remove Hilda from his house."

"Which she has not the means to do," Portia rejoined.

"Then she would have been better off waiting until they *had* married. Then Hilda would have inherited the Hall and the Allenbys would once more be masters of their own domain."

"But that would have polluted the Allenby line," Portia argued. "What if Hilda conceived a child in that time? The Allenby blood would have been tainted with his."

Her expression was smug, but try as I might, I could not believe it. "It is madness," I said finally.

"And who is to say the old woman is not mad?" she asked. "Think how they live. She is alone up here, with only another old woman and an oafish farm manager for company, and two daughters who are scarcely better than children. Ailith spends all day scurrying meekly behind her mother and stitching at her needlepoint, while Hilda wanders the moors like a madwoman and talks to chickens. They have buried the last male heir of Grimsgrave, and they have only themselves left, the remains of a noble and illustrious family. Isn't it at all possible Lady Allenby would rather let their name die out than mix it with lesser blood?"

"It is possible," I said slowly. "But there is another Allenby still unaccounted for." I told her about Wilfreda, her quiet, bookish ways, and her desperate flight from Grimsgrave with the artist commissioned to paint her portrait. "Her name was unpicked from the family tapestry," I finished. "They would rather pretend she never existed than admit she married beneath her."

Portia nodded. "Mark me, Julia. Lady Allenby was determined not to let another of her daughters go astray, and her only recourse was to attempt the life of the man who attracted her."

I shuddered. "It seems so much more terrible, you know. I cannot imagine what a person must think, picking the mushrooms so carefully, wiping them and slicing them and bottling them just so, placing them carefully upon someone's plate, all the while knowing what you mean to do with them. No one quite in her right mind could do such a thing."

"Well, I have always said northerners were not trustworthy," she reminded me. "And Yorkshire folk are the maddest of the lot."

I thought of Deborah at the inn, and gentle Mrs. Butters, and Godwin, rough but kind for all his country ways. "Oh, I don't know," I said finally. "I think people are much the same wherever you go. Some of them good, some of them clever, and some of them with the devil in them."

"The trick is learning to distinguish the difference," my sister added.

"Indeed. There is one more thing," I began, and told her about the mummified babies I had discovered in the priest's hole. She gaped at me, horrified.

"Julia, that is beyond belief. Why on earth would Redwall Allenby have such things? And why keep them squirreled away behind the chimney?"

"Probably because they are so horrid. If you had mummy babies, would you advertise the fact?"

"But that is precisely the point. If I were the type of person to keep mummy babies lying about, I shouldn't think I would mind if people actually knew it," she pointed out.

Puggy let out a great, flatulent noise and I turned away. "But what sort of person collects mummified babies in the first place?" I asked.

"We are arguing in a circle," Portia noted with maddening logic. "Mummified children are collected by the sort of people who would collect mummified children."

"I feel a headache coming on, Portia. We have established that Redwall Allenby had rather peculiar tastes. Now, we must determine why. Were the mummies merely a curiosity, like the baboon and the cat? Or were they collected for a more sinister purpose?"

Portia arched a cool brow. "Like what?"

I began to tick the possibilities off on my fingers. "Medicinal properties, public demonstration, speculation…"

My sister waved a hand. "Your cart has galloped apace of your horse. Let us begin at the beginning. Medicinal properties?"

"Mummy dust has been used for medical compounds for centuries to cure a variety of ailments. One of the more disgusting facts I have recently learned."

Portia pulled a face. "You mean people *eat* them?"

"Drink them, actually. A pinch of mummy dust in an embrocation of other assorted ghoulish ingredients. Just imagine how much power a superstitious peasant mind might attribute to powdered mummy."

"I suppose," she said slowly. "It was not so long ago that desperate syphilitics tried drinking from virgins' skulls to cure their affliction."

"Yes," I said lightly, trying not to dwell in the long shadows of previous investigations. There were things I had learned that I had never told my sister, and never would.

"Public demonstration," I continued. "Remember the unrolling we attended at the Duchess of Ottley's? It was grotesque, but I am told the scientist who procured the mummy was paid a fantastic sum for the evening's entertainment, particularly because the mummy was red-haired and therefore a rarity. Imagine how much more might be demanded for unrolling a pair of children."

Portia shuddered. "Go on. You said speculation."

"Hm, yes. The unlikeliest of all," I told her, "but entirely possible. What if Redwall looked at his coffin, empty and therefore less valuable? And what if he then decided to fill it, and thereby increase its value? Procure a pair of mummified children and etch some appropriate inscription into the cartouche. It would be a very simple matter to find another buyer then, one who would be willing to pay a great deal more than Redwall would have had to put up in the first place."

"Possible," Portia said. She lapsed into silence then and I considered my theory. It fitted very well with what I had learned thus far of Redwall Allenby's character. Opportunistic, resourceful, perhaps a little weak, and entirely ruthless when it suited him. I could well imagine him piecing together a superbly-fashioned hoax to fleece an unsuspecting lamb of a buyer. I made a note to delve further into Redwall Allenby's notes and diaries. Whatever became of the

Allenby ladies at this point, I would finish this investigation, I promised myself.

"What will become of Lady Allenby?" I asked suddenly. In spite of her attempt on Brisbane's life, I hated to think of her turned over to the authorities to hang for her crime. She was so old, so fragile. But even as I thought it, I pictured her gnarled hands cupped tightly over the head of her walking stick, her firm carriage, her indomitable will, and my pity withered a little.

Portia shook her head. "Brisbane has not spoken of it. It is for him to say, you know. Perhaps he will not tell the authorities at all. She is very old."

Much as I did not like the idea of Lady Allenby in the hands of the law, I did not like the notion of Brisbane settling his score himself any better. His notions of justice were usually quite sound, but I wondered at his ability to remain impartial where the Allenbys were concerned.

"I must ask him." I rose then and Portia and I made our way back toward the house. The empty east wing cast long shadows over the grass, stretching out to meet us. Or capture us, I fancied. I could not imagine ever feeling entirely comfortable in the house again, and although I still admired the elegant lines and solid workmanship, it would always hold horrors for me. I was so reluctant to return to it that we walked the long way round the pond, watching the wind stir the reeds and ruffle the surface of the black water.

"That pond wants a fish," Portia said roundly. She put Puggy down to romp, but all he managed was a wheezing cough as he stumped toward the house.

"That pond wants filling in," I returned. "It is bleak and unwelcoming. Just like the rest of this place. Don't you feel it?" I turned on my heel slowly, taking in the empty wing, the crumbling stone, the weed-choked gardens and brackish pond.

"It is a bit austere," Portia admitted. "It just needs a bit of work. A little repointing of the stone, rebuilding the east wing—"

"An exorcism."

She pushed me. "Don't be feeble. It could be a very nice house with some effort and a good deal of money. Brisbane could make a very nice home here."

Indeed he could, I reflected, but not one that I would ever live in.

"Portia, about Jane," I began.

She shook her head, and for an instant, the cool mask of self-possession slipped. Her anguish was so complete, so raw, it seemed like a trespass to look upon it. I dropped my eyes. "No, Julia. Jane has left for India. It is quite finished, and if I have to talk about it there is every chance I may never recover. Do you understand?"

I said nothing more. I whistled to Puggy and followed Portia inside, pulling my cloak more tightly about me as I entered and closed the door behind me.

THE NINETEENTH CHAPTER

Like a dull actor now,
I have forgot my part, and I am out,
Even to a full disgrace.
—William Shakespeare
Coriolanus

"Brisbane, you cannot live in this room with Morag tasting your food and Minna jumping like a hare every time there is a knock at the door. You must make a decision about Lady Allenby. This situation cannot go on indefinitely," I told him.

We were alone in his bedchamber two days later, after supper. Rosalie had returned to her cottage to collect some fresh supplies, while Portia was endeavouring to be kind to Ailith by spending the evening looking at her doll's house. Valerius had finally persuaded Hilda to let him begin work on a new henhouse for her little flock. Morag and Minna had agreed to leave Brisbane for the evening on the condition that I remain in his room at all times and surrender my post to Morag when he retired. She had laid a pallet across the doorway and intended to sleep there to guard him. Her devotion to him was beginning to alarm me.

He was still abed, but his nightshirt had been changed and he had grudgingly permitted Morag to shave him. He had a handkerchief pressed to his jaw.

"Am I still bleeding?" He pulled the handkerchief aside and I inspected the wound.

"Not much. But the one on your cheek has opened again. Here, let me," I said, taking the handkerchief and pressing it firmly against his cheek. "Why on earth you let Morag shave you is beyond my comprehension. She is singularly unsuited to the task."

"I was bored."

"Do not shrug. You've opened it again. Be still, and listen to me. You cannot leave matters indefinitely. Something must be done about Lady Allenby."

He touched my wrist, and I suppressed a shiver. "It will be. I have made arrangements already. When you were under Rosalie's sleeping draught, I dictated instructions to Minna, and Godwin took her to Howlett Magna to the telegraph. The matter will be out of my hands very soon."

I clamped my mouth shut, determined not to speak. My resolve did not last. "You were quite busy whilst I was out of the way. You mean to see her hang then? Brisbane, how could you? She is old and ailing. She might well be out of her mind, not in the sense that you or I might notice, but somewhere deep within. She cannot really have meant to kill you, not in the same fashion as a person who takes up a knife and stabs another to the heart. She mayn't even have meant to kill you at all," I pointed out, warming to my theme. "She might only have meant to make you ill and miscalculated how dangerous the mushrooms were. Or how many you would eat. You can be quite greedy when it comes to food, I've noticed. You ought to be more restrained. You could run to fat when you get old."

"Are you quite finished defending the woman who tried to murder me? You would make a delightful witness for the defence, you know." His lips were tight, but I did not believe he was entirely put out with me. I blotted at his face again.

"You're all right now." I handed him the handkerchief. "If there is nothing I can say to change your mind—"

I moved to the door, but before I could leave he gave a great sigh. "A convent. She is going to a convent. In Ireland. There is apparently some connection with the family. It was founded by an Allenby lady a thousand years ago or some such rot. In any event, I have sent to the mother house in Dublin, and a very discreet abbess replied that they would dispatch a pair of sisters from the convent to fetch her. They have even," he said, his lips twitching in what I assumed was amusement, "promised to pray for my soul in perpetuity for showing such compassion to an old woman who now has time to atone for her sins before she must stand in judgment before her Maker."

I hardly knew what to say. How like him to resolve the entire situation so neatly and so appropriately. And how like him to torment me a little before taking me into his confidence.

"When does she leave?"

"Tomorrow. I was naturally not inclined to spend any

more time than strictly necessary under the same roof as Lady Allenby once she confessed."

"Her poor daughters," I murmured. "They will be quite lost now."

Brisbane's expression turned thoughtful, but he said nothing.

I shook my head. "I still cannot quite take it in. That elegant old lady, willing to kill you."

Still he did not speak, but a muscle moved in his jaw, and I realised he was angry, far angrier than I had guessed.

"I would like to see her before she goes," I told him.

He nodded and Morag returned, effectively putting an end to our conversation. I left him then, his expression thoughtful and his eyes fixed on the view of the moor from the window.

The next morning after breakfast, I paid a visit to Lady Allenby. Mrs. Butters had told me she was still in her room, receiving no one. I gathered my nerve and tapped on the door, calling softly to her.

"Lady Allenby, it is Lady Julia. May I come in?"

She made no reply, but I opened the door and slipped in, closing it behind me. Lady Allenby was kneeling at her *prie-dieu*, her full skirts spread about her like a still pool of black water. Her rosary was clasped in her hands, and her lips were moving. Her gaze did not waver from the crucifix on the wall. I waited several minutes as her hands moved over the beads, counting them off one at a time.

At last she reached the end and crossed herself.

"I apologise," she said faintly. In spite of my horror of what she had done, I went to her and helped her to her feet. She gave me a grateful smile, only faintly tinged with cynicism.

"You are kind," she said, looping the rosary at her belt and regarding me closely. "You do not like me, and yet you help me. That speaks of the virtue of compassion. Something of the divine dwells in you, my child."

Already she spoke like a nun. She seated herself in a straight-backed chair and waved me to another opposite. I settled myself, feeling strangely awkward, as though I were a pupil summoned before an exacting headmistress. I tried to compose myself and remember why I had come.

"I do not think you came to gawk at the would-be murderess," she remarked softly. "Was there another purpose?"

I shook my head, wondering why I found the interview so difficult. She was in the wrong, and yet she had managed with a coolly superior look and a few choice words to make me feel entirely at fault.

She sighed, and when she spoke it was with exaggerated patience. "Do you want to know why I did it, or how? Life with him will be extraordinarily difficult, you know. It might suit you to know the method. Just in case you have need of it," she finished coldly.

I rose at once. "It was a mistake to have come," I told her, my tone as icy as hers. "I thought to understand you, but there is nothing to understand. I ought to have known you for what you were the day you told me about the bees. You were ruthless to them, and you were ruthless to Brisbane."

She curled her lip at me, scorn written in every line of her countenance. "My dear girl, now you know the true legacy of the Allenbys. Ruthlessness has always been our byword."

She began to laugh then, laughing until she wept, great, wracking sobs. She motioned angrily for me to leave her, and the sound of her weeping was still ringing in my ears when I left her.

I descended the stairs, intending to take a brisk walk across the moor to calm myself, but there was a stranger standing in the hall, a small travelling bag at her side. She was dressed in a plain black habit, the coif perfectly starched and blindingly white. I wondered vaguely how she had managed to keep herself so tidy on her travels.

"Sister?" I began, moving toward her. She had been looking about the panelled hall with great interest, but at the sound of my voice she turned, her eyes wide, her lips set in a half-smile.

"I rang the bell, but no one came. I thought no one would mind if I let myself in," she began.

"Think nothing of it," I assured her. "The master of the house, Mr. Brisbane, is still abed," I said, glossing lightly over the reason for her visit.

She nodded, the smile fading. "I am Sister Bridget," she said suddenly, thrusting out a hand. I took it, introducing myself and explaining briefly as I could that I was a friend of the new owner. Her hand was warm in mine, the palm hard and edged with calluses. It was a sturdy hand, formed by hard labour, and it suited her, for she was a tall, solid sort of woman. I doubted she spent her days singing in the chapel choir. This was a woman who served God literally, toiling in the fields or labouring in the kitchens, I decided.

"I hope you have not travelled alone, sister. I thought there was a pair of you coming to collect Lady Allenby."

The nun's eyes drifted up to the ceiling again, where pale shadows of crowned A's were barely visible overhead.

"Aye. Sister Dolores. She thought to stay in Lesser Howlett and let me come alone. She did not fancy a walk across the moor, and Godwin Allenby was kind enough to fetch me," she said with a faint smile.

Brisbane had given no instructions regarding the nun, and I was just wondering what I ought to do with her when Minna appeared.

"Mr. Brisbane said as the sister has arrived, if you would be good enough to show her into the great hall to wait, he will come," she said, bobbing curtseys at me and to Sister Bridget, to the nun's obvious amusement.

"He ought not to be up and about yet, but if I tell him so, he will only argue. Very well, Minna. Tell him we will await him there."

She scurried off and I turned, but Sister Bridget was already moving, looking about her with avid interest.

"It is a lovely house," I said, not quite truthfully, "but it has seen some difficult times lately. The furnishings are gone, but there is one relic of the family who built the place."

I nodded toward the mouldering tapestry on the wall. Sister Bridget gave a little intake of breath and went to it, putting out a fingertip to trace the lines of embroidery. She ought not to have, but it was not mine to protect, and truth be told, it was in sorry enough condition as it was. I wondered what would become of it now. I supposed Ailith and Hilda would live together in the Bear's Hut with Mrs. Butters, but I doubted there would be a wall in any cottage large enough to accommodate it.

"Moths have been at this," Sister Bridget said finally, touching a series of tidy little holes. "And likely the damp as well." She scraped a fingernail over the patch that had been picked out, pulling loose a tiny golden thread. She held it out to me, smiling.

"One gold thread. The only remnant of a lost girl," she said softly.

I blinked at her, comprehension dawning at last. "You are Wilfreda Allenby."

She smiled, and in her wide honest face, I saw none of the ruthless cunning of the Allenbys. They were nature's aristocrats, beautiful and merciless. This girl had kindness in her face and good humour, and I found her altogether more attractive than her far lovelier sister. She reminded me of Hilda, but there was a pleasantness to her countenance, a contentedness that spoke of satisfaction with her place in the world.

"I am," she said roundly. "And I think you know more about my family than a stranger might. Tell me quickly, is Mrs. Butters still here? I am gasping for a cup of tea and one of her little plum cakes."

I managed a nod. "I am sure she would be only too happy to provide you with refreshment. Forgive me, you've had a long journey. I ought to have offered straightaway."

She waved a hand. "It can wait a moment. I am too much a coward to leave this room quite yet."

With a rush of sympathy, I realised what she meant. She was at Grimsgrave to collect her mother to do penance for attempting a murder. That would have been difficult enough, but added to that was the strangeness of coming home after so many years away.

"How long has it been?" I asked her.

"Very nearly twenty years. That was why I came alone. Sister Dolores thought I ought to face my ghosts on my own. She is very wise."

"Did Godwin know you?"

"Oh, aye, he knew me well enough. I could not bring myself to ask him after my family. We talked rather a lot about sheep on our way here. I understand they are disappearing. They never did that in the old days." Sister Bridget gave me a smile then that was so sad, so wistful, I wondered how I could ever have thought her merry.

"Has it been so difficult then?"

She groped for her words, choosing them carefully. "Not always. Most of the time it has been peaceful. I have known real serenity, Lady Julia, and that has been a gift. I will not know it again. I had thought Grimsgrave and my family were in my past, and I find they are in my present as well. I will not make that mistake again. We are what we are, blood cannot be undone."

"Were you close to your family?"

She said nothing for a moment, and I wondered if I had offended her. But the wide, clear brow was furrowed slightly, and I realised she was thinking carefully.

"No, I do not believe that I was. We were never the ideal, you know. Never what one thinks a family ought to be. Father was always too busy carrying on with his magistrate's duties, making quite certain everyone followed the law to its strictest interpretation. Mother was distant—living in the past, I think, when the Allenby name meant something. We were kings, once upon a time, and for my mother, time has stood still. We were never permitted to make friends with the other children. We never even played with Godwin. We had only each other, and yet…"

She paused and I looked at her encouragingly.

"Have you brothers and sisters, Lady Julia?"

"Nine, actually."

The fair brows lifted. "Indeed. Then perhaps you will understand. Even amongst one's siblings, one can be entirely alone."

I thought of my place in the family as the youngest daughter. Only my brother Valerius was lesser, and yet he and I, who ought to have been allies, had often been at odds. I had known the close affection of Benedick and Portia, but some of the elder children were far removed from the nursery by the time I made my appearance. The eccentricity of my family had made it easy enough to justify holding them at arm's length when I was so inclined.

"I think so," I told her.

"It was that way for me. I was the eldest, and I was a disappointment. Both of my parents were certain I would be a boy, an heir for Allenby. And when Redwall was born, I was dispensable."

Such was the legacy of primogeniture upon the female psyche, I reflected bitterly.

"And when Ailith was born?"

"Oh, more disappointment, of course. They would have liked another son to secure the line, but she was so beautiful, even from birth. It was as if everything pure and lovely in the Allenby blood had been perfected in her. I never saw a more striking child, although truth be told, Redwall was extraordinarily handsome himself. Hilda was nothing but an

DEANNA RAYBOURN

afterthought. No one ever paid her much attention. I was the odd one out," she said with a wry smile. "With a peasant's face and a sturdy gait, always with an argument or a truculent mood. My mother despaired of ever making a lady of me. All I cared about were books. I thought for awhile that Redwall and I might be good friends because we shared a love of learning, but he had no use for me."

The words were spoken conversationally, with no regret, no bitterness. A simple recitation of facts that must have wounded her deeply at the time.

"The truth is Redwall was so obsessed with anything Egyptian. He simply could not be educated in any other subjects. Father ran off a dozen tutors for failing to teach him simple mathematics. He was a stubborn boy. I think being fussed over, having so much made of him as the heir, rather ruined his character. He was not always a pleasant child, and Ailith always followed where he led."

I thought of the mummified children hidden behind the chimney and wondered if Sister Bridget knew precisely how unpleasant her brother could be.

"He was given to playing pranks, and I am sorry to say, the tricks were usually cruel ones, at someone else's expense. He stole the note I left for Mama, explaining my decision to join a convent. He told her I had eloped with an artist."

"That is monstrous," I breathed.

Sister Bridget shrugged. "He did a dozen things worse, I am certain. He was angry that I left, that I was willing to reject the Allenby name and all that it stood for, and he wanted to hurt me. He thought that maligning my reputation would be the best way, but in truth, it was the only weapon he had. He could not harm me. I was in a convent. All he could do was spread gossip about me, and I was immune to his venom."

"But Lady Allenby, she must have been quite devastated. The thought of her daughter taking the veil might have given her some comfort. At least, the comfort of knowing you were safe and happy."

"Oh, Redwall would not have cared about that. He was angry with Mother because she would not give him the funds to go to Egypt. It was before he attained control of the estate, under the terms of Father's will. He was dependent upon Mother for everything then, and I think it galled him to have to ask for every last farthing. He was angry with her, angry with me. It was a rather efficient little revenge really."

"And has Lady Allenby never learned the truth? Even now?"

Sister Bridget shrugged. "I do not know. If Redwall confided in anyone, it would have been Ailith, and she would never have gone against his authority, even after his death."

"Why did you never tell Lady Allenby yourself? You might have written."

She gave a short, unpleasant little laugh. "My dear lady, you clearly did not know Redwall. He collected the post himself. He wrote to me once, and only once, to tell me what he had done and to assure me that it was futile to think of writing to Mother because she wanted nothing to do with me." She gave me an apologetic look. "I was younger then, and I believed him. I went to the head of my order for guidance, and she counselled me not to write, as thinking on my temporal family would only serve to interfere with my conventual life. For the most part I obeyed," she said with a wry little twist of the lips. "But once or twice I did send a letter, appealing to Redwall's better nature. Unfortunately, he did not have one."

I thought of the note in his diary about correspondence from *SB*. Sister Bridget, the sister who had renounced all material wealth and the legacy of the Allenby name.

"What a beastly young man," I said, forgetting for a moment that he had been her brother.

She smiled. "He had his moments. But you must recollect I intended to leave the world behind in any event. The convent was my home, and that was where attention must be paid."

I must have seemed dubious, for she touched my arm lightly.

"I would not have you think entirely ill of my brother. Redwall could be quite charming as well. And so generous. I remember once when I found a bird, a young pheasant with a broken wing, Redwall helped me to bring it home and care for it. When it died, I sobbed over it for days and Redwall promised to bury it for me, so that I should not have to do it myself. He saved me one beautiful feather from its plumage. And another time, when I was sent to bed without supper for some childish transgression, Redwall threw his own supper out the window, and Ailith's as well, and said if I did not eat, neither would they."

She leaned toward me, her tone conspiratorial. "I would have preferred if he had just shared his, but that was Redwall. He always liked a grand gesture, and Ailith was always so content to play the consort, pretty and docile and standing in the shadows. And poor little Hilda, always overlooked."

She sank into a reverie for a moment, and the silence stretched between us, comfortable and peaceful. After several minutes, she collected herself and smoothed her habit.

"I am sorry. I am unaccustomed to talking so much. It fatigues me, in a way I did not expect. I am responsible for the gardens at the abbey, and I often spend whole days in silent contemplation."

"What a lovely thought," I told her. "I will leave you now. Is there anything I can do to make you comfortable while you wait?"

She shook her head. "No, thank you. I would like only a little solitude, if that could be arranged. A few moments of contemplation would be most useful."

I nodded and went to the door. I lingered a moment as I pulled it closed, watching Sister Bridget, the prodigal daughter come home. She slid to her knees, but did not cross herself, and unlike her mother, she did not finger her rosary. Instead her eyes were fixed on the tapestry where her name had been so carefully unpicked until only a single golden thread remained to show she had ever been born.

I went to the kitchen to find Portia and Mrs. Butters chatting soberly over cups of tea. Ailith was nowhere to be found, and I took the opportunity to apprise the others of Sister Bridget's identity.

"Bless my soul," said Mrs. Butters, her face alight. She had been sunk in gloom since Lady Allenby's confession, but the prospect of seeing Sister Bridget roused her like the arrival of the prodigal son. "Miss Wilfreda come home. 'Tis like she were raised from the dead, like tha' fellow, oh, what were his name?" She frowned, drumming her fingers on the table.

"Lazarus?" Portia hazarded.

"Tha' is the one!" Mrs. Butters beamed. "You are clever,

my lady. Yes, indeed. I had thought her dead, I did, for many a year. What a turn it will give the mistress to see her alive again. And to go and live with her in the convent, I cannot imagine it."

"Yes, quite the coincidence," Portia remarked, arching a brow at me significantly. I gave a quick, sharp shake of the head to silence her, but I might not have bothered. Mrs. Butters was off again.

"Always loved my plum cakes, did Miss Wilfreda. I have just one put by in the larder. Oh, I must go and see to it. I left it a few days past now, and I do hope the moths have not got at it."

She hurried away and Portia blinked at me. "Moths? Isn't it too early for moths?"

"Portia, never mind about the moths." I darted a glance at the door. "You must meet her before she leaves. She is quite something. I spent quarter of an hour in her company and felt so peaceful, I think I might well join an order on the way back to London."

"I shall forward your post and adopt your pets, shall I?" my sister asked.

"Yes, and you may have all of my clothes," I told her generously.

Portia snorted. "Your clothes? I would sooner give them to Florence to use as birthing cloths."

"They were all made by *your* dressmakers," I reminded her, but she waved a hand and I lapsed into a sulky silence.

Just then Brisbane entered, fully dressed in a fine black coat and a black silk neckcloth wound tidily about his throat. His shirt was neatly buttoned, and although his hair would never be orderly, it was less tumbled than usual. He was paler than I would have liked, and there were new hollows carved beneath his cheekbones. He had lost weight through his ordeal, although I noticed his coat still tugged across the width of his shoulders.

"Where is she?" he asked without preamble.

"The old great hall, as you asked. She wanted a few moments of solitude, to pray I think. Brisbane, you ought to know, Sister Bridget was Wilfreda Allenby. She is Lady Allenby's eldest daughter."

"I know," he said, shooting his cuffs.

I stared at him, and Portia merely sipped at her tea, looking from me to Brisbane with avid interest. I think she smelled a quarrel brewing between us.

"Kindly explain," I directed him.

"I know Sister Bridget is Wilfreda Allenby," he said slowly. "I have known it for months. I traced her whereabouts some time ago and was already in communication with the abbess in Dublin. When it became necessary to remove Lady Allenby, it was a simple matter to arrange it."

My mouth was agape and he huffed an impatient sigh. "For God's sake, Julia, how do you think I managed to arrange this so quickly from a sickbed? I am a competent man, but I am no conjurer."

"How very clever you are," I said sweetly. "And how stupid of me not to have known, but then you take great delight in amusing yourself with my silliness, don't you, Brisbane?"

His lips tightened. "Julia Grey, I have no intention of quarrelling with you now. Nothing I have done was with the thought of making you feel foolish. In fact, nothing I have done has anything to do with you. Now I am telling you, leave it be."

He turned on his heel and stalked out. I turned to Portia, fairly sputtering in my rage.

"That is why I gave up men," she said ruefully. "They can be so very difficult."

"I was packing to leave when he fell ill," I confessed. "I was through with him, with his tricks and games, with all of it. I was quite shattered when I thought he would die. I thought it would change things. Clearly, it has not. I suppose I ought to leave now."

Portia tipped her head quizzically. "I thought there were mysteries afoot here? Questions unanswered? Puzzles undetected? You cannot really expect me to believe you would rather leave here, not knowing the truth."

I recognised the tone. She was cajoling, the way she had always done when she wanted something of me and suspected bullying would not work.

"Stop it, Portia. Don't you want to go back to London, too?"

She went white to the lips, but when she spoke, her voice was steady. "Not now. Jane is gone, Julia. Forever. I have nothing to hold me in London, and in fact, I rather think a diversion might be quite welcome at present."

"Portia," I murmured, reaching for her hand. She let me pet her a moment, then drew herself up briskly, tucking her emotions away.

"So, what is it to be? Shall we endeavour to sleuth about and lay some of the ghosts of Grimsgrave Hall, or shall we slink back to London like whipped dogs?" She thrust out her hand.

I pulled a face, but clasped her hand in mine to seal the

bargain. "Very well. We will stay until it is finished," I told her, not entirely happy about the arrangement. God only knew what fresh humiliations Brisbane could conjure for me. But knowing that I had meant to leave him gave me a little more power than I had had before. I made a mental note to keep my trunk packed in any event.

THE TWENTIETH CHAPTER

Sigh no more, ladies, sigh no more,
Men were deceivers ever,
One foot in sea, and one on shore.
—William Shakespeare
Much Ado About Nothing

The departure of Lady Allenby was accomplished with a great deal less excitement than I would have expected. Godwin had told Ailith and Hilda of their sister's arrival, and the ladies met in the entry hall where we had all assembled to bid farewell to Lady Allenby. Ailith embraced her sister with warmth, but Hilda greeted Bridget awkwardly, and I realised that they had not seen one another since Hilda was a young girl. It was a sober moment.

Valerius came to stand in the shadows next to Portia, and I took the place next to them. Mrs. Butters was weeping softly into her apron as her mistress descended the great carved staircase for the last time. Lady Allenby was dressed in one of her usual wide gowns of deepest black, a rosary at her belt. Ailith had packed for her, the smallest bag imaginable, with the few things she would need for the journey. Once at the convent, God and the good sisters would supply her needs.

To my astonishment, Brisbane himself had gone to fetch Lady Allenby from her room. I do not know what words they may have exchanged, only that she leaned heavily upon him as they moved down the stairs. When they reached the bottom, she turned to him, her impressive height bringing her very nearly eye-to-eye with him.

"You have shown me more compassion than I deserve, Nicholas Brisbane," she said, her imperious voice softened by something that sounded like gratitude. "One day, when you have need of it the most, and deserve it the least, God will repay you."

He gave her a short, sharp nod and in that instant she raised one gnarled hand to make a quick sign of the cross over his bent head.

She turned instantly, lifting her chin and surveying the rest of the assembled company. "Of the dark deeds done in this house, I say only this, that I am responsible, and I will spend the rest of my life atoning for them, and begging God's benevolent mercy upon my poor sinner's heart. And although God has no cause to listen to a transgressor whose failings are legion, I will pray for each of you in the long dark evening of my life."

The words were purest melodrama, but they seemed heartfelt, and oddly touching as well. As she passed, Lady Allenby gave each of us a brief nod, as if committing our faces to memory. It felt strange then, to know I would never see her again. In spite of what horrors she had perpetrated,

I felt a surge of pity for her, and I hoped that her convent would be a place of refuge and repentance for her.

She said nothing to her daughters. There was a sigh of recognition when she looked upon the plain, placid features of Sister Bridget, and I suspected Brisbane had told her of Wilfreda's return. She lingered a moment before Ailith and Hilda, her expression as sorrowful as the Christ before which she knelt each day, and I knew she must be grieving for how thoroughly she had failed them. She was leaving them adrift in the world whilst she found a safe haven in her Irish convent, and I wondered if she would ever forgive herself for that. And more to the point, if her daughters would.

Sister Bridget took charge of her then, and it was Ailith who shut the door behind them. Hilda, her complexion reddened from wind and emotion, dashed angry tears from her cheeks and turned to me as if to speak. But she turned instead and fled to the garden, slamming the door as she went. Valerius followed hard upon her heels, and I hoped she would take some comfort in his company. He was seldom tactful, but his intentions were always good.

Ailith said nothing. She merely shook her head sorrowfully and looked neither to the left nor right as she slowly ascended the stairs.

"Those poor girls," Portia breathed. "Whatever will become of them now?"

I shrugged. "They will go to live in the Bear's Hut with Mrs. Butters, and that will be the end of them."

That afternoon I walked across the moor to Rosalie's cottage. Portia stayed behind, pleading a headache, and I was secretly glad of it. I was eager for some fresh air and I wanted to talk to Rosalie alone. She opened the door before I even put my hand to the little gate in the stone wall, as if she had been expecting me.

"Good afternoon, lady," she said, stepping aside. The cottage was as tidy and cosy as ever, but I noticed her hearth-rug was empty. I mentioned it to her.

She gave a shrug. "Rook prefers Brisbane's company, so I let him go where he pleases. He may return, he may stay at the Hall. It is no matter."

I was glad she introduced the subject of Brisbane, for I had not yet fixed how to go about learning what I wanted to know.

"You were marvellous when he was ill," I told her. She gave me a fathomless, familiar look.

"I think we will need something stronger than tea for this chat, eh, lady?" She went to the beautifully painted cupboard and took out two tiny glasses, thin as paper and decorated with a design of Venetian gilt. She took out a bottle as well, dark green and felted with dust. When she had poured us each a glass of thick, amber liquid, she lifted hers to me in silent salute. I returned the gesture and sipped, gasping a little as the liquid slipped down like molten glass.

"What is this?" I asked when I recovered my breath.

"A mixture of my own making. Brandy, and a few other special things."

"Very tasty," I remarked, taking another sip, this one smaller and I took the time to roll it over my tongue, tasting honey and something more elusive.

She drained her glass and poured another for each of us,

then sat forward, resting her elbows on the gaily-printed tablecloth. "You've questions in your eyes. Ask them."

"I hardly know where to begin."

"At the beginning, child."

I took another sip, feeling its warm Dutch courage suffusing my bones. "When Brisbane was poisoned, Minna came to fetch me and I thought of the different means by which he may have come to harm. I thought of the mushrooms of Lady Allenby and Godwin's arsenic for dipping the sheep. And I thought of your poppy-red syrup, and I had no way of knowing which of the three of you might have wanted him dead."

"You took a chance," Rosalie said. "You are bold, Lady Julia."

"I was not bold," I confessed. "I was terrified. I knew if I made the wrong choice, he would die. It was that simple. And I chose you, without even knowing why. Until later, when I had long hours full of dreamless sleep, and I woke knowing what I ought to have pieced together before."

I paused and she looked at me expectantly, her mouth curved into a faint smile.

"I chose you because I knew you would never harm your own kin. Brisbane is your nephew, isn't he?"

The smile deepened. "He is. My poor little *chavvo*. Not quite a Gypsy, not quite a *gorgio*. When he was a child it made him very bitter. He used to say he would never fit into either man's world, neither the Gypsy's nor the *gorgio's*. And I always told him it was because neither of those worlds was big enough to hold him. I taught him that he carried what was best of both inside him, and to be proud of what he was. Or I tried," she finished with a sigh. "His mother, she was not so kind to him. I have never known another woman so beautiful as my sister. But neither was there a woman as cruel as Mariah Young. She was many years older than I was, the eldest of our mother's children, while I was the youngest. I was fifteen when he was born, and his mother wept and cursed him for being the son of a faithless man. Do you know about Black Jack Brisbane?"

"Good Lord, he sounds like a pirate."

"He was no better. He took what did not belong to him, usually women. They came willingly, make no mistake, for he was the handsomest man I have ever known. Quite a match in looks for Mariah, and in temper. They were a tempestuous couple. They never lived together for more than two months running. Always the fighting, the screaming, the throwing of dishes and breaking of chairs. Always Mariah ran away and Jack would bring her back. Her brothers and cousins learned not to interfere. My own husband, John-the-Baptist, still carries a scar upon his neck from coming between them."

"Jack stabbed him?" I breathed.

"Mariah," she corrected with a grim nod. "Jack had been choking her, and John-the-Baptist thought to impress me with his bravery. We were not married then, but he thought I was pretty," she recounted with a tiny smile. "He jumped into the fray and pulled Jack off of her. And quick as a cat, Mariah went for *him*, cutting him with the blade she carried in her skirt."

She gave me a stern look. "Whatever *gorgios* say of us, you must believe that we are not all like that. We are a passionate people, but we do not like to fight. We are peaceful and loving, but Mariah was always the devil's child, and Jack was just the same. They were alike as brother and sister, the same faults, the same witch-black hair and the same peculiar way of looking right through a person. I always wondered if Black Jack's mother was quite a lady, or if perhaps she had had an indiscretion with a travelling tinker," Rosalie said with a meaningful lift of her eyebrows.

"In any event, by the time Nicholas was ten, he had had enough. His father tired at last of Mariah's tricks and left them for good, and Nicholas had taken a lifetime of abuse from his mother. He did what any good Roma does when the welcome is a cold one. He packed his little bundle and he struck out on a new road and he did not look back. It was many years before I saw him again, years of loss and pain, for both of us."

I waited, and she went on, speaking more to herself than to me. "They say the Roma came from Egypt, and that is why they are called Gypsies, that we came dancing out of the pharaoh's lands, summoning our luck with magic spells and telling fortunes in teacups. That is a faery story for children. Even we do not know where we come from, but the Sight is a true gift, one that has been handed down for centuries, and for as long as the women of the Young family have travelled this isle, there have been those of the blood who knew things before they came to pass. Mariah was one of those. I was never blessed with the gift, but Mariah was exceptional. She could tell a woman was quick with child before she had even missed her courses. She could watch the way the moonlight fell on a man's face and know he would die within a fortnight, and she passed her gift to Nicholas, the first male of our line ever to have the Sight."

"He fights it," I told her. "I have watched him struggle against it. He thinks—I don't know—that it is superstition or something out of a story to frighten children with. He does not see it for the gift it is."

"Many do not," Rosalie pointed out. "Can you imagine what it must be, to know things before they happen, and yet so often be powerless to stop them?"

"He is not powerless," I argued. "He could do a great deal of good if he only accepted the visions and acted upon them. Instead he fights them with all of his might, ending up with migraines so ferocious he doses himself with all sorts of monstrous things. I have seen him take absinthe and hashish, and God knows what else, all because he will not admit what he really is."

"And what is he?" Rosalie prodded gently.

"The most extraordinary, maddening man I have ever known," I said, feeling exhilarated and a little deflated at the same time.

"And you believe that just because you are willing to accept him for what he is, that others will be as broad-minded?"

I opened my mouth, then snapped it shut. "Of course not. You are quite right. They would clap him in an asylum the first time he tried to tell anyone what he saw. I am a fool."

She shook her head, the golden coins at her ears glinting in the light. "Not a fool. A woman in love, and that is a very near thing."

"Am I so very obvious?"

She was kind enough not to laugh.

"Thank you for not answering," I said with a touch of asperity.

We fell silent a moment and I was struck by how companionable it was. We were from very different worlds, Rosalie Smith and I, but we were kindred spirits.

"How did you know I was his aunt?" she asked finally.

I shrugged. "The initials on your knife. RY. I thought it stood for Yolande or some other second name, but then I realised it might well be your maiden name, Young. And then Godwin actually referred to you as Rosalie Young. I did not pay it mind at the time, but I thought of it later."

She nodded. "I have known him since boyhood. He used to bring his pets to me to nurse them back to health."

I shook my head. "I still cannot imagine that you have lived here so long."

"Ever since Mariah died," she said softly. "John-the-Baptist married me even though he knew I would never travel with him, not so long as Mariah's boy was out there, lost in the world, with none of his kin to know him."

I stared at her, scarcely comprehending what she had just said. "You have been here since Brisbane ran away? He ran away from here?"

"We were camped out on this very moor, just below Thorn Crag. Sir Alfred hated the Gypsies on his land, but he liked to keep us where he could watch what we did. He thought we would behave better under his thumb," she told me, her eyes slanting maliciously. "We made more trouble here than any other two places combined. But Nicholas was not happy. He left here, running away, and Mariah went out of her head. There were legal troubles and she died of a broken heart. There was no one left to wait for him. The chemist had died and this cottage was vacant. Sir Alfred agreed to rent it to John-the-Baptist and me, provided we marry in the church. We did, and I told John-the-Baptist to go on. I knew he could never leave the road, and I could not leave this place, not so long as there was a chance that Nicholas would come back and need to find his people."

I swallowed hard against the lump in my throat. It was perhaps the most extraordinary tale of sacrifice I had ever heard. I only wondered if Brisbane appreciated it.

"Did you never see him then? Not until he came to Grimsgrave in January?"

"Bless you, of course I did. He has come before, a dozen times since he was grown. He found me when he was barely twenty, and he insisted upon paying for the rent on this cottage himself, although if you ask him, he will deny it. He has been good to me."

"But if he found you, why didn't you join John-the-Baptist and the rest of your family on the road? Why do you still live here, in such isolation?"

Her gaze slanted again, this time with all the Byzantine mystery of her people. "Because my destiny is not yet done here, lady. I am called to stay until the earth itself moves and gives up her dead. That was the last prophecy Mariah ever uttered, and I will remain until it is done."

The words chilled me, and although we moved on to speak of other things, pleasant, harmless things, my blood did not warm again until I left her.

THE TWENTY-FIRST CHAPTER

When a world of men
Could not prevail with all their oratory,
Yet hath a woman's kindness overruled.
—William Shakespeare
Henry VI, Part 1

When I had taken the turning at the crossroads toward Grimsgrave Hall, I paused to
look back across the moor, and just then
caught the faint toll of the Grimswater bell.

Without thinking, I set off across the moor toward the
black lake, heedless of the prickly furze and heather, striding
over the spongy ground.

"Julia!" Behind me I heard Brisbane's voice, carried on the
wind. He was only a dozen paces behind me, and before I
could reply he was upon me. I waved him to silence, but it
was too late. The bell had quieted.

"Bother!" I muttered, puffing out a sigh of frustration. I turned to Brisbane. "Did you hear it?"

"Did I hear what?" he asked, his gaze sweeping the empty horizon.

"The bell," I told him, my voice edged with impatience. "The one that lies beneath the waves of Grimswater. You must have heard it."

Brisbane shrugged. "What bell? Julia, you must have heard the moor wind. It can play tricks upon the ears."

"There is a village buried under Grimswater," I told him. "There is a bell there that tolls when an Allenby is to die. Surely you've heard of it," I finished.

I turned to set off again toward Grimswater, but Brisbane took my arm and spun me round.

"I am not interested in local superstition, and I did not trouble myself to walk all this way to chase after imaginary bells," he said sharply. He paused for breath, and I realised the long walk had tired him. He was still recovering from the poisoning, and I ought to have had a care for his health, I chided myself. I was even generous enough to overlook his pointed reference to "imaginary" bells.

"Of course. Shall we walk back together? We could take it quite slowly, in stages, if you like?" I offered.

He shot me a nasty look. "Oh, and then will you tuck me up in bed and feed me rice pudding? I am not an invalid, Julia. I am perfectly fine, only a bit fatigued."

I bit off the sharp reply that rose to my lips. I had seen him suffer the effects of ill health often enough to know that he bore infirmity with even less grace than most men.

"Then let us by all means stand out here on a freezing cold moor and discuss world events," I said sweetly.

He glowered a little, but came straight to the point. "I want you to continue to work in the study. You have the catalogue, but it must still be compared to the present collection to see if any pieces are missing. I will require a proper catalogue when I go to sell it."

"I do not think I want to help you." I raised my chin a little, making a point of looking over his shoulder at nothing in particular.

"Don't be stubborn. You look quite mulish and that is never an attractive trait in a woman."

I resisted the urge to put out my tongue at him, and sighed instead. "Brisbane, why must we always quarrel like children? You are the most impossibly arrogant man I have ever known."

He looked genuinely surprised at my remark. "I would not seem arrogant if you occasionally did as you were told," he said mildly, stroking the dark shadow of a beard at his chin. He had been clean-shaven when he had groomed himself to meet Sister Bridget. I supposed he needed to shave twice a day if he meant to be really tidy.

"Have I ever given you reason to believe I was the sort of woman who would do as she was told?"

"You did once," he told me, his impenetrable black gaze fixed on my face. "When I first met you, you were a quivering little mouse. You did precisely as you were instructed, and I thought you were the dullest woman I had ever met."

I laughed and he nodded. "You have changed. Once upon a time you would have flown at me for making that observation."

"I am older now," I said.

His expression was thoughtful. "No, it isn't just that. Do you remember when you wanted to embark upon that first investigation and I warned you it would change you forever? You have seen death now and evil, and the ways it can twist a soul into something unrecognisable. There was something childlike about you when our paths first crossed. I feel as though I murdered that girl with my bare hands," he said finally, a faint edge of bitterness cutting through his words.

I put a hand to his sleeve. "I did not want to be that girl any longer. I was sleepwalking through my own life, didn't you know that? I wasn't happy. I wasn't unhappy. I scarcely even existed. I did not really care about anything, least of all myself. Now I feel alive every moment. I care for everything, and right now," I said, warming to my theme, "I care for Ailith and Hilda Allenby."

He raised a brow, but I hurried on before he could speak. "I know Hilda has been rude and Ailith is rather vague, and I know your dislike of the Allenbys runs deep, but I am asking you, please, give the collection back to them. They have nothing, they are nothing. Their own mother was taken today for attempting an unspeakable crime, and they will never see her again."

I stepped closer still, my hand tightening on his arm. "You showed compassion to Lady Allenby in letting her retire to a convent. I am only asking the same for her daughters."

A tiny smile played over his lips as he glanced down at my hand. "Do you mean to win me over with feminine wiles? I must admit it is a more diverting notion than your usual method of screaming at me like a fishwife."

I did not rise to the bait. I simply looked at him. "Please."

He caught his breath, a slow smile warming his features. "My God, you are trying to seduce me."

"I am not," I said primly. "I am merely trying to get your attention."

He bent swiftly and kissed me hard, pulling back so suddenly I nearly toppled over. "I believe I have already made it quite clear that you have my attention."

He strode past me then down the path toward Rosalie's cottage. I was still gaping after him when he turned back, his hands thrust in his pockets like a schoolboy.

"Oh, and the reason I came to find you was to ask you to finish cataloguing the collection for Ailith and Hilda. They will want the sale completed as quickly as possible. They will need money to furnish the Bear's Hut."

I could not speak. I simply stared, openmouthed as he gave me a wink and went on his way, whistling a bit of Paganini as he went.

When I returned to Grimsgrave, I hung my cloak upon the peg and went in search of my sister. I found her in the maids' room, crouched over a panting Florence, very much in Godwin's way as he crooned to the little dog. They had arranged her in a snug box with a nice warm blanket and placed her near the fire. On the bed, Mr. Pugglesworth was lying on Morag's pillow, snoring wetly.

I motioned to Portia to join me in the bedroom, gesturing for her to close the connecting door.

"Anytime now, Godwin says," she told me. "We shall be aunties. Or I suppose you will be a grandmother," she amended, regarding me curiously.

I narrowed my eyes at her. "So would you," I told her tartly.

"Oh, I hadn't thought of that! I suppose I ought to buy them presents then. Perhaps little collars?" She looked more cheerful than I had seen her since her return, and it occurred to me that it might be a very good notion to keep her too busy to dwell on Jane's departure.

"That would be lovely, I am sure. But what is Godwin doing here? It is wildly inappropriate, you know."

She rolled her eyes at me. "Honestly, Julia. Have you no sense of *occasion*? I do not know the first thing about whelping pups, do you?"

"No," I admitted. "But all of our dogs pupped in the stables. I imagine the grooms took care of matters."

"And so Godwin will for us," she promised. "He is extremely knowledgeable about animals, you know. He is a trifle worried that Florence might be too small to deliver them safely. Puggy is rather plump."

I was astonished. It was the first critical word I had ever heard out of Portia regarding Mr. Pugglesworth.

I heard a little yip then and I cringed. "I cannot look. Go and help him if he needs anything. And, Portia," I called after her, "tell him to do what he can for her. I have grown rather fond of the little horror."

She nodded, her expression serious as she slipped into the adjoining room. There were various scufflings and moist noises and in the end I could not bear the suspense. I fled the room, determined to be useful elsewhere.

I had no desire to see Morag—I dreaded telling her about her pillow to begin with—so I went to the study instead. I thumbed through the official catalogue, the one Brisbane had kept hidden beneath his bed. It was a comprehensive document. It described each of Redwall's purchases, the entries inscribed in his own hand in excruciating detail. Everything was there, date of purchase, dealer's name, the date and condition of arrival. It made for surprisingly fascinating reading. I recognised many of the entries straight off, greeting them as old friends. There was a statue of Thoth, the ibis-headed god and judge of the dead. Then a pair of vases, alabaster and gracefully curved as a maiden's hip.

I thumbed a few more pages, idly perusing the entries. The bulk of them dated to the years between 1866 and 1885 when he had been travelling, mostly in Egypt it seemed, although he had apparently been willing to travel quite far afield to secure a purchase. His journeys were carefully noted, some to Paris, others to Morocco, even one to America. Anywhere his beloved antiquities were likely to turn up, Redwall Allenby had been there.

"Little wonder he frittered away a fortune," I murmured. Granted he had travelled to many inexpensive destinations; one could live far more cheaply in Paris than in London, for instance, and it was customary for gentlemen in need of retrenchment to go abroad to live. But many of his destinations had been so remote, it must have cost him the earth to get there, to say nothing of the expense of shipping his purchases home.

And all the while, there was the upkeep of Grimsgrave to be settled as well, although it was apparent he had neglected that particular duty shamefully. If even a quarter of his expenses as a collector had been put into the house, it might even now be able to pay its way, and need never have been sold, I reflected.

Or was that what Redwall Allenby had wanted all the while? It was a horrible but intriguing thought. He had spent freely, profligately even, and no man in his right mind could have mistaken the rapid, inevitable shift from one column to the other in the ledgers. His estate had been decimated, and since it was not entailed, he must have realised it was his to do with as he pleased. The sale of it, even as a ruin, would have brought him thousands of pounds of capital. Had that been his scheme all along? To spend his liquid assets, and then begin on the estate itself? I wondered how long the proceeds of the estate would have lasted him if he meant to live on them. And what was the point in assembling such a massive and comprehensive collection without the house to display it?

I rubbed at the spot between my brows, feeling a headache gathering behind my eyes. I had been squinting at Redwall's handwriting for too long in uncertain light. There were delicious smells wafting from the kitchen, and my stomach gave an indelicate rumble. I made to close the ledger, but as I did, an entry I had not noticed caught my eye on account of its brevity. It was early on in the ledger, under the heading for 1886, shortly after Redwall returned to England.

17 February: Two caskets of natron have arrived from source. That was all. No mention of who the source might be, nor from whence the natron came. I thought quickly, remembering from one of the volumes I had perused that natron was a natural salt, found in the Wadi Natrum in Egypt. Its only use was mummification.

I sat back in the chair, clasping the ledger to my chest. It was unthinkable, and yet I was thinking it. *The mummified babies in the priest's hole.* It was possible, I thought, with a sudden sick twist in my gut.

I had to find the natron, I decided. That was the first, logical step. If the natron was still here, both barrels full, I must be wrong, and I would thank God on my knees for it.

Just as I rose Brisbane entered, his hair windblown from coming across the moor, dark crescents shadowing his eyes. He took one look at my stricken face and came straight to the point.

"What is the trouble?"

I put out my hand with the ledger. "Natron. He ordered two barrels of it from an unnamed source two years ago."

I said nothing more; I did not need to. Brisbane scrutinised the ledger, then drew in a deep, shuddering breath.

"We must search for the natron," he said finally. "If it is intact—"

"Then Redwall Allenby did not make a habit of mummifying babies," I finished. He gave me a grudging nod.

"Precisely. We will search after supper if you are up for it," he said, his tone lightly mocking.

"I am perfectly well, thank you," I told him, although in truth I was feeling rather wilted and longed for my bed. A good plate of supper and a few strong cups of tea would restore me, I promised myself. And a stiff whisky.

We separated then to wash for supper, and I went to look

in on my pups. I tapped lightly at the door and Godwin opened it, looking a bit the worse for wear. His hair was standing out around his head in great gold tufts and his expression was jubilant.

"Four strong, healthy pups," he told me. "All born alive, and all taken to the teat," he announced proudly.

"Indeed?" I said, my voice a trifle faint. "How splendid."

"Aye, an ugly bunch, but charmers all the same," he said. He stepped back so I could peek at them. They were all nestled against Florence, nursing happily while she looked down at them with a faintly embarrassed expression. They were ugly, I admitted to myself. They mixed Puggy's protuberant eyes and lumpy head with Florence's long nose and skinny legs. It was not a prepossessing combination, but they were winsome in spite of it.

Portia entered then waving several lengths of silk ribbon.

"I've brought yellow for the girls and this lovely green stripe for the boy," she announced. Godwin guffawed and I gave her a repressive look.

"I rather think we could see the difference without ribbons," I pointed out. She ignored me and began to tie a pretty bow at each pup's neck.

I turned to Godwin. "Thank you for your help. I am really very grateful. You must choose a pup for your own if you would like one to keep."

His blue eyes danced merrily. "Would I not? There is nothing grander than a new wee pup in the house." He nodded toward the fattest of the lot, a peculiar mottled thing with fur that managed to be black, brown, and white at the same time.

"I'll have tha' lad there, if you don't mind," he told me. Portia tweaked its bow, shooting me a dark look as she did so.

"Excellent choice," I told him. "You may have him as soon as he is weaned." Portia grumbled a little, and I fancied then I knew what ailed her.

Godwin tugged his forelock then, in his mischievous little gesture of respect and took his leave. I turned to Portia. "I mean to keep one myself to keep Florence company, and you ought to have one for Puggy."

She brightened instantly. "I cannot decide," she announced. "Of course, Godwin took the biggest and the only male, but this one here has the prettiest markings. Isn't she lovely? Or perhaps this one?" She was asking questions, but expected no answers, and I was grateful. There were too many questions to answer at present, and the most horrible of them was whether or not Redwall Allenby had done something unspeakable to a pair of infants in the name of science.

THE TWENTY-SECOND CHAPTER

Upon such sacrifices, my Cordelia,
The gods themselves throw incense.
—William Shakespeare
King Lear

The evening was a strained one for conversation. Godwin tried his best to talk of pleasant things, but Hilda would have none of it. She merely curled her lip at him and took the first reasonable opportunity to escape to her room. Valerius watched her go, his expression thoughtful as he worked on the plans for the henhouse, labouring with a pencil and rubber over the same drawing until it was sprawling and grubby. Portia prattled on about the puppies and kept dashing upstairs to peek at them. Brisbane was unusually quiet as was I, and I fancied we were both thinking of the coffin lying in the priest's hole. As soon as the clock struck the hour, we made our excuses to each other, and even Godwin seemed pleased to make an early evening of it.

I looked in on Portia and the pups and listened to Morag grumble for a full ten minutes about her room being turned into a puppy nursery. I appeased her by promising her my pillow in exchange for her nasty one and hastened back downstairs. In the short time I had been upstairs, Brisbane had managed quite a lot. As there was little room to manoeuvre in the study, he had given up part of his bed-chamber for our task. The writing table had been swept clean of paper, pens, inks, and blotters, and in their place was a clean sheet and a few instruments, the looks of which I could not like. There were wickedly sharp scissors, blades, hooks, and something that looked like a double-headed corkscrew. I only hoped we would not have need of it.

For lighting he had gathered as many lamps as he could find and stoked up the fire, with the effect that the room was uncomfortably warm. To offset this, he had opened a window to the cold evening air.

He was just bringing in the coffin when I arrived. He did not greet me, but placed it carefully atop the sheet and dis-appeared back into the study for a moment, returning with a notebook and pencil.

"I locked the door," he said in reply to my questioning look. "I thought it best if we were not interrupted."

I nodded and took the notebook. The entire affair was putting me painfully in mind of the occasion upon which Brisbane and I had conducted an informal post-mortem together. He had been recovering from his bullet wound at the time, and I had had to function as his hands. The memory of it still chilled me.

"I'll take notes, shall I?" I asked brightly.

Brisbane had already stripped off his coat and waistcoat and loosened his collar, dropping his discarded neckcloth over the end of the bedstead. He was folding back his cuffs, baring strong brown wrists when he noticed I was staring at him. I ducked my head instantly and began to scribble nonsense into the notebook.

"You have seen me often enough without my shirt. I did not think it would distress you to watch me take off my waistcoat," he remarked, tucking the cuffs into neat points.

"I am not disturbed, and you are quite right. I have seen altogether too much of you," I retorted, still not daring to raise my eyes.

In fact, it had disturbed me, but not in the sense he thought. My husband had never disrobed in front of me, and the times I had seen Brisbane without his shirt—and there had been several—I had come upon him already disrobed. I had never been a witness to the slow, graceful gestures, the unveiling of solid male flesh like a glorious statue being revealed for the first time.

With an Herculean effort, I pulled my thoughts back in line and stepped a little closer to the cool breeze from the window.

"Are you sure you can see properly from there?" he asked.

"Oh, yes, perfectly," I lied. I made a hasty sketch of the coffin while he removed the lid and laid it aside. When I was done I held it out at arm's length to gauge its likeness and decided it looked more like a loaf of bread than a coffin. I sighed and turned to a fresh page.

Brisbane was bending over the coffin, inspecting the little remains carefully. I crept closer as he leaned nearer still, running his gaze over every inch of the tiny, linen-wrapped bodies. He put a hand into the coffin and slid it under the first child.

"I shall lift the body out and I want you to hold it while I look underneath."

"Why can't you simply put it down on its face?"

"Because I do not wish to damage it further. There may be some clue in the wrapping, and I would like to at least make a cursory examination. Now hold out your arms."

"No," I said stepping backward. "I won't."

He flicked one quick glance of those imperious witch-black eyes at me. "Yes, you will. Now put down that note-book and take the child."

I made a rapid calculation. Either Brisbane and I could stand and argue for some minutes and I would end up holding the child, or I could capitulate now and save us both the time and aggravation.

I dropped the notebook and held out my arms. He laid the child gently in them, and I felt a queer, sick lurch in my stomach. He went onto his knees and peered up at the underside of the mummy.

"Oh, do hurry, Brisbane. It is awful," I murmured.

To his credit, it was but a moment before he relieved me of the grisly burden and replaced it onto the table. He gave me an odd look, but said nothing.

We spent the next several minutes examining the linen wrappings and the tuft of blond hair at the top.

"I must know for sure," he said finally. "The lozenge pattern of the wrappings is one I have never seen before. I think whoever prepared this child for burial created it, and there may be other clues as well if there are the usual amulets inside the wrappings."

The next half hour was one of the most gruesome of my life. Each layer of linen had to be carefully unwrapped, every inch of the fabric scrutinised for clues to the child's identity. I knew what Brisbane and I both suspected, and I knew how desperately I wanted to be wrong. Inch by inch, layer by layer, the linen was unrolled. It gave up a pair of amulets, a peculiar knotted image and an animal, both fashioned of gold.

Brisbane held them up to the light. "It is a *tyet,*" he said. "The Knot of Isis. Common enough."

He passed it to me, and I saw a resemblance to a few pieces I had seen in Redwall's collection already. Brisbane laid the other aside and proceeded with the unrolling.

I scarcely dared to look now, but I could not betray my squeamishness a second time. It was oddly out of character for Brisbane to invite me to participate in an investigation with such good humour; I was not going to let him regret it.

"At last," he said softly, lifting the last bit of linen free and laying it aside. What remained was barely human. It was clearly a perfectly formed child, born at its full gestation, or very nearly. There was no deformity, no violence upon it, save for the damage inflicted by the rotting coffin. The rest was grotesque, yet oddly peaceful. There was something timeless about the tiny face, a nobility I would not have believed possible. The skin was perfectly dried and stretched taut over its features, giving it the look of some ancient deity come to rest in a faraway land. I could not take my eyes from it.

Brisbane looked away for a moment, then at me, his jaw hardening into an expression I knew quite well.

"This mummy is not ancient," he said flatly. "I would put it at perhaps two years, and likely less."

I said nothing for a long moment, wishing he was wrong, and knowing he was not.

"I knew he was a devil, but even I would not have thought him capable of this," he said, his voice thick with anger.

"You are quite certain about the age of the mummy?"

He gave me a vicious look and I waved him off. "Very well. You are certain."

"Yes, I am," he returned coldly. "Those wrappings were no ancient pattern. The amulets are wrong, and there is no heart scarab, not even a place where one ought to have been. And even if the mummy were not wrong for an Egyptian, it is quite wrong for four thousand years ago. Look at the skin, Julia. It is barely dried. Look at the hair. It is bright gold. *Gold.* Not a colour one usually associates with Egyptians, as you pointed out to me."

"I know," I said, spreading my hands. "I just wish you were wrong. I wish I did not know that a man could be capable of such things."

Brisbane dropped his head, his hands braced on the table. After a deep, shuddering breath, he looked at me, his eyes on a level with mine. "Men are capable of every evil. I should have thought you would know that by now."

"It is one thing to know it intellectually. It is entirely another to see a dead child that has been butchered for someone's amusement," I snapped.

We were both breathing hard, angry and disgusted, and perfectly willing to take out our bad tempers upon one another.

"I do not know it," I said finally. "I thought I did. I thought

I understood evil after the last two investigations. This is some new wickedness I could never have imagined. You don't think he killed them deliberately?" I asked, still clinging to the hope that Redwall might not be quite the monster I feared.

To my relief, Brisbane did not laugh. "No, this child was dead when the mummification was begun. There are no other signs of violence. It is likely it died of natural causes."

"How do you—never mind. I do not want to know," I amended hastily. "But if he did not kill them, where did he get them?"

Brisbane shrugged. "If we want to know that, we must examine the other child." He gave me a sharp, searching look. "Are you up to it? You went quite white when I handed you the first."

"I am perfectly fine," I told him. "Go and get the other." He took me at my word and turned to retrieve the other mummy, and I was glad. If he questioned me further, I might have told him that when he had put the mummified child into my arms, all I could think was that the first time he had laid a baby in my arms it was a cold, dead, lifeless monster. It had not seemed a good omen for any happiness between us.

The examination of the other body yielded little more information, save one interesting fact: the children appeared to be twins. They were remarkably identical in appearance, even after enduring so invasive and grotesque a procedure as mummification. One was a boy, one a girl, but their features were astonishingly similar, and both had the same curling, gilt hair, and each was missing a lock, shorn close to the head, to what purpose we could not say. The second child had been buried with the same amulets, wrapped in the same pattern. There was no doubt they had been mummified by the same hand, and it seemed certain whose hand it must have been, particularly as there was not a speck of natron to be found in the study. We turned over bowls and peered into baskets and barrels, but nothing remained of the preservative salts Redwall Allenby had ordered.

When we had put the study back to rights, Brisbane laid the babies out carefully next to one another for purposes of comparison. The amulets were arranged next to them, identical golden talismans, the Knot of Isis and the other, a stylised animal I could not identify. I put a fingertip to one of them gingerly.

"What animal is this meant to be? Some sort of livestock," I hazarded.

"A ram," Brisbane said grimly.

"A ram?" I straightened, my mind racing. "You don't suppose this could be some sort of clue?"

"In what way?" he asked, studying the children's heads closely.

I smothered a sigh, irritated that he could not tear himself away to give a moment's consideration to my idea. "We believe Redwall mummified these children. The question is where did they come from? Whose children are they? And I am suggesting that those amulets might present us with a starting point."

I had his attention now. He looked up from the tiny blond heads and gave me a shrewd glance.

"As a joke on Redwall's part? Or something else?"

"Who knows? Perhaps he paid for the children's corpses and did not like to leave them completely unidentified after he had conducted this monstrous experiment. If it was an experiment," I fretted.

"It was." Brisbane spoke with perfect confidence. "He wrote several articles on the subject for various Egyptological periodicals. He had a mania for the subject. He was extremely well-informed, and made quite a name for himself before he was twenty. All of his writings were limited to the rituals of embalming and mummification. I believe he began with a snake. The last article he published was about a cat he had successfully mummified. It was only a matter of time before he moved on to humans."

"That is revolting."

"That is science," he returned, nodding toward me meaningfully.

"If you are referring to my brother's experiments, I can only point out that Valerius has aspirations to becoming a physician. And *his* patients have all been willing to be butchered, unlike these poor babies," I finished, wilfully overlooking the fact that I had once suspected my own brother of graverobbing to support his studies.

Brisbane was considering the mummies thoughtfully. "So let us suppose Redwall decides to take the next obvious step in his studies of Egyptian embalming. He brings home from Egypt an embalmer's kit, orders natron, and is wise enough to conceal his source, even in his own journal. He has only to find the babies."

"Why babies?" I put in suddenly.

"They are smaller, quicker to embalm. And he could

handle them by himself. It takes at least two men to mummify a fully-grown man."

"No, why *babies?* As in more than one," I asked again. "Why two of them? Why not just one?"

Brisbane shrugged. "For purposes of comparison, I presume. Take two infants of the same age and subject them to the same procedures. Store them for a certain period of time, then unroll them and see which has survived intact and figure out why. Perhaps he altered the formula slightly between them. Embalmers in ancient Egypt devised their own compounds of resins and aromatics to use upon the dead. If Redwall was attempting to perfect the art of embalming, it would have served him very well to use two formulae and compare the results."

"True," I said slowly, still fitting the pieces together. "But that leaves us with the question of where the babies were procured. Let us assume he did as you suggested and embalmed the children as some sort of hideous experiment. He would need a secure place to store the bodies for a fixed period of time—years, I imagine."

Brisbane nodded. "Certainly. I should think at least a decade if he was quite serious about determining the rate of decay. Longer, if possible."

"And what would have happened to Redwall if the mummies were found before he had an opportunity to conclude his experiment? Presumably he would have unrolled them, recorded his results, and then buried them secretly somewhere. He could not simply leave them tucked away behind the chimney forever."

"Yes, he could have," Brisbane argued. "You only found

them by chance. They might have lain there undisturbed for years yet. His death was untimely. He had no reason to suspect he wouldn't have years left to finish the experiment."

"But what would have happened to him if they had been found prematurely? By someone who would have turned him over to the authorities?" I demanded.

"Putting aside the fact that Redwall Allenby himself was the magistrate, if the mummies had been discovered in his possession, he might have been charged with graverobbing."

"Not a serious offence in and of itself, but devastating to his family. Think of the scandal."

"I think the Allenbys believe they are above scandal," he said slowly. "But I confess I am intrigued. Carry on."

"Redwall would have known he was taking a risk in keeping the children here. What if he left some means of identifying the parents upon the children as a way of proving he did not actually kill them?"

"You think the parents turned them over to him willingly?"

I spread my hands. "How else could he have acquired them? The corpses of twin stillborn babies are not exactly littering the roadsides, Brisbane. Either a desperate and impoverished parent sold them, or a dishonest gravedigger thought to line his pockets by pretending to bury them and then selling them off—the churchyard!" I cried suddenly.

Brisbane blinked at me. "You do have the most alarming processes of ratiocination," he said. "What churchyard?"

"The one at the chapel ruins," I explained. "If there is a gravestone there for these children, we will know where they came from. We will know their parents' names, and when they died. And we can rebury them," I said with satisfaction. "The chapel was Roman Catholic—do you think it matters?"

Brisbane rubbed a hand across his face. His eyes were heavy, and the lines at the corners were more pronounced.

"Julia, you are galloping ahead, as usual. We must proceed in a more orderly fashion. We know the children were mummified, that is all. We may conjecture they were embalmed by Redwall Allenby, but beyond that we simply do not know. Explore the churchyard if you must, but for the love of God, be careful."

I blinked at him. "Careful? What possible danger can there be at this point? If anything we would be doing the children's parents a service by returning them."

"Would we? What if the parents did sell them to Redwall for an experiment? Do you think they will want us uncovering that fact? More to the point, those children have gold hair, just like all the Allenbys. And," he added, picking up the animal-shaped amulet, "this is not just any type of livestock. It is a ram."

I inhaled sharply. "Godwin. If the amulets were put there as a hint to the parents' identities, the ram would point directly to him. He is a sheep farmer. And the children had gold hair," I echoed.

"Now do you see how dangerous this could become?" he demanded softly.

"We do not know, Brisbane. It is only the wildest speculation at this point, as you just pointed out."

"In any event, I do not want you alone with him."

I flapped a hand. "He is no danger to me because I am no danger to him, at least not insofar as he knows. I will be careful and discreet, but if I leave off speaking privately with him, it will raise his suspicions."

One black brow winged up. "Are you in the habit of conversing privately with him?"

"Yes, upon occasion," I said, exasperated. "He is a part of this household for better or worse, and it would be a strange thing if I did not."

Brisbane rubbed at his temple. "He seeks you out, doesn't he?"

"From time to time. Brisbane, are you quite all right? Why are you pressing your head like that?"

"Because it hurts," he muttered through gritted teeth. His eyes had glazed, and I realised with a start that he was in the beginning stages of a migraine.

"Lie down," I ordered. It was a mark of his disorientation that he did so without question. He sat heavily, then stretched out, averting his eyes from the fire. I moved to blow out the candles and extinguish the fire as best I could, dousing it carefully with water from the washstand.

Hastily I bundled the babies back into their coffin, heedless of either my revulsion or the dignity they deserved. I dropped one set of amulets into the coffin, and slipped the second set into my pocket before turning back to Brisbane. The room was chilly, but too smoky to risk shutting the window. Instead I took up his dressing gown and laid it over his shoulders. It was a heavy silk affair, weighty as a king's robe and I hoped it would keep out the worst of the chill.

"Thank you," he said, ending the words on a groan. He fisted his hands and put them to his eyes, grinding against the pain. The few times I had seen him suffer the headaches before, they had come on more gradually, over the course of hours or even days of increasing pain and sensitivity to light. This had struck him with the force of an axe blow, and I wondered how long he had been fighting it off, or if perhaps his recent illness had hastened its onset.

I knelt in front of him and put my hands to his, bringing them down. "Brisbane, I want you to do something."

He groaned again by way of reply.

"I want you to give in. Stop fighting the vision. That is why the pain has come. Just let go and see what will become of it."

"No," he growled. He moved to pull his hands away, but I held them fast.

"You must. Brisbane, listen to me. I know the visions are terrible. I know they show you things you do not want to see. But the headaches are more of a curse. You dose yourself with God knows what sorts of vileness to keep them at bay, and it only hurts you more. Just give in to the vision and see what you are meant to see."

He tugged again at his hands, but still I held them fast, and I fancied he did not resist as strongly. I rose up on my knees and put my lips near his ear.

"I will not leave you," I whispered. "I promise. I will stay with you until it is done, and I will not let you come to harm."

He opened his eyes then and I saw a torment there I had never seen on any human face. "You do not know what you are asking," he said thickly.

"I know that if you do not do this, you will keep killing yourself with hashish and absinthe and whatever is in that red syrup of Rosalie's. Can that sort of a life be enough for you?"

"It has to be," he told me. "The visions—" He broke off

then, and with a renewed strength he tore free of my grasp and put the heels of his hands to his eyes.

I sat back and waited. After a long moment, he rose with a tremendous effort of will, and thrust himself up from the bed. He stumbled toward the washstand and took up a bottle of poppy syrup. I did not try to stop him. He unstoppered it and drank off a deep draught from the bottle. He did not look at me as he returned to the bed, falling heavily into sleep almost as soon as he dropped onto it.

I sat on the cold stone floor for a long time, watching him sleep, peaceful now, and free of his pain. The room grew colder, and I rose, stiff and aching. I took the coverlet from his bed and draped it over him, and brushed a stray lock of hair back from his brow. Poets say that men look like children when they sleep, but Brisbane did not. His breathing was so slow, his pallor so complete that he looked like the effigy on a prince's tomb, carved from marble, perfect and unchanging.

There was little for me to do before I left his room. I wedged the coffin under the writing table and draped it with the sheet, hoping that small attempt at subterfuge would keep it from sight.

And then I took the little bottle of red syrup and poured the remains out the window, poked up the fire, and closed the door behind me.

THE TWENTY-THIRD CHAPTER

We are yet but young in deed.
—William Shakespeare
Macbeth

The next morning I left the house early after checking in on the growing menagerie in the maids' room and telling Portia to look in on Brisbane. I did not particularly want to be the first person he saw when he realised his supply of poppy syrup had been tampered with. I simply told Portia he had been unwell the previous evening and had taken a sleeping draught, neatly glossing over the fact that he had drugged himself into oblivion.

I ate a quick breakfast alone, stopping only long enough in the hall to collect my cloak and make certain the little gold amulet was still in my pocket. I had just gained the orchard path when I heard a voice behind me, calling me to stop. I turned, fixing a smile to my face.

"Good morning, Miss Ailith, you are about bright and

early." She fell into step next to me, although I did not relish taking her with me to search the graveyard, it occurred to me this was a rather good opportunity to question her discreetly about a few matters.

"I am glad I found you," she told me. She looked better rested than I would have thought possible, her eyes clear and her expression serene. The loss of her mother had not affected her as deeply as I would have expected, but I wondered if perhaps Ailith had known her mother was unbalanced in the mind. They had lived so closely together, she must have seen some sign of derangement in her, or malice or wickedness or whatever one might call it. Perhaps she was relieved that her mother's domination of her was at an end.

"I have been thinking," she went on, "that it seems quite silly for you and Lady Bettiscombe to share a bedchamber. Now that Mama is gone—" She paused to clear her throat, then continued on stronger. "Now that Mama is gone, the largest bedchamber is unoccupied. I thought perhaps you or Lady Bettiscombe might prefer to take up residence in that room."

I thought of the bloody crucifix and the weeping saints and suppressed a delicate shudder. "I am quite comfortable in the room I have at present. Portia might like to move, and I should like *for* her to move, I cannot deny it. She snores, although if you tell her I said it, I will call you a liar."

Ailith's lovely mouth curved into a smile. It was one of the few times I had seen her truly happy, and the difference in her was remarkable. If she had been striking before, she was supremely beautiful now.

She closed her eyes and turned her face to the rising sun, drawing in great lungsful of air. "It is going to be a beautiful day, Lady Julia. Can you not feel it? There is a lightness now, a freedom that was not there before."

It was as I suspected then. Little wonder she had been vague and meek. Trapped under the thumb of a woman capable of such viciousness, her character had surely been held down, stunted as a flower in a shaded garden, choked by weeds and yet yearning for the sun. There was hope for Ailith Allenby now that she was free of her mother, and I made up my mind then to help her in any way that I could.

"Yes, I think it will be a beautiful day," I replied firmly.

She opened her eyes and regarded me for a moment, tipping her head to the side. "You are in love with Brisbane, aren't you? Oh, careful! You might have twisted your ankle. Did I startle you so much?"

"No," I lied, smoothing my skirts and rolling my ankle around in a circle to make certain I had not wrenched it. "I am quite all right. I suppose I am. Does that concern you?" The words were direct, but I endeavoured to make my tone civil.

She smiled. "Not at all. I was indiscreet when I talked of Hilda's intentions, as well as my own past with him. I hope I did not hurt you. You have been so very kind to me." I said nothing and she went on, her voice dreamy. "Mama was furious at the idea that Hilda meant to marry Brisbane. He is a half-blood Gypsy, far beneath our status," she told me, her expression serious. "She would never have permitted such a match, but I never imagined she would take such steps to prevent it."

I thought of my own conversation with Lady Allenby and her assurance that her daughter would not marry Brisbane, her prodding of my own hopes in that direction. I felt a sharp stab of guilt that my discussion with her might have prompted the attack on Brisbane.

Ailith shook her head. "I think I have always known there was something quite apart about her, something different. I pushed Hilda, you know, in spite of Mama. I knew she hated the idea, but I did not care. I looked after her for so many years, and she never thought to provide for us, not properly. There were no marriages arranged, no trips abroad, no friendships. It did not matter to me. I love the moor, and I should never want to leave it. But Hilda, oh, how she hates it here. She ought to have a life of some sort, some money to travel, a chance to get right away and really live." She broke off, burying her face in her hands. "So I pushed her toward Brisbane. I thought Mama would come to accept it. And instead she nearly killed him because of it."

She lifted her face, tears sparkling like tiny gems on the dark gold of her lashes. "Can you forgive me, Lady Julia? I never thought she was capable of such monstrousness. I only meant to bring her to our way of thinking, and I was stupid, thoughtless. Please, say that you forgive me." She took my hand in hers and squeezed it hard.

"Of course, my dear," I said faintly, slightly taken aback by the passion of her outburst. "None of us know precisely what the consequences of our actions might be. Your concern for your sister is quite commendable, and under the circumstances, I might well have done the same myself. We will speak no more about it."

"Oh, you are good!" she cried. "I feel free as a newborn

child." She smiled broadly, then clapped a hand over her mouth to hide her immodest pleasure. She was almost giddy, but I felt a little chill at her words, and thought of the newborn children lying in their wrappings behind the chimney breast of her brother's room. Had she known, had she any reason to suppose what he was capable of? She had suspected her mother's villainy; had she intuited her brother's?

Once at the graveyard, Ailith stopped to pick daffodils, gathering a great armful as I pretended to idly peruse the gravestones, all the while searching for some monument that might lend a clue to the identity of the dead children. Mindful of the fact that they might have been merely recorded on a parent's stone, I read them all as carefully as I could, casting the occasional glance back at Ailith and keeping my demeanour casual.

At length, I had come to the end of the little graveyard and had to concede there was nothing to be found. The children were not mentioned, either on their own markers or those of some family member. They had not been stolen from the Allenby graveyard then, I surmised. That left the village churchyard as a possibility, and I made a note to search it as soon as possible.

I turned to find Ailith just bending over to lay her bundle of daffodils at the foot of Redwall's gravestone. She paused a moment, her head bowed, then gave a great sigh of release it seemed to me. She caught my eye then and smiled.

We arrived back at the Hall to find the place at sixes and sevens, with Brisbane tearing at his hair and shouting at Portia in the kitchen while she brandished a spoon at him and shouted back. Ailith scurried to her room, and I envied her heartily.

"I do not care if she has gone to the devil," Brisbane shouted, "but I want her back immediately!"

"Do not raise your voice to me, you oaf!" Portia yelled back at him. "Do you think I have any control over what my sister does?"

It had been some years since I had heard Portia lose her temper, and I was never particularly enthusiastic about seeing Brisbane in a pet. I tiptoed past the open door, but not quickly enough. They turned as one and saw me, and before I could make my escape, Brisbane lunged.

He caught me by the arm and began to herd me toward the study.

"I am so glad you found her," Portia called after him. "Perhaps she can teach you some better manners."

"Not bloody likely," Brisbane ground out through gritted teeth. He pushed me through the door and slammed it behind us.

I smiled up at him brightly. "Good morning, Brisbane. You do seem livelier than when I saw you last."

"Livelier? I ought to turn you over my knee right now and give you the beating of your life. Do you have any idea what it feels like inside my head just now?"

I thought for a moment. "Well, I don't imagine it can be hurting too terribly or you wouldn't be shouting."

"Quite right," he said, clipping his consonants sharply. "It is dull as cotton wool in there because you saw fit to throw out my only means of controlling the pain."

His fingers were still tight about my arm and I pried them

free, rubbing at my flesh. "I think you've bruised me. I do not understand. How is the pain gone if I threw out the poppy syrup?"

"Because when I woke in the middle of the night to swallow another dose, I had no choice but to do as you wanted me to in the first place."

I caught my breath. "The vision."

"The vision," he said. In spite of his anger, I thought he looked quite well. The shadows beneath his eyes had gone, and his pupils were clear and undilated. Even his colour looked better to me.

"Was it very awful?" I asked him finally, dreading the answer.

"Awful?" his voice was thick with sarcasm. "Not at all. The merest ramble in the park. I can't think why I didn't throw out my remedies sooner and simply enjoy them."

I bit at my lip and he jerked back his cuffs, baring his arms to the biceps.

"Do you see those marks? They are from the hypodermic syringes when I used to inject cocaine. Would you like to see the scars on my back where a Chinese doctor used to apply hot glass cups to draw out the devils? Or the tiny slashes on the backs of my knees where an Austrian specialist once bled me by nicking my veins with a scalpel?"

His fury was palpable now, and building. I took a step backward, but there was no retreat. The wall was behind me, and Brisbane in front of me, implacable and enraged. He planted his hands flat on either side of my head and loomed close to me, his face inches from mine. It was not the first time we had stood thus, but it was the first time I had ever seen him regard me with such naked contempt and I shrank from it.

"Do not pull away," he ordered. "You ought to face the consequences of what you have done, for once in your life. You thought you knew better, didn't you? You thought you would fix me by forcing me to confront what I really am."

I turned my face aside, but he grabbed my chin in his hand, holding it hard, forcing me to meet his eyes. His voice dropped to a harsh whisper.

"And what if I am a monster? Did you ever wonder that, Julia Grey? Did you ever ask yourself what I might really be capable of?"

I stared at him, lips trembling a little as I searched his face for some sign of the man I had known. I knew his features as well as my own, from the scar high on his cheekbone to the hard curve of his jaw, and yet there was nothing familiar in this face.

I lifted my hand and touched a fingertip to his cheek. He jerked backward as if I had scorched him, dropping his hand from my face. He shook his head slowly, as if emerging from a dream.

"Do not push me too far, Julia. You have meddled with me in ways I ought never to have permitted. But I will finish what I began here, and you will not interfere with me again."

He turned on his heel and left me then. I slid to the floor, my legs powerless to hold me. I sat there for a long time, turning over the words he had said, his coldness, his resolve, the chilling glitter of his eyes. But what I remembered most vividly was that even as his right hand had gripped my chin so cruelly, forcing me to face him as he raged at me, his left hand had stolen into mine, clasping it with all the desperation of a drowning man.

THE TWENTY-FOURTH CHAPTER

Rage must be withstood.
Lions make leopards tame.
—William Shakespeare
Richard II

That afternoon I collected Portia after dinner and told her we were going into the village proper.

"Ought we to ask Valerius?" she inquired. "He has been spending every waking moment with Hilda, and her peevishness is beginning to wear off on him. He's becoming sulky. He has struck himself twice upon the thumb with a hammer in building that henhouse, and has raised four blisters. It has not improved his temper."

"Not this time. I want to get right away, and I do not think I could endure him if he's in a mood. May we go alone?"

"Gladly," Portia said, pinning her hat firmly onto her head. "Anything to get out of this place. You know, when Brisbane is angry, it creates quite an *atmosphere*."

"Yes, I had noticed," I returned, shoving her out of the door. She complained about Brisbane for the better part of the walk into the village, rather a relief to me as all that was required of me was the occasional nod or murmur of agreement.

As we reached the village, footsore and thirsty, she stopped and turned to me. "I just realised what it felt like when he was shouting at me," she said, trying unsuccessfully to hide a smile. "He felt like one of the family."

"Very funny," I told her, turning toward the little stone church in the village. There was a statue in front of St. Agnes with her lamb.

"I mean it," she replied, hurrying to catch up to me. "He sounded exactly like Benedick in one of his rages," she said, referring to my favourite of all our brothers. "Do you suppose he might be related? Distantly, of course. Perhaps through the connection to the Duke of Aberdour. Weren't Mama's people related somehow to the Comyns? And the Comyns are connected to the Aberdour line, I'm certain of it."

"All the aristocrats on this island have intermarried so much I am quite sure we are related to everyone above the rank of baronet," I said absently.

"It isn't healthy," Portia commented. "Father always says inbreeding will be the downfall of the monarchy, and the aristocracy as well. Bad blood always tells, whether it's horses or dogs or men," she added, echoing one of Father's favourite sentiments.

"Or sheep," I finished, thinking of Godwin's travails with the flock at Grimsgrave.

We pushed through the little gate and I began to scrutinise the markers. It was a far more daunting task than inspecting the tiny chapel graveyard. The graves here went back at least three hundred years, although I reminded myself only markers carved within the last year or two were of interest to me. I looked for anything that might have a bearing on the identity of the little mummies: stillbirths, twins, women dead in childbed.

Portia peered over my shoulder. "What are we looking for?" she asked suddenly. "I thought we were simply making our escape from Brisbane's bad temper."

"Not exactly," I told her, moving slowly from one stone to the next, squinting at the grimy, obscured carving. "I am looking for babies, twins actually, stillborn or died shortly after birth. A year, or perhaps two or even three years past. See if you can find any."

Portia shrugged and did as she was told. We walked the rows slowly for the better part of an hour, rubbing moss away from old gravestones and occasionally stopping to read an interesting epitaph.

"Nothing," she said finally, straightening as we reached the end of the last row. "Not even a child under the age of four in this lot. Why do we care, incidentally?"

I told her quickly what conclusions Brisbane and I had drawn from the discovery of the mummy babies, and that I thought to expand the investigation by an examination of the churchyard. Her eyes were enormous by the time I had finished explaining that we no longer believed them to be ancient specimens, but rather the sinister remains of a recent crime.

She punched me lightly on the arm. "Julia Constance Desdemona Grey," she began.

I rubbed at my arm. "That was unnecessary. I am sure you have left a mark."

She folded her arms over her chest and put out her underlip, her expression mulish. "It isn't fair, you know. Aunt Hermia has her prostitutes to reform, Father has his Shakespearean society, Valerius has his medical studies. And now you seem to trip over mysteries wherever you go. I want a hobby."

"Perhaps you could take up painting kittens?" I suggested. "Hooking rugs? Needlepointing?"

She sat down on a gravestone marked *Cecily Potts, Beloved wife of Thomas.* "I mean it, Julia. I intend to take up something *useful.*"

"I don't know that what I do is particularly useful," I said slowly. "I've nearly got myself killed more than once, and Father has had to step in both times to make quite certain the scandals did not become fodder for the public. I imagine he would rather I gave up sleuthing altogether and sit quietly in the corner improving my French."

"French is *passé,*" she commented without a trace of irony. "Italian is much more of the moment. Or perhaps I ought to take up something more active, like stalking pheasant."

"Darling, one doesn't stalk pheasant. One shoots pheasant and one stalks deer," I corrected, putting out my hand to her. She pulled a face. Country pursuits had never been of the slightest interest to her even when she lived in the country. "But right now I would quite like to know where those babies came from. And I imagine Mrs. Potts would be greatly relieved if you got off of her."

Portia took my hand and we made our way to the gate,

chatting idly. It was not until we had nearly reached the gate that we looked up and realised we were not alone.

"Lady Bettiscombe! Lady Julia!" It was Deborah from the inn, waving over the gate, smiling. "I saw you pass from the window. I told my mam it was the ladies from Grimsgrave come to the village, and we hoped you would stop in for a cup of tea. She would so like to make your acquaintance."

I thought of how deliciously full of local gossip old women were likely to be and smiled.

"We should like nothing better," I told her. Portia nodded graciously to her and Deborah hurried off, calling over her shoulder that she would lay the tea things and we must take our time.

"Are you quite serious?" Portia hissed when Deborah was scarcely out of earshot. "Do you really want to spend teatime with an old woman we do not know?"

"Do you know of anyone likelier to know who might have borne twins within the past two years than an elderly woman?" I returned. Comprehension dawned on Portia's lovely face and she gave me an approving look.

"You have a gift for deviousness," she told me. I was not entirely sure it was a compliment.

We were received at the inn with the warmest of hospitality. Deborah fluttered around, apron flapping as she guided us to the snug, warm parlour where we had taken tea upon our arrival in the village.

"Here the ladies are, Mam," she called out. She gave us an apologetic look. "Mam is a little hard of hearing. Lady Bettiscombe, Lady Julia, my mam, Mrs. Earnshaw. Mam, here are the ladies to have tea with us," she said, raising her voice.

The elderly woman seated by the fire looked us up and down, nodding. "Handsome girls and they know it," she said to herself.

Portia smothered a laugh as Deborah threw an apologetic look over her shoulder. "Do forgive her," she whispered. "She doesn't realise what she says half the time."

We were given chairs by the fire, ours drawn into a cosy semicircle with Mrs. Earnshaw's. The old lady was dressed in the fashion I had noticed in the village, the full skirts and plain caps of the mid-century still popular with the local ladies. Her dress was of plain, serviceable brown stuff, but she had pinned a pretty brooch of carnelian to the neck of it to secure her lace collar. They were the only touches of frivolity in an otherwise plain and sober costume. Her hands were a bit swollen with arthritis and her eyes were faded and rheumy, but still sharp and I fancied there was little she missed.

"I am so pleased to make your acquaintance," I told her, smoothing my skirts over my knees. "Earnshaw is quite a famous name, thanks to Miss Brontë. I did not realise there were Earnshaws in this country."

Mrs. Earnshaw gave a sharp nod. "Aye. And Heathcliffs and Eyres, as well. Proper little thieves, those Brontë girls."

"Did you know them?" Portia asked. Deborah, who had been hovering in the background, apparently judged us on safe footing, for she left us to fetch the tea things.

"They'm from Haworth way," Mrs. Earnshaw said, as if the distance of some six miles was all the Earth to her.

"You have never been to Haworth?" I asked.

"And why would I?" she demanded. "There'm naught to see in Haworth thee could not find here," she told me firmly.

"Quite right," Portia seconded. "Lesser Howlett is a very fine village. My sister and I have just been walking the churchyard, admiring the gravestones."

Mrs. Earnshaw blinked. "Tha's a curious habit, tha' is. Londoners," she snorted.

"We are actually country-bred," I corrected with a smile. "We were reared in Sussex."

"Sussex is near enough to London," Mrs. Earnshaw advised me. "'Tis all the devil's pleasure ground, is it not?"

Portia coughed, disguising a laugh. Mrs. Earnshaw gave her a sharp look, but I hurried to reply.

"That it is," I agreed. "Society seems more wholesome here in the north."

She nodded, mollified. "Aye. There is soberness here, and a respect for righteous ways."

"Indeed," Portia murmured.

"Of course," Mrs. Earnshaw went on, "even here there has been wickedness, and the devil will work his craft wherever he finds the tools."

Just then the door opened and Deborah returned, bearing a tray that must have weighed an hundredweight, loaded with bread and butter and small cakes and sandwiches and pots of tea and little dishes of jam. It looked hearty and comforting, like a nursery tea, and I would have been thoroughly pleased had Deborah not interrupted her mother just when she had seen fit to drop such an interesting titbit into conversation.

The next quarter of an hour was taken up with pouring out and the dainty selecting of cakes and sandwiches, although there was no polite dithering for Mrs. Earnshaw.

She heaped her plate as high as any youth might have done, taking a goodly portion of everything on offer.

"You were talking of wickedness," I reminded her with little subtlety when she had finished her first plate and replenished it.

She nodded, finishing a delectable little ham pie that I wondered if Mrs. Butters could replicate. "Aye. Wickedness. Not among the God-fearing folk of this village. Nay, we are sober, respectable folk who know one way, and that is to work hard and to obey God. But there are others who think themselves above such things."

Portia and I exchanged quick glances, but not quick enough. Mrs. Earnshaw noticed and waved a hand.

"Not you, my ladies. You've got goodness in you, I can see tha'. Tell me, d'ye give to those tha' have need of it in your village in Sussex?"

"Of course," Portia said roundly. "There are always baskets at Christmas, and whatever the farm folk need is always attended to."

Mrs. Earnshaw nodded in satisfaction. "Thee has been brought up properly to know thy duty. But there's those that were born here have not."

"The Allenbys?" I asked. Mrs. Earnshaw gave me a slow, meaningful wink.

"Aye. Born to the manor and they keep to the manor. No thought to help the villagers, save when it suits them."

"Well, perhaps their circumstances are strained," I put in. It was not my place to salvage the Allenby reputation, but Ailith and Hilda did still have to make their home amongst the villagers, however removed they might like to think themselves.

Mrs. Earnshaw gave a sharp cackle. "Strained? Oh, my girl, there was a time when the Allenbys were rich as any lord between here and the border. And what did they do with it? Not a bit of good. The poor of this village went without shoes or coal or meat, while they prospered on the backs of the miners. 'Twere a black day for folk here when the mine collapsed, but there were those who wondered if we might not be better working for anyone besides the old devil, Sir Alfred."

"He was not a popular figure then?" Portia put in. She reached out and helped herself to a third slice of parkin.

"Nay. A Roman he was, and yet every Sunday he came to sit in state at St. Agnes, not to worship God, but to see us and be seen in turn. He wanted us to know he was watching, always watching, just like God."

"He sounds like a religious zealot," I commented. Mrs. Earnshaw laughed, sounding like a rusty squeezebox.

"Bless you, lady. There were no religion in him. There were pomp and popish ways, but no Christian virtues. He played the man of God, but there was no godliness in him. He was a vengeful, brutish, lustful man, and this village was not sorry when the devil took his own."

"Lustful?" The word struck a chord. I had heard of Sir Alfred's harshness, but this was the first I had heard of something darker. "Do you mean he took his *droit du seigneur* with the local girls?"

"I don't know about tha'," Mrs. Earnshaw said, her mouth twisting bitterly, "but I know he forced himself upon whatever girl he fancied, maiden or wife, and when there were bastards to be had, he gave them nothing for it. The day they carried him to be buried at Allenby chapel, there were naught but dry eyes in this village, I can tell you."

A hundred questions trembled on my lips, but none of them were appropriate.

Just then the door opened again and Deborah entered, followed by another person who stood behind her in the narrow doorway.

"I do hope your ladyships will not mind. My sister has just come, and she so wanted to make your acquaintance. She's a governess down Manchester way," she added with an unmistakable note of pride.

"Not at all. Do bring her in," Portia instructed.

"Lady Bettiscombe, Lady Julia, my sister, Jerusha Earnshaw." Deborah stepped aside and there stood a girl so like her, I blinked. Jerusha dropped a curtsey as Deborah laughed at my expression.

"Aye, lady. Jerusha and I are twins."

Twins with golden hair and bright blue eyes, I noted. I smiled at the newcomer. "Miss Earnshaw, how delightful to make your acquaintance."

I glanced at Mrs. Earnshaw. There was no mistaking the pride on her face at having two such pretty daughters, but there was something else flickering behind her eyes as she looked into mine. Mrs. Earnshaw was wary.

But before I could determine why, Miss Earnshaw had claimed my attention. Unlike her mother and sister, she did not affect the clothing of the mid-century. Her skirts were fashionably slim and she even wore a tiny bustle, although one perfectly in keeping with her position. Her clothes were serviceable and neat, and her expression wore a clever watchfulness I had not seen in her sister.

"Miss Earnshaw, do join us for tea, won't you? I should so like to hear about your position. A governess, your sister says?"

If Miss Earnshaw thought my curiosity odd, she gave no sign of it. She sat and accepted a cup, her gestures neat and economical. She would not be noticed, but she would notice everything, I wagered.

"Thank you, Lady Julia. Yes, I have a post in Manchester. My employer owns several factories there. He is in textiles."

"He's a townhouse in London, and an estate outside Manchester," Mrs. Earnshaw put in with a satisfied nod. "Jerusha has the keeping of his two daughters, good girls too, and the lady of the house is generous to her. Give her Sundays off, and a half-day Wednesdays, as well as one weekend every other month to come home. And she pays the railway fare as well."

A ghost of a smile touched Miss Earnshaw's lips. "My employers are very generous," she agreed.

Mrs. Earnshaw leaned close, darting her eyes around as if to make certain we were alone in the room. "The lady is ill, she is. She'll never make old bones, and then who will be mistress, I ask you?"

Portia murmured, "Oh, my," at this juicy bit of scandal in the making, but Miss Earnshaw merely sipped at her tea. "That is quite silly, Mam," she told her mother. "Mrs. Bellingham is perfectly healthy, and I have no designs on a dead woman's shoes."

She was unruffled as a mill pond, and I found myself warming to a woman who could maintain her serenity in the face of such a mother.

"Is it your first post, Miss Earnshaw?" Portia inquired.

"No, my lady. I have kept myself since I was seventeen. I took a post teaching in a school, but found I preferred working with a smaller number of pupils. The work is often more demanding in such cases, but it is far easier to gauge one's success."

"Oh, well, you wouldn't have had any success with us, would she, Julia? We went through a dozen governesses and still cannot speak more than two languages each, nor can we do our sums. Our educations were frightfully neglected," Portia confided to her.

I did not bother to contradict my sister. Efforts to educate us had been spotty, but rather effective. We were terrible at sums, that much was true, but I still retained a fair smattering of Latin while Portia could discourse freely on the sciences.

"The Allenby ladies seem quite accomplished," I put in, rather clumsily. "I wonder what sort of education they employed in schooling their children? Did they have governesses and tutors?" I gave Miss Earnshaw a wide-eyed look, but out of the tail of my eye I saw her mother dart a glance between us, her fingers plucking at her skirts.

"I believe Sir Alfred saw to the education of his children himself. Lady Allenby schooled the girls, while Sir Alfred taught his son."

"Surely not Egyptology," I said, thinking aloud. "I do not remember hearing that Sir Alfred was interested in such a subject."

"He wasn't interested in anything tha' could not make him money," Mrs. Earnshaw put in bitterly.

"I believe," said Miss Earnshaw, drawing attention away

from her agitated parent, "that Sir Alfred's interest in Egyptology was a passing one, the sort of thing he toyed with for a season or so. He had many such interests—Roman ruins, the history of the Popes, that sort of thing. Sir Redwall's interest went much further and he continued his studies independently."

"How interesting," I said, noticing that Mrs. Earnshaw had taken another biscuit onto her plate. She had not eaten it, but was crumbling it slowly to bits.

"Julia," Portia said, nodding toward the shepherdess clock standing upon the mantel, "it is quite late. We shall be very tardy getting back to Grimsgrave."

"How silly of me. We have far overstayed ourselves, but the company and the refreshments were so delightful," I said, smiling at Mrs. Earnshaw. She returned my smile, but I fancied she was not sorry to see us go. We gathered our things and bade her farewell, and she was careful not to invite us to return. I wanted to speak privately to Jerusha, but we had lingered as long as we dared, and I wondered if there would be some pretence I could manufacture to bring her with us to Grimsgrave.

Deborah ushered us out of the cosy sitting room and down the stairs, chattering all the while. We thanked her for her hospitality, and when we had reached the bottom of the stairs, I realised Jerusha Earnshaw had followed us.

"May I walk with you as far as the path to Grimsgrave?" she asked, reaching for her hat.

"Of course," I told her, immensely relieved that I had not had need to fabricate a reason to invite her along. We waved to Deborah and started down the village street. Dusk had fallen and the windows of the shops were shuttered and dark, while the windows of the houses were bathed in warm yellow light.

"It *is* late," I told Portia. "At least the moon is rising."

Just ahead of us, the moon hung low on the horizon, round and white as a pearl. The gravestones of St. Agnes' churchyard were silhouetted against it like a picture from a child's book of spooky tales.

"I do hope you won't think too harshly of Mam," Miss Earnshaw began, coming straight to the point.

"Why on earth should we think badly of her?" Portia asked.

"Because she lies so," Miss Earnshaw said with no trace of embarrassment. "She likes to pretend that Deborah and I are legitimate, but of course we are not. We are Sir Alfred Allenby's bastards, and everyone in the village knows it."

I stumbled over a cobblestone, catching myself quickly.

Miss Earnshaw was looking at me with cool, smiling detachment. "Are you quite all right, Lady Julia?"

"Quite, thank you," I returned crisply. "But I confess I am rather impressed with your briskness. Most people would not find it so easy to come to terms with their illegitimacy."

Miss Earnshaw shrugged. "It is of no consequence to me. The crime is not mine. It is Mam's and Sir Alfred's. Why should Deborah and I be any less worthwhile simply because our parents chose to conceive us out of wedlock?"

"You are a very modern thinker," Portia put in, admiringly.

"It is simple common sense," Miss Earnshaw rejoined. "A person ought not to be held accountable for any errors made by others. My parents may have committed double adultery, but their transgressions have nothing to do with me."

"Mrs. Earnshaw did allude to Sir Alfred being less than gallant in his conduct with women," I offered. "Perhaps your mother's crime was only in catching the eye of an untrustworthy man."

Miss Earnshaw's expression warmed to amusement. "I think not, Lady Julia. Did you not notice the carnelian brooch at her throat? It was a love trinket from Sir Alfred when Deborah and I were born. She never takes it off. If he had forced her, do you think she would still remember him so warmly? Nay, he was a rogue, but he was a handsome one, golden-haired and strong. The man who raised us, Richard Earnshaw—Amos' father—was a miner, small and dark. His mother's people had come from Wales, and he had the look of them. Deborah and I are cuckoos in the nest to be sure."

We walked along in silence for a moment, and I was struck by this woman's self-possession. She had been born into circumstances more unlike my own than any I could imagine, and yet she was poised as a duchess.

"Did Sir Alfred ever help with your education? With maintenance?"

Miss Earnshaw shrugged. "He died the year after we were born. He left us a small sum of money. Deborah used hers to help our half brother, Amos, buy the inn. I used mine to go to school. I wanted out of this village, away from the clacking tongues, the whispers behind our backs."

She took a deep breath and shook her head. "I always forget what it is like, how small, how dark, how closed. And then I come back, and it quite takes my breath away. I will come until Mam dies, and then I will not come again," she said with an air of finality.

A sudden thought struck me and I turned to her. "This Richard Earnshaw, he was a miner?"

A slow smile ripened on her lips. She knew precisely where I was leading with my question. "Yes. And he was killed when the mine collapsed. It was ten years after Sir Alfred died. Deborah and I were only eleven. It was a terrible blow. He never once treated us as though we were less than his own. He sang us songs of the Welsh hills and taught us to stand proudly, even when the gossips in the village were whispering our names."

"It must have been a tremendous loss to your family when he died," Portia put in.

"It was. Mam had the keeping of us, so she did anything she could to feed and clothe us. She went into service at Grimsgrave Hall as a chambermaid."

I stared at her. It was difficult to read her features through the deepening gloom. "That must have been a trifle awkward, with your mother working for Lady Allenby."

"Oh, I think it must have been why she was employed in the first place. Lady Allenby is a God-fearing woman. She would not let her husband's children starve, even if they were the fruits of sin."

I said nothing, but I wondered if Miss Earnshaw would be quite so quick to praise Lady Allenby if she knew what horrors she was capable of.

"Sir Alfred must have been rather young when he died," Portia put in suddenly.

"Just over forty," Miss Earnshaw corrected. "Not young, but not long past his prime."

"Was it sudden?" I do not know what prompted Portia's questions, but I was suddenly interested in the answers.

"Yes, rather. There was actually quite a bit of talk at the time. The villagers said he was cursed to death."

I stopped in my tracks. "Cursed?" I said, my voice barely audible.

"Yes. He was the local magistrate, as befitted his position as the largest landowner. He had bound over a Gypsy woman for trial, and when he did so, she cursed him. He was dead within a fortnight. It was all anyone could talk about for months. She cursed the chemist as well, and he died several months later, of fear, some said."

"What became of the Gypsy woman?" Portia asked.

Miss Earnshaw shrugged again. "She died as well, as soon as she delivered her curse. Never even made it to the trial, poor thing. Pity, she might well have been set free."

"Curious," Portia offered. "One would think the death of the Gypsy woman would have lifted the curse."

We had reached the path then that struck off toward Grimsgrave Hall. I put out my hand.

"It has been a pleasure, Miss Earnshaw," I said, my mind galloping ahead. "If you have a mind to call at Grimsgrave while we are visiting, we should so enjoy meeting you again."

Miss Earnshaw shook my hand soberly and gave a little shake of her head. "I think not, Lady Julia. I do not believe I would be comfortable in my father's house knowing that, but for a few words said in church and a bit of paper, it might have been my home."

"You do know that Lady Allenby is no longer in residence?" I asked, delicately skirting the issue of why.

Miss Earnshaw's expression did not vary. "Yes. It was a nine days' wonder when she left in the company of two nuns from Ireland. For a rest cure for her rheumatism, it seems. Folk said that one of the nuns looked very like her eldest daughter, Wilfreda, who eloped with a painter many years past."

"That is not the truth of it," I protested, but Miss Earnshaw merely smiled.

"This is Lesser Howlett, Lady Julia. The truth does not matter half so much as what people *think* is the truth."

"I quite understand," I said, inclining my head.

Portia made her goodbyes and we left Jerusha Earnshaw there, standing at the moor gate, smiling into the darkness.

THE TWENTY-FIFTH CHAPTER

Is there any cause in nature that makes these hard hearts?
—William Shakespeare
King Lear

Portia and I made our way back to Grimsgrave Hall, chattering most of the journey.

"I cannot believe Mrs. Earnshaw," Portia began once we were out of earshot of the woman's daughter. "So righteous and godly, and all the while, she's borne a pair of illegitimate daughters to Sir Alfred Allenby for all the world to see."

"She did not have much choice about the world seeing once they were born," I pointed out. "They are tall and blond with blue eyes. Anyone would have known them for Sir Alfred's daughters. I knew there was something familiar about Deborah, but I did not realise until just today it is because she is so very like Ailith Allenby."

"But more to the point, we now have proof the Allenbys run to twins."

I nodded. "Yes. Twin babies with blond hair, walled up in Grimsgrave Hall. There seems little room to doubt those children are Allenbys. The question remains, who is the father?"

"Godwin or Redwall," Portia said promptly. "And I shall plump for Godwin. He has an earthy sort of character. He's robust and always slightly flushed, as if he had just come from rogering the milkmaid in the haymow."

I gave her a little push. "There are no milkmaids at Grimsgrave. But I know what you mean. He is indeed earthy. From the impressions I have been given, Redwall seems an altogether different character. Studious, scholarly, more interested in his cold-blooded experiments than seducing the village maids."

"Besides which we have heard nothing of intemperate habits," Portia observed. "One teatime's conversation and we know that his father was a rogue. Wouldn't we have heard at least a whisper of scandal about Redwall if he'd been making free with the local maidens?"

"Just think of it," I said slowly. "Redwall embalming children that were actually related to him. Even if they were Godwin's, they would still be a sort of cousin."

"How perfectly disgusting you are, Julia. It is frightful to think of Redwall embalming children of any variety, let alone family."

I stopped and put a hand to her sleeve. "So, let us work from the likeliest hypothesis—Godwin Allenby fathered a pair of bastard twins upon some hapless girl, and then gave them to his own cousin to experiment upon."

We walked in silence awhile, each of us pondering the

DEANNA RAYBOURN

same thing, I think. Godwin was a likeable fellow, and it was oddly painful to think him capable of such callous behaviour to his own children.

"Perhaps they were born dead," Portia put in hopefully. "Without a proper postmortem, there is no way of determining what really happened. You said Brisbane believes they were not killed by violence, and I want to believe it, too. Oh, Julia, the other possibility does not bear thinking about."

"He is a farmer," I said slowly. "Think how many times he must have laid a killing hand to a struggling lamb or a starveling calf. He would view it as a necessity, no different than culling the weakest of the litter if the children had no prospects of a good life."

"But why should they have no prospects?" Portia demanded. "If he lay with a village girl and got her with child, why should he not marry her? He is not so far above the local folk as all that."

"Isn't he? He is still an Allenby. Think of them, Portia. All of them, nursed on that overweening pride, not of the normal variety, but the mad sort. They've got their obsessions and their delusions, and they think they are so far above everyone else because their grandfather forty times over was a Saxon king. Do you honestly believe Lady Allenby would have sat idly by while Godwin married an unlettered farmer's daughter? And who else is likely to have fallen victim to his seductions? Jerusha Earnshaw is, as far as I can see, the only properly educated young lady in the entire village and she fled it as soon as possible. If the Allenbys wished to preserve the exclusivity of their blood, they would never have permitted Godwin to commingle his with the local folk."

"I suppose you are right," Portia said finally. "But what if the mother died in childbed? The birthing of twins can be difficult, particularly if it was her first pregnancy. If she died, her family would want the scandal quieted down, wouldn't they? And it would suit the Allenbys as well. Pay the girl's family a suitable sum to keep their silence and then dispose of the children themselves."

"Is it possible to keep such secrets in a village?" I wondered aloud. "We always knew everything that happened in Blessingstoke," I reminded her. "That is why we never dared misbehave in the village. The news would have reached Father before we'd even returned home."

Portia stumbled over a stone in the fitful moonlight and cursed. "Perhaps it isn't likely," she conceded. "But it is possible. And we've no theory as plausible as that one."

"I suppose. I still think if villagers were involved, there would be talk of it. You know the old saying, three can keep a secret if two are dead."

Portia stopped suddenly and turned to face me, her complexion pale as the moonlight that shone upon it.

"What did you make of that tale Jerusha Earnshaw told us about Sir Alfred, dying by a Gypsy woman's curse?"

I kept walking, schooling my expression to serenity. "I think it proves my point about village gossip. They tell the most outlandish stories. I have no doubt that one in particular was embellished and embroidered in the retelling until it hardly resembles the truth anymore."

Portia hurried to keep pace with me. "I don't know. Jerusha Earnshaw struck me as an extremely sensible woman. I cannot imagine she would believe it if it were a faery story."

"Did she say she believed it?" I asked lightly. "I thought she was just repeating village tattle. Besides, she was a year old when Sir Alfred died, by her own admission. She would have hardly been in a position to know these things for herself."

"I suppose," Portia said at length. We topped a rise just then, and the moor stretched out ahead of us, silvery-white and rustling, like a wide ghostly sea. In the distance lay Grimsgrave Hall, black and hulking as a ship adrift on moonlit waves.

"It is horrible," Portia said. "And I do not know why it should be. It is actually quite a pretty house in broad daylight. But under that moon…"

"It is sinister," I agreed, steeling myself to return to it. Lady Allenby was gone, the danger to Brisbane was past. And yet knowing what Godwin had likely done to his own children made me reluctant to stay there. I wondered what it would take for Brisbane to return to London and leave this place to its ghosts.

"Tuppence for your thoughts," Portia said at last.

I shook my head slowly. "I was just thinking of Brisbane, and why he feels compelled to stay here. It reminded me of something Father once told me when Bellmont was being difficult, just after I was widowed. He said Bellmont was turning forty, and it was a hard age for a man because that is the age when he looks at his life and realises whatever he is is all he will ever be."

"Why did you connect that thought with Brisbane?"

"He will be forty this year," I told her, arching my brow significantly. "Perhaps he has something to prove to himself." Or others, I thought privately.

"Speaking of Bellmont, I saw him in London," Portia said. "His family were just preparing to leave for an extended visit to the Duke of Driffield's country seat. Nothing formal has been announced between Driffield's girl and our nephew, Orlando, but matters are quite far advanced. Bellmont cherishes hopes that this visit will seal the match. Parliament is sitting, of course, so Bellmont could not accompany them, but he means to come up when he can," she finished.

I stared at her. "Driffield. His seat is in Yorkshire, in the East Riding. Do you mean to tell me—"

"Yes, dearest." She patted my hand. "Bellmont will be in Yorkshire very soon. And he means to call upon us here whilst he is in the north."

I let loose a stream of colourful language I had learned from my brother Benedick.

"You have conjugated that particular word most incorrectly, but I quite agree," Portia told me. "If it is any consolation to you, I propose we put him in Lady Allenby's bedchamber for the duration of his stay. I will be quite happy to share with you again, and he can spend his nights being stared awake by a bleeding Jesus."

"I can think of no one more deserving," I said sharply. This was a new worry I did not need. Bellmont's presence at Grimsgrave would effectively end my involvement in the many mysteries I was ravelling out. He capitulated often enough when Father exerted his influence, but we were far from London, and if Brisbane wanted me gone, Bellmont was entirely capable of packing me off. There was no hope for it, I decided, lengthening my stride and taking in great lungsful of fresh moor wind. If I wanted to solve the mysteries that swirled around Grimsgrave Hall, I would have to do it myself, and before Bellmont came. There was no time to waste.

Brisbane had been irrationally pleased that Portia and I had gone to the village, and thoroughly annoyed when we returned.

"I had rather hoped you had both come to your senses and gone home," he commented nastily upon seeing us.

Portia merely put out her tongue at him and proceeded to instruct Mrs. Butters to lay our supper. He retired to his room then, to sulk no doubt, which was just as well. I had much to think about, and Brisbane was frequently a distraction.

True to her word, Ailith had removed Portia's things to Lady Allenby's chamber, and I ought to have had a peaceful night's rest. Instead, a hundred questions tangled in my mind, keeping me wakeful long past midnight.

At length I fell into a long, pointless dream about picking mushrooms with Rosalie and Rook while Godwin sat on a riverbank, playing mournful tunes on a flute and Ailith arranged furniture made of acorn caps and twigs in her dolls' house. Back and forth Brisbane strode on the horizon, never moving farther away, never coming closer. It was a maddening dream, and I felt oddly unsettled when I rose.

If nothing else, the dream suggested a visit to Rosalie might be in order, and I set off for the little cottage on the moor shortly after breakfast, leaving the rest of the inhabitants of Grimsgrave to their various occupations. Portia was reading—a thick, densely-written tome about India. Minna was stirring up a pudding under Mrs. Butters' watchful eye whilst Jetty turned out the larder for a thorough scrubbing. Morag could not be shifted from her post with the pups, clucking over them like a doting mother hen. Valerius was busy hammering upon the new henhouse with his sore hands, watched closely by a nervous flock of chickens who seemed to disapprove of his plans. Ailith applied herself to her mending, and I kept to my plan and turned my steps to Rosalie's, bearing a basket with a fresh ham pie, courtesy of Minna's efforts in the kitchens.

But before I reached the moor, another notion struck me. The person most likely to illuminate Redwall Allenby's character was his sister. Not Ailith, she had been too fond of him. Her simple, sisterly affection may well have blinded her to his faults. No, it was an altogether more critical observation I wanted.

I found Hilda in the garden, tucked in the limbs of an apple tree, her feet dangling just above my head.

"I am reading," she told me without looking up from her book. "Leave me be."

"I would like to speak with you, Miss Hilda. Will you come down, or shall I come up?" I called pleasantly.

She regarded me suspiciously. "You would, wouldn't you?" She sighed and snapped the book closed, shoving it into her pocket. "Very well."

She scrambled down, neatly as a monkey, then stood in front of me, her shoulders rounded down, hands thrust into her pockets.

"Valerius is no carpenter, but he seems to be making quite good progress on the henhouse. I don't wonder it will be finished soon."

"The chickens were perfectly happy with the old house," she said flatly.

"Then why did you permit my brother to build them another?"

She gave shake of her head as an impatient pony will do. "Because I am humouring him. He has been kind to me and he wants to do this."

I was impressed in spite of myself. "You astonish me, Miss Hilda. Most people recognise the importance of giving. Few understand the importance of letting others give. Yes, Valerius is a bit of a fixer. Nothing gives him greater pleasure than to think he's been useful. It's a family failing," I mused, reflecting briefly how much satisfaction I had had in solving the little mysteries I had encountered.

Her gaze narrowed. "You have not come to discuss the chickens. What do you want of me?"

"I want to know about Redwall."

Emotion of some sort flickered over her face, but I could not read it. "Why?"

"Because I would like to understand his character," I temporised. "I have been fascinated to work on his collection, and I want to know more about the man who built it."

She put her head to the side, her cool gaze running over me from booted feet to the locks I had pinned into submission behind my ears. "You are untruthful, Lady Julia. But it doesn't matter. I will tell you all you need to know about Redwall. He was selfish and greedy, and whatever evil you can conceive, he was capable of its execution. Our father was cruel and amoral, and Redwall was his equal. He had no sense of duty or propriety, and I did not love him. I did not even like him."

She stopped then, her breath coming quite fast. It was a

lengthy speech for her, and I gave her a moment to compose herself.

"Do you remember a coffin, an Egyptian lady's coffin, in his collection? I believe it was owned by your grandfather first," I said at last.

If the change of subject unbalanced her, she did not betray it. "Yes. It was the first piece in Redwall's collection. He unrolled the mummy without the slightest bit of scientific method, I am sorry to say. He quite destroyed it," she finished bitterly.

"When was the last time you saw the coffin?"

Hilda shook her head. "Years ago, before he left for Egypt. Probably when he unrolled the mummy. I imagine it was thrown back in the storeroom after that. I told you, I was not permitted to touch his things," she said coldly.

"I understand. Thank you," I said, giving her a cordial nod. I walked around her then to the moor gate.

"Why do you care?" she called after me. "Let the dead bury the dead, or haven't you heard that?"

I turned. "Yes, but I find they so often don't."

It was a cool, grey morning, the air freshening over the moor, the sort of weather that might burn away into glorious sunshine by noon, or might just as easily turn to lowering skies and thick, black clouds. Still, I hoped it would hold as I wished to speak with Valerius before I ventured out to Rosalie's cottage. I made my way to the poultry yard to speak with my brother.

"Valerius!" I cried over the din of his hammering. He waved and dropped his hammer, barely missing his foot. His face was grimy with dust from the chickens and he looked nearly as disreputable as Godwin usually did.

"I was hoping to speak with you and Portia," he said. "I thought I could tell you both at the same time, but I suppose I will have to face you down separately."

He looked serious, sober even, and I put out a hand. "Val, what is it? Are you ill?"

He smiled and linked his arm with mine, a rare gesture of affection. "No, I wanted to talk to you about Miss Hilda."

I gave him a little pat. "Excellent. I came to discuss that very subject. I thought to give you a word of warning."

His expression sobered. "Julia, I must stop you there, for I will hear no word against her. I have quite made up my mind. I mean to ask Miss Hilda to marry me."

"Are you quite mad?" I asked, pulling my arm from his. "Val, you cannot. You hardly know the girl."

"I know her well enough," he countered roundly. "I know her character. She is honest, as honest as the earth. She has a good mind and—I know you will not believe it—but she can be quite funny at times."

"And this is your basis for marriage? The most important decision you will ever make," I argued.

His colour rose a little. "I can think of worse reasons to marry," he said. If his words pricked like thorns, I believe it was unintentional.

I stared at the toes of my boots, torn. "I feel I ought to counsel you, to point out that marriage ought to be based on sounder reasons than those you offer."

"Why don't you then?" he asked.

"Because I am a fool. I know property and family and

common interests are supposed to be the pillars of a good match, but I cannot preach to you what I do not believe myself. I married for security and look what became of me. I was the Mistletoe Bough bride."

Valerius' warm hand closed over mine. "I am glad you understand."

"I did not say that," I warned him. "In fact, I object, strenuously, for the *opposite* reason. Val, you cannot take a wife so dispassionately, as if you were ordering soup from a menu. Life is far too long to spend it shackled with someone who does not—"

I broke off and looked away, suddenly embarrassed. He prodded me. "Someone who does not?"

"Someone who does not rouse your passions," I said in a burst of bravado. "Tepid affection or an overdeveloped sense of chivalry are no proper reasons for marriage. Surely you must see that."

He turned to me, mouth agape. "Chivalry? You think I mean to rescue her?"

"Of course you do. What other reason could there possibly be? Valerius, I have seen the dancers you admire. I know your tastes well enough. If you have ever kissed a girl who was not tiny and brunette and buxom, I will eat my basket."

His cheeks wore a painful flush. "Bellmont was right about you. Your association with Brisbane has coarsened you. I cannot believe you would notice such things, much less speak of them."

"Why?" I demanded. "Because I am a woman? What hypocrites you men are! You and Bellmont could happily spend an entire evening judging the opera chorus like a pair of horse dealers, and yet I am vulgar because I am willing to speak of what you ought to know well enough. For God's sake, Valerius, you have studied medicine! If you do not appreciate the fact that women have passions as well as you, then you are not fit to treat them."

He swallowed hard, his jaw set. "This discussion has become both uncomfortable and unprofitable. I see no need to prolong it. I intend to offer my hand to Hilda Allenby."

He turned on his heel and left me then, scattering chickens as he went. I hurried out onto the moor in a bad temper, an incipient headache lurking as I walked, hoping my interview with Rosalie would be more productive than either of my previous conversations.

As I drew nearer, I could hear a thin thread of violin music reaching out over the waving grasses of the moorland. It was a Gypsy tune, quick and lively, beckoning me onward. When I reached the wicket gate, Rosalie threw open the door, rosy and smiling.

"Lady, come and meet my husband!" I handed her the basket with my compliments, and she thanked me. She stepped back and I entered the cottage. Standing in front of the window was a Gypsy man of middling height, wiry and dark, with dancing black eyes and handsome features. There was a sharp intelligence in his eyes, and even a touch of flirtation as he drew his bow across the violin on one last, dancing note.

He was dressed in traditional Roma garb, with breeches tucked into soft leather boots to the knee, his shirt gaily patterned with checks and a scarlet handkerchief tied neatly about his neck. He wore a waistcoat, buttoned to show off his trim waist, and he sported a pair of handsome, lush moustaches, liberally oiled.

When he saw me, he doffed his flat cap and swept a courtly bow. "Good day to you, my lady. I am John-the-Baptist Smith."

I smiled and extended my hand. "How do you do? I am Lady Julia Grey."

He smiled back at me, his teeth flashing beautifully white against his olive skin. "Oh, I know you, lady. My Rosalie tells me all."

"Indeed? Then I shall be glad I have confessed to no crimes," I said lightly.

Rosalie did not laugh, but her husband roared, slapping his knees. "Tea, Rosalie love," he called, and she moved to put the kettle on.

"You should take Rook for a walk on the moor," she told him when she had done. "He returned yesterday, and he is pining for some attention. The tea will be ready when you return."

It was subtly done, but both John-the-Baptist and I knew it was an order, not a request. It amused me to find that Rosalie wielded such power in their relationship, but as John-the-Baptist took down his coat and whistled for the dog, I realised it was probably only because he permitted it.

"A singular fellow," I commented when he had gone. "And a likeable one."

"Indeed" was her only reply.

"It is a rare man who would consent to have a wife he could see only once or twice a year," I said, keeping my tone casual.

She shrugged. "Some men would see it as a blessing. No one to nag constantly, no one to spend his money."

"Oh, I don't know. I rather think John-the-Baptist would prefer your presence, don't you?"

She sat then, heavily, and gave me a sigh. It sounded like a breath of surrender, and I knew it was time to ask the questions I wanted answered.

"Why didn't you tell me Sir Alfred Allenby was the man responsible for putting Mariah Young in gaol?"

Rosalie's face had settled into lines of fatigue, or was it despair? There was something old and tired about her, and for the first time I realised how much of her youthful vigour was an illusion. There were spots on the backs of her hands, just a few, and there seemed to be more silver threads among the black of her hair.

"Yes, the Allenbys and the Youngs have a long history," she said finally. "Our destinies were intertwined long ago, and even now we are not able to break free."

"Of course you could," I said sharply. "Brisbane has only to sell this place and you to go travelling with your husband. No one is keeping you here."

Rosalie laughed, a dry, brittle, mirthless sound. "She does. *She* keeps me here. I swore an oath to her, and I am bound by it, as firmly as by the strongest iron chains."

"Are you talking about Mariah? Rosalie, she has been dead for thirty years. You owe her nothing. If there ever was a debt or obligation, you have certainly paid it by now."

She shook her head, her expression mournful. "You do not understand. The blood oath is a thing which cannot be broken, *must not* be broken. I am bound to remain here until it is done."

"Until *what* is done?" I demanded, my frustration rising. I had had my fill of half truths and enigmatic tales.

But she merely shook her head again, turning her wedding ring round and round on her finger, the slender band of gold mellow in the firelight.

"It was my fault," she said finally, her voice barely above a whisper.

"What was your fault?"

"Laudanum." She spoke slowly then, each word delivered painfully, as if being wrenched from her. "She suffered so from the headaches. I wanted her to be free of it. I gave it to her the first time. But she took it so often, too often. And she needed more and more to keep the pain at bay. That last day, she needed it so desperately, and I would not get it for her. We quarrelled, and I told her if she needed it—" She broke off, closing her eyes, her hands fisted in her lap. "I told her if she needed it she would have to steal it herself."

"Oh," I breathed, finally understanding at long last the burden of guilt Rosalie Smith carried upon her shoulders.

She opened her eyes. They were tearless, but full of pain, and I hated myself a little for opening such wounds.

"She was seen, and when they made her turn out her pockets, there it was."

She spread her hands helplessly, and I took one in my own. "Rosalie, it was not your fault. Mariah made her choices, and they were not good ones." I thought for a fleeting moment of Brisbane and his devils, wondering if it was even possible for him to avoid his mother's fate. I tightened my grip on her hand. "Rosalie, what is in the red syrup you gave to Brisbane? Is it poppy?"

She shook her head. "No. I would not give him syrup of poppy. He wanted it, but I knew it would destroy him. It is dangerous, the poppy—the hedge witch's laudanum. I gave him a special mixture of lettuce and skullcap, with a little colouring of beetroot so he would think it made of poppy. It will soothe a headache and induce sleep, but it is not dangerous."

I sagged in my chair, boneless with relief. "Thank God for that," I murmured. "I threw his out. I thought it was poppy. If you have more, I ought to take it to him."

"He has already been," she told me. The kettle had begun to boil and she rose to prepare the tea, moving slowly, as a woman underwater. "He came this morning to fetch it." She flicked me a sidelong glance. "You are meddlesome, Lady Julia. But from the best motives, I think."

"Of course from the best motives," I snapped. "I do not want anything to happen to him."

She spooned leaves into the teapot and poured in the water. I noticed something else in there as well, a few starry borage flowers. I said nothing. I could use whatever courage I could find, I decided.

"Something has already happened to him," Rosalie said, bringing the pot to the table. "He had a vision this morning, a gruesome one."

I felt a cold prickle down my neck. I hated to think that my actions had caused Brisbane to suffer, no matter how maddening he could be.

"What sort of vision?" I asked, my voice unnaturally high. But I had already guessed.

"He saw Death, lady. Dressed in black and gliding over the moor, waiting to collect a new soul as the moon waxes full."

Rosalie spoke then with all the theatricality of her people, imbuing each word with horror. She paused to allow the full dread to overcome me, then poured out a cup and pushed it toward me.

Defiantly, I drank it off, scalding and bitter. "Then his visions are singularly useless," I told her. "Death is everywhere."

"Indeed," she said, sipping at her tea, looking markedly more composed than she had a few moments before. "Death is everywhere. I only wonder if you will know him face-to-face," she finished darkly. And then she smiled her slanted, enigmatic Gypsy smile, and I wondered if I liked her quite as much as before.

THE TWENTY-SIXTH CHAPTER

Fortune, good night;
Smile once more, turn thy wheel.
—William Shakespeare
King Lear

As soon as I left Rosalie's cottage, I spied John-the-Baptist returning, Rook hard upon his heels, frisking in the soft heather. John-the-Baptist called a greeting and I paused on the path, waiting for him to join me.

"Tha women's gossip is all finished?" he asked, smiling knowingly.

"Are women ever finished gossiping?" I asked by way of reply. Rook nuzzled my knee and I bent to pet his rough white head.

"The dog likes you. He doesn't usually take to *gorgios*," John-the-Baptist remarked.

"We are old friends now, Rook and I." I straightened,

brushing the dog hairs from my skirts. "You must be very glad to see Rosalie again."

He nodded. "Aye. It's been too many years apart. But there's an end to that."

"You mean to take her with you this time?" I wondered if Rosalie knew that. She seemed perfectly content to remain where she was, mired in guilt and bound by a promise to her dead sister.

"I do," he told me, folding his arms over his chest in a confident gesture I had seen so often upon his nephew. "This business here is done, or it will be soon."

My hand stilled of its own accord. "You know this for a fact?" I wondered then if he had spoken to Brisbane, if perhaps he knew something more of Brisbane's plans than his own aunt did.

"My sister has the sight. She told me this will be the end of things," he said, his brows lowering ominously.

"Ah, yes. When the moon waxes full, I have heard," I returned waspishly.

A small smile played about his lips, nearly hidden by his moustaches. "You do not believe in the sight?"

"Oh, no, I believe. I have seen it often enough to know its power. It would just be helpful if the sight could be more *specific*," I complained.

John-the-Baptist gave a little snort of laughter, but said nothing.

"You knew Brisbane as a child," I said suddenly, remembering Rosalie's tale of how John-the-Baptist had intervened in a quarrel between Brisbane's parents.

He gave a nod, and the kerchief at his neck fell an inch

or so, baring the flesh. I could see a thin white line, the legacy of his interference. It marked him still.

"I taught the boy to sit a horse like a centaur and to play the violin as if it were part of his own arm," he said proudly. "Rosalie and I had no children. The boy was like my own."

"It must have been quite a wrench for you when he left," I hazarded.

Again, that slow secret smile. "A wrench? Lady, I gave him the money."

My expression must have betrayed my surprise for he gave a roar of laughter, startling the dog. "We are not like *gorgio* folk," he reminded me. "A boy is a man when he can keep a wife. And Nicholas had wit. I knew he could survive." He shook his head. "Lady, you look doubtful, but I tell you the truth. Nicholas was more of a man at ten years old than I was at twenty. He took care of himself because he was forced to it. Life for a *poshrat* in our tribe is not easy, particularly if his father is the *gorgio* parent. He would never have been fully accepted."

I recognised the word *poshrat*. It meant a half blood, and it was never used by the Roma as a term of affection.

"You mean your own people did not consider him one of them?"

"Never," he said flatly. "This is why marriage between your people and mine is not encouraged. Life is very hard for the children, more so if the mother is Roma. It is her duty to keep the blood pure and not marry outside of her own people."

I gave a sigh of exasperation. "And so the children are punished, when it is through no fault of their own that their blood is mixed?"

He lifted one shoulder in a shrug. "It is the way. I am not so particular. If the boy was born to my wife's sister, he is a Rom, that is my way. But I am only one man in the tribe. I cannot change the old ways, and I would not want to. I did what I could for him, and I helped him to leave. I never told Rosalie, but believe me when I say it was the best."

"I suppose it was," I said slowly, thinking of the life Brisbane had made for himself.

John-the-Baptist must have intuited my thoughts, for he threw his arms wide. "You see what he is now? A *gorgio* lord, even if he does not bear the title. He owns land and the other *gorgios* treat him with respect. It is not our way, but it is the *gorgio* way. If he must live in their world, he must be better than they are."

I took his point, but there was no possible reply to such a statement. Brisbane, as a half blood, would always be judged by a different standard, by both his Gypsy family and the English he lived amongst. It struck me as a formula for an incredibly difficult and lonely life.

"My tea is ready," he said. "I leave you now." He lifted his cap to me and I offered my hand.

He smiled in surprise and took it. His own hand was wide, the fingers long as suited a violinist.

"You are a lady of many surprises," he observed, giving me a mischievous smile. "I wonder what secrets you know."

"Not as many as I would like," I told him truthfully.

He laughed again. "Do not wish to know what is hidden," he advised me. "Things that are kept in locked cupboards are not worthy to be seen."

He left me then, whistling for Rook to follow. The dog

gave me a mournful look and trotted obediently away. As they moved, I heard the sound of the Grimswater bell, beckoning faintly. John-the-Baptist did not turn, but Rook pricked up his ears and paused a moment, then put his head down and followed his master.

"I will see at least one mystery in this place solved," I muttered, gathering up my skirts and picking my way hastily over the moor toward Grimswater. The ground was softer here, the mud clutching at my shoes and hems like soft, grasping fingers. I jerked myself free time and again, never quite making headway as I zigzagged over the ground, searching for a safe, dry path.

I thought that keeping to the low clumps of moor grasses would ensure safe footing, but no sooner had I stepped upon a promising bit of gorse than the ground gave way beneath me and I sank nearly up to my knees in squelching black mud.

"Damnation," I said. I wriggled my legs but they were stuck fast in the mud.

I heard a voice behind me.

"Lady Julia, are you quite all right?"

I glanced over my shoulder. Godwin was bounding toward me, light-footed as a damsel, springing from tussock to tussock until he reached me, not even breathing heavily.

"Godwin, thank God. I am quite stuck," I told him, looking ruefully at my legs.

He clucked at me and bent swiftly to remedy the situation. He looked up at me, his hand poised near my leg.

"May I?" His lips were twitching with amusement, and I thumped him on the back with a fist.

"Yes, you lummox. I don't care about propriety just now. Get me out!"

He bent again to his task, wrapping his hands firmly about my stockinged thigh and pulling slowly and evenly until the leg came free with a sickening sucking sound. There was a gush of black water and the hole filled again, swirling peaty mud about my other leg.

"Do not put tha' foot down again," he warned. "Thee'll only be stuck fast again. Wrap your arms about my back and keep tha' foot free of the ground."

I obeyed, but in spite of my little lecture about propriety, it was an awkwardly intimate position to occupy. His back was broad and warm under my arms, and I could feel the play of the heavy muscles as he gently worked my leg free. There was another great sucking sound as the earth rendered up my leg, dripping filthy water from my sodden boot and stocking.

Godwin turned and scooped me up easily. "Put tha' arms about my neck. I'll carry thee to solid ground, and then we'll see if thou're hurt," he said, cradling me gently as he had the pups. We had not far to go, and I did not argue with him. It was rather pleasant being taken care of, and so long as I did not make a habit of it, I did not see the harm.

In a very few minutes we had regained the path. He set me gently on my feet and spent quite a long time examining my ankles and knees for injury, feeling both carefully with surprisingly deft hands.

Finally I twitched my skirts down with a brisk gesture. "I *think* that will do, Godwin," I told him repressively. "I am quite all right, and I thank you for your timely rescue. I might have been stranded out there for hours."

The prospect was not an enticing one, but what he told me next chilled my blood.

"Tha' might not have survived at all," he said, his expression sober. "There are mires on the moor, and some of those spots have no bottom, nought but pools of mud tha' go on forever, right to the centre of the earth. Sheep have been lost on the moor before, and people, too, from time to time. Did no one say thee must keep to the path?"

I thought I remembered Ailith saying something of the sort, but I could not recall. "Perhaps. I had no idea it was all that dangerous. Thank you for intervening. My thoughtlessness put you at risk, and I am sorry for that."

He flushed with pleasure and embarrassment. "'Twas nothing. I've known these moors from boyhood. Besides, I would have done it twice over to save thee. I want you to think well of me, my lady."

He ducked his head, almost bashfully, and I gave a little cough, uncertain how to respond. Whatever admiration Godwin harboured for me, surely he knew nothing could come of it.

But perhaps I could use it to my advantage, I thought suddenly. I reached into my pocket and drew out the object I had been carrying.

"Godwin, do you recognise this?" I opened my palm, and lying flat, glowing burnished gold in the morning sun was the amulet of the ram.

His eyes widened and his tanned face went white to the lips. He took a step backward and looked at me in horror.

"Where did you get tha'?"

I held his gaze with my own. "I think you know where I found it. And the other, just like it."

He shook his head, angrily, as a child will. "I have never seen tha' before."

I took a step closer, raising my palm to his eye level, forcing him to see it. "Godwin, you are not that accomplished a liar. You have seen it. Tell me where."

He shook his head again, and when he spoke, his voice was clipped and completely lacking in the warm northern burr to which I had become accustomed. "I have never seen it before. And I have work to do. You can find your own way back to the Hall."

I stared after him as he broke into a run, taking the moor path in great, loping strides. I shoved the amulet in my pocket, nearly ripping the seam in my frustration. I had mishandled the situation badly. It had not occurred to me that he would be so horrified by the sight of the amulet. I had thought to surprise him, to startle him into telling the truth. I had not counted on his abject terror at seeing it.

I turned my steps toward Grimsgrave Hall, determined to find answers at last.

Not surprisingly, Brisbane was out when I arrived back at Grimsgrave. There was no sign of Godwin either, and I went to my bedchamber to freshen up a little. Grim quorked at me from his cage, but whether it was a greeting or a scolding, I could not tell.

I opened the little door of the cage and clucked at him,

encouraging him to come out, but he merely fixed me with a cold, beady eye.

"Good morning, Grim," I said formally, but he continued to look just over my shoulder, ignoring me with all the cool hauteur of a fine gentleman. A scolding then.

"Very well, sulk if you must. I am going to have a think," I told him. I reclined on the bed, hoping a few moments of meditative silence would help me to put the pieces together.

Still, nothing seemed to fit quite properly, and after a quarter of an hour I gave up and got something to read. Redwall Allenby's travel journals would be just the thing, I decided. He had left for Egypt just after the mine had collapsed and shortly after the disappointment of unrolling the ruined mummy. It occurred to me that he might well have alluded to his experiments in his first journal, and I opened it, skimming the spiky letters in faded brown ink. His writing style was painfully pedantic, with regular, dutiful recordings of what he ate, how long he slept, and even his toilet habits. I cringed a little as I skipped over them, searching for some mention of anything of significance.

But there was nothing, I soon realised. I reached for the next journal, and the one after, and these were more detailed, but just as disappointing. His travels had broadened to the Americas, to other parts of Africa and Europe as well as he trailed each new purchase related to Egyptology. He seemed to make many varied and interesting acquaintances, but none of his connections deepened to friendship, and there was a distinct air of superiority when he spoke of them. He was the worst kind of traveller, I reflected sourly. The entitled Englishman, considering himself lord of all he surveyed, and looking down on everything and everyone with marked contempt.

But as the journals went on, I noticed one change. There was frequent mention of money troubles, of requests on the part of his mother for funds for Grimsgrave, and his repeated annoyance that he should have to maintain an estate he no longer occupied. His spending was curtailed, expenses were curbed, and at last, to his outrage, he was obliged to accept a post with an expedition if he hoped to return to Egypt for the 1884-1885 season.

"The Evandale expedition," I murmured, tracing his endlessly dull recitation of the facts surrounding the equipment of the party. There were lists of supplies, innumerable complaints about poor accommodations and slights to his dignity. I skipped over the greater part of them, turning a dozen pages at a time. The first thing of interest was a tiny set of sketches, not very well-rendered, but perfectly recognisable. One was a ram of Osiris, the other the *tyet* of Isis. Underneath were scrawled the words, *Seven Days*. Something stirred in my memory, but only distantly. I turned the page, reading as Redwall railed against the members of the expedition, lambasting Lord Evandale for a fool, and naming the Comte de Roselende as his greatest enemy.

I have known him from childhood, and although I have the power to inform Lord E. that he has accepted employ under a false identity, I have said nothing. I have seen his black eyes upon me, and I know he realises I have recognised him. I have him in my power, and he wonders, even now if I mean to do him harm. He is a fool. I do not care what becomes of him. He is less than the dirt beneath my feet. Petty revenges will not distract me from my true purpose here: I will make great discoveries this season, discoveries which will ensure the recovery of my fortune, and the Allenby name.

I sat up as I read the words. Redwall Allenby rarely noticed anyone whose path crossed his. The fact that he found an enemy in Egypt was highly interesting. That was the season of his disgrace, I realised quickly, the last season he had spent in Egypt before returning home to England, and a premature death. He had been wrong not to fear his enemy. Whoever he was, Redwall had apparently estimated him badly.

I turned the page to read more, but it was blank, and in its place was clipped a photograph, smudged and grimy, but still clear enough. It was a group photograph, the Evandale expedition in that fateful year when Redwall Allenby was disgraced and drummed from Egyptology forever. I found Redwall at once, in the back of the group, tall and handsomely blond, perhaps only a slight twist of the lips betraying his annoyance at not being seated next to Lord Evandale in the front of the group. Lord Evandale's feet rested on a stuffed lion, and his expression was one of jovial *bonhomie*. Clearly he was no enemy to Redwall; he had not the temperament for it, and his face was like a child's, open and guileless. He was obviously delighted to be financing an expedition, and he had gathered his staff about him like an indulgent parent. I studied the other faces carefully, but none were familiar, save one. The man standing next to Redwall Allenby. He was muscular and well-formed, perhaps an inch taller than Redwall. He sported a luxuriant black beard, and across his firm waist stretched a watch chain, its slender length hung with a coin struck with the head of a Gorgon. The reverse of the photograph was labelled in Redwall's familiar hand, and I only turned it over to confirm what I already knew. Redwall Allenby had identified the tall, dark man beside him as St. John Malachy-LaPlante, the Comte de Roselende. But of course, I knew him as Nicholas Brisbane.

THE TWENTY-SEVENTH CHAPTER

Forbear to judge, for we are sinners all.
—William Shakespeare
Henry VI, Part 2

I stared at the photograph for a long time, feeling oddly light, as if my head was stuffed with cotton wool. I had known Brisbane loathed the Allenbys. He had even told me himself that he had been in Egypt, masquerading as an Egyptologist. Why had I not connected the points sooner? Brisbane had been the instrument of Redwall Allenby's disgrace and destruction.

Sickened, I closed the journal, shutting Brisbane's clever, calculating face away. I turned onto my side, thinking hard. The feud between their families was an old one. Sir Alfred Allenby had been responsible for seeing Brisbane's mother put into gaol where she died. Did Brisbane hold the rest of the Allenbys accountable for what one of them had done?

He must have, I thought fiercely. He had insisted upon

Lord Salisbury purchasing Grimsgrave Hall for him when a dozen other properties might have done just as well if not better. Properties in excellent condition, near to his business interests in London, properties with no ghosts or scores to settle. But Brisbane had chosen none of them. He had insisted upon having Grimsgrave, knowing the Allenby women would be at his mercy, dependent upon him as completely as Mariah Young had been upon the clemency of Sir Alfred Allenby.

And because Sir Alfred had shown no mercy to her, none would be given to the Allenbys, I realised with horror. Brisbane had marked his time, dangling the promise of a snug, pretty cottage in front of them, but forcing them to live under his roof, beholden to him. Until from frustration or anger or thwarted pride, Lady Allenby had attempted his life, giving him the perfect pretext to send her away. That he had not had her hanged ought to have given me a flicker of hope, but it did not. Brisbane was a subtle and clever man with a fair measure of hot Gypsy blood. He had been schooled in blood feuds since childhood. If he wanted an enemy to suffer, a quick snap of the hangman's noose would be too quick, too easy. How much more terrible to be immured in the stone walls of a convent, knowing nothing more of the outside world, but remembering every day that one's child and one's beloved home were still in the hands of a sworn enemy.

The very notion turned my stomach to water, and I was glad I had not eaten dinner. I relived every moment I had spent with Brisbane since I had arrived at Grimsgrave, every anguished glance he had given me, every time he had demanded my return to London. He did not want me to witness what he had become, to know what monstrousness he was capable of. How many times had he warned me he was bedevilled? And fool that I was, I had not listened. I had believed the passionate kisses, the warm, demanding hand in mine, and I had not believed him capable of real evil. But then, the poets tell us love is blind, I thought bitterly, and for all his sins, I loved him.

And as soon as I had constructed the case against him, I demolished it. "No," I told myself firmly, "it is not possible. He is no monster." I had known Brisbane in many and varied circumstances, and even though I knew him to be clever and dispassionate enough to be the architect of a revenge scheme, he was not vicious. I would not believe, even if I heard it from his own lips, that he would truly harm the Allenby women for the sins of their kinsmen.

But I had to know precisely what his intentions were toward Ailith and Hilda, and the only way to bring an end to the matter was to clear away all of the mysteries in that gloomy house. There was a legacy of pain and treachery in that place, and there would be no future for any of us if I did not expose it at last.

I closed the cage on Grim and hurried out of the room. The door to Ailith's room was closed and I tapped on it, shifting my weight impatiently. She called for me to come in, her voice serene as ever.

She was sitting on the floor, arranging dolls in her dolls' house. I went to her and knelt, startling her.

"Ailith, I wanted to talk to you, about Redwall and Brisbane—"

I broke off as I looked at the dolls in her hands. A pair of babies, tightly swaddled, with identical shocks of golden hair, hair identical to that shorn from the mummified babies in the study.

I rocked back on my heels, thinking hard. "They were yours," I said flatly. "The babies were yours."

She did not look at me. She merely continued to fuss over the tiny dolls, stroking their silken locks. "Yes. They were taken away from me as soon as they were born. I never even held them."

She laid them into the pair of cradles in the nursery she had so lovingly prepared. I felt a rush of horror and sympathy for her. She had given birth to children she had never even been permitted to hold. I thought of Lady Allenby and her flinty pride, Redwall and his horrible experiments.

"Were they stillborn?" I asked her, keeping my voice low and gentle.

She shook her head, her golden hair falling free. It was the first time I had seen her without it bound tightly into a coronet. She looked younger, and terribly vulnerable.

"No. They were alive when they were taken from me. I heard them cry."

"Who took them?" I asked, although I thought I knew the answer.

Her head came up then, her eyes flashing with anger even after all the years that had passed. "She took them. Godwin knows. He was there."

She ducked her head again and busied herself with tidying the little nursery of make-believe. I could not quite take it all in. It had been Godwin after all who was the villain.

Father to illegitimate children, doubtless goaded by Lady Allenby, he had been a party to giving them to Redwall to be immured forever, burying their secrets and shame with the bodies. Little wonder he had behaved so strangely when I had confronted him with the ram amulet. It must have been like seeing the very ghosts of his children resurrected. I wondered what would become of Ailith should the truth be revealed. I knew Brisbane would not deliberately harm her, but I could not say with perfect certainty that he would help her either. Perhaps the enmity between their families ran too deeply for that. No, it would be left to me to save her if I could.

I put an arm around her, noting that she had lost weight. She felt little more than skin and bones. My pendant slid out from my neckline and her eyes fixed on it, watching it swing back and forth, like a sleepy child watching a candle flame.

"That is Medusa, is it not?" she asked, putting out a finger to touch it.

I tucked it away and gave her a patient smile.

"Ailith, I wonder if you would not like a little rest. Perhaps we could go away. A trip to the seaside. Would you like that? I have a fancy to see Whitby. It would be such fun if you came as well. And Hilda and Portia. We could invite them, and make it a little party of hens, what do you say to that?"

Ailith shook her head. "There is no money for such trifles," she said sadly. "There is no money at all."

"Oh, do not mind about that. I will make all the arrangements. You must come as my guest. Would you like to visit the seaside?"

She nodded slowly. "Someone will have to mind Hilda's chickens. You will tell her to find someone to mind the chickens, won't you?"

Her gaze was flat and childlike. I coaxed her toward the bed. "Of course. Why don't you lie down now, and I will settle everything. Have a nice rest, and we can be gone in the morning. I will even have Minna pack for you. You need do nothing at all."

She climbed onto the bed and lay atop the coverlet. Her eyelids drooped, but then flared open. She put out a hand to mine.

"You are so very kind, Lady Julia," she murmured.

"It is nothing," I told her. "Rest now, and do not worry about anything."

She nodded and turned onto her side, curling into the pillow. In one hand she clutched the little pair of dolls with the bright gold curls.

I hurried from her room to the poultry yard. Hilda was pouring out fresh water for the chickens who were clucking irritably at her feet.

"Oh, be quiet, you bloody monsters. Can't you see I am doing you a favour?" she muttered.

"Miss Hilda, I should like a word," I told her.

She flicked a glance up at me but did not pause in her labours. "If it is about the proposal I have had from Valerius, it is none of your concern."

I smoothed my skirts. "Your impertinence notwithstanding, I quite agree. I have made my feelings known to Valerius. What he chooses to do is entirely his own affair."

She straightened, her thin upper lip curled. "Hardly an enthusiastic endorsement."

I spread my hands. "Did you expect me to feel differently? You have scarcely uttered a civil word to me the entire time I have been here, and you have made your intentions to marry another man quite clear. Naturally I am concerned if the lady my brother plans to wed is motivated solely by mercenary interests."

"Mercenary?" She threw the pail to the ground. "Oh, I like that. Val has told me something of your past. Tell me, would you have married Edward Grey if he hadn't had tuppence to rub together?" she demanded.

"Of course not," I told her. Her expression of triumph faded to one of astonishment. "I married Edward because we were friends, because I wanted an establishment of my own, because I was tired of being a spinster and a laughing-stock. If he had not had money, our paths would never have crossed. I moved then in rather more exclusive circles," I finished apologetically.

"Well, at least you are honest," she said, deflating a little.

"One ought to be, when speaking of such things," I replied. "And in perfect honesty, I do not wish you to marry my brother because I think you cannot make him happy, and I believe he would fail you as well. His intentions are of the very best sort, but he is a somewhat unhappy young man because he has no proper occupation for his time. Until he is settled within himself, he will be no sort of husband. That is my opinion, but I meant what I said. I have spoken to Val, and now I have spoken to you. I will say nothing further on the matter, and if you choose to marry, I will welcome you as a sister."

She curled her lip again, a singularly unattractive expression, and I longed to tell her so.

"Very well, believe me or don't. I do not care. I am more concerned about Miss Ailith."

Her eyes widened, but her gaze slid from mine. "Why?"

"I believe she is quite fragile at present," I said slowly. I did not know how much Hilda knew of her sister's ordeal, but it was not my place to disclose it. I must tread warily. "She has been in low spirits since your brother died. I think the departure of your mother has had a dampening effect upon her, and I detect signs of melancholia. I proposed to her a rest cure at the seaside. I would like you to come as well, as my guests, of course," I finished hastily lest she refuse on monetary grounds.

She stooped to retrieve her pail. "That is good of you," she said grudgingly. "But I think not. It would be best if Ailith stays here."

She drew an apple core from her pocket and tossed it to the hens, clucking softly at them.

"Hilda, I must disagree. Your sister seems changed, childlike. She must be looked after."

Hilda turned then and fixed me with a pitying stare. "Looked after? Ailith is more capable of looking after herself than anyone I have ever known. The devil himself could not stand against her."

I blinked. "You do not understand. I am not at liberty to reveal everything, but I can say that your sister suffered a tragedy when your brother was lost, and the recent upheavals in your family have not helped in her recovery. She needs gentle treatment and a rest cure if she is to be restored."

Hilda's little hands fisted at her sides. "The only treatment my sister needs is a hangman's noose."

She clamped her mouth shut as if to bite back the words. I moved toward her.

"What do you mean?"

She dropped her head, but I took her shoulders in my hands and shook her hard. "What do you mean?" I demanded again.

Hilda wrenched her arms from my grasp. "She was the one who attempted Brisbane's life, not Mama. She was the one who put the mushrooms onto his plate. She took a toadstool from the wood and sliced it up and mixed it with the mushrooms Mama bottled last year."

Blackness crept into the edge of my vision and I blinked it away. I felt terribly cold, as if I had just swum in a lake of icy black water.

"Why?" I whispered.

She shook her head, her expression mutinous. "I have said too much already. But you must go. Leave this place and make Brisbane go with you." Her voice broke on a sob. "I know I cannot marry Valerius. You will not want to have your brother connected to a murderess. I know her for what she is. I have always known her. She will not harm me, but she hates Brisbane. And you as well. I beg you, leave."

I pressed my temples to stop the roaring inside my head. "I cannot believe this. I thought her vulnerable—"

Hilda gave a ragged sob then, and to my surprise, she permitted me to embrace her. She cried like a child, great gasps of emotion that tore at my heart. There was so much raw feeling under that brusque exterior, it was like holding some newborn, quite awkward thing.

I held her until she stopped. She pulled back suddenly, wiping the moist places of her face on her sleeve.

"I am sorry," she said finally. "I do not know what came over me. I am not usually such a blubberboots."

"I don't imagine you give way to emotion very often," I ventured.

"Not unless it is anger," she agreed. "It is so much easier that way. I am so tired, you see. So tired of being here, year after year of my life just unrolling behind me with nothing to show for it. I've no education, no career, no family or home of my own. Nothing to show that I have ever set foot on this earth. When I am gone, there will only be a stone to mark that I was here, and even that will crumble in time."

There was no pity for herself in her voice, only the flatness of resignation, and I realised she and Valerius shared precisely the same affliction. They both wanted desperately to matter in a world that took no notice of them. Perhaps they were better suited than I had thought.

But this was no time to worry about their romantic prospects. I needed to talk to Brisbane, and the sooner the better.

"I will go and find Brisbane," I told her. "He will know how to get to the bottom of—" I broke off as something in the tail of my eye caught my attention. "He must be out on the moor. I will find him. Go and close the door before the chickens get out." The door in the stone wall that led to the moor path was slowly swinging open in the wind.

Hilda went white to the lips. "I shut it myself. Someone has been listening to us."

She looked at me in horror. "Ailith," she whispered. "Julia, she will kill him. She means to, and now that she knows I have told you, she will stop at nothing." Her eyes rounded and she clutched at me. "Valerius is out on the moor. He went for a walk. If he thwarts her…"

I gave her no time to finish the thought. I was through the door and on the moor path before she finished speaking. She was hard behind me, urging me faster.

We broke into a run, and I cursed my stays as they bit into my sides. But every minute counted now, and I was determined to keep pace with Hilda as we raced over the moor, mindful of the boggy mud and the low thorny bushes snatching at our skirts. She led the way, hurtling along like a modern Atalanta.

From time to time as we ran I looked up toward Thorn Crag, but I could see no one. I thought I saw a flash of movement just once, but it might have been a trick of the light. The clouds were lowering over the moor, weather that Yorkshire folk call wuthering. A moor mist was rising, and I blessed it, for if it shrouded the top of Thorn Crag, it hid our approach as well. We climbed as quickly as we dared, hoping the descending fog would muffle our movements.

It was very dark now, the afternoon sun blotted out by the thunderous black mass of cloud that hung low and threatening. The rain started to fall as we ascended the crag, making the rocks slippery and dangerous and more than once we fell heavily. Hilda was bleeding from her hands and I from a particularly nasty cut above my cheek, but we did not stop, nor did we slacken our pace. We forged on, wiping blood and rain from our faces. We climbed on our hands and knees in some places, clinging to the steep path only through force of will.

I smothered a scream when I put out my hand and felt a face. It was Valerius, unconscious, his complexion deathly pale, bleeding freely from a wound to his temple. There was a rock next to him, jagged and blood-stained.

"You must stay with him," I told Hilda. "Bind the wound, and hold it fast."

It is to her everlasting credit that she did not argue. She knelt swiftly as I stepped past him, sending up a desperate, incoherent prayer as I did so. He was in God's hands now, and Hilda's, and there was nothing more I could do for him.

I looked up the path, dashing the rain from my face. There was one more ledge to climb, and I did so, peering around the last boulder, steeling myself for what I would find when I reached the top.

It was unthinkable. Ailith was perched on the very edge of the crag, her cloak whipping behind her on the wind. She was sobbing, her hair streaming wildly, like a maenad's, and she clutched a dagger in her hand, the obsidian blade of the Egyptian embalmer, taken from her brother's collection, doubtless snatched up before she left Grimsgrave. Brisbane was perhaps ten paces from her, his back safely to the rock, his hand held out in front of him as if to push her. Blood was streaming from a cut to his brow, and I realised she must have landed at least one blow with her blade.

"You are a monster," she shrieked, her voice carrying on the wind. "You deserve to die for what you have done," she cried, edging farther away from him. She trembled on the very rim of the drop now. "Do not come closer!"

Brisbane advanced purposefully, stealthy as a lion. He put out his hand. "I want to watch you die, Ailith," he said, in a voice I had never heard him use before, cold and commanding. I had underestimated his hatred for the Allenbys, I realised. Here before me was the proof of it, Ailith pleading for her life and Brisbane, coolly preparing to deprive her of it.

At that moment I stepped from behind the rock. Brisbane's head jerked toward me, his eyes locked with mine. He said nothing, but I understood him perfectly. In the space of a heartbeat, I made my choice.

I rushed at Ailith, throwing wide my arms to embrace her and twisting as we fell so that we landed hard upon the ledge.

As we fell, we rolled, so that Ailith was on top of me, the tip of her knife wedged firmly into my stays. She pushed herself up slowly, her eyes burning with rage.

She wrenched the dagger from my stays and brandished it just as Brisbane leapt. He had caught her by surprise. He could move as swiftly as a cat when he liked, but what he did to her was not graceful or lovely. It was brutal and almost faster than the eye could see. He snapped her wrist back, breaking the bone and forcing the dagger from her hand. She screamed and would have fallen to her knees but for Brisbane's grip. She cursed and spat, but he held her fast as I struggled to my feet, holding my side where the knife had dented my stays. I stood next to Brisbane, keeping a wary eye upon Ailith, who had gone suspiciously quiet.

"Are you hurt?" he asked me in a low voice, never taking his eyes from Ailith.

"Just a bruise, nothing more," I told him.

"Good." He tightened his grip upon Ailith's arm. "If you had hurt her, I would have thrown you off this crag and smiled as I did it. As it is, it will be my very great pleasure to watch you hang."

He paused and wiped the blood from his face with his free hand. "Ailith Allenby, I am holding you for the attempted murder of Valerius March," he said flatly.

"And yours," I told him, prodding him in the ribs. He winced a little, and noticed then the ever-widening red stain on his shirt. "It was she who poisoned you, not Lady Allenby."

"Yes, I did know that," he said. He spoke to me, but his gaze never wavered from her face. "That was why I sent her mother away. Lady Allenby was in as much danger from her as I."

Ailith laughed then, doubling over and screaming her mirth to the teeming skies. It echoed over the moor and rolled back to us. There was madness in that laughter, and I wondered I had not seen it in her before.

"You stupid man, even now you don't understand, do you? You're still the filthy ignorant Gypsy brat you always were. I am an Allenby, a daughter of kings. I am not subject to your laws," she told him, raising her chin high and staring at him with all the disdain of an empress.

She looked at me then and gave me a little smile, and I knew what she meant to do. I could not have stopped her, even if I had wished to. There was no time.

With her uninjured arm, she gave Brisbane an unexpected shove, catching him off guard and rocking him back on his heels. Then she straightened her back and simply stepped off the side of the crag. There was no mad laughter now. There was only the long, deathly drop and the faint tolling of the Grimswater bell through the soft, muffling rain as Ailith Allenby fell to the rocks on the moor below.

THE TWENTY-EIGHTH CHAPTER

Be just, and fear not.
—William Shakespeare
Henry VIII

It was a difficult job getting Valerius off the crag. The wound to Brisbane's chest was shallow but bleeding freely, making rather a mess of things until I demanded a knife to cut my skirt hem to make a bandage. He handed me Ailith's knife and I felt my stomach churn at the sight of it. But I put my hand to the grip and sliced through the tweed, hacking off enough cloth to bind Brisbane's wound until he could be properly stitched.

Brisbane hefted Val onto his shoulders, his teeth gritted against the pain that must have seared his ribs. But he held my brother steady and set his face against the rain and the wind to carry him to Rosalie's cottage as it was the nearest shelter. Hilda followed, her eyes red with unshed tears. She did not look back at the broken body of her sister.

Without speaking of it, we hurried as fast as we dared to the cottage. John-the-Baptist hastened out to help and he and Brisbane carried Val in between them. Rosalie bustled about, collecting what she would need to nurse them both and to attend to the rest of us.

I sat by the fire, bone-tired and drenched to the skin, pressing a cloth soaked in calendula water to my cheek. Rook the lurcher came to sit with me, putting his head onto my lap. He did not seem to mind when my tears dampened his fur, and I stroked him for what seemed like hours. I kept reliving that terrible moment when I had rounded the boulder on the crag and seen Brisbane, menacing and vengeful, and Ailith, teetering on the edge of the crag, giving every appearance of pleading for her life. It would have been so easy to have made the wrong choice, I reflected. It was only by the smallest chance I had not.

"Lady." I looked up and there was Rosalie, holding out a warm wrapper of bright scarlet cotton. "I have already made Miss Hilda change. You must get out of those wet things. You will catch your death. I have brewed a posset for you, and John-the-Baptist has hung a curtain. You can change there. Let me look at your cheek."

Gently, she pulled the cloth away, and peered closely at my face, then nodded. "It will not even swell. I will give you a salve of calendula and thyme. It will help you to heal. Use it often, and there will not even be a scar to remind you."

I did not think I should require a scar to remind me of the day's events, but I was too tired to argue.

She coaxed me to stand and I saw that Val had been settled into her little bed, his head neatly bandaged, his tanned face still too white and unnaturally still.

"Will he—" I did not want to ask it.

She patted me. "He will be fine, if God wills. We have done all that can be done."

Hilda was sitting perfectly still in a chair next to the bed. She was dressed in a bright green blouse and blue skirt, the colours incongruous against the moment. She did not look at me, nor did she speak. She simply sat, staring at Val's pale face.

I turned then to see Brisbane, stripped to the waist, sipping something that steamed in the cup, something bitter from the expression on his face. His uncle was plying a needle and thin silk thread, neatly stitching up a long, shallow gash across his ribs.

I swallowed hard and Rosalie patted me again. "There is no one with a better hand to the needle than a Gypsy harness-maker," she told me firmly. She steered me behind the curtain, and when I made no move to lift my hands, she came with me, briskly undressing me and rubbing my skin with a rough towel. My skin was tingling by the time she had finished, and I was warm for the first time since I had seen Val lying broken on the crag. Rosalie helped me into the wrapper, knotting the sash snugly at my waist. She cleaned the gouges on my hands and cheek then, careful not to hurt me. Then she unbound my hair and brushed it until it crackled.

"There. Now for your posset," she said firmly. She seated me next to the fire again and gave me a steaming cup like the one Brisbane was drinking from. It *was* bitter, full of tea and herbs and something potently alcoholic. I felt energised and much the better after I drank it.

John-the-Baptist set the last stitch and Rosalie handed

Brisbane a pot of salve to daub onto the wound. He obeyed and she bound it neatly with clean strips of white linen while John-the-Baptist brought him a fresh shirt and cleaned the cut to his brow. We looked rather more reputable then, and Rosalie brewed tea and ladled out mugs of hot soup as John-the-Baptist departed to take a message to the Hall.

I had no appetite for soup, but drank my tea, feeling a hundred years old and saying nothing. Hilda was finally persuaded to take some posset, but she drank less than half of it, letting the rest of it grow cold in the cup.

Brisbane did not speak either, and Rosalie asked no questions. She knew the answers would come soon enough, and I almost dreaded the arrival of my sister when we would have to explain what had happened on Thorn Crag.

Rosalie brewed tea for everyone and was just putting out new bread and butter when John-the-Baptist returned with Portia and Mrs. Butters, Minna and Godwin in tow.

I roused from my torpor. "Portia, dearest, why have you brought the entire household?"

She shrugged. "It hardly seems fair to keep them out of it now. It is a family affair, and Godwin is an Allenby." She took a little stool next to me and dropped her voice. "And apparently Godwin and Minna have an understanding," she told me, lifting her brows significantly. "We shall have to write her mother."

I thought of Godwin standing before me on the moor path after he had helped me out of the boggy mud. *I want you to think well of me,* he had said. And I thought of how badly I had misinterpreted his interest in me. He might well have acted the part of the country gallant, but he did not want *me;* he wanted my approval of his match with Minna. I shook my head, wondering how many other things I had misunderstood since I had come to Grimsgrave.

Rosalie found low stools for Minna and Godwin, while Mrs. Butters took the last chair at Portia's insistence. John-the-Baptist stood a little distance apart, but Rosalie came to sit with the rest of us at the table. It was quite a snug fit for the cottage, but I felt comforted at having so many of us there, and I fancied the others felt the same.

It was Brisbane who spoke first. He looked from Godwin to Mrs. Butters as he addressed them.

"Godwin, Mrs. Butters," he said softly, "I am sorry to tell you Ailith Allenby is dead."

Mrs. Butters said nothing for a long moment. Then she nodded toward the cut on his brow, a thin, wicked slash that only enhanced his resemblance to a pirate. "Is tha' her handiwork?"

Brisbane nodded.

"I am only sorry she harmed you before she died," Mrs. Butters replied calmly. "I will not pray for her. The devil looks after his own, so the Scriptures tell us."

I blinked at her and Portia gave a little gasp which she covered with a cough, but not successfully. "I thought that was Shakespeare," she murmured to me.

Mrs. Butters turned to her, her expression one of mild surprise. "Have I shocked you, Lady Bettiscombe? I am sorry for it. But Ailith Allenby was wicked, through and through. She always was, even as a child, and Redwall was just the same. It was bad blood, you know. A little weakness in a family is a small matter. A tendency to melancholia, or a love of drink, these may be overcome by fresh blood coming into the line. But the Allenbys seldom married outside of their own. They insisted upon maintaining the purest blood in Britain, and they paid for it."

Her expression took on a faraway look, as if she were telling a faery story to children. "I saw it in Sir Alfred's mother when I first came to Grimsgrave. She were elderly then and nearly an invalid. But she lived in mortal hatred of cats. Whenever one came to Grimsgrave, she drowned it herself in the pond. I daresay tha's what gave Lady Allenby the idea."

"Lady Allenby?" I asked.

Mrs. Butters' smile was infinitely sad. "The twins, my dear. Ailith's children. Lady Allenby drowned them in the pond in front of the house, just after they was born."

Brisbane went a shade paler under the olive of his complexion, and Portia and I exchanged shocked glances, but Rosalie's expression did not change.

"You knew she had been pregnant," I said suddenly. "You gave her raspberry leaf tea when I first came here."

Rosalie nodded. "She bore the twins last year. She was too old to bear for the first time, and the birth tore her womb. It has never been strong since. She used to come to me for remedies. The raspberry leaf was soothing."

Portia shook her head. "Ailith bore illegitimate twins? And her mother killed her own grandchildren? I cannot take it in. They must have all been mad as hatters."

"They were," I said softly, casting a glance at Hilda. She was silent, her head resting against the back of her chair, her eyes closed. I went on. "Mad enough to let Redwall embalm the children and make mummies of them. But he left clues in their wrappings, a pair of amulets, the knot of Isis and a golden ram. They were tokens to symbolise the parents. The knot of Isis stood for Ailith, the tall, golden goddess. And the ram stood for…" I glanced at Godwin, the sheep farmer who had been so poorly used by his cousins. I cleared my throat and proceeded. "The ram was the symbol of the god Osiris, the husband and brother of Isis, and it stood for Redwall Allenby."

Hilda gave a low moan of disbelief and dropped her head into her hands. Portia stared at me. "Ailith Allenby gave birth to twins fathered by her own brother?"

"Yes," I told her, gaining confidence as I finally remembered what had stirred in my mind when I had seen the little sketches of the Isis knot and the ram in Redwall's journal.

"Redwall left a clue in his journal. He sketched the knot of Isis and the ram and beneath it he wrote, *Seven Days*, the title of an Egyptian love poem." I paused and cleared my throat, then began to recite.

Seven days since I saw my sister,
And sickness invaded me;
I am heavy in all my limbs,
My body has forsaken me.
When the physicians come to me,
My heart rejects their remedies;
The magicians are quite helpless,
My sickness is not discerned.
To tell me "She is here" would revive me!

I glanced around to see a mixture of horror and revulsion and sadness on the faces gathered in the little cottage. "Egyptian love poems often used the terms 'brother' and 'sister' when referring to lovers," I finished. "But Redwall meant them quite literally. He must have begun his seduction of Ailith even before he returned home from Egypt. She was his golden goddess, his sister-queen, and to his mind, she was his only worthy consort."

"Madness," Portia breathed.

"But it is true, isn't it, Mrs. Butters? It makes sense, really. They were always together, thick as thieves when they were children. Only the Allenby pride, twisted to madness by now, would not let them marry outside of their own blood. And Redwall began to study Egyptology. There was a strong precedent there for fraternal marriage. The gods did it, and so did the pharaohs. Cleopatra married two of her brothers. It was a means of keeping the blood pure and the power within the family. And so these two beautiful, mad individuals came together and conceived a pair of twins."

"Yes, it is true," Hilda said, opening her eyes slowly. She rose and came to the table, moving as stiffly as an old woman. Godwin stood and she took his seat, leaving him to stand next to the fireplace. She began to speak, and it was akin to watching a purge. The words flowed out, slowly at first, then faster as she released them.

"They were lovers. I saw them at it once, at the chapel by the river. They had always been close, and when he left for Egypt, Ailith was the one he wrote to every week, without fail. I do not know if it was the distance that blunted him to the fact she was his sister, or if it was his illness."

"His illness?" Portia prompted softly.

"Malaria. He contracted a virulent form of it," Brisbane put in. "He was dosing himself with quinine, massive amounts."

"Oughtn't that to have made him better?" Portia inquired.

"Not the amount he was taking. The cure can be worse than the ailment. He was already suffering from a touch of deafness and spells of dizziness, as well as hallucinations. I warned Lord Evandale that he wasn't to be trusted in that state. Lord Evandale sent his doctors, but Redwall would have none of it. He was too far sunk into his depravity by then."

"It was a pretext," Hilda put in bitterly. "An excuse for him to do what he liked. Mama indulged him so, and Ailith did as well. Only I saw him for what he truly was—a monster. But I never imagined that there might have been children. It is too horrible to be believed."

She lapsed into silence, and I resumed the thread of my narrative. "I wonder if Ailith was horrified when she realised she was going to bear a child? Perhaps it had all been a dream to her, something not entirely real, a bit of play-acting. A romance of sorts for a girl with a romantic imagination who had never had a lover. And then she knew she would have to tell her mother what had happened."

"She was not horrified," Mrs. Butters corrected, her chin quivering with indignation. "She was *proud,* proud as the devil she was. She actually thought her mother would understand. She and Redwall went to her hand in hand. They wanted to go right away together, to start anew and pass themselves off as man and wife. Lady Allenby persuaded them to stay. She told them Ailith would require nursing after the birth, and tha' she was the one best suited to do so discreetly."

"But she did not approve, did she?" I asked.

Mrs. Butters shook her head. "Tha' was when her religion became an obsession with her. She prayed for hours on her knees, until sores opened and when she could no longer kneel, she lay right on the floor before the Crucifix. She never said, but I think she was praying for God to take the child before it was born. She shut Ailith in her room and told everyone she had taken a bad chill and must not be disturbed. And every day she went on her knees to beg God to intervene. Ailith delivered twins, healthy, beautiful children. It must have seemed to Lady Allenby as if God himself had forsaken her. But she knew what she had to do."

Mrs. Butters paused in her story, looking into the depths of her teacup. "She took the babies from Ailith. She told her they must be cleaned before they could be swaddled. And she carried them out to the pond and drowned them, praying over them all the while. Then she took them back inside and dried them and gave them to Redwall. She told him sometimes healthy babies die for no reason. He were out of his mind with grief and sickness. He would believe anything she told him. He wanted to preserve them forever. He began to mummify them."

She nodded toward Godwin. "You knew. Ailith had been able to hide her pregnancy for a very long time. She favoured those wide, old-fashioned skirts, she did. But at the end, you knew she was carrying. You're a clever lad and you've seen enough ewes at lambing to know what breeding looks like.

You listened at doors and peered in windows as well, and you knew what had happened. You went to Redwall and Redwall promised you a sum of money to be quiet, did he not? He also promised to leave you the farm in his will," she added.

"A promise he didn't keep," Godwin put in, his face flushing.

"Did you know about the children, Godwin?" I asked him. I thought of Ailith's insistence that he had been there, but she had said quite distinctly that "she" had taken her babies. I wondered which version was the truth. Godwin's eyes held mine for a long moment, then he nodded.

"Aye. And I would not have thought it possible, but Redwall hated me the more for it. The thieving bastard would have cheated me. He meant to take the gardener's cottage from me, told me so just before he died. He would have turned me out to starve if he'd lived."

Minna, completely unconscious of the fact that her betrothed had just confessed a very sturdy motive for murder, patted his arm consolingly.

I turned suddenly to Brisbane. "Did you know whose children they were?"

He fixed me with a steady look from those deep black eyes. "When I saw the amulets together, I knew."

"Why didn't you tell me?" I demanded, but he said nothing more. His quarrel with the Allenbys was long and deep and he had done his best to keep me at a remove from it. Perhaps he had meant to use the information against Ailith, I surmised, or perhaps he simply had not decided what to do with it.

"She knew you meant her harm," I told him. "That is why she poisoned you. It was not Lady Allenby at all. With one stroke, she thought to remove you and see her own mother hanged for the crime. A perfect revenge upon you both."

"Except that I did not die," Brisbane said softly.

"No, you survived, and in an unexpected act of clemency, you did not turn Lady Allenby over to the authorities. You sent her to a convent," I finished.

"For her own protection," Brisbane said. "Ailith planned to destroy us both, and her initial plan would have done it. Once she was thwarted, there was no telling what she might do. If Ailith Allenby was so determined to see her mother hanged, then she would likely try again. I had to get her straight away from Grimsgrave. That left Ailith only one victim to vent her wrath upon."

I stared at him, scarcely comprehending his carelessness. "You rage at me, but you are without a doubt the most headstrong, wilful, obstinate, *reckless* man I have ever known."

Brisbane did not rise to the bait. He merely shrugged, wincing a little at his stitched ribs. "She had to try, and she did today on Thorn Crag. I had not expected a direct attack, and my failure to anticipate her nearly cost Valerius his life."

"She might have poisoned you again!" I pointed out, aghast.

"Not likely, my lady," Minna chimed in. She was still holding Godwin's hand, stroking it gently. "Mr. Brisbane did ask me to prepare all of his food from a store I was to keep locked in the pantry. I was never to leave it unattended for a minute, and if I stepped away, I was to throw it out and boil an egg for him instead. Eggs is hard to tamper with," she said sagely. Then she gave a sheepish little smile. "Poor Mr. Brisbane has eat a lot of eggs recently."

Brisbane gave her a warm smile. "You did very well, Minna," he told her, and the girl blushed deeply.

I felt a surge of anger and battered it down. It was maddening that he had entrusted himself to Minna and not to me, but given my complete uselessness in the kitchen, it was probably all for the best.

"What happened today on Thorn Crag?" Portia asked.

Brisbane did not look at me. He stared into his cup as he replied, his words clipped. "Valerius came to Thorn Crag to speak with me. He wanted to discuss a private matter and thought we would not be overheard there. It was pure bad luck he was still there when Ailith arrived. She attacked him with a rock, leaving him unconscious. Then she came at me with a knife she had taken from Redwall's collection, an Egyptian embalmer's knife," he clarified.

He reached into his pocket and drew it out, laying it in the centre of the table. Light gleamed off the black obsidian blade. There were gods and goddesses wrought in small gold figures on the grip, with a chain of images set within a cartouche. It looked like something one might use to practise the dark arts, and I turned away.

"Julia arrived just as I disarmed Ailith and she fell from the crag," Brisbane finished smoothly. He flicked me a significant look, then let his gaze slide away. I opened my mouth, then closed it sharply.

"Miss Ailith fell?" Mrs. Butters asked.

"Miss Ailith fell," I told her, my voice ringing certain.

The process of moving us all back to Grimsgrave in the rain was slow and torturous. Valerius had roused a little, and taken some broth. Rosalie offered the use of the cottage to nurse him, but we decided it would be more comfortable and suitable for everyone if he were removed to the Hall. John-the-Baptist was dispatched to the Gypsy encampment to secure horses and willing hands. They came, a dozen Roma men, dressed in high boots and checked neckerchiefs, leading glossy horses whose tails and manes were plaited with silken ribbons that hung limp with the rain.

I glanced around just as we left the cottage to find Brisbane. I watched as he mounted a borrowed horse in one fluid motion. He caught my eye then, and held my gaze for a long moment. Then he turned his mount in the direction of Thorn Crag and kicked it hard in the flank. Portia prodded me then as we moved to the horses the Roma had provided for us.

"Where is Brisbane going?"

I did not meet her eyes. "Someone has to bring Ailith home," I told her.

I turned away then and John-the-Baptist laced his fingers to provide me a mounting block. I hefted myself onto the back of a sweet little piebald mare and turned her head toward Grimsgrave.

We must have looked a mad sort of parade as we rode slowly back to the Hall, a motley crew of injured and heartsick. The Gypsies, always superstitious about matters relating to death, were sombre and said little. From time to time I searched a face, wondering if any of these were cousins or uncles of Brisbane's. Here and there I caught a resemblance, in the curve of a high cheekbone or the imperious profile. John-the-Baptist rode next to me, keeping one hand on my bridle and a careful eye upon my face. I must have given him cause for worry because he heaved a great sigh of relief when he helped me to dismount in the forecourt of Grimsgrave.

He pressed my cold hands, startling me with his sudden gesture. "You will be fine now, lady. You are safe here."

I looked up at the bleak façade of the Hall, then at the dark waters of the pond, and shook my head. "I do not think I will ever feel safe here. This is a house of too many secrets and too much pain."

He smiled his gentle smile, his moustaches curving upward. "Lady, a house is merely stones. And this house holds no horrors now."

I did not believe him, but I smiled to be polite and thanked him for his kindness. He ducked his head. For an instant I thought I detected the faintest trace of a blush staining his cheek. But darkness had fallen, and in the fitful light it was impossible to tell.

He mounted his horse again and whistled to his kinsmen. Two of them had carried Valerius inside and they returned, taking up the reins of the spare horses. They rode off then, saying nothing, but lifting their hands in farewell.

Hilda had hurried inside with Mrs. Butters to attend to Val, and Portia and I were left quite alone in the suddenly empty forecourt. My sister put her arm about me in an unusual and welcome gesture of affection.

"I cannot believe you and Hilda were stupid enough to trail a murderess to Thorn Crag," she scolded. "You might have been killed."

"We had no choice," I said simply. "She meant to kill

Brisbane and very nearly Val as well. There was no time to bring help."

We moved slowly into the hall.

"I still cannot believe it. She was such an odd, fey creature, at times reserved and elegant and at others almost childlike," Portia said.

"And cunning," I pointed out. "It was she who gave me the journals her brother kept in Egypt. She knew I would eventually recognise the photograph of Brisbane and deduce that he had been responsible for Redwall's disgrace. Perhaps she thought I would leave then, go back to London and leave the field clear for her to murder Brisbane at her leisure."

I gave a great shudder and Portia herded me upstairs as I talked, giving Morag quick instructions and seeing me safely into bed. Morag asked no questions, but I knew from her expression she would expect a full disclosure of the day's events the next morning. She brought up a cup of hot milk with honey and left us alone again. Portia fussed with bed-warmers and stoking up the fire before she drew up a chair and made me finish my tale.

"What happened after Redwall mummified the children?" she demanded.

"He planned to sell the estate and raise more funds, perhaps to leave with Ailith after all, but he died before he could do so. Lady Allenby and her daughters were left with the house, but no money at all to keep it. They were forced to sell it, and most of the furnishings and art. Only Redwall's collection was kept."

"I wonder why?" Portia mused.

I yawned broadly. "Sentimental value? Or guilt perhaps? We shall never know…." My voice trailed off then.

"Sleep now, Julia. I will go and sit with Valerius. If there is any news, I will come."

I wanted to nod, but my head was far too heavy. I thought I felt the brush of lips to my brow. Before I could respond, I fell fast asleep.

THE TWENTY-NINTH CHAPTER

We must not make a scarecrow of the law.
—William Shakespeare
Measure for Measure

rose sometime later, when the fire had fallen to cold grey ash and the moon had risen high above the crag. I could just make out the cool white glow of it, though the rain still fell softly against the windowpane. I slipped my arms into my dressing gown, tiptoeing silently down the stairs.

The door to Brisbane's room was ajar, as though he expected me.

"You ought to be abed," I told Brisbane. He was stretched out upon his bed, book in hand, still dressed, even to his mud-splashed boots and his uncle's shirt.

He laid aside the book.

"I cannot sleep," he said simply. A glass full of amber liquid stood on the mantel and he rose and took a deep draught of it.

I put out my hand. "Whisky?"

"From my great-uncle Aberdour's personal stock," he said, handing me his glass. I took a long sip, feeling its shocking warmth clear down to my toes.

"God bless the Duke of Aberdour," I said faintly. I handed the glass back to him and he finished it off.

"Where did you put her?" I asked. His knuckles were white against the glass.

"The inn. That is where the inquest will be held, so it seemed the simplest." He flicked me a glance. "You will have to give evidence. I am sorry for it, but there does not seem to be a way around it."

I folded my hands together. "Very well. I am sure it will not be so very terrible. We will say she fell, since that is the story we have already told. It will save a verdict of suicide being returned, and she will be buried in hallowed ground. Perhaps that will give her mother some comfort."

Brisbane stared at me, his black eyes wide. "You are the most singular woman I have ever met. You threw yourself at a murderess today and yet there you sit, cool as a duchess, calmly plotting to perjure yourself in front of a coroner's jury."

"What would you have me do? You are the one who said she fell. If that was not the story you wanted told, you ought not to have told it," I pointed out waspishly.

He shook his head and poured out another measure of whisky. "You really do not understand, do you? You have been so insulated from the world you do not have the faintest notion what the jury will make of you."

I blinked at him. "Of me? Why should they make anything of me? I am simply Julia Grey."

He gave a short, sharp laugh. "Simply Julia Grey." He downed the whisky in one go, clearing his throat as he put down the glass. He folded his arms over his chest, gingerly, so as not to pull at his stitches.

"Julia, you have broken almost every convention known to society. You are a widow, yet you do not wear black. I am a bachelor, yet you stayed as a guest in my home without a chaperone. You were alone with me on the crag when Ailith died. Read that, with the worst possible construction, because that is what the jury will do."

I considered it for a moment, then shook my head. "Nonsense. I realise it looks bad, but when they understand that Valerius was here—"

"Valerius was not here," he corrected. "Not for a matter of days. Neither was Portia. And if they have a mind to question her character as a witness, how long do you think it will be before they discover her relationship with Jane?"

"Oh, that needn't be a problem. Jane is gone. She left Portia to marry some man she met in London. She is off to India."

"That is beside the point," he said, grinding his teeth. "She is a woman of known immoral habits, that is what they will say. Do you want that in the newspapers?"

"They wouldn't dare," I whispered.

"Julia, you are not in the south. Your father's title carries little weight here. He cannot simply come in and fix everything up for you as he always does."

I bristled. "Father doesn't always fix everything up, thank you very much. I do make some rather good decisions."

Brisbane passed a hand over his face, fighting fatigue and frustration, no doubt.

"The March name is not hallowed here. He cannot head off the damage that might be done. Only I can," he finished softly.

"You? What can you do?"

He stared at me for a long moment, and when he spoke, his words were weighted, as if he had chosen each one with exquisite care.

"In order to protect your character—and your sister's—we will have to present a fiction to the jury. We will have to pretend to be betrothed."

I said nothing.

"We will say there was opposition from your family because of my low birth and my connections with trade. Your brother and sister came to lend respectability to the match in spite of your father's disapproval. We will tell them we meant to marry when the Hall was restored to order, only there was more work than we had anticipated. We had fixed the date for next week and were preparing to elope to Scotland. We will say Ailith suggested a picnic luncheon on the crag to celebrate our impending nuptials, but the weather turned foul and when we went to descend, she slipped and fell. It was a tragic accident, and that is all."

"What about Hilda?" I asked faintly.

"Hilda will do anything to keep the true story from becoming known."

I tipped my head. "You are rather fond of her, aren't you?"

Brisbane shrugged. "She is alone and defenceless, and she is as much a victim of this bloody family as those babies in the coffin."

I suppressed a smile. "I knew it. I knew you could never really harm a defenceless woman. You are the most virtuous man I know."

He sputtered. "Virtuous? I cannot think that that is a word that I have *ever* heard in relationship to my character. You are quite mad."

"I am not," I said stoutly. "I am perfectly serious."

"Julia," he began patiently, "there are certain expectations of behaviour in every civilized society. The fact that I observe them does not make me virtuous. It makes me no better than the next man."

"Rubbish. What virtue is there in a man who demonstrates goodness because he has been bred to it? It is his habit from youth. But a man who has known unkindness and want, for him to be kind and charitable to those who have been the cause of his misfortunes, that is a virtuous man."

He shook his head, wonderingly. "You are a singular woman, Julia Grey. You persist in seeing me as the man you want me to be."

"No," I corrected him. "I see you as the man you want to be."

He looked away sharply and took another sip of his whisky. "Thank you for that."

I primmed my mouth. "Yes, well." We both fell silent for a moment until I cleared my throat and wiped at my eyes. I assumed a brisk tone. "And what of your escapades on the moor? Surely you do not expect me to believe you were really playing at being a sheep farmer. What were you about at all hours, creeping about on the moor and receiving secret correspondence?" I asked, reminding him of the letter he had sealed so secretively in my presence.

"Mines," Brisbane said shortly. "There is still silver and lead under this land, I know it."

I quirked a brow and he pulled a face.

"Very well," he said. "I do not know. It is merely an intuition, but it springs from sound logic. Romans mined here, and there are traces of where they worked, if you know how to look for it. I instructed Monk and he set himself up in Howlett Magna as a visiting schoolmaster, complete with false whiskers. That way he had an identity established to account for being in the neighbourhood. We met once a week upon Thorn Crag or at the Bear's Hut to discuss our findings."

I stared at him, mouth agape. "That is astonishingly clever. But why the secrecy?"

Brisbane shrugged. "I did not want the village to know what we were about. If we found a mine, it would have put half the village back to work. It seemed cruel to raise their hopes only to dash them. Not only cruel, dangerous. They nearly stoned the Allenby who closed the mines, remember." His mouth shifted into a grin. "You gave poor Monk quite a fright when you arrived, you know. He spotted you across the street and dove into a linen-draper's lest you recognise him and give it all away."

I thought back to the odd elderly man with the curious limp I had seen in Howlett Magna.

"So there are no mines?"

"None that we have found," he said, his tone regretful. "And the estate itself has no resources beyond three sheep."

"Three sheep? You and Godwin spend every day out of doors looking after *three sheep*?"

He gave me a grim smile. "I needed a plausible reason to be away from the Hall," he said. "And Godwin doesn't want me to know that he has been systematically selling off the sheep to put something by should I turn him out."

"Thievery!" I breathed.

Brisbane shrugged. "I can hardly blame him. I would have done precisely the same under the circumstances. He has not been paid in three years, you know. So I pretended to believe there were more sheep on the moor and to spend my days looking for them. I could hardly tell you that Monk and I were searching for traces of Roman mines. We took it in turns to sit upon the crag, surveying the moor with a glass, both of us careful to keep out of Godwin's way. It was highly methodical and perfectly useless," he finished in disgust. He gestured toward the little flasks and bottles of his scientific equipment. "I have even experimented with the soil, and still we cannot find precisely where the veins rest under the moor. We have been so close."

I thought of the day I had sought Brisbane on the crag and wondered if he was quite alone. Monk must have been there then, comparing observations with Brisbane in their futile quest.

"All these months," I sympathised, "and nothing to show for it."

"Yes, well, it doesn't much matter now, does it?" He paused, as if marshalling his thoughts. "You did not answer me."

"About what?" I blinked at him.

"About pretending to be my fiancée," he said in exasperation. "Will you do it?"

I fought the urge to sob. It hardly seemed fair that I was being asked to pretend to be his fiancée when he might have proposed to me outright and been able to tell the truth to the coroner's jury.

I swallowed hard and smoothed out the skirts of my dressing gown. "As you have made it clear you are acting out of the noblest concern for my own reputation and that of my sister, it would be churlish of me to refuse," I said formally.

He inclined his head, matching my coolness with a dispassionate chill of his own. "Good. If we mean to make this plausible, we should tell no one it is a fabrication."

"You mean I have to lie to Portia and Valerius."

"They will forgive you when the truth comes out," he said dismissively. "After all, it is for their own good."

At that moment I felt an overwhelming urge to throw something heavy at his head. I left him instead. Maiming him would be a very poor start to our betrothal, sham or not.

I lingered in bed the next morning, nursing my physical ailments and hiding from my sister. A spectacular violet bruise had blossomed across my ribs from the blow struck by Ailith's knife against my corset. Morag helped me to dress, buttoning me into the only ensemble I owned that did not require a corset. It was a casual affair of bottle-green velvet, more suited to entertaining privately at home than being seen in public, but it was the best I could manage under the circumstances.

She told me Valerius had been awake for hours and had taken a nice bowl of beef tea and cursed Portia for fixing a fresh bandage too tightly about his head. In defiance of convention, Hilda had sat with him through the night and had finally retired to her own bed for some needed rest.

Morag said nothing of my erstwhile betrothal so I judged the story had not yet made its way belowstairs. My sister was another story altogether. No sooner had I seated myself at the table for breakfast than she pushed away her empty plate and fixed me with a sour smile.

"I hear congratulations are in order. Shall I buy you a wedding present? What would you like? A nice set of fruit knives, perhaps?"

Mrs. Butters bustled over with a plate of piping hot eggs and bacon, a rack of crisp toast, and a steaming pot of tea. Jetty was weeping quietly into her apron in the corner. Apparently, she had taken the news of Godwin's betrothal to Minna rather hard.

I took my first exquisite bite of breakfast and savoured it before turning to Portia.

"Don't let's be peevish. You always thought Brisbane and I would make a match of it."

"Yes, well, I didn't think you would be so furtive about the whole business. Brisbane said you have had an understanding since he left Bellmont just before Christmas."

My mind whipped back to that last moment, full of unspoken yearning, when we knew we would not see one another for a long time, if ever. I thought of what he had said to me, his lips against my hair, and what he had told me later still, when he lingered at the door. A woman could easily interpret such things as declarations, I reasoned, although I knew perfectly well if Brisbane ever proposed there would be no need for interpretation. He would be forthright as a bull in his intentions.

"Don't sulk, Portia. You've a nasty crease, right between your eyes. It's *aging*," I added maliciously.

Instantly she brightened. "Still, I think you might have told me. When do you mean to marry?"

I shoved another forkful of food into my mouth to buy myself a moment. "We have not really discussed it," I told her.

"I should think sooner rather than later," she told me sagely. "Neither of you is very young, after all."

"I am only thirty!" I protested.

"And Brisbane is nearly forty. If he means to settle down and start a family, he ought to get to it."

I shoved my plate away, feeling rather desperate to turn the conversation to another topic, *any* other topic.

"Mrs. Butters, what perfect eggs. So light, I cannot imagine how you do it."

Mrs. Butters, who had been lingering discreetly in the background, came near with a fresh rack of toast. Portia took a piece and began to break it to bits in a desultory fashion. Mrs. Butters beamed at me.

"Thank you, Lady Julia. I have always taken great pride in my eggs."

"With excellent reason," I said, giving her a grateful smile.

Portia, who had been lost in thought, perked up suddenly. "Mrs. Butters, will you stay on now that Lady Julia is going to be mistress of Grimsgrave?"

I groaned, but neither of them paid me any mind.

"I should think Lady Julia would be an excellent mistress," Mrs. Butters said kindly. "But perhaps she would care to engage her own staff."

I smiled at her again. "Mrs. Butters, you are tact incarnate. And pay no attention to my sister. No firm plans have been made at present. Nothing will be decided until after the inquest," I told them both, taking in Portia with a glance.

Portia gestured toward an empty chair. "Mrs. Butters, I should very much like you to take a cup of tea with us."

Mrs. Butters demurred, as any good servant would, but eventually Portia's powers of persuasion won out over her diffidence. She retrieved a plain cup, not a prettily flowered one such as those that had been laid for us, and poured out a tiny measure of tea, sweetening it heavily.

"Toast?" Portia offered, graciously waving toward the toast rack.

Mrs. Butters shook her head firmly. "I could not, my lady. Really."

Portia accepted this refusal and pushed no further.

"Now then, Mrs. Butters, I am very interested in Miss Ailith. There are unanswered questions, you know. And I think you can supply the answers."

I smothered another groan and took a sip of tea instead. How like Portia to go directly to the horse's mouth, no matter how discomfited the horse.

"Well," Mrs. Butters began slowly, "a servant does see rather a lot. And I have been here a very long time."

Portia nodded, beaming. "Precisely. And a valued member of staff is practically one of the family."

She was pouring on the cream rather thickly now with

that sort of flattery, but Mrs. Butters merely gave her a muted version of her old twinkle and sipped at her tea.

"When did you realise there was an unnatural closeness between Miss Ailith and her brother?"

"Portia!" I scolded. "Is that really necessary?"

Portia flapped her hand at me. "Really, Julia, don't be so provincial. Mrs. Butters and I are women of the world. We can discuss such things without embarrassment, can we not, Mrs. Butters?"

Mrs. Butters was thoughtful. "I think it was always there, that attachment. Even when they were children, there was something secretive and strange about them. Miss Wilfreda, she was as plain as milk and easy to read as an open book. Miss Hilda was much the same, but she was smart as a whip, and always fretting that she could not go to school. Always hidden away somewhere with a book, she was. But Miss Ailith, she was wild as moor wind and Master Redwall was just the same. Whatever she directed him to do, he did. He was her slave."

I cocked my head, curious now, in spite of myself. "Do you mean Ailith initiated the relationship, not Redwall?"

Mrs. Butters shrugged. "I do not suppose we will ever know. But I would not be tha' surprised. I know she was deeply in love with him. She never forgave Lady Allenby for sending him away."

"But she must have realised, she must have *known*, what they did together was terribly wrong," I protested.

"Did she? Miss Ailith always believed there was another set of rules for her, if indeed there were any rules besides her own will. She took what she liked, and when she was done with it, she destroyed it. That was the sort of person she was."

Mrs. Butters' eyes grew misty with remembrance. "She loved the little chapel by the river. I think that might have been where those poor babies were conceived. It was Miss Ailith's special place, you know. It was like a tiny palace, and she liked to pretend she was a queen in the ruins of it. Yes, it would have done very well for their trysts."

I shuddered. "She was monstrous."

"Perhaps," Mrs. Butters said evenly. "She might have been born with a flaw in her character, like a pulled thread in fine piece of silk. Never able to be mended, no matter how much one tries. Or she might have been flawless, and twisted by human hands."

"Her mother's," Portia added.

"And her father's, and her brother's as well. Too many people too willing to acquiesce to her every whim. Such indulgence can warp even the best character, while hammering against a strong character will only hone it to its truest self," Mrs. Butters observed.

I thought of Brisbane, bashed and knocked by every circumstance life could throw at him, and I thought of the man he had become in spite of the trials he had suffered. And then Ailith Allenby, with such natural advantages and a cosseted upbringing, would have been the agent of his destruction if she could have managed it.

But I dared not say those things aloud. There were too many stories circulating at present, and none of them was the whole truth. The jury at the inquest would be given no hint that anything at Grimsgrave had been amiss. A simple, tragic accident, they would call it, and the case would be closed.

The inhabitants of the Hall knew better. They knew Ailith's character, and they knew she had intended harm when she set off for the crag. She had hurt Valerius, almost mortally, and attacked Brisbane and myself before falling to her death. Only Brisbane and I knew the full truth, and it was a secret we would hold between us.

As so often happens with my sister, she intuited my thoughts and asked the question I had been hoping would slip her mind.

"Why would Ailith want to kill Brisbane? First the poisoned mushrooms, then following him to the crag? It makes no sense."

Mrs. Butters looked at me, but I let my gaze slide away as I forked up another bit of breakfast.

"She wanted to be revenged upon her mother for the loss of her children. We discussed that yesterday," I said easily, passing smoothly over the true motive, the motive I had not even discussed with Brisbane yet, but the reason I believed to be the truth. "Lady Allenby was usually the one who prepared the bottled mushrooms. It would be an easy matter to convince a jury that her mother had wanted to dispose of Brisbane in order to regain control of her property, or some such nonsense. Believe me, Ailith would have given testimony to some plausible motive while weeping crocodile tears over her mother's fate."

"I wonder if Lady Allenby did kill Redwall," Portia mused. "I asked Valerius about quinine this morning. He shouted a bit because his head hurt, but he did say that if Redwall had already been dosing himself heavily with the stuff, it would have been an easy matter to strengthen the dose to a fatal one."

"Madness," I muttered. "I cannot believe that elegant old woman was capable of murdering her own son." But even as I said it, I realised I did believe it. She had taken bold, drastic action when Ailith delivered a pair of incestuous, illegitimate twins. What else might she have been prepared to do to prevent sin and scandal from polluting the atmosphere of her home?

THE THIRTIETH CHAPTER

The gods are just.
—William Shakespeare
King Lear

The inquest proceeded precisely as Brisbane had predicted. The coroner and the men of his jury journeyed out to the crag to see for themselves the location of Ailith Allenby's death. Then they retired to The Hanging Tree to view the body and conduct the inquisition of the witnesses.

Brisbane was called first, and must have made a tremendous impression upon them. He had dressed carefully in sombre black, but for him the choice was not merely appropriately doleful. Black always lent him an elegant authority, and coupled with his skin, still pale beneath its olive cast, and his imperious black gaze, he was a formidable witness. He took great care when he moved not to betray any sign of the wound he had sustained to his ribs, moving with all the grave dignity of an elder statesman and bearing a striking resemblance to Grim. I noticed that he had permitted a lock of hair to tumble over his brow, neatly obscuring the thin cut from Ailith Allenby's knife. I was not permitted to hear him give testimony, and I waited in the upper sitting room alone, twisting my gloves into knots as I listened to the low rumble of masculine voices rising and falling through the floorboards at my feet.

At length there was a scratch at the door and the coroner himself appeared. He was an elderly man, with great flyaway tufts of candy floss white hair and the most impressive set of eyebrows I had ever seen. His manner was gentle and very kindly, and he put me in mind of a country parson.

He gave me a rheumy smile and nodded as I rose.

"Lady Julia Grey? Née March?"

"I am she," I said, my voice holding steady. I put out my hand and he took it in both of his. I offered him a chair next to mine and we settled ourselves. He watched me from under those spectacular brows for a long moment, so long in fact that I wondered if he had fallen asleep. But then he cleared his throat and came to the point.

"My dear, I have never approved of the questioning of ladies when it can possibly be avoided. Now, if you will disclose to me what you meant to tell the jury, I will confirm to them that Mr. Brisbane's testimony has been corroborated, and there will be no necessity for you to display yourself before the gentlemen of the jury."

I smoothed my skirts, hardly knowing how to reply. "I am not afraid to do my duty, sir. I am perfectly willing to be questioned before the jury."

He shook his head, wisps of untidy white hair fluttering about his ears. "Oh, no. I would want no granddaughter of mine forced to such an exigency, and I will not ask it of a granddaughter of Mercutio March."

I stared at him, a slow smile spreading over my face. "You knew Grandpapa."

He nodded. "We were at Eton together. Such a character, he was. Oh, he ought to have been too grand to notice the likes of me. He was already the earl, and in command of a great estate. I was sent there on charity subscriptions and wore third-hand clothes. But he stopped me being flogged by one of the older boys, and I never forgot it."

He paused, smiling at his recollections. "I saw him once, many years later, in London. He was riding past in his carriage, a grand equipage it was, with footmen and plumed horses and his coat of arms blazoned on the door. I was standing on the kerb, waiting to cross. I would never have presumed to make myself known to him, but he knew me. He made the driver stop the carriage and leapt out to embrace me and call me friend."

He drew a handkerchief from his pocket and wiped at his moist eyes. "He called me friend, Mercutio March, the earl. And I made up my mind that I would never allow any opportunity to do him or his family good pass me by."

"I see," I said, folding my hands in my lap.

"Now, I understand Mr. Brisbane is your betrothed?"

"Yes," I said, my throat going suddenly dry.

"Then we may assume that whatever he told us is what you yourself witnessed and are prepared to swear to?"

"Yes," I affirmed.

"Ailith Allenby fell from Thorn Crag?"

"Ailith Allenby fell from Thorn Crag," I echoed.

"And there is no question of suicide?" he asked. I hesitated and he went on, quite oblivious to my pause. "I dearly hope not. Suicide is a dirty and desperate business. One never likes to have a verdict of suicide returned."

I was struck then by how he had phrased his last question and I gave him a gracious smile and squared my shoulders. "No, sir. There is no question in my mind whether Ailith Allenby committed suicide or not."

He beamed at me and reached out to pat my hand. "Very good. Now I have only to tell the gentlemen that you have corroborated Mr. Brisbane's story, and there will be no need for you to be questioned." He paused. "I do hope you will not think me too forward, but I hope you have had that cut on your cheek attended to. It would be a shame for so lovely a face to be marked."

I put a hand to my cheek, brushing one gloved fingertip over the souvenir of that fateful day on Thorn Crag.

"Not at all," I told him, smiling. "You are very kind."

He was quite pink to the tips of his ears, and it occurred to me that he was really rather flirtatious.

He rose and bowed deeply. "Thank you, my dear lady. You have been most helpful."

He scurried out then, after several more protestations of goodwill and gratitude on his part, and I was left alone, staring into the fire and reflecting that Brisbane had been quite wrong: even here, in the wilds of Yorkshire, the March name still carried the day.

The coroner's jury had business yet, and I waited upstairs

for Brisbane. A few minutes after the coroner left me, there was another scratch at the door, this time it was Miss Jerusha Earnshaw bearing a tea tray. I exclaimed in surprised pleasure to see her.

"Miss Earnshaw! I thought you would have returned to your employer's house by now."

She placed the tea carefully on the little table at my elbow and gave me a rueful smile. "I am afraid my mistress is rather given to the habit of gossip. She read about Miss Allenby's death in the newspapers and wants me to stay until the inquest is finished and I can provide her with the most complete story."

The words were correct, but there was a thread of disapproval. Jerusha Earnshaw might not mind sharing a titbit or two with me, but she did not much care for gossiping with her mistress.

I looked at the tea tray, puzzled. "There is only one cup. Don't you mean to join me?"

Her mouth was prim. "I would not dream of imposing, Lady Julia."

"Don't be silly. Go and fetch another cup. I would be glad of the company. If you like," I finished feebly, realising how imperious I had sounded.

But if I had been bossy, Miss Earnshaw did not mind. "I will be but a moment."

She fetched another cup and returned swiftly. I motioned for her to pour out and she did so with the same deft economy of motion I had come to expect of her. Her gestures, like her words and even her clothing, were just right, never too bold or too retiring. She was an unusually comfortable person to be around, an invaluable quality in a member of staff. For a moment I regretted not having children merely because I could not engage her.

"Miss Earnshaw, I confess, I had an ulterior motive for inviting you to take tea with me, beyond the pleasure of your company."

She did not seem at all surprised. "You want information."

"What makes you say that?"

She sipped placidly at her tea, and very good tea it was. Indian, with broad black leaves instead of the weedy dust that is so often used instead.

"You are a naturally curious person, Lady Julia, if you will forgive the observation."

"Oh, entirely," I told her, reaching for a scone.

"And the last time we spoke, I sensed a certain frustration. I think you would have liked to have asked me more, but you were hampered by the presence of Lady Bettiscombe."

"Miss Earnshaw, you are a witch. I adore my sister, but there is some business too private even to share with her."

She offered me a subtle smile. "I am, to the public eye, a miner's daughter from a thoroughly insignificant village in Yorkshire with an indifferent education. I would never have risen to the position I now occupy without learning first the complementary skills of observation and discretion."

One could make a similar comment about Brisbane, I reflected. "Very well, I wish to know things."

We settled in for a chat then, and I asked her many questions. Some answers she knew, others we were forced to cobble together from bits and pieces she had collected over the years. In the end, I believe we pieced together a fair representation of what had happened so many years ago in her little village, what ghosts had been raised, and which ones still walked their uneasy path.

"Thank you, Miss Earnshaw," I said at length. "You have been most helpful. If there is ever anything I can do for you—"

Her gaze sharpened, and I smiled. "Ask."

"Well, I have put a bit of money aside. I mean to open a school for young ladies. Not a finishing school, but a proper school where girls may learn mathematics and the hard sciences as well as dancing and deportment. I realise it is a radical proposition, but if your ladyship could perhaps mention it to a friend or two, should they have daughters to educate…"

She trailed off hopefully. I waved a hand. "It would be my pleasure. In fact, I would be happy to write a general letter of recommendation. You may use it in your advertisements, for whatever it is worth."

She thanked me effusively, and I thanked her again for the tea and the conversation, and I think we both parted feeling quite kindly disposed toward the other. I was waiting alone by the time Brisbane finally came to collect me. He looked exhausted, his face drawn with fatigue.

"Are you ready?"

I rose at once and collected my things. "Of course."

"Thank God," he said fervently. "I want to get the hell out of here."

Brisbane's language was frequently inappropriate, but there was an urgency to his tone that I had not often seen before. His pace was rapid as well, and by the time we reached the path to Grimsgrave, he was nearly a dozen steps ahead.

I stopped by the stone wall and waited. After half a minute he realised I had not kept pace and returned to fetch me, clearly battling his temper.

"I am sorry," he ground out through clenched teeth. "I did not mean to rush you. I want to get back to Grimsgrave."

"Quite all right," I told him with a smile. He offered his arm very civilly and I took it. He matched his steps to mine with great deliberation, and as we walked I felt the tension ebbing from him. The fresh moorland air blowing about seemed to clear the cobwebs and the anger away. The muscles under my hand relaxed, and the tightness at his jaw eased.

"I was rather surprised at not having to testify," I began.

He snorted. "Yes, well, it seems I underestimated the power of the March name."

I shrugged. "It is an illusion, really. People think it means something to be the daughter of an earl, so they treat you differently. And then you come to expect it, and they think it is because you are an earl's daughter, and really it's only because you have *always* been treated differently that you expect it in the first place."

Brisbane shook his head. "That is the most convoluted piece of logic I have ever heard."

"No, it isn't. And you are capable of some rather twisty logic yourself."

"Such as?" He quirked one glossy black brow in my direction.

"Such as permitting a would-be murderess to remain under your roof to attempt your life again just so she could be caught in the act. You seem to have entirely forgot that she might well have succeeded," I pointed out acidly.

He shrugged. "Oh, that. I took precautions, you know. I am not completely helpless."

"No, but you are reckless, as headstrong as any member of *my* family. I daresay it is bad breeding. The Aberdours always were rather flamboyant."

"And my mother's people," he put in. "Not exactly the reticent sort."

"True," I agreed. "They are a singular people. I quite like your aunt and uncle. Tell me, is Rosalie very like your mother?"

It was the first time I had raised the spectre of Brisbane's mother in conversation. He answered, but only after a moment, and his voice was low.

"Yes, I suppose she is. Same colouring, same graceful gestures. But there was something otherworldly about my mother. Rosalie is as plain as salt, for all that she is a Gypsy."

The fact that Brisbane could have described Rosalie thus was an excellent indication of his upbringing. Rosalie Smith was one of the most exotic creatures I had ever known. Mariah Young must have been something out of myth.

We walked on in silence for a moment, but his arm was tense again under mine.

"Portia asked me why Ailith was so determined to kill you," I began conversationally. "I told her it was because she meant to set up her mother to hang for your murder, but that is not the whole story, is it? No, I think she meant to punish you for ruining Redwall. You did, didn't you? During the 1884-1885 expedition? You needn't bother to deny it. I saw the photograph of the expedition party. You look rather dashing with whiskers. I wonder that Lord Evandale trusted you near his daughter. The poor girl must have been quite smitten."

Brisbane said nothing and I continued on, keeping my tone light. "It must have been terribly easy to bring Redwall down into disgrace. Was he stealing from Lord Evandale? Or selling faked antiquities as genuine? It hardly matters now. Evandale became suspicious, but he had so many new members to his expedition, he could not pinpoint the criminal. He asked you to join his excavation team and unmask the villain. You did so, with alacrity. It must have been so tempting to arrange proof to condemn him, but I don't believe you did. I think you waited until he betrayed himself. I think the evidence you presented to Evandale was entirely genuine."

"You seem to think very highly of my character," he said mildly, but his arm twitched beneath mine.

"No, I think you enjoyed the cat and mouse game too much. I believe you are completely capable of arranging for his culpability the first day. It would have been so easy for you. You are clever and deft and the coolest liar I know. Poor Redwall wouldn't have stood a chance if you had simply picked the lock to his room and cached a necklace or statue under his pillow. But watching him go to pieces was rather more satisfying, wasn't it?"

"Yes, it was," he agreed.

"You had months together, over the long Egyptian winter, toiling in the hot sun and lingering over group dinners, and all the while you watched him. He was confident at first, believing he had the measure of you, had *you* at a disadvantage. How immensely pleasurable it must have been for you to watch him disintegrate as the truth slowly dawned upon him—you had come to Egypt for revenge."

Brisbane's expression turned to one of disgust. "You have a febrile imagination, Julia. Redwall Allenby did nothing of the sort. Until the day Lord Evandale expelled him from the expedition, he thought I was in his power. He underestimated me completely."

I thought for a moment. "He was a singularly stupid man, wasn't he?"

"He was. And he was already ill, desperately so. When Lord Evandale dismissed him, he was devastated. He knew it was the end of him in the Egyptological community and he went home to die, it is as simple as that. It is a measure of his depravity that he thought to defile his sister first."

I gave him a reproving look. "It is not really that simple, is it? I cannot believe you never took the opportunity to let him know why you had come."

"I let him know every day," Brisbane said with a savage little smile of satisfaction.

"How?" I asked.

"Can't you imagine? You saw the photograph."

I thought of the images I had seen, captured in that one brief moment, stilled forever. I shook my head. "No. How did you signal your thirst for vengeance to Redwall?"

"'Thirst for vengeance?' Ye gods, Julia, you ought to be writing thrillers of the lowest variety."

I gave him a little poke in the ribs, but I must have caught him on the bad side. He stumbled and righted himself, looking very pale.

"I am sorry, Brisbane. But I was right, wasn't I? You did go to Egypt for revenge, and you had it. I finally put it all together today. I had heard of course that your mother was bound over for trial for stealing a bottle of laudanum. I knew she cursed the judge, Sir Alfred Allenby, and the chemist as well. That was Mr. Butters, wasn't it? Poor Mrs. Butters. I wonder if she ever realised it was your mother who cursed her husband."

"Of course she knows," Brisbane said, gritting his teeth a little and holding a hand to his ribs. "She used to make griddlecakes for me when I was a boy."

"Remind me to ask her what you were like as a boy. Incorrigible, I should imagine."

"Thoroughly."

His tone was light, but I knew he dreaded what was coming next. I dreaded it as well. I did not want to open new wounds, but so long as they poisoned him still, there was no hope for us. The only way for him to face the future was to put the past squarely behind him. I only hoped he was capable of it.

"But it was something Jerusha Earnshaw said that made all the difference."

"Jerusha Earnshaw?" he asked, but I knew it was a bid for time. I gave him a repressive look.

"The innkeeper's sister. She told me the charges against your mother would have likely been dismissed at the Assizes because the witnesses against her were a pair of children. Ailith and Redwall Allenby."

His jaw hardened and his handsome mouth twisted into something most unpleasant. "Did she tell you why? Did she tell you it was because of me?"

I stared straight ahead as we continued to walk. It was easier somehow if I did not have to look directly at him as I exposed his demons.

"Well, it was," he went on. "Ailith was not even ten, and the most accomplished liar I had ever met. I did my best to stay away from them, Ailith and her brother both, but sometimes our paths crossed. One day I went swimming in the river, where it flows calmly by the graveyard. Ailith and Redwall came upon me and began their usual habit, taunting and calling abuse. I ignored them until I realised Ailith was holding up a pendant of mine I had left on the bank with my clothes. It had been given me by my mother. She told me stories about the lady engraved upon it, a beautiful and terrible lady. I used to wonder if the woman on the pendant was my mother. It was my dearest possession. And there was Ailith Allenby, swinging it from her fingertips, saying she meant to keep it, even if it was an ugly piece of Gypsy trash."

I had the oddest fancy then that Brisbane did not even remember I was there, he was speaking almost to himself, in a low hollow voice, his eyes unfocused, as if he only saw the past.

"I leapt out of the river and charged at her. I pushed her down and took the pendant back, and told her if she ever touched anything of mine ever again, I would kill her. Redwall tried to stand up for her, but I shoved him into the river. It might have been funny, a stupid children's quarrel, but for the look on Ailith Allenby's face. It was not the face of a child. It was the wilful evil of some devil straight from the pits of hell. I knew then she meant to do something terrible. And, coward that I was, I packed my things and I ran away."

I had guessed some of what Brisbane told me, but I had not anticipated that. "I thought you ran away because the Gypsies would not have you as one of them."

Brisbane came slowly back to himself, as if the sound of

my voice had roused him. "They have more generosity than you credit them with. I was my mother's son, and she was a powerful woman. I looked just like them, I rode and picked pockets and made harnesses as well as any other Gypsy lad."

"You picked pockets?"

He shrugged. "Once in a while and only from people who could spare it. My mother's people are resourceful."

Not quite the word I would have used, but I was not surprised he still felt warmly toward his maternal family.

"And after you ran away, Ailith Allenby took her revenge upon your mother instead."

He nodded slowly. "I am to blame for everything that happened to her. The least I could do was see her avenged. It's come full circle now."

We walked in silence a moment, and then I had a sudden start of realisation. I put a hand into the neck of my bodice and drew out the pendant Brisbane had given me, incised with the head of Medusa, a beautiful and terrible woman. I tucked it away, hastily. There was no need to ask. I knew now precisely what I meant to him. What I had always meant.

Just then he turned to me, and I felt a surge of joy. The past had been exorcised. I felt lighter and a hundred years younger. We were betrothed, as far as the world knew. *This* was the moment then, when it would all come right.

"I just remembered, I put notices in the newspaper of our engagement to lend the lie more veritas," he said, his brow furrowing.

"Yes," I said encouragingly. My breath felt tight within my lungs.

"I forgot to post the retractions. They ought to be printed

as soon as possible. It would be more believable if you sued me for breach of promise, but the whole thing will go away more quickly if we just let it be."

I swallowed hard, concealing my disappointment. "Of course. Breach of promise suits are so terribly louche, I always think."

He stood for a long moment, staring at me, searching my face, and when he spoke it was without pretence and every word was its own tragic poem. "There is no money, Julia. Not a farthing. I've put everything I had into Grimsgrave. I was convinced there was a fortune under this moor, if only I could find it. I was a fool," he said bitterly.

"I understand," I said hollowly, but of course I did not. It was a very great irony that the fortune my husband had left me stood between me and my only happiness. "I could give it all away, you know. I am sure there is some home for elderly cats or something that would quite appreciate the money."

He laughed, and I heard the sharp edge of despair in the sound, and perhaps anger as well. "I will not touch you again. It isn't fair, to either of us."

I nodded. "I won't kiss you either. You might get ideas and I am a very respectable widow."

We stood a foot apart and yet with worlds between. He reached out then and crushed me to him, heedless of his newly-stitched ribs. I clasped my arms around him, holding him as tightly to me as my own flesh.

"For the love of God, don't cry," he ordered, his face muffled by my hair. My hat had gone tumbling over the moor, bowled along by the wind, but I did not care.

"I won't," I promised. "But I am feeling rather fragile, so you might want to look away in a moment."

He pulled back, and I saw a thousand emotions warring on his face. He seemed to be memorising my face, his eyes lingering on each feature in turn.

Finally, he released me. "Ailith will be buried the day after tomorrow. I will make arrangements for you and Portia to return to London the following day. I will be closing up the house. I am leaving England for a while."

"For how long?" I asked him, determined to keep my composure.

"Until I am quite recovered from you," he said evenly.

"When will you return?"

"Never."

He turned and left me then, walking slowly toward the village. I stared after him for a long time, until I could no longer see the strong form and the witch-black hair tumbling in the wind. And then I turned and set my face for Grimsgrave Hall.

THE THIRTY-FIRST CHAPTER

All gold and silver rather turn to dirt.
—William Shakespeare
Cymbeline

And so Portia and I made our preparations to return to London. I expected her to pry and fuss, but she took one look at my face and put me straight to bed with a hot whisky.

The next morning I gathered up Redwall Allenby's things, the journals and photographs and the little amulets from the babies' coffin. I replaced them in his desk, wondering if they would ever again see the light of day. I almost opened the priest's hole, but in the end I left the children where they lay, hoping they were at peace. Brisbane would have to make arrangements for them to be buried secretly.

Mrs. Butters was subdued as she prepared breakfast, and I do not think anyone was inclined to eat. I picked at some eggs, and tried not to think. Portia fed bits of York ham to Puggy, coaxing him to eat from her hand.

"Puggy's off his feed," she complained. "I think he would rather be upstairs with Florence and the pups."

To our mutual surprise, Puggy had turned out to be a devoted father. He doted on Florence, offering her the choicest titbits of food and permitting her to use his favourite cushion. He growled when anyone came near his little family, and had even nipped Morag when she touched one without his express permission.

"I do not see how we can keep them apart," Portia said, offering Puggy a spoonful of coddled egg. "Do you mean to come back to stay with me, or will you go straight down to the Rookery?"

I thought of the peace of the countryside in Sussex. The Rookery was the charming little house Father had presented me with as a Christmas present. My devoted butler, Aquinas, had written that all was in order and I could finally take up residence whenever I liked. I would have as much quiet and solitude as I wanted, I thought.

And perhaps more. The city, with all of its heady diversions, might be a better distraction at present. But the thought of my family, pressing dinner invitations and outings upon me, made my stomach hurt. I wanted to be alone, but not alone. I wanted to pour out my hurts and frustrations, and I wanted never to speak again. In short, I was at war with myself.

I shrugged at Portia and idly buttered my toast. "I do not care. I suppose I will stay for a little while with you."

"You needn't sound so enthusiastic," she said waspishly. "I am no more thrilled about the prospect than you, I assure you."

I would have put out my tongue at her, but it was simply too much effort. Mrs. Butters brought another rack of toast, although we had scarcely touched the one on the table. I think she simply wanted to keep busy.

"Mrs. Butters, what will become of you? If Mr. Brisbane is closing up Grimsgrave, where will you go?"

She gave me a brisk nod. "You needn't worry about me, Lady Julia. Mr. Brisbane made certain I would be taken care of. I have a sister in Leeds. He has said he will arrange for my transportation to her when he is ready to leave Grimsgrave. I have put a little something by, and I will be perfectly all right."

"I am glad to hear it. At least someone will," I said peevishly.

"And Minna," Portia put in.

I lifted a brow. "What do you mean?"

"Hasn't she asked you yet? She means to stay here and marry Godwin Allenby."

"Out of the question," I told her. "I know they have an understanding, but he cannot keep a wife."

"You will break the girl's heart," Portia said softly.

I sighed. "I have promised her mother to take care of her, Portia. I have thought it over carefully, and I cannot leave her with an impoverished husband, no matter how much she loves him. If he cannot provide for her, he cannot have her."

Portia looked to Mrs. Butters. "I do not suppose Godwin has a tidy sum put by as well?"

Mrs. Butters shook her head sadly. "I regret not. I have

grown rather fond of that girl. She would have trained up as an excellent housekeeper. Her cookery is very solid, and she has a head for figures."

"What if we took Godwin back to London?" I suggested. "He could find employment, something reliable and steady. Then when he has saved enough, he can approach her mother for her hand."

Mrs. Butters clucked. "Oh, no. Tha' would never do. Godwin is an Allenby. He belongs to these moors. He would never live in a city. I think it would kill him."

She cleared away a few of the dishes then, and Portia and I regarded each other across the breakfast table.

"We are a couple of sour old women," I told her.

"But you are right, even if I hate to say it," she said. "We cannot let her marry for love if it means she will starve. What if she had children? How would they keep them? I was stupid to think it. I just wanted a happy ending for them," she finished wanly.

"Because we neither of us have ours?" I asked softly.

She nodded and we fell silent.

"Then we will have to give her a dowry," I said finally. "We will each put up fifty percent. Name a sum that will settle them, either as far as purchasing a small farm and a herd to stock it, or a business in the village."

"We cannot offer it directly," Portia warned, and I bristled.

"I know that. It would be insulting to them both. We will have to disguise it as an inheritance. We can make Brisbane give it to Godwin, say it was a legacy from Ailith's death."

"But Ailith's property would go to Lady Allenby," she pointed out.

I waved her aside. "Nuns cannot inherit property," I told her loftily. "At least, I do not think they can, and if they can, we will simply have Brisbane tell him otherwise. We'll make up some story about Hilda getting a sum as well. I hardly think Godwin will question such a piece of good fortune closely."

Portia's eyes lit up and we haggled then, even drawing Mrs. Butters into the business. The three of us worked the sums and argued over the details, but in the end, we devised a settlement that seemed suitable without being too generous. There was also the question of how to present the money. We agreed to leave it to Brisbane, and Portia volunteered to apprise him of our plan while I began to pack.

I do not know what was said, or how. I only know that by suppertime, all was decided. Minna flew out of the kitchen as I was coming down the stairs. She was still holding a ladle in one hand, dripping sauce upon the flagstones as she clasped me in an embrace.

"Oh, bless you, my lady! I know you did this. Miss Ailith hated him, she would never have left him money. But I know you and Lady Bettiscombe did this between you. How can I ever thank you?"

She was sobbing freely now, and I disengaged myself gently. "If you keep crying, you will water the sauce and ruin supper."

She wiped her eyes on her apron and shook her head. "I cannot believe it. I just knew we wouldn't be able to marry, not with us having but a shilling between us. And then when Mr. Brisbane told us, it was like a miracle, like the world just cracked open wide and everything I ever dreamed of was inside."

She hugged me again, fiercely, and flew off to the kitchens, leaving me feeling fairly staggered. I was the daughter of an earl, I thought bleakly, born to privilege and wealth most people could not even hope to imagine. And in that moment, I would have happily traded places with a little maid who had everything I did not.

Ailith Allenby was buried quietly in the graveyard of the ruined chapel. There were no hymns, no weeping, only the soft patter of the rain that fell upon the coffin. The grave had been dug the day before, and I noticed that Brisbane and Godwin were conspicuously absent for a long period of time before the burial. They never said, and I never asked, but I saw the grave was rather shallower than one might have expected and the bottom of it was freshly packed, as if something else had been buried before Ailith's coffin was lowered into the ground. No one else seemed to notice anything amiss, and I murmured a prayer for the souls of the lost babies as well as their unfortunate mother as the clods of earth covered her at last.

It was a small and solemn group that wended its way back to Grimsgrave under a cluster of black umbrellas. Hilda and Mrs. Butters served as chief mourners in the absence of Lady Allenby. Brisbane had sent word to Lady Allenby of Ailith's death, but she had not replied. Perhaps she was already too deeply entrenched in the solitude of her convent life, or perhaps she struggled with the twin burdens of guilt and relief: guilt at her own crimes and relief that the daughter who was bent upon her destruction was dead.

There had been a letter from Sister Bridget, brief and to the point. All of Ailith's personal property was to be given to the poor of the parish "that she who had done so little good in her life, might do some in death." Harsh, but not inaccurate, I thought. Hilda refused to deal with the matter, so Mrs. Butters saw to the removal of her things. I wondered if somewhere in the village a little girl would be awed at the gift of the elaborate doll's house, never dreaming what it had meant to Ailith's twisted mind. The doll's house was uninhabited when it left Grimsgrave. The tiny infant dolls with their unmistakable gilt hair had been laid in Ailith's coffin. I could not imagine leaving them in the toy house, and destroying them seemed somehow wrong. Yorkshire folk believed that suicides walked the earth, never resting in their graves. It seemed a primitive sort of magic to leave the dolls with her, but perhaps she would lie quietly.

After cakes and wine at Grimsgrave, everyone dispersed. Portia went to play with the puppies, Mrs. Butters to rest, and heaven only knew where Brisbane had got to. Valerius, still weak from the blow to his head, was dozing by the fireside, and I found Hilda in the room she had shared with Ailith. It was barren now that Ailith's things were gone. A little trunk stood open under the window and it was half filled with Hilda's books and unbecoming tweeds. In spite of the recent tragedies, there was a new serenity to Hilda that she wore well. She even smiled a little in welcome as I settled myself on a chair.

"I am glad you have come," she said, and I believed her.

"I wanted you to know that I am leaving tomorrow. Miss Earnshaw has offered me a post in her school. I am to live on the premises in Manchester and help her establish the curriculum. And when the pupils come, I am to teach modern languages and ancient history. Miss Earnshaw is not at all troubled by my lack of formal education," she finished, blushing hotly. "She says even though I am self-taught, I am well-suited to such a post."

"A very good fit, I think," I told her. "So you are leaving the moor at last."

She nodded. "I do hope Minna will see to my chickens," she said with a tiny smile.

"Perhaps you will have a flock at the school. You can teach the girls poultry-keeping skills," I suggested. "Every woman ought to have her own money, even if it is just a bit from the eggs."

Her smile broadened then. "Perhaps we will. It is a useful skill at that." She faltered then, and I could see that she was steeling herself for what she was about to say.

I spoke first. "Have you told him?"

"No, but I did write him a rather good letter. I even quoted a bit of Donne. He'll like that."

I nodded. "Yes, he will. My brothers all have a weakness for poetry, I'm afraid."

She looked up sharply then. "Do you think he will come after me?"

I thought a moment, then shook my head. "I think not. My brothers share a love of poetry, and a rather pliable character. They would all rather languish in their heartbreak than do anything useful about it. You've made rather a lucky escape, if you ask me. Valerius may take up writing sonnets, and that would be a tragedy indeed."

I spoke lightly, but I knew Valerius would feel the disappointment keenly. It was the first time in his life he had truly played the man, and I pitied him. He had so much compassion, so much tenderness to give. He had been badly thwarted in his choice of profession, and now he was to suffer yet another defeat.

Hilda straightened her shoulders then, and for the first time I saw the proud, stiff carriage of the Allenbys in her. "It would be too easy, you know. That's the trouble. If I married him, I would be safe and comfortable, and I would go on feeling as though I were wrapped in cotton wool. I am terrified of going to Manchester. I am terrified of living in a little room and making my tea on a spirit lamp. I am terrified of teaching. And that is why I must."

I knew only too well the feeling of being wrapped in cotton wool. I rose and offered my hand.

"Fear is how you know you are alive, my dear," I told her.

She took my hand and tipped her head to one side. She was actually rather pretty now that she wasn't scowling at me, and I understood why Val had thought her attractive. It was an interesting face, and one that promised great character.

"Are you afraid, Lady Julia?" she asked at length.

"Every day," I told her, thinking of a future without Brisbane. "Every day."

After I left Hilda, I set off amid lowering cloud to bid farewell to Rosalie and John-the-Baptist. Portia and I were

almost completely packed and would be up before cockcrow
to make the long journey by road to the village with our
trunks in time to catch the train to London. There was so
much I wanted to thank Rosalie for, and I knew I would miss
her terribly.

The rain was teeming down by the time I reached the
cottage. Its lights glowed through the darkening gloom of the
afternoon, beckoning with such homely warmth I nearly wept.

"Oh, don't be feeble," I told myself firmly. "You are merely
tired and a little melancholy. A hot cup of tea and some good
company, and you will be right as rain."

I set my shoulders against the wind and pressed on, nearly
slipping over the flat rock at the turning of the path, and
then almost falling against the door as a strong gust blew
against my back.

"Lady Julia!" Rosalie exclaimed. She ushered me in,
already rubbing at my hands and face with a towel. "You
ought not to have come today. The storm grows stronger."

"I wanted to say goodbye," I explained, my voice muffled
by the towel.

She finished wiping my face and took my wet things.
Only then did I realise she was not alone. I had expected
John-the-Baptist, but not Brisbane. He was standing at the
window, looking out at the moor, his back to the room. He
must have seen me coming for some distance, time enough
to school his reaction. He did not turn.

"Good afternoon, lady," John-the-Baptist said cordially.
He rose and offered me his chair by the fire.

I held up a hand. "No, I cannot stay. I merely wanted to

come and tell you both goodbye. I am leaving tomorrow, quite early."

Still there was no reaction from Brisbane. The set of his shoulders betrayed nothing. Was he angry I had come? Or was he as shattered as I by the idea of parting forever?

"I am sorry to hear it," John-the-Baptist said. "We will wish you a safe journey."

Rosalie went to the painted cupboard and returned, pressing a small silken bag into my hands. Like the first she had given me, it was lumpy and hard, and hung on a bit of velvet ribbon.

"Another charm, this one to keep you safe," she told me. "It is full of things which call down the protection of God, and it has been blessed by a powerful *shuvani*."

"You?" I asked, looping it about my neck.

She smiled and lifted her chin. "Of course."

We forgot ceremony then. She embraced me, pressing me close to her heart. "Do not fear the road before you, my dear. Only those who step boldly tread the right path."

I smiled at her enigmatic words. A true Gypsy to the end, I thought with great affection. I shook hands with John-the-Baptist, who then bowed with a flourish.

"Safe journey, lady," he told me.

I hesitated, then held out my hand for my wet things. It was a struggle to put them on again, for they were cold and heavy now, but I managed, and gave them both a smile that was rather braver than I felt.

I left, but Brisbane had never even turned. He could watch my back then as I left, I thought angrily, striding firmly through the wicket gate and slamming it as I went. I was not watching my steps. Between my irritation at Brisbane and the flooding rain, it was difficult to see, and my toe caught the flat rock at the crossroads.

"Why doesn't someone move this bloody thing?" I demanded, kicking it hard.

I do not know if it was my petulant gesture that dislodged the stone, or if the ground was so sodden the merest touch would have caused it to crumble like cake, but it did. One moment I was standing on solid ground, the next, I was hurtling into the opened earth, my feet and arms flailing as I fell. My scrabbling hands caught at a root and I hung, suspended, feet dangling helplessly over an abyss. I dared not look down. I screamed for help, and before the echo of the word had even died away, there was Brisbane. He must have seen me fall. There was no other way he could have managed to reach me so quickly.

"Thank God," I sobbed. He lay flat on his stomach, doubtless tearing open the stitches in his ribs, but he never gave the slightest hint he was in pain. He turned over his shoulder to shout something, and I fancied John-the-Baptist was anchoring his legs. He reached down with both arms, almost, but not quite reaching me.

He cursed soundly, then reached back with his left hand to secure a better grip. He stretched out his right hand and just caught my wrist, holding it fast.

"I cannot hold on, and you cannot lift me with one arm," I said, kicking my feet in a vain attempt to find some purchase on the wall of earth in front of me.

Brisbane gritted his teeth against what must have been a

tearing pain in his shoulder. Rain dripped from his sleek black head and he held on to me with an iron grip.

"Trust me," he said, infusing his words with every emotion he felt but had never dared to say.

"I do," I told him, realising I trusted him more than any person I had ever known. My life was literally in his hands, I thought wonderingly, and yet I knew I would be perfectly safe.

And then he dropped me. Without preamble, without discussion, he merely opened his hand and let me fall. I was too startled even to scream. I landed with a thud some four or five feet below where I had been dangling.

"Well, I suppose I am well-served for not looking down," I thought sourly. There was some commotion above, and in a moment Brisbane descended smoothly by means of a rope, holding a lantern that threw wicked shadows across the planes of his face.

"You might have warned me," I told him with a peevish scowl.

"I didn't want you to have time to be frightened," he said simply, but his tone was distracted. He was circling slowly, raising the lantern to throw its feeble light along the earthen walls.

Suddenly, his expression turned grim and he put out his free arm. "Julia, I want you to move quickly but very carefully. Climb onto my back and hold on. We have very little time."

"Time for what?" I demanded, pushing myself up. It was only then that I realised I had landed on something rather firmer than the soft peat mud of the moor. "Brisbane, this is wood. Proper planking. What on earth was this doing below that flat stone at the crossroads?" I asked.

"Julia, now!" he ordered, and I obeyed. He whistled and there was a creaking groan from the ropes as we slowly began our ascent.

I pressed my face against the collar of his shirt. It smelled quite good, I thought idly. A whiff of something citrussy, perhaps bergamot.

We inched upward, at last coming to the rim of the hole. "Be careful here, the ground is not firm," he told me. I scrambled gracelessly over him and collapsed, feeling the firm turf beneath me. Rosalie darted forward, wrapping me in her arms and crooning over me. It seemed rather a big fuss over something that had in the end been so minor, but I let her. John-the-Baptist stood a few feet away, the rope harnessed firmly about his middle, stretching taut as he continued to haul Brisbane to the surface.

"What an extraordinarily strong man your husband is," I remarked to Rosalie.

Just then, the earth itself seemed to collapse. The hole where I had disappeared opened up, the walls crumbling inward with a great roar that sounded like the end of the world. Rosalie and I were knocked to the ground, and lay, clutching the sodden grass until the trembling of the earth subsided. John-the-Baptist had fallen flat upon his back, the rope snapped in half.

I screamed Brisbane's name and scrambled as close as I dared to the edge of the crater that now scarred the face of the moor. John-the-Baptist looped an arm around my waist and hoisted me backward. "It is not safe, lady. If there is a way out, he will find it."

I struggled against him, but by the time I kicked my way free, Brisbane had hefted himself over the edge, covered in peaty black mud, his expression dumbfounded.

"Oh, thank God," I sobbed. I threw myself at him, heedless of the mud.

He held me tightly for a long moment, still clearly stunned by his experience.

"What is it?" I asked. "What did I land upon?"

"A coffin," he said.

He looked straight at his aunt and she gestured toward me. "We will talk inside. Lady Julia will take a chill."

Brisbane moved swiftly to cut her off, placing himself squarely in front of her.

"We will talk now," he said to Rosalie. "That is my mother's coffin."

Rosalie looked at John-the-Baptist, but he merely shrugged. Rosalie turned back to Brisbane, her expression inscrutable.

"Yes, that is where Mariah Young was buried. At the crossroads."

"A suicide," Brisbane said flatly. "You told me she died in gaol."

"She did. She hanged herself with her own petticoat," Rosalie said sadly. "And they buried her there, with a stake through her heart so that she would not walk."

Brisbane turned to walk off, but Rosalie caught his arm, leaving me standing some little distance apart.

"That is why I stayed. For my own penance. I had a hand

in my sister's death, we all did. The chemist, those terrible children, Sir Alfred. When Mariah hanged herself, Sir Alfred believed the only way to break the curse she had laid upon him was to make amends to me. He let me have this cottage, and he had them lay her at this crossroads so I could always watch over her. And now the earth has moved, and she has spoken to us at last," she said, her eyes shining.

Brisbane stared at her. "Are you quite mad?"

Rosalie began to weep then, or to laugh. The sounds were very alike, and she rocked, holding herself. "Oh, my dear boy. Did you not even see that for what it is?"

She pointed at the hole, and I realised she was not mad. She was entirely, completely, beautifully sane.

"It's a mine!" I cried, stumbling toward the edge to peer down into it.

Brisbane caught me, an arm about my waist, and we looked in together. I could just see timbers, the beams heaved into place perhaps by the Romans themselves so many centuries ago. And through the thick soft black peat mud of the walls, I could see the rain cutting through the earth, exposing the dark metallic veins.

"Lead?" I guessed, hardly daring to hope.

"Silver," Brisbane corrected. He looked at me then, a slow smile spreading over his face. "A silver mine. On my land."

I threw myself at him for the second time in as many minutes. "Shall I get down on one knee?" he asked, after an extremely interesting interlude. I noticed Rosalie and John-the-Baptist had moved a little distance away to give us some privacy.

"You haven't asked Father yet," I reminded him.

"Oh, good God. I don't think I can face that."

"Let's just run away to Gretna Green," I said, pressing my lips to the enticing spot where his jaw met his neck.

"Absolutely not," he said roundly. "Your family would string me up from the nearest tree. No, if we are going to do this thing, we shall do it properly. At Bellmont Abbey or in London, I do not care. You arrange whatever you like and I will be there," he said, brushing the sodden hair away from my brow. "And we will go wherever you wish for our wedding journey," he said, his eyes lighting with sudden mischief. "Even to the ends of the earth with you in a white petticoat."

I poked him hard in the ribs. "You did hear me."

"Every word."

There followed another extremely interesting interlude during which I completely forgave him for hearing my impassioned plea when he was unconscious. And after it was concluded, I ventured a question.

"Would you really have let me go?"

He took my hands and tucked them into the pocket of his coat. "You are cold. We ought to get you inside."

I prodded him again. "Would you?"

He tipped his head to the side, his hair thoroughly soaked and sleek as a seal's. "Would *you*?"

I nibbled at my lip. "Well, I was planning a rather sizeable donation to Aunt Hermia's Reformatory for Penitent Women," I admitted.

"How sizeable?"

"A few hundred thousand pounds. Just enough to reduce

me to the status of barely respectable widow. I might have even had to take employment," I told him.

"What are you fit for?"

"I thought perhaps I would make a very good partner in detection for a certain inquiry agent of my acquaintance," I said, running a finger along his underlip.

He grabbed at my hand and pressed a kiss to my palm. My knees felt suddenly weak and I think I may have clung to him a little harder. "Partner? I thought assistant."

I gave him a repressive look. "If we are going to do this thing," I said, deliberately turning his words back on him, "then let us have it clearly understood. We are equal partners. Both of us now have money to contribute, and both of us have rather unique talents. I think we would make admirable partners."

"We always have," he said, and that simple declaration meant far more to me than the one he made a moment later, which was a little more poetic and a great deal more private. He had just concluded this romantic little speech with an extremely expert kiss when we heard approaching hoofbeats, muffled by the moor and the rain.

We looked up to find a small party approaching, and to my astonishment, I realised it was my brother Bellmont, accompanied by his eldest, Orlando, and a gentleman and young lady I did not know.

"Driffield," Brisbane called. The Duke of Driffield raised his hat in spite of the rain, smiling broadly.

"I say, when Bellmont told me a fellow named Brisbane

owned this place, I hoped it was you. Told him you were always a good fellow to know."

Brisbane walked over and the two shook hands. Bellmont was staring in disbelief, his mouth agape.

"Hullo, Monty," I called cheerfully. "Orlando, how are you, dearest?"

Orlando dismounted and came to give me a kiss, very correctly ignoring my bedraggled state. "Very well, thank you, Aunt Julia. May I present my fiancée, Lady Harriet?"

The young lady had a pleasant, rather horsy face and an excellent seat. I smiled at her. "Lady Harriet, do forgive Orlando. He's never been very good at introductions, but he is marvellous at chess. I am his aunt, Lady Julia Grey."

She nodded, smiling broadly. "Oh, we do not stand on ceremony. We prefer country manners. How d'ye do?" She turned to her father who was chatting amiably with Brisbane. "Father, this will do quite well. The moor is excellent for hunting, and I think the village could do with a little benevolent work. The drains looked rather wanting."

Her manner was brisk and managing, and I looked affectionately at Orlando. If anyone needed managing, it was he. The boy did have ambitions, solid ones, and eventually he would be Earl March, a position of great authority and responsibility. He was well-intentioned, but neither as solid nor as articulate as his father. A firm wife, practical and efficient, would be the making of him.

"But the house," his Grace of Driffield interjected doubtfully.

Lady Harriet waved a hand. "Can be put right with a bit of work. The east wing wants restoring, of course, and there will have to be a new stable block built. The old one is far too distant from the house. It will not serve forever, of course. Once we have children to be launched and Orlando is settled in Parliament, we will need to be in London regularly and it may be too far removed. But for the first fifteen, twenty years, I think it will suit us quite nicely."

Lady Harriet seemed like a very determined young lady, and I fancied that whatever she turned her hand to inevitably came right.

"The estate comes with an excellent cook and a superb farm manager," I put in, slanting Brisbane a mischievous glance. I had a feeling Mrs. Butters could be persuaded to remain at Grimsgrave, particularly now that so many of the ghosts of the place had been put to rest.

"And Gypsies," Bellmont put in. He had been remarkably silent, but nothing had escaped his notice.

Driffield brushed this aside. "I always let them camp on my land. Bad luck not to, you know."

He waved a courteous hand to Rosalie and John-the-Baptist who had maintained some distance from our visitors.

Driffield nodded toward the hole. "Bit of trouble?"

"Not at all," Brisbane said coolly. "It is a mine, actually. We mean to open it again. So I am afraid I cannot sell the estate. My apologies, Lady Harriet," he added with a nod in her direction.

"A mine will be excellent for the local folk," she said. "Must keep the villagers employed." Clearly the duke had raised her to take a keen interest in the lives of those dependent upon their goodwill. "Perhaps we can sort something out and purchase the house itself, but lease the moor for purposes of hunting if we promise not to interfere with the operations of the mine?" she asked hopefully.

Brisbane smiled. "You have a fine head for business, Lady Harriet. And I am certain something can be arranged."

"Excellent," said the duke, clearly relieved that his imperious daughter was not to be thwarted. He seemed to see me for the first time and I was aware of the wide streaks of mud across my costume and my hair, dripping wet and hanging free of pins.

"Do forgive my appearance, your Grace," I began, but Driffield merely waved a hand.

"Think nothing of it, good lady. I admire an athletic woman who is not afraid of a little dirt in the pursuit of sport."

Bellmont choked a little, but I smiled graciously.

"Yes, I am terribly athletic," I agreed.

I went to my brother and raised my face for a kiss.

He obliged me and I whispered into his ear. "Get down and shake hands with Brisbane. He is going to be your brother-in-law."

He opened his mouth, then shut it abruptly, the little muscle in his jaw working furiously. "I suppose there is no point in trying to talk you out of this disaster?"

"None whatsoever."

He paused a long moment, then asked, "Will he make you happy?"

Bellmont's wide green eyes were anxious, and I put a hand to his face, smiling up at him. "Do I look happy?"

He studied my face, took in my entire figure from filthy

clothes to abominable hair. "I have never seen you more radiant," he admitted. He kissed the top of my head and slid from the saddle.

He went to Brisbane and extended his hand. "I understand congratulations are in order, brother," he said stiffly, and I knew precisely what that gesture had cost him.

Brisbane accepted his hand and I went to stand beside my betrothed.

"I only hope you know what you are getting into," Bellmont said with a sigh.

"I am quite certain," I told him tartly.

Bellmont lifted a brow. "I was talking to Brisbane."

He shook his head and remounted, leading the way back to Grimsgrave.

THE THIRTY-SECOND CHAPTER

In time the savage bull doth bear the yoke.
—William Shakespeare
Much Ado About Nothing

There is little more to say; I married him. The words are familiar, but the simplicity of them holds the whole world within. We married on Midsummer Day, in the little church of St. Barnabas at Blessingstoke, with my father's dearest friend, Uncle Fly, the vicar of Blessingstoke, to perform the ceremony. Most of my family were present, which meant the day was little short of Bedlam.

As it was my second marriage it ought to have been a quiet affair, but nothing to do with the Marches is ever quiet. My father smiled through his tears as he gave me away, and the little church was crowded with my relations and Brisbane's Scottish uncle, the Duke of Aberdour, nearly ninety and almost totally deaf. He shouted through the service, demanding to know what we said until Brisbane roared at him, "I just promised to endow her with all my worldly goods, now be quiet!" To which the duke replied, "I didn't know you *had* any worldly goods," and subsided into muttering for the rest of the ceremony.

In fact, Brisbane had rather a lot of worldly goods. The mine had apparently been closed when the Romans were driven out of the north, and never opened again until the weight of Mariah Young's coffin and the sodden earth had broken it open. In death, she had given her son the means to live his life as he pleased, and it felt like a benediction from the grave. Brisbane had defiantly reburied her in the chapel graveyard at Grimsgrave, flouting church authority, but then Brisbane was never one to observe rules he does not respect. Rosalie promised to lay flowers when they journeyed past each summer, for she returned to the road with John-the-Baptist. I did not know if we would ever see them again, but I knew she would keep her promise to Brisbane.

The Duke of Driffield settled matters quickly, paying a generous sum for the remains of Grimsgrave Hall and engaging Mrs. Butters and Minna and Godwin. Minna was training to be the housekeeper under Mrs. Butters' tutelage. Mrs. Butters, who might have held the post herself, was content to remain in the kitchen, and Godwin was very nearly beside himself at the handsome flock of sheep the duke permitted him to purchase with an eye to re-establishing the livestock. Work had already begun at the house by the time Portia and I left, and a new lightness had come over the place. The first thing Lady Harriet had done was burn the tapestry of Allenbys, claiming it was ugly and full of moths. She might have been right. It seemed a little sad to destroy the record of such a long and noble lineage, but I thought of all the pain and suffering that lineage had caused, the slow descent into madness, and I was glad for Lady Harriet. Even if ghosts walked at Grimsgrave, they would never stand against her sound common sense and practicality. When I last saw Grimsgrave, Lady Harriet was having the black pond in front of the house drained to make a flower garden.

Portia agreed to take Florence, as Puggy would not be separated from his little family. I still had Grim, and Brisbane had acquired Rook, the lurcher, who refused to travel with the Gypsies, but simply lay down in the road until Brisbane came to fetch him. I did not know how we were going to manage travelling with him, but he was surprisingly delicate in his habits, and I grew fond of him very quickly.

The wedding itself was arranged with tremendous speed and very little trouble. I simply let my sisters fuss over the details and spent every moment I could with Brisbane. They dressed me in a very suitable, elegant gown of heavy lavender silk, a nod to the mourning I no longer wore, and a wreath of lavender blossoms in my hair. I did not wear a veil, and by the time the dancing was finished, the lavender had broken to bits, twining in my hair only to fall out later in Brisbane's hands, like so many pieces of confetti. Brisbane was dressed in beautiful black, with the purest white shirt and waistcoat, a picture of elegance in spite of his tumbled hair and the slight shadow at his jaw.

We stayed the night at my little house, the Rookery, with no one to wait upon us. I dismissed Morag for the night, and sent Aquinas up to my father's home at Bellmont Abbey. We were alone, finally, and I stared at the ring upon my left hand, a slender band of diamonds.

"I told you I didn't need diamonds," I chided him. "Plain silver would have been enough."

"It is plain silver on the underside, and I had it engraved," he told me. He slid it off my finger and rolled it in his fingers, catching the light.

A chain of letters had been incised inside, "'HIIii116,'" I read aloud. "Another Shakespearean code, and a simple one."

"You know what it means?" he asked, settling me onto his lap. I put one arm about his neck and held out my other hand for him to replace my ring.

"*Hamlet,* of course. 'Doubt thou the stars are fire, doubt that the sun doth move, doubt truth to be a liar, but never doubt I love.'" I put my brow to his. "I have never doubted it, you know. Not really. But it is a lovely quote."

He slanted me a wicked look. "Well, it was either that or *All's Well That Ends Well,* Act One, scene one, line two hundred twenty-one."

I furrowed my brow. "I do not remember that one."

He slid an arm under my knees and rose effortlessly to his feet. "'Get thee a good husband, and use him as he uses thee.'"

I was still laughing when he kicked the bedroom door closed behind us.

What followed was a revelation. It is astonishing that so simple a thing can change everything, but there it is. Before we went into that room, the world was as it has always been, but by the time I awoke, long afterward as dawn was just beginning to silver the shadows, my entire life had changed. I stretched and yawned, sinuous and satisfied as a cat. It woke Brisbane who opened one eye and grinned at me sleepily.

"You have ruined that corset in your haste," I told him severely. "That was French lace, you know," I added, mourning the loss of the beautiful pale violet confection. I had ordered it from Paris at great cost and worn it precisely once.

"I'll buy you another. Besides, it is nothing compared to my complaint. You snore," he said thickly.

I hit him with my pillow, sending a shower of feathers into the air. One settled on his shoulder and I blew it off. "I do not. You must have been dreaming of another wife."

He took the pillow and put it under his head, leaving me nowhere to rest mine except his chest. I nestled there, one hand toying with the crisp, dark hair that spread toward his belly. Another interlude, *vastly* more interesting than those on the moor, took place and the sun was fully up by the time we had concluded our exchange of affections.

"We haven't even talked about the wedding trip yet," I said, yawning broadly.

Brisbane quirked a brow at me in a gesture I knew so well. "If that was where your thoughts were, remind me to apply myself more thoroughly next time," he said with a touch of asperity.

"Oh, no. I only thought of it after, I assure you. If you apply yourself more thoroughly I don't think I will be fit to leave this bed," I consoled.

He nodded. "That is better. As to the wedding trip, I have had Monk on the Continent, scouting suitable destinations. He seems to think Venice would be lovely, or perhaps a villa in Greece?"

I stared at him. "Monk has been looking for a house? For us?"

"Of course. You don't think I would marry you and drag you off to someplace, sight unseen? I trust him implicitly. He always thinks to inquire about things like hygienic arrangements," Brisbane said, raising a brow significantly. "I gave him a list of places I compiled months ago and sent him off to look them over."

"I cannot believe you have been thinking about this marriage, *planning* this marriage for months."

He put a hand through my hair, twisting it around his fingers. "I have been planning it since that first interview in your study at Grey House, a few weeks after Edward's death. You were all wide eyes and tart tongue, and you insisted to me Edward could not have been murdered."

"You are joking," I said, tickling his chin with a lock of my hair.

He shook his head, wrapping his arms about me and pulling me closer still. "I seem to recall you are the one always telling me to respect the sight," he said, only slightly mocking.

"You had a vision? About me?" He did not answer at first, and I began to nip at him with my fingers until he replied.

"Ow, yes, stop that, you vicious little beast. I had a vision of you, the first time I stepped into Grey House, the night Edward died. That was why I kept staring at you while he lay on the bed, convulsing between us. I had seen you standing before me, your hand in mine. I could not hear what was said between us, but there was a sense of belonging to you, as if I had always known you somehow, and you had been waiting for me. It came as rather a nasty shock to realise you were already married."

"Why were you so cold to me then? I thought you quite hated me."

"I hated what was happening to you," he said, brushing a bit of hair out of my eyes. "I knew you would suffer when he died. Besides, I never quite thought of myself as the marrying sort."

I stared at him, comprehension dawning. "You were afraid of me."

"Quite terrified," he said, smiling. He kissed my palm then, and I settled back against him.

"I cannot imagine that," I told him. "You, so coolly disdainful and dismissive. Terrified of me as I stood trembling in front of you, thinking you were the most alarming man I had ever met. I cannot believe you have ever been afraid of anything."

"It was a rather novel experience, I assure you," he said, tracing a path along the small of my back. I thought of the journey that had brought us together, the earl's daughter and the country-bred Gypsy lad, and I marvelled at the workings of fate. So many little turnings along the way, and if either of us had taken a different path, we would never have found one another.

"Tell me," I commanded. "Tell me about your adventures. I know you have been to China, to Egypt. I want to know it all. Tell me about the Orient first. Is it very exotic?"

Without warning, Brisbane, my partner and now my husband, rolled me smoothly onto my back and put his lips to my ear. "Later," he said, applying himself enthusiastically to the conjugal arts.

"But I want to know about China," I said, laughing as he did something rather new and thoroughly enjoyable.

He drew back, looked at me with those mesmerising witch-black eyes. He put a firm finger across my lips. "That is a tale for another time."

* * * * *

DEANNA RAYBOURN

Silent on the Moor

A Reader Group Guide

We hope you enjoyed this novel
by Deanna Raybourn.
See the discussion questions on the
following pages to further enhance
your reading enjoyment.

QUESTIONS FOR DISCUSSION

1. Although Julia and Nicholas are a Victorian couple, they have a very modern problem: his career versus their relationship. In what ways does his work complicate their future?

2. Hilda Allenby speaks bitterly about how difficult it is to be a woman and subject to the whims of men. What are some examples of this in the book?

3. The Allenbys have let down the villagers of Lesser Howlett by not fulfilling the responsibility they have toward the locals. How do they fail in their role and what impact does this have on the family and the community?

4. Jane gives up her relationship with Portia in order to assume the more traditional role of wife and mother. Is she right to do so?

5. Nicholas and Julia both rely to varying degrees upon intuition. How does this play into their decision making?

6. The Allenbys are devoted to the memory of their ancestors. How is this pride manifested in the inhabitants of Grimsgrave Hall?

7. Hilda Allenby chooses employment and uncertainty over marriage with Valerius March. Why?

8. Julia Grey is not a traditional Victorian woman. Discuss the qualities that make her unconventional and whether these qualities make her relatable to a modern reader.

9. The tragic story of Mariah Young has repercussions into the next generation. Discuss.

10. Will Julia and Nicholas be able to sustain a working relationship or will they find this problematic?

Acknowledgments

One of the loveliest aspects of being a writer is having the opportunity to acknowledge the debts I owe. Great appreciation and tremendous thanks:

To my family: my daughter, who provides endless companionship, laughter and very often food, my mother, who tidies everything up—including my manuscripts—and my husband, who makes it all possible.

To my agent, Pam Hopkins, a woman of tenacity and good humor whose skills at hand-holding, negotiating and talking her writers down from ledges is unsurpassed.

To my editor, the stylish and demanding Valerie Gray, who never rests unless she has my best.

To my friends, particularly those who traveled great distances, hosted me, shepherded me through their cities, or made multiple trips to events, most especially Vanessa, Sherri, Kim, Stephanie, Jerusha, Suzanne, Kristin, David, Tyler, Sali and my beloved godfather, Billy.

To those who have given technical assistance and shown exceptional professional generosity: Chris Wallbruch, Dr. Sandra Hammock, Shea Titlow and Dr. Gregory Davis.

To all the unsung heroes and heroines of publishing, the many hardworking people through whose hands my books pass and are made better and who work so tirelessly to get my books into the hands of readers—editorial, marketing, sales, public relations and production. Most particularly, I would like to thank Emily Ohanjanians and Nancy Fischer for their elegant and attentive contributions to the editing process, and Michael Rehder for the exquisite new covers.

To the many booksellers who have shared their enthusiasm with their customers and converted them to readers.

To the readers of blog and books who have been so generous in their praise and kind in their compliments. I have shared my stories with you, and in return you have shared your stories with me. Thank you.

"To say that I met Nicholas Brisbane over my husband's dead body is not entirely accurate. Edward, it should be noted, was still twitching upon the floor…"

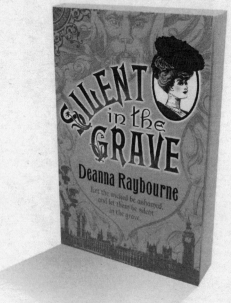

London, 1886

For Lady Julia Grey, her husband's sudden death at a dinner party is extremely inconvenient. However, things worsen when inscrutable private investigator Nicholas Brisbane reveals that the death was not due to natural causes.

Drawn away from her comfortable, conventional life, Julia is exposed to threatening notes, secret societies and gypsy curses, not to mention Nicholas's charismatic unpredictability.

"There is a dead man stinking in the game larder. I hardly think a few missing pearls will be the ruin of this house party."

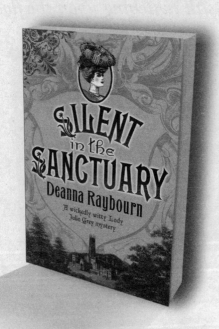

England, 1887

Christmas festivities at Bellmont Abbey are brought to an abrupt halt by a murder in the chapel. Blood dripping from her hands, Lady Julia Grey's cousin claims the ancient right of sanctuary.

Forced to resume her deliciously intriguing partnership with the enigmatic detective Nicholas Brisbane, Lady Julia is intent on proving her cousin's innocence. Still, the truth is rarely pure and never simple…

www.mirabooks.co.uk